C000024177

VANGUARD RISING

A.C. HADFIELD

BINARY BOOKS LTD

ACKNOWLEDGMENTS

I would like to thank the following wonderful people for all their help and input. Their combined efforts helped make this book a reality. Thank you!

Aaron Sikes, Paul Lucas, Ryan MacGavin, Pauline Nolet, Krista Walsh, Dusty Crosley.

1

SFSA Shuttle Rubicon,
en route to Jupiter's moon Europa

When death arrives, what is the final measure of a life?

Is it the sum of wealth accumulated? One's humor? What brave deeds one has completed? For many, it is those things and more, but for Gianni Mazzari, it was what one discovered about life, existence, the universe. What absolute truths were revealed. And he knew he was close to sealing *his* measurement as one of the greatest people to have ever existed.

He sat forward in the space shuttle's seat and stared with wide-eyed wonder into the void of space as he noted that, in over a hundred years of colonizing the solar system, humans were still the highest form of biological life—for now.

Gianni had always wondered what it would mean if humanity discovered something more advanced. And now, as he approached, he speculated what the strange signals he had recorded from the Europa relay would lead to.

The spectrum of hypothesis stretched from an alien uplift to humanity's doom, and a thousand speculations between.

A part of him, the scared boy he was as a child who would look out from Atlas Station and shrink away from the possibilities, wanted to instruct his shuttle's AI pilot to slingshot around Jupiter and head back to the relative safety of the inner planets.

Another part of him, the element that signed up to the Solar Federation Space Agency, ignored his childhood fears and instead brought up the image of Europa on the large wraparound cockpit screen.

Although the probes had found no life in its vast oceans, the Jovian moon would provide a base for future deep-space exploration missions. He'd seen high-resolution imagery of Europa before from the SFSA missions, but to behold it in context with Jupiter dominating the great expanse behind was something else.

Europa was a pale, light-gray bauble, its surface decorated by tendril filaments the color of tobacco, its stature a tiny mote, orbiting the all-seeing oculus of its gravitational master.

A breath caught in his throat as awe overtook him. This would be his view for the next few months, and a more inspiring one he could not have wished for.

He'd thought this moment would never arrive.

That the management at the space agency refused to listen to his theories meant he'd had to go it alone. Upon discovering the signal, he had deciphered it as some kind of communication, although the language, if it was such thing, remained indecipherable.

Whatever it was, he would be the one to claim the

discovery. And here he was, approaching the shining pearl in the expanse, a stepping-stone to greater discoveries.

No longer would those at the head of the SFSA be able to ignore him.

"Sarah," Gianni said, activating the ship's AI, "I can't see the astronomy structure. I thought I'd see it from here."

"We're currently obstructed by the orbits. The AstroLab will be visible within the next fifteen minutes. Do you want me to magnify when we're in view?"

"Yes, thanks. Are all other ship functions working normally?"

"Affirmative. All systems are normal."

They modeled the AI's voice on his sister, Bella. The SFSA training he had undergone—before deciding to go rogue—had instructed him it'd be beneficial to his mental wellbeing to have a familiar voice to accompany him during the two-week journey from Atlas Station.

The concept worked. Too a point. It freaked him out on occasion, primarily during the interstitial moments of waking and sleeping when he would think he was back home on Atlas Station as a child, running through the level with Bella, getting into trouble. He and his sister had taken very different paths since then, and he'd never been so far from her as he was now.

It was but a small sacrifice to make for scientific discovery.

For a place in human history.

"Sarah, how long until we dock?"

"ETA two hours. Reducing thrust to half g."

Gianni yawned and raised his arms, flexed the muscles. He shifted beneath the straps around his shoulders. He couldn't wait to dock with the AstroLab and stretch his legs. He settled into the crash couch as the gravity reduced within the shuttle. Head back, he looked up at the view from the external cameras. He shook his head, a smile stretching across his face. *I'm going to do it. I'm really going to do it. They'll remember this day forever...*

Then the image of Europa before him darkened as though a great cloud had passed between it and the sun.

"What the..."

A shadow crept across the moon's pale surface. The screen flickered before fragmenting into a billion pixels of static. Gianni leaned forward and readjusted the AV controls to no effect. The lights within the cockpit cut out, and the rumble of the engines ceased, bringing complete silence.

"Sarah? There's no thrust. You were only supposed to reduce it to half g. What's going on? Sarah? Do you hear me?"

No response.

His pulse quickened. His breath came short and rushed. He focused on the disaster protocols he had drilled so many times during the training months.

First step—activate the backup power.

He eased the straps off his shoulders, floated away in the microgravity. Using the foot- and handholds, he pushed himself over to the manual backup switch and pulled down on the red handle. The *Rubicon's* reserve generator kicked into life, flicking the screen back on. He instantly regretted it.

A high-pitched wail pierced through the speakers, making him wince with pain. The screen's image shifted and blurred as though he were drunk. It then shut off, and the ship rocked with a sudden violence, causing the airlock warning alarms to blare out.

Something had entered the shuttle from outside.

With shaking hands, he dragged himself to the rear of the cockpit, mashed his palm against the emergency transmitter button to set it to record and broadcast as per the protocols.

The bulkhead door between the cockpit and the rest of the shuttle opened.

He screamed for Bella, for Sarah, for God.

But the reply came from none of those.

2

Asimovia
Luna Colony District

Screw this colony, Harlan Rubik thought. Screw all the people in it. But most of all, screw Santos Vallan. Harlan kept up his mental diatribe as the transport ship lowered on Luna base's elevator and prepared to dock.

The fugitive murderer, Santos Vallan, had led Harlan on a chase halfway across the Solar system, exhausting all his patience and relaxed disposition during a two standard-week period. Harlan's dislike for Santos and the Luna colony could only be matched by the disdain he felt for the transportation system that had tested his stoical learnings to their limits. He'd had to rely on memories of the verbal lessons from his now-deceased mentor, Marius Rubik, from whom he had taken his surname, replacing the assigned name of 'Doe', as per the protocols applied to vat-born orphans. Even with those wise words, Harlan's composure was stretched taut and threatening to snap.

The old clunker, an ancient Kenmore Group Hyper-

Ferry, had dawdled through space from Ceres to Mars and then over to Atlas Station and finally to Harlan's destination: the industrial colony of Asimovia on Luna. The decrepit ship shuddered violently, connecting to the colony's dock. The amber lights flickered and settled to just above a nauseating level of dimness.

Stale, scrubbed air pumped into the carriage, mixed with dust particles from clogged filters to create a thick, unpleasant atmosphere. He coughed, his throat already dry from the two-day journey. Sweat pooled on his forehead and dripped from the back of his neck, soaking his collar.

The public area—according to a quick scan, the data of which displayed on his heads-up contact lens display—seated some two hundred and thirty-three travelers. As one, they shuffled to life, roused from the bench seats that ran lengthways down the carriage. A hubbub of noise rose from the dozens of languages, dialects, and slang of the Sol-Fed citizens as they stood and stretched their tired limbs.

Video screens above the seats—responsible for giving everyone a stiff neck during the journey, because hell will freeze over before there's eye-contact made on a ferry—displayed the bleak monochrome buildings that formed the Asimovia industrial complex, spreading ever vastly across Earth's moon's dusty surface.

Twenty-two other ships lay dormant in the dock. Gangway tunnels, flowing from a central hub, attached to their airlocks like the tentacles of some great mechanical beast. In the distance of the rocky gray moon, a neon sign flashed, promising unregulated off-world gambling. Despite this anachronism, the stakes and potential winnings were not for money like in the old days; gambling on Luna, or anywhere else, was for favors—the currency of choice within the Solar Federation that all the cool kids now called the Sol-Fed.

The rise of robots and computers handled the majority of jobs, meaning there was little reason for a monetary system anymore. And yet that desire within humans to gamble hadn't died out. And wherever there was desire, there was someone, or some mechanism, to turn it into profit. Those profits were calorie privileges and access statuses now. Despite that, it never failed to surprise Harlan how people created their own alternative forms of currency, whether it be unrecognized bitcreds, time, favors, or his personal favorite: contraband from the dying husk of Earth.

Although a given access status provided the individual with everything they needed for a decent standard of living according to their level of status, there were still some who wanted more—yet another hangover from humankind's consumerist past.

That was where the unofficial bitcreds came in. If one preferred their own ship, for example, they had to pony up hard cash in the form of the digital currency accepted by the system's network of criminal syndicates. Unless one was connected to a business-privileged family, one did not get a ship from the Sol-Fed resource distribution system. Harlan rued the fact he was not entitled to his own transport, hence having to travel on decades-old, ramshackle public services.

As a person with investigative authority, Harlan couldn't be seen trading in bitcreds publicly. Favors were fine and, to an extent, so was Earth-sourced contraband, as long as he didn't flaunt it. Which, of course, he didn't. He had a few choice collections—books, twenty-first-century vinyl records—and his personal favorite: clothes.

The black leather biker's jacket and the once-trendy blue overalls he wore came from Earth. They'd once belonged to an NYPD detective called Larry Schneider according to the label stitched inside the garments.

Harlan often imagined himself as Larry's reincarnation. He would wonder what it was like in Larry's time, before Earth became uninhabitable. How did they manage to do anything with such huge populations and inferior technology? They were real detectives, unlike most of the silicon runners today procuring off-the-shelf digital algorithms to solve cases for them.

A booming crunch broke Harlan out of his thought process and echoed down the carriage, followed by the loud clang of the airlock connection, the force of which rocked the ship hard to one side.

An elderly lady, dressed in rags, stumbled forward. Her arthritic, clawed hands grasped for the pole but swiped through the air and whacked against the dirty metallic floor.

Harlan knelt down, reached out for her.

She slapped his hand aside instinctively, presumably thinking he was after the small pouch of personal knick-knacks hanging from her waist. "Get your paws away from me."

"I'm sorry," Harlan replied. "I didn't mean to... I was just trying to help."

The rest of the carriage looked at him with suspicion. The woman glanced up and blinked, clearing the rheum from her eyes. Her pupils dilated, then narrowed.

Enhanced autofocus. A pre-Migration model.

"You're a stoic," she said, pushing herself up to her knees before scrutinizing him again, then, with a short laugh of derision, added, "Not sure what a stoic wants from this cursed place. It's all hedonists and capitalists out here."

"I've business to attend." He held out his hand once more.

This time she took it, hauled herself to her feet. Now that she was close, Harlan recognized her perfume. It was the same scent his estranged wife, Leanne, used to wear.

Even though she'd been gone for nearly a decade, that scent never failed to bring back a wash of memories and emotions—some good, some bad, all of them a kick in the guts.

The old woman looked him up and down. "Business, eh? That makes sense now. I've been watching you since I got on from Atlas Station. Did you know you chatter in your sleep?"

Harlan didn't know this, but then, having lived on his own for as long as he had, he'd no one to tell him. Even his embedded peripheral, the AI companion Milo, hadn't picked up on it. Harlan kept Milo switched off during transportation; he didn't want to stick out from the crowd too much and blow his cover. Talking to one's self, even in this day and age of illicit brain-mods, was frowned upon. Peripherals were not officially permitted.

As a silicon runner—the only officially sanctioned investigative service in the Sol-Fed—he took his cover as an important aspect of his job; not that anyone seemed to give a crap these days. Most runners went around dressed in shiny clothes and sunglasses, thinking they were something special.

People didn't respond well to that. A plain-clothed stoic, though? People opened up to a stoic, trusted them. Harlan used that to his advantage, although it seemed this woman had the advantage over him—or maybe she was just crazy. Lots of them about these days too.

Interplanetary travel could really mess with some people, push them to the edge.

"What did I say in my sleep?" Harlan asked, deciding to play along.

"That'll cost you two favors."

"Sorry, lady. I'm all out of favors."

She smiled, shrugged. "Fine, I'll give you this for free." She moved closer and spoke into his ear, her breath smelling of cheap, synthesized garlic. "The person you seek disembarked into the colony's hedonist bar two standard hours ago, on a shuttle. You will owe me, Harlan Rubik."

"And you would know this how—and how do you know my name?"

A horn blared, indicating that they had arrived at their destination and the airlock was ready to go. The crowd burst into life, grabbing their luggage from overhead bins. They moved like a wave, surging past Harlan and the old woman toward the exit at the rear of the ship.

A large man bumped into Harlan's shoulder, knocking him down to the bench seat.

When Harlan stood back up, the old lady had gone, swept away by the crowd, apparently eager to go about her business. But as he moved toward the exit, he still couldn't see her in the brightly lit security lounge. What the hell had happened, and where'd she go? And how did she know he was tracking someone? Whatever. He had a lead and figured it wouldn't hurt to follow it up. Regardless, Vallan was still out there somewhere.

AN HOUR LATER, his search bearing no fruit, Harlan was sitting at the colony bar, empty-handed—apart from a shot of the local booze, aptly named Moon Shine. He slammed it back and swore aloud as it burned all the way to his feet.

While his body decided how to cope with that, he thought about the old woman again. When he hacked into the ferry's manifest, he could find no one matching her description.

To make matters worse, her information—whether real or imagined—hadn't helped him in his search for Vallan. Although he had no idea what the murderer looked like, he had a digital profile to check against. None of the humans in this bar, or the surrounding infrastructure, remotely fit that analysis.

He had a trace program running on the colony's transport database, looking for any matches to Vallan's many IDs. It was a long shot, but it was all he had for now. He switched on his peripheral to check its status.

— *Evening, Harlan,* it said, the voice sounding directly in his brain as though it were some random thought reaching out to him through the ether.

"Any progress on the trace program?"

— *Nothing. Vallan must have spoofed a different ID chip. We're going to need a new profile.*

"Damn it." Harlan slammed his palm on the bar top. "It took weeks building that. How could he have changed it so soon after leaving Atlas Station?"

— *Your guess is as good as mine.*

Typically, Harlan wouldn't speak out loud like this in public to his peripheral, but he was tired, a little drunk, and no one around him within the small lunar colony bar could give a shit. They were too busy living on the edge, indulging in the only thing they wanted: hedonistic pleasure as they drank, drugged, and danced in with complete abandon, burning through their life vitality like it was the latest consumer drug.

Harlan shifted his weight on the bar stool and took another shot of Moon Shine. Apparently, the drink was supposed to be the finest liquor on Luna, but to him it tasted of disappointment with hints of bullshit—and yet he continued to drink.

The abbot working behind the bar received the network notification from Harlan's glass that the drink was running low. The V2 robot whirred toward him, bottle held between fingers that weren't at all convincing as it waited for Harlan's permission to pour another shot.

That was the problem with V2s: they looked like robots, despite the sophisticated neural intelligence going on under the hood.

Sure, wheels for legs and multiple manipulators for arms didn't exactly try to convince anyone they were human, unlike the V3s, but still, there was something odd about them, as if their makers, the self-replicating V1 units, had a penchant for retro aesthetics.

It was possible, Harlan thought, given how the entirety of the Earth's computing and transmission data was backed up on the Quantum Computer Array a hundred or so years ago. With every abbot plugged into that massive cache of data and culture, it wasn't beyond the realm of possibility that the V1s picked up on humans' 1950s and '60s robot design cues.

"No more, thanks," Harlan said, letting the abbot sweep up the empty glass and wheel away to serve some sweaty, pupil-dilated kid so young he probably didn't even remember what abbot stood for.

Harlan always remembered, however.

Abbot: Artificial Biomechanical roBot.

To kids these days, the V3s weren't even robots.

— *You're getting maudlin,* Milo warned. *Time to get back to work.*

"And what exactly do you suggest?" It bothered Harlan

that the AI peripheral could detect his emotional state. It helped in many situations, but sometimes a man's mind ought to be an inviolate sea where no vessel could trespass.

— *Walk that shit off and then think. We know Vallan's here; we just need to go about this logically. This ain't your first rodeo.*

"You're right. I can't sit around here anymore."

The magnets in his boots clicked on and off as he walked across the dingy bar to the exit. His hips and spine ached. Just an hour of Luna's microgravity had already brought changes to his body. He pictured his bones losing density, becoming hollow tubes of chalk.

How people stayed here for the long term, he could never guess. At least on Atlas or one of the other stations, you had near-Earth-like gravity, not to mention protection from the sun's radiation. Being stuck here inside the colony was like being a caged animal: at some point everyone wanted out, to be on the surface. But even with the best equipment, he knew there were still too many dangers for that to be viable for any length of time. If it wasn't Luna's untrustworthy landscape trying to kill you, radiation, temperature, and failing equipment were waiting to finish you off.

Harlan shook his head and stepped across the threshold, leaving the bar and its awful music behind. He turned right into a corridor that would lead back to the hotel complex. The walls were terra-cotta orange; the yellow lights hidden behind slits across the ceiling gave it a sense of warmth that was otherwise absent from Luna's surface.

He took three steps, and then something crunched underfoot, preventing the magnets from locking on. He held his leg aloft in the microgravity and looked down. Splayed out on the light-gray surface of the magnetized floor were eight spindly legs, each about a centimeter long and connected to a small, bulbous black body.

The surface of the spider shimmered.

— *What have you found, old chap?*

"Not sure yet..."

Harlan stepped back and knelt down to investigate. The leather of his biker's jacket creaked as he reached inside for a pen with which to poke the spider.

"The thing's definitely dead, although there's no blood or secretions of any kind. The body's made from a chitin-like material with the texture of fine honeycomb."

— *It's artificial.*

He poked a little harder, cracking open the carapace. He instructed his contact lenses to zoom into the small creature, magnifying its insides. A series of tiny chips and PCBs confirmed its artificiality.

"It's top-quality work." Harlan admired the technical proficiency to have created such a thing.

— *Probably came from one of the spy guilds on Galilei Station.*

"Aye, looks like it." Galilei was the name designation for Station Six: a notorious hive of scum and villainy. A place that Harlan, through no choice of his own, had become intimately familiar with over the years due to the development of his relationship with Gabriel Salazar, the head honcho for one of the many syndicates and a fan of old-school detective novels. It was that connection that had drawn the two unlikely men together, the latter proving to be the most useful of informants.

Harlan activated his brain-computer interface, reached out to network with the device. *Offline.* It seemed as if he had inadvertently crushed it to digital death. Didn't mean he couldn't get something from it though; just meant it'd take a little while longer. He gathered the spider and placed it in a small vacuum-seal bag—one of the many forensic items within the multitude of pockets of his now-old-fashioned overalls.

— *You know who else frequented Galilei in the last month?*

"Vallan. Commonality isn't necessarily causality."

— *No, but it's a big damn coincidence, is it not?*

The peripheral had a point. Harlan brought up his augmented-reality overlay and programmed an algorithm based on the natural surface texture of the floor. A light-blue blanket appeared at his feet, stretching out across his full field of vision. He zoomed the scene, switched the AR to show him anything that didn't fit the texture.

Bingo! There, before him, starting from where he had first crushed the spider, tiny red dots led down the corridor and back into the bar.

The damn thing had been following him.

Finally, a new lead.

A man's guttural scream punctured Harlan's elation. The sound came from deep within the industrial complex. Harlan set his jaw and headed toward the sound, knowing that if Vallan was down there, he'd have no way out—which applied equally to them both.

One way or another, this case would definitely be settled.

3

Earth Restoration Project Facility
Northeast Greenland

I rena Selles pressed her hands to the glass window on the top floor of the facility. It was cold to the touch. Frost lingered at the edges of the panes. Outside, the science complex looked entirely alien in its surroundings with its white domes and tunnels amongst the dirt tracks and forest. Spring had well and truly sprung, despite the odds. Greenland appeared to be living up to its name beneath the striking cyan sky, with barely a cloud to smudge this day's canvas.

Although she'd been here against her father's will for nearly three standard weeks, she still got a thrill from its beauty—even if her arrival couldn't have been more harrowing. The image of those bodies on the ground at the base of the entrance, their arms outstretched...

At first sight, they didn't look human; their limbs were distorted and their skin was like bark.

They were a stark reminder of what had happened to

those who were left behind after the Great Migration. Left to slowly branch off from Homo sapiens. The offspring of humankind's attempt to reconfigure its genetic foundations in order to be more resistant to all the Earth's ills: irradiated lands, poisoned food supplies, extreme temperatures, and the worst of the lot: Arctic flu.

Homo adversus, the genetic engineers had called them.

The pinnacle of human potential.

In just a few generations, adversus—or earthers as most people referred to them given they had literally inherited Earth—had not just evolved to the planet's worsening conditions, but had devolved into little more than animalistic creatures whose primary focus was survival at all costs.

Irena sighed, then drew a deep breath. She turned from the window, straightened her white coat, and walked across the light, airy room to her desk. The holographic screen sensed her approach, cleared her security, and displayed an image of Earth from space. She had set this as her screensaver as a reminder of why she was here: to find a way to fix the weather, diminish the effects the nuclear fallout damage, and perhaps help develop a cure for the flu that ravaged the planet.

Although she could do little directly regarding radiation or influenza issues, her weather-modeling skills had won her a scholarship as a young teenager. A decade later, at the age of twenty-three, she had secured a place here, at the Earth Restoration Project facility.

The lead scientist, Dr. Osho, believed her models and scientific thinking would be applicable to the other areas of the facility, citing how Irena's theories on weather systems could be applied to the spread of viruses. Irena was unconvinced, but was happy to help wherever possible. The facility had many bright minds on the project. Perhaps they would see applications for her theories more easily than she.

"Are you daydreaming again?" a familiar voice said from the elevator on the far side of the room, the glass doors lit from within by a pale blue light.

She hadn't even heard the doors open, but was pleased to see her guest.

"Darnesh, I'm always daydreaming. It's how I got here. The question is when are you going to start dreaming?"

The older, bearded man smiled and zipped his hooded sweater up to his chin as he walked over to her desk. "It's cold up here," he said. "You do know you're allowed to turn the heating systems on. The solar array is fully operational."

"Feels warm enough to me," Irena said. "Not always that warm on Atlas, so you develop a thick skin. You're just getting too comfortable."

"Too much time on Earth will do that to you," he said. "Well, as long as you stay inside, of course. We had three more of the savages feed on the dead this morning."

Darnesh stroked his unruly gray beard. His light blue eyes shone out from beneath wiry eyebrows. His hair was unusually thick for his age and rested shaggily on his shoulders.

"You know they can't help it," Irena said. "I think it's unfair to call them savages—they can't help what the virus did to them."

The older man sighed and sat on the edge of her desk, crossing his arms. "Aye, I guess you're right, but when you see them up close, feeding on their own kind... it's difficult to empathize, even if it is my job to find a cure."

"You don't think they're too far gone?" Irena asked, taking a seat.

The older man shrugged. "The computer models

suggest not, and we're still no closer to a vaccine than when we started three years ago. But at least we know what we're dealing with now. Perhaps we'll get a breakthrough when we least expect it—like your weather model."

Irena blushed and turned away.

She'd always had an issue dealing with praise.

What came easily to her seemed to be so difficult for others, which made her seem somehow superior, yet she felt inferior to everyone. Her abilities came to her through great effort. It was just that others often didn't see all the hard work she'd gone through to get to the point where she could strategize, analyze, and conclude quickly. She'd had to sacrifice a decade or more of her life to develop those skills.

All the other scientists here worked hard every day to get where they were.

"I'm sorry," Darnesh said. "I didn't mean to embarrass you. I came up to see how you're doing with your latest project. Dr. Osho has me on report duty today—she wants to collate statuses while the abbots are working over at the relay station."

"I saw them go out yesterday," Irena said. "Good thing they're abbots; I doubt we'd have many volunteers to go out there. My father sends me daily emails warning me to stay inside, stay safe. I'm sure he thinks I'm an idiot and somehow unaware of the dangers."

"I understand, though. My daughter is working on the Mars colony research center. Not a day goes by I don't worry something's going to happen."

Irena let it hang for a moment, not wanting to go further into that particular topic. She'd been under her father's influence all her life, and even escaping to a dead planet hadn't stopped him from influencing her feelings.

"Okay," she said. "Report time." She gestured her hands

across the control surface and brought up the statistics from her most recent weather model, which she swiped toward Darnesh. He received the transfer onto his thumb chip.

"Thanks." He stood up to leave but stopped and turned back to her. "There was one other thing."

"Oh?"

"You heard about Romanov, right?"

"I heard he went outside into the woods."

"Yeah, and didn't come back. He was found this morning. In various pieces. Seems as though he went mad and let the earthers feed on him voluntarily."

Irena put her hand to her mouth and resisted the gut response. "That's awful."

"It's an unfortunate business; he should have been sent back to his home station two months ago. He'd been down here too long. Despite the state of this planet, it still has a hold over us... Don't let yourself get trapped like that."

"I... won't," she said, unsure of what else to say. She had briefly studied the plight of what were now called the earthers before she had arrived at the ERP. They were mythologized across the stations and colonies, and depending on the goal of the conversation, demonized. These poor, doomed creatures, the perfect metaphor for unintended consequences, were nothing more than reactive animals trying their best to survive a harsh, hostile planet. That Romanov had purposefully allowed himself to be... consumed could be looked at as incredibly stupid, the act of an insane mind, or, in some philosophical quarters, the ultimate expression of compassion.

A brief, uncomfortable silence stretched taut for a moment before Darnesh remembered himself. "I'll see you later. Don't work too hard."

With that, he returned to the elevator and disappeared from view.

Barely an hour had passed when Irena's wrist terminal bleeped with a notification.

Dr. Osho wanted to see Irena immediately in the facility's rover depot regarding an emergency situation.

Irena wasted no time. She dashed across the room, entered the elevator, and gestured to the control panel to take her down to ground level. As she descended, she willed the butterflies in her stomach to stop. Surely there was a good reason for this. Osho didn't do things for the sake of it, did she?

WHEN IRENA ENTERED the rover depot, she realized she was the last. A group of others were waiting for her, and all stared at her as she entered.

Darnesh was there, along with Siegfried. In addition were Kestro and Ortsek—the two V3 abbots who looked like a pair of ravens with their beady eyes and dark, straight hair. In front of all of them stood Dr. Osho. Although a small woman of Chinese descent, she commanded the group through sheer charisma and an aura of authority.

"Irena, you're here. Good, come in; we've got work to do."

Irena joined the group. No one said anything. Even Darnesh wasn't giving anything away with his expressive eyebrows.

"Okay, listen up, everyone. Whatever your plans were for today, they've changed," Osho said. "We received a distress signal from the abbots up at Station Nord Relay. Their rover is too damaged to repair, and they've lost all connection to the network and regular communications."

Irena's stomached flipped. "We're... going outside?"

"That's what I said. We're going in the secondary rover. We've got a weather window of about eighteen hours. That's more than enough for us to recover the abbots. Everyone, put on your hab suits and load up the rover."

With that, she spun on her heel and strode across the darkly lit depot toward one of the rovers. The two raven-haired abbots, whom Irena had yet to form any kind of relationship with since she'd arrived, shared an inscrutable look as they followed Dr. Osho.

Siegfried and Darnesh likewise wasted no time.

Irena had to almost jog to keep up with them. "Is this normal? I thought the abbots are self-sufficient—can't they just fix the rover and return? Can't we send a service drone?"

Without turning his back, Siegfried shrugged. "I'm sure Dr. Osho will explain. Keep up; we don't want to waste time."

This was all happening too fast. No one told her she would have to venture out of the facility. She was here for science, not exploration or rescue missions that could be handled by drones or abbots.

But if they were going to rescue abbots... What could have happened?

She didn't want to become another Romanov.

She rushed to keep up and joined the others at the eight-wheeled rover.

With its glass canopy, it looked like a giant pill on wheels. A V2 abbot arrived with a pallet of hab suits. Darnesh helped Irena into hers. "Climate controls are in the suit's OS," he said, his voice coming through the internal communication systems embedded into the helmets.

Irena thanked him and set the temperature to a comfortable sixteen degrees Celsius.

Dr. Osho approached Irena, checked her suit fitting, and nodded.

"Dr. Osho, are you sure you want me to go with you? I'm not sure what I can offer. I have no experience with damaged equipment..."

"I want you with us. It's a learning experience."

"But the service drones—"

"All allocated. It's not just a rescue job, my girl. When we're there, we're going to be installing some new q-bit analysis cores to upgrade the station's prediction models. That's why I instructed the abbots already there to stay put. We can't risk losing them. And that could happen if they simply returned on foot—poor Romanov succumbed to..."

"What about lifting them out with the tri-copter? I don't mean to question you—"

Dr. Osho took Irena by the elbow and led her to the rover, adding, "Our tri-copter is no good up there. It's too densely forested and the winds too unpredictable. Besides, we'll need the abbots' help to get the q-bit cores online, and together we should be able to fix whatever damage has caused the network outage. It'll be good for you to see what the observation station is like. You'll probably have a few shifts there over the course of your stay."

"Right... I see." Irena's head buzzed with the speed of everything as she took a seat in the front. The abbots had finished loading the rover. Siegfried and Darnesh had got in, sitting in the row behind her. Osho finished the loading, took the seat on Irena's left, and pulled the curved glass canopy shut.

"Okay, we're ready to go," Osho said. "Strap in, everyone, the route can get bumpy."

Irena strapped her safety belt around her body and breathed against its auto-tightening pull. The electric motors of the rover wound up, and the vibrations shook through the chassis. The vehicle's computer locked on to their destination and piloted the crew away from the Earth Restoration Project facility.

Osho smiled at Irena, her old hazelnut brown eyes little more than thin slivers behind crinkled lids. At a hundred and twenty, she looked not a day over sixty. Irena hoped she would wear as well in another eighty-six years.

If she survived, that is.

"Don't look so worried," Osho said. "These days, this kind of task is considered routine."

"So was a frontal lobotomy once," Irena responded.

A series of chortles came from behind her. When she looked over her shoulder to nervously smile at the two men, she recognized her own tension in their eyes.

"At least we have the weather for it," she said, trying to lift the mood.

"For now," Darnesh intoned, his words heavy with a foreboding Irena really didn't appreciate. Siegfried and the two abbots were more focused, their expressions neutral behind their visors.

"It's amazing to think this was all barren tundra just a few generations ago," Irena said. She turned her attention to the front windshield and made no effort to hide her awe. "You wouldn't even think there was a problem with the planet looking at all this."

"I don't know," Siegfried said. "It's not normal to have tropical-born trees growing this far north in the Arctic. That in itself represents a problem, does it not?"

She wanted to respond to him but bit her tongue. There was no point adding more tension. Tall, thin trees reached toward the bright sunshine, creating a tunnel with a rich blue circle at its center. Their woody limbs reached up as if they were faithful members of a congregation beseeching their lord. But Irena could not help but see the color of dead skin in the trees' dull bark.

That same image, of decaying flesh, rose up in Irena's mind: the bodies she had found upon first arriving at the facility. Three earthers dead at the base of the entrance tower. Their arms stretched out, palms flat against the white ceramic walls as if prostrating themselves against the gates of heaven for salvation, but finding only impotent pity.

She closed her eyes, willed the image away, and then cast her gaze back on the blue sky. The scene had already changed, however. A diaphanous sheet of fragmented altostratus cloud scudded by, suggesting in its mercurial fashion that rain was on its way.

"You see that?" Irena said, pointing upward.

The other scientists looked up through the glass rover ceiling.

"Bad weather's coming," Darnesh grumbled, his voice that of a preacher warning his congregation of the coming apocalypse. That metaphorical ship had sailed long ago, however.

"Okay, everyone, let's just remain focused," Osho said. "We've forecasted clear weather for at least the next eighteen hours. It's just a small cloud formation. We'll be back at base enjoying cold beer and hot food long before any rain falls."

Irena wanted to ask, "What if the forecast was wrong?" but clenched her jaw tight and said nothing. Instead she looked out the glass canopy, watching the landscape go by as the rover made its way farther north.

Movement caught her attention.

A shadow in the trees shifted in their direction.

Something was following them—or perhaps she was just imagining it, letting her fear get the better of her. She thought about saying something, but the tension was already high, and she didn't want to risk the embarrassment of mistaking it for one of the few remaining animals that roamed the lesser-radiated areas. She looked away, focused on her terminal, deciding it'd be a better use of her time to go over some datasets and try to forget about being outside, on Earth, while something stalked them from the shadows.

4

Harlan jogged down the corridor toward the sound of the scream. The tiny spider footprints were here also, indicating where it had originated before following him into the bar. The AR display showed him the external and internal climate among other metrics.

Now that he was higher up in the colony, just a few levels away from the moon's surface, the temperature was dropping. He pulled his biker's jacket closer around his body and increased his walking speed.

The smart-magnets weren't conducive for anything more than a brisk walk; they couldn't activate and deactivate fast enough for a sprint, and the corridor's narrow and low ceiling meant that it wasn't advisable to switch them off and try to float through.

The red dots turned left at a junction.

Thick cords of pipework and conduits met at the bulkhead and twisted off into the depths of the colony. Several of the strip lights overhead thrummed, their luminosity pulsing as though the place had a heartbeat. His own, according to his monitoring systems, had increased steadily until it now rested at nearly eighty percent of his maximum.

Low gravity and claustrophobic tunnels were clearly as effective a workout as his regular callisthenic routine back on Atlas. Sweat pooled beneath his mechanic's overalls despite the chill. He wiped his hand across his brow and over his close-shaved head.

No wonder humanity had replaced maintenance workers with VI abbots. Must have been hell in the days before the Great Build when humans had to construct their own rockets and other space exploration equipment.

Even worse for those before them, having to toil in mines and factories.

Harlan mentally saluted all those men and women and chased the red dots until he came to a door leading into a workshop. It featured a security panel where the abbots would attach themselves to gain access. He reached into one of his many pockets, pulled out a slim black card, barely the size of his thumb, and placed it against the control surface.

He waited as a green dot blinked—indication that it was connecting to the Quantum Computer Array for verification of the ID.

Harlan set a reminder to himself to thank the shady dealer who had hooked him up with the skeleton key that allowed him to skirt the outer security protocols of the QCA. It was well worth the five favors Harlan had agreed to barter for the device. Especially as the dealer only had one more favor to call in.

Harlan pushed the door open slowly, using all his augmented senses to reach out within the darkened room beyond. His system showed metrics pertaining to magnetic fields, temperature fluctuations, sources of electricity, light degrees, humidity, oxygen levels, and early warning for toxins.

All came back unchanged. Negative.

The room was effectively dead.

Taking his ID card, he eased the thick metal door open further with one shoulder, his weight on his back foot, ready to dive out of the way if stealth or masking technology somehow fooled his sensors.

Still nothing.

Satisfied it was safe to enter, he stepped over the threshold and switched on the light. The same rhythmically pulsing lights doused the small workshop in even, white light from all angles to ensure no shadows. Important for delicate electronic tasks.

The area was large enough for half a dozen abbots.

Steel worktables took up the center while other ad hoc stations and cabinetry lined the walls. On the tables were five electronically controlled mechanical devices in various states of disrepair. Wires, chips, and other equipment lay strewn about, as though the engineers had sudden reason to leave.

The stench of solder and grease hung in the stale air. There was no sound of air scrubbers here. Who needed clean air when the workers didn't even breathe?

The red spider dots terminated at the far-right corner of the room.

A single desk, bathed in light from a three-sided surround, was set flush against the wall. An abbot lay slumped in front of it, one arm bent forward as if reaching out for something.

Harlan closed the door and stepped closer to the abbot. It appeared someone had struck the V3 unit on the back of the head, causing a gash in the skull approximately fifty millimeters long and twenty wide. Purple coolant dripped from the opening, soaking the abbot's gray and yellow engineer's uniform.

"I doubt it knew anything about it—the scream was just a programmed response."

— *Even if it did know about the attack, would it care?* Milo asked.

"Let's not get into a debate of whether abbots have consciousness."

— *Then get on with your work. There's a terminal there.*

Before Harlan reported the destroyed abbot to the maintenance division for recycling, he continued his search and located the diagnostic terminal. His AR layer showed multiple smears on the glossy surface. A human wearing gloves must have handled it recently. If an abbot had used it last, their prints, like miniature right-angle mazes, would have shown instead. In all his years, he'd never heard of an abbot breaking the law, let alone covering their prints like this.

— *You can use the terminal to connect to the spider.*

"I know, I'm not a rookie. You'd be a much greater help telling me things I don't know. Isn't that why I paid twenty favors to have you installed?"

— *It's cute you think that's all you paid.*

"What's that mean?"

— *I thought you wanted me to tell you something you didn't know?*

"Stop playing games or I'll switch you off."

— *Your sanity, Harlan. You paid with your sanity.*

"Get lost." Harlan was tiring of Milo's jibes. He wished he'd paid extra for a more professional model of peripheral instead of one programmed by some snarky code-ninja.

Harlan stepped up to the desk, placed the semi-crushed

spider on the worktop and activated the terminal. The machine booted up within a few seconds, and he checked the log files. Although there were instructions sent to the spider's address, there was something else: a set of directives to the QCA.

"This is not good," Harlan said, looking back at the abbot, the picture becoming clear in his head. "Why would someone destroy an abbot?" he asked, mostly rhetorically.

— *To use their unprotected chip ID to gain access to the QCA.*

"Right. Many people have tried and failed—the encryption is too strong— but look at this."

He scanned the list of instructions from the terminal. One thing stood out that chilled him to the bone.

— *Someone's written a virus that's breached the QCA's first layer of security,* Milo said.

"Yeah, and look what it's done."

Harlan gestured across the terminal to show the virus' source code, the program still fresh in the memory of the dead abbot—its backup power would be good for another few weeks.

— *Holy crap.*

"Holy crap indeed. The virus has taken over the controls of another abbot somewhere. Whoever's behind this has managed to crack the autonomous sovereignty of abbots. This could reignite the war... and if the virus cracks the rest of the QCA security layers, it would give someone complete control over the entire population of abbots."

— *A ten-million-strong robot army...*

Harlan downloaded the data he had found and removed the chip from the dead abbot's head. He'd take it back to the office for further analysis. He turned to gaze around the room, wondering how Vallan was tied up in all this. Was it his job to upload the virus to the QCA via the now-dead abbot?

It made sense. The spider was used to spy on Harlan so Vallan would know if he was being followed. So where was he? And why have something like a spider do the work? Vallan must have known it would have left tracks. He could have hacked into the Luna base's security systems, set up a facial-recognition tracking program....

"Why am I here?" he mumbled, stalking about the room, tapping a finger to his lips.

— *You're here because of spider tracks and the scream from the abbot, dumbass.*

Harlan repeated that to himself a number of times, without the insult.

Milo was on to something, but it couldn't quite form into a coherent thought. Harlan stopped pacing, closed his eyes, and focused on those two facts, going backwards from his current location, trying to extrapolate meaning.

The spider... the scream... Vallan's target...

And then it hit him.

"It's me," Harlan said. "Damn it. I'm the target."

He rushed for the door, but it was already slamming shut. It locked into place with the loud clunk of the maglocks activating. He spun around, saw a shadow move across the table. His heart rate spiked, but his controller throttled it to eighty percent maximum.

A controlled dose of adrenalin entered his bloodstream. His vision narrowed and his senses heightened. He swung around, trying to get a visual on his adversary.

— *Above you.*

Harlan looked up.

Sprawled between beams like a spider himself, Santos Vallan peered down at Harlan through a semi-translucent face mask. The assassin was wearing a chameleon suit, helping him blend in. No wonder Harlan hadn't registered any living creatures in there; the suit would have blocked his scan.

Thinking back, Harlan realized Vallan had probably been on the same transport ship.

He had been led here all along. Harlan was always the target. The hunter now the hunted.

In the microsecond it took for all this to process, Vallan pulled a palm-pistol from a holster and pointed it at Harlan's head.

Harlan's upgraded reflex system kicked in, and he dived to his right as a near-silent '*thwup*' sound fired close, the round penetrating the steel wall with a punctuated clang.

Another shot, this time closer, grazed the edge of Harlan's boot.

He scrambled beneath the workbenches and pulled a Taser from his biker jacket's inner pocket. From under the table, Harlan saw the shadows shift quickly.

Vallan had fallen to the floor in almost complete silence.

Before Harlan could get a visual, the lights went out.

And then came the mocking laughter.

"Dearest Harlan," Vallan said, his voice disguised and scattered by the chameleon suit to prevent location, "looks like you got yourself into quite the situation."

"I've alerted security," Harlan said, willing his contacts to activate their dark-vision feature—a feature he'd been meaning to get fixed. Sometimes the contacts worked, sometimes they didn't, and this was not the time he wanted them to fail.

— *Keep him talking. Buy some time for me to sort your dark vision.*

"Don't lie to me, Harlan. I thought we had a better relationship than that."

"The only relationship we have is good guy to bad guy."

"And which is which, I wonder?"

Harlan's enhanced hearing wasn't helping locate Vallan via his voice, but there was a barely audible sound of textile on steel—Vallan's feet moving deftly over the floor—which gave Harlan the sense that Vallan was now on the right-hand side of the room, by the dead abbot.

"You really have to ask?" Harlan said, using his voice as a cover to spin around and face the right direction.

"You have a greater body count than I. Though only by one."

"And you're looking to draw level, is that it?"

"Depends who that one is." Vallan laughed again.

The assassin fired another shot, this time striking the leg of the workbench, forcing Harlan farther back.

— *Okay, got it. Just don't waste any time.*

Harlan's night vision flickered on. The scene before him glowed in various values of green. The assassin's chameleon suit didn't show up, but the absence of it did, reversing its usefulness. A black form shifted through the green landscape, dodging behind cover, and preventing a clear shot.

"It was you on the transport ship, wasn't it? Disguised as the old woman," Harlan said, trying to buy a few more seconds.

"Ah, yes, I'm surprised it took you so long to figure that out. Always the gentleman ready to help old ladies. One day that will get you into trouble... oh, it looks like today is that day."

"Maybe..."

The form shifted a few inches out of cover.

Harlan leaned out from under the workbench and fired his Taser.

Vallan grunted and stumbled back, the chameleon suit taking the brunt of the charge.

Harlan scrambled forward and fired again.

The assassin yelled and swung a foot up, catching Harlan in the jaw. The force knocked him against the workbench, but he rebounded off it and used the momentum to slam his heavy magnetic boot down.

The boot struck against the assassin's chest, knocking his arms back.

Another kick slapped the weapon from his hands.

Harlan pressed the Taser to Vallan's head and was about to pull the trigger when the lights came on and the door swung open.

"Hold it," a deep voice boomed out. "Luna security. Drop the weapon."

— *Finally, the cavalry has arrived. Oh, while you were hiding like a baby, I hacked the communications relay to send a message to Luna's security. You're welcome.*

Harlan dropped his weapon, held his arms up, noticing that Vallan had a monofilament blade in his left hand—Harlan would have been dead before he had even pulled the trigger. And he hadn't even seen it.

Half a dozen armored security abbots quickly entered the room. They lifted Harlan up and pulled him aside. He explained the situation and showed the security officer the warrant for Vallan's arrest along with his silicon runner identification.

Three of the security abbots held Vallan as they read him his rights. They were about to arrest him when Harlan exerted his authority and jurisdiction. The abbots handed

Vallan over to Harlan after they had removed any weapons from his person.

"Thanks, guys," Harlan said. "You got here just in time."

Vallan remained silent.

— *Well, are you going to take off his mask, or what? I'm dying to know what this scumbag looks like*, Milo said, echoing Harlan's own curiosity.

For years Vallan had gone about his business without anyone directly identifying him, which was what made him so difficult to track.

Harlan removed the mask and gasped.

"Leanne?"

Vallan was his wife.

5

I rena checked her watch. They'd travelled for four hours and twenty-five standard minutes through the woodland. The going had been worse than anticipated, but finally they'd arrived at Station Nord.

The small brick facility housed a single satellite dish that beamed data to and from the Quantum Computer Array, which floated in the Lagrangian point between Earth and its moon. The building used to be a refueling depot during humankind's first forays in colonization, but when the computers and robots got sufficiently smart, they had taken it upon themselves to re-purpose it as a central server for all their operations.

"The station looks out of place in the dense forest," Siegfried said.

"The front bay is open," Darnesh said, pointing at a steel door swinging in the breeze. "The abbots must have seen us arrive."

"They have names," one of the raven-haired abbots in the back said.

"I'm sorry," Darnesh said. "I meant no offense."

"Let's not sit around arguing about human-abbot relations," Osho said. "The weather's taking a bad turn. Let's get in and prep the q-bit cores. The sooner we get them installed, the sooner we can get back to base."

Everyone got out of the rover. Siegfried and Darnesh took the two q-bit cores into the station. The two abbots faced out to the woodland, rifles slung over their shoulders.

The sight made Irena shiver. She hadn't seen the weapons until now and hadn't thought they would need to be armed. But given that she'd noticed a shadow following them in the woods for the majority of the journey, she wasn't unhappy to know that Osho had arranged for some security provisions.

Still, seeing a pair of abbots with lethal weapons filled Irena with a sense of unease.

Her father had often told her stories about the abbot uprising and the short war that had followed. Although there hadn't been a single incident of abbot-on-human violence since then, Irena had always been nervous around them.

"Go," Kestro said to her, nodding toward the open bay door. "We'll follow you in."

Irena hesitated for a moment, but realized they weren't going to move until she did, presumably for her own protection. She thanked them awkwardly and headed into the station. Before she reached for the door, however, a thought occurred to her. She considered it out loud. "Where's the other rover?"

Osho, who was standing in the shadow of the facility, turned to face her. "That's a very good point. Kestro, Ortsek, would you mind checking the perimeter, see if it's parked on the other side? We really ought to assess the damage to see if we can drive it back with us."

The two abbots split up and proceeded to circle the station.

"Miss Selles, if you will—we'll need your help," Osho added.

Irena hurried, not wanting to annoy her superior.

Inside, the base was in darkness. It was only ten meters square on the ground level and featured a central spiral staircase leading into the laboratory area. Panels of computer equipment and workstations lined the walls. A couple of office chairs lay strewn about as if abandoned. Two doors were visible on the back wall. One of them hung open on its hinges.

Through the filtered helmet on the hab suit, Irena smelled the faint scent of burnt plastic. No one else mentioned it, so she put it down to her imagination.

"Why is it so quiet in here, and why are the lights off?" Irena asked.

"The generator's down," Darnesh replied as he struggled up the spiral stair with a bulky q-bit core in his arms. It weighed about twenty kilos, all dark and shiny and filled with niobium superconductors.

Magic boxes, her father used to call them. And the problem with magic, he said, was that it didn't exist; it was all an illusion. This was all prefaced with the unspoken notion that she was wasting her time. He, and her mother, would have rather she followed them into politics. The thought had never once appealed to her. For her, science and technology were eminently more useful. But, illusion or not, the q-bit cores were a pain to fit and cohere with the rest of the system. They'd be here for hours—longer if the generator needed repairing.

"Dr. Siegfried," Osho said, "attend to the power supply when you've found the other abbot team, would you, please? Irena, come with me through here. I would like to show you something."

Irena followed Osho through the open door on the ground level. The room was barely large enough for two people to stand side by side and only twice that long. On the far wall hung a holographic display. On the two other walls were paper printouts.

Osho switched on the lights attached to the side of her helmet.

Irena did the same, kicking herself for not realizing earlier. This whole place made her nervous and unable to think logically. She hated that feeling of not being in control.

"Here's some data from the atmospheric seeding program," Osho said, indicating a particular long piece of paper pinned to the wall. "When we get the computers back online, I'd like you to go through these and see if the reports will help shape your models."

Irena took a cursory glance at the data and knew without thinking about it that it would be of no use to her. Seeding the atmosphere could only do so much; she had modeled it years ago and quickly realized they'd need other tools if they were to cool the environment enough.

Earth had passed its no-return zone back in 2083 CE. Experts had predicted temperature rises of around four degrees. They had no idea that the catalyst would happen, sending temperatures six degrees over the threshold in just a few short years, or the increasing rise—until nuclear winter from the Last War settled across vast tracts of the planet.

Irena had anticipated it would take at least another fifty years to implement the technology to reverse that. The Mars colonists in Bujoldia were making some interesting breakthroughs with atmospheric conditioning, but even with the abbots for the labor and the QCA to crunch the numbers, it would require significant time.

Osho turned to face Irena, the lights shining into her face mask, glaring into her eyes. "You've already figured it out, haven't you?" she said, her old eyes widening with amazement.

Irena blushed under the scrutiny and shook her head. "I can't say for sure; I'll need to run the numbers properly."

"I can sense it in you. Your body language says it all. This is why I wanted you here. You have a gift, my girl, and you will do wonders with it. Come on, let's help the old guys with those q-bit cores before they start complaining about what a slave driver I am."

Irena smiled and turned to exit the room.

Osho went first and got five paces in front when she suddenly stopped as though she had walked into a wall. Her whole body shuddered for a moment.

"Doctor, what is it?" Irena asked, inching forward.

Her light beams reflected off something dark on Osho's right shoulder.

Dark and red.

Blood smears.

Osho stumbled backward. The prone, bloodied form of Siegfried collapsed in front of her. His helmet had been removed, the ragged edges of his suit coated in blood. Farther behind Siegfried, Darnesh careened down the spiral staircase, gripping his throat.

Irena shouted and sprinted toward him, but it was too late.

He too collapsed to the ground. She removed her glove and checked for his pulse with a shaking hand, but there was nothing.

Osho screamed.

Irena looked back to see the doctor pointing up to the next floor. An abbot, not Kestro or Ortsek, stepped onto the staircase, pointed a rifle at Dr. Osho and shot three times, sending her body stumbling back.

"Run," Osho whispered with a gurgled voice. "Save yourself."

Irena was caught with indecision: save Dr. Osho or follow orders.

A bullet striking her in the hand made up her mind. She threw her arm back in reaction, her wrist terminal flying off. She made to reach for it, but another shot blasted out.

As pain pulsed through her body from the wound, she sprinted as fast as she could out of the building and into the open. "Kestro, Ortsek, do you hear me?" Her shouted words came between panicked breaths.

No reply.

Another shot came from inside, presumably to finish off Dr. Osho.

Irena spun around and pushed the doors closed before taking off around the building to find the other two abbots. She did find them—ripped to pieces and lying in a heap against the damaged rover. The vehicle had been completely ruined; all the tires were slashed, and coolant was seeping out of the motor bay.

If only they had checked first.

Around the far side of the station, Irena found the rest of

the original abbot team—all were dismembered and stacked in a pile behind the station.

Fear and panic threatened to overwhelm her. The suit was suddenly too small, obstructing her movements, making her too hot. She pulled the helmet off and threw it to the ground, tears coursing down her cheeks, her body shaking.

Next, she zipped it down the middle and stepped out of it. Freed of its bulk, she continued around the station until she came to the corner. She peered around it and saw the other rover.

If she could get in, she could engage the autopilot back to the facility. She tiptoed forward, readying to sprint. The armed abbot was reflected in the rover's glass dome. He was lying in wait, rifle trained on the vehicle. Waiting for her to walk into her death.

She stumbled behind the brick wall, pressing her back against the cold stone. She let out a sob. She shook because of the pain in her hand. Because her friends had been brutally murdered. And because now she was alone on an abandoned, decaying Earth.

But most of all because an abbot had gone wrong. Badly wrong.

The sound of footsteps squelching in the mud came from around the corner. She held her breath with an effort and forced herself to find composure. *Look at the data; analyze the facts; leave emotion out of it for now.*

It was the only way she'd survive. Without her terminal to call the ERP facility, or send a message to one of the stations, she was completely vulnerable and alone. Survival was now her singular responsibility.

First things first, find a weapon. She looked around and found nothing of use.

Okay, second option: run.

She'd have to run into the wilderness and keep running until she could find help, even though that represented a new kind of danger. The shadows she had seen chasing them on the way to the station were clearly earthers. She faced a terrible choice: face a deranged and armed abbot or head into the woods and chance her luck with humanity's cursed children.

The sound of the rover's tires being slashed and a gun being loaded made up her mind. She took a deep breath, pressed her palms against the wall, and pushed off at a sprint into the trees, fear and determination to survive flowing through her body and keeping her legs pumping.

Behind her, twigs snapped.

The abbot fired at her. The bullet whistled past, slammed into the trunk of a tree.

She twisted and turned, dashing between the trunks, dodging in and out, and trying to get as much woodland between her and her attacker as possible. After a few moments, she realized the abbot was no longer firing at her. With her heart pounding and every breath burning her lungs, she stopped and chanced a look over her shoulder.

And stifled a scream.

The dying light of dusk barely illuminated a pack of four earthers in ragged clothes, their long hair matted with leaves and twigs. They hunched over the prone form of the rogue abbot as they ripped it limb from limb, trying to find some sustenance and looking dismayed when all they found were servos, artificial muscle, and electronics.

One of them looked up to the sky, sniffed, and turned to face Irena.

The stare from those mad, wild blue eyes froze her in place until the horror of what had happened hit again like a lightning strike. She turned and ran deeper into the woods, determined to find safety but only seeing more shadows shifting in the trees ahead of her, closing in.

6

L eanne had said nothing to Harlan during the trip to Atlas Station.

He couldn't believe that, after all these years, he'd found his ex-wife and that she had turned out to be the notorious killer Santos Vallan. Harlan had watched her in the cell at the back of the transport ship during the six-hour-and-thirty-five-minute standard journey.

She'd steadfastly refused to speak to him, had refused to explain where she had been all these years, and refused to explain why she'd become a hired assassin.

She had barely aged during the last ten years, presumably the work of cybernetics from her contacts on Galilei. Despite himself, a small part of Harlan was still attracted to her. A part of him wanted to believe this was some terrible mistake and that he wasn't her target.

"You have to talk to me at some point," he said.

He crossed his legs and leaned back into the uncomfortable transport ship seat.

Three other cells in the ship contained petty thieves and

small-time criminals, none of whom had visitors, leaving Harlan the only one there.

Leanne sat on her bunk and brought her knees to her chest. Her bright green eyes stared at Harlan with a mix of confusion, hatred, and what he thought was amusement.

"You think this is some kind of game?" Harlan asked. "It isn't. This is your life on the line. You'll be executed for your crimes. And there's nothing I can do to help you unless you speak to me. Tell me what happened to you. Did someone put you up to this? Are you working for some kind of criminal organization? Or is this some sad fantasy you're living out? The all-powerful assassin?"

Leanne ran a hand through her short-cropped brunette hair and pressed her lips together, as though preparing to say something.

Harlan leaned forward, ready for her words.

She simply smiled and rested her back against the wall of the cell.

— *You still have your Taser,* Milo said. *Perhaps a little encouragement would get her talking.*

"My AI assistant believes I should torture you with my Taser to get you speaking," Harlan said, reaching inside his biker's jacket and removing the weapon.

He flipped it over in his hands as though it were a child's toy.

"Is that what it's really going to come to? Because if it is, then trust me, I have enough anger in me that tasering you into submission will actually be quite therapeutic."

Leanne rubbed her forehead, easing the tension from her face. She glared up at Harlan and approached the glass security wall. She looked down at him as though appraising him, perhaps seeing if he would actually go ahead and torture her.

Harlan had no such intention, but knew within himself that if he did start, he probably wouldn't be able to finish.

Leanne had hurt him as much as anyone or anything had in his life.

He still carried that hurt within him and used it every day. His belief was that his anger was the sole reason why he was motivated to bring justice to the solar system. It was a way for him to exorcise the injustice she'd inflicted upon him when she left with no explanation.

They stared at each other for what seemed like an eternity until, finally, Leanne spoke.

"You weren't my first option as a target," she said. "But you just couldn't help yourself, could you? You couldn't leave it alone. Hell, I even left you clues, but you are so intent on justice you couldn't see them."

"Would it have killed you to have told me you were Vallan?" Harlan said.

"Yes, it would have. You do not understand what is happening in the solar system right now. There are things way beyond us. Like you, I'm just a pawn in the game. My killing you would have been a mercy compared to what is coming."

Harlan stood and slapped his hands against the glass barrier.

Leanne flinched and stepped back.

"That's bullshit," Harlan said. "Stop hiding behind cryptic claims. If you wish to live and avoid execution, talk. I will never stop hating you, but a tiny, withered part of me never stopped loving you. Take this opportunity. Tell me what you know—and maybe that'll keep you alive."

Leanne took a half-step forward, raised a hand to the glass screen, but then dropped it to her side and sat back on the bench, shaking her head. "No," she said. "You don't understand what you're asking. I can't."

"Damn it, Leanne. You leave me with no alternative."

Harlan turned his back on the glass screen and left the cell compartment, taking his seat within the commuter carriage.

They were less than a quarter of an hour away from docking at Atlas Station. The feed showed their approach. A familiar tourist video played, quoting the facts to newcomers, although there were few these days who hadn't either been born on Atlas or visited it from one of the many colonies or the other six stations.

An abbot with long blond hair spoke with all the plastic charm in the world. "Welcome to Atlas Station. Atlas is home to five million humans and abbots. It is forty-five kilometers in diameter and ten torus-levels high. Each ring has ten levels within it to make over one hundred comfortable habitable areas.

"In old 'money' it cost well over one hundred trillion, but shortly after its initial build, the abbot and space-based construction technology rapidly reduced the cost to where a financial economy wasn't necessary; everything humanity and abbotkind needed was already out there in space. They mined most of the material from the moon and asteroids within the Belt. Using mass drivers and construction docks, the automated abbots made quick work of the manufacturing, securing a new home for the descendants of the now-ruined Earth."

Harlan couldn't help but think this all sounded like abbot propaganda: the machine entities promoting themselves as the savior of humanity.

They seemed to forget who had designed and built them.

A small tug-like shuttle flanked them and escorted their ship to the dock on level three. The old transport ship altered its arc, plumes of thrust ejecta blooming in space like miniature versions of the geysers from Saturn's moon Enceladus.

The transport ship docked without incident this time, and the port authority checked the ship's manifest. Fifteen standard minutes of administrative procedures later, Harlan had given them his identification and authority to transport a criminal.

Leanne remained silent during the journey throughs the silicon runners' HQ on level five of Atlas Station. As Harlan escorted her through the office, a dozen of his colleagues, busy at work at their terminals, turned to face him and applaud.

Some cheered the fact Harlan had brought Santos Vallan to justice, while others chatted amongst each other, casting furtive glances.

It was clear some of them had recognized Leanne as his ex-wife.

Some veterans in the office had been there when Harlan had had his breakdown. Those looked at him with a mix of surprise and pity, no doubt confused about how to react. Harlan didn't blame them; he had mixed emotions about the situation, too.

Harlan placed Leanne into a holding cell and returned to his cubicle, ready to write up his report and present his charges to the Sol-Fed justice system.

His boss, Hugo Raul, was waiting for Harlan and indicated that he should join him in his private office. Harlan followed and closed the door behind him. Hugo sat at the ornate desk in the bright room. A window overlooked level five of the station, showing a scene of busy citizens going about their business, trading and moving to and from their places of work.

To them, this was just another day.

To Harlan, it was a turning point in his life. But instead of closure for an old wound, it had become a complete reversal.

Hugo eased his elbows onto the desk and leaned forward. His thick black eyebrows met in the middle as his forehead creased. His bald head shone beneath the overhead LED lights. A contemporary suit fitted him like a glove, showing his still-fit form despite him having hit his centenary.

"Well, Harlan, this is an unusual situation," he said, his deep voice resonating.

"Yeah, you can imagine my surprise. Turns out I was the target after all that chasing around."

"That's not what I'm talking about," Hugo said. "I'm talking about the fact that Santos Vallan is your ex. I find it difficult to believe you wouldn't have had any idea after all these years that it was her."

Most times, Harlan appreciated Hugo's bluntness. It meant he could manage his silicon runners with no bullshit, but this insinuation just pissed Harlan off.

After everything he had been through, it wouldn't have been too much to expect Hugo to show some sympathy for his situation or perhaps congratulate him on a job well done.

"Look, boss, this is as much of a surprise to me as it is to you. Do you really think if I knew Leanne was an assassin, I would have stayed quiet all these years? You know how much that bitch hurt me."

Hugo leaned back in his chair and arched his fingers. "I guess so," he said. "I trust you. It's just the governors are riding my ass these days for results. Leanne has caused untold collateral damage over the last few months. Her killing an abbot has caused a major diplomatic crisis with Asimovia, and they're pointing the figure of blame at you."

"I did my best. I'm not sure what else was expected of me. We should be thankful that it was only an abbot she killed. She was with me on the transport ship for two weeks and had the opportunity to kill any number of the few hundred people there. That this was all a setup to get to me meant that we actually reduced any collateral damage if her controllers had other ideas for her."

Hugo got out of his chair, turned his back, and looked out the window. He paced back and forth. There was something else on his mind. He wasn't usually this distant.

"Boss, listen, I'm not stupid. I can tell something's going on. You wouldn't bring me in here to tear a strip off me for a job I did well. Why don't you just come out with it?"

"I want you to drop this case. Leanne is involved in something much larger. I don't know what yet, but I just got off the phone with the governor of Asimovia, and he's escalating this to the House of Messengers for debate."

Harlan stood and leaned against the table. "You've got to be kidding me. She's my ex. Who better to follow this case than me? I know her. I can get the information from her. We can find out who she's working for and what this other business is about. Damn it, Hugo, let me do my job."

Hugo turned to face him and placed his hands in his trouser pockets. "I'm sorry. It's out of my hands. Besides, I've got another task for you."

"I don't want another job. I haven't finished this one yet. Don't treat me like some newbie. I'm one of the most experienced runners you have. Let me do this."

Hugo sighed and ran a hand over his head. He sat down

and gestured to Harlan to also sit. "If I could, I would, Harlan, trust me. But you'll be interested in this other case; it's something that can put your considerable skills to use while all this business with Asimovia blows over."

Realizing he was getting nowhere, Harlan sat back in his chair and resigned himself. If Hugo was being pushed from someone above, that was way beyond Harlan's privilege level.

That didn't mean he couldn't check in with Leanne and see how the case was going. Harlan had a few more tricks up his sleeve than Hugo knew.

"What is the case?" Harlan asked, accepting his reassignment.

"An abbot has disappeared. But not just any abbot. We're talking about one of the first ever V3s. One of the QCA founders. Fizon."

"Holy shit. That's huge. When did Fizon go missing?"

"A few days ago. I knew I'd get your attention with that one. It'll be good for you to take your mind off Leanne. We don't want a repeat of what happened before."

Harlan controlled an outburst. He didn't appreciate being reminded about that time of his life, and it was unfair of Hugo to use it as a way of manipulating him.

"Fine. I'll take the case. Send me the brief, and I'll get on it right away."

"You'll be starting this afternoon. We've got a meeting with the governor of Asimovia first and then disciplinary action for the death of the abbot. I will do all I can to make sure this doesn't end up on your record. And if you do this new case, well, that will go a long way to improving your current standing. But hear me when I say this, Harlan, this is likely your last chance. Your previous three cases have all ended up with considerable collateral damage and the deaths of civilians. If it wasn't for me, they'd have fired you even before *this* case. So please, for the sake of your career, do as I say and find this missing abbot with no more death and destruction."

"Sounds like I have no other option."

"No, you don't. Go home, get some sleep, and be back here by 1500 hours. And don't do anything stupid in the meantime."

"Fine. I'll see you later."

Harlan turned and approached the door, but Hugo stopped him. "I'm serious, Harlan. Don't screw up this last opportunity."

Harlan said nothing, opened the door, and headed home, contemplating his future if he failed and wondering what degrading task they would assign him.

If they kicked him out of the silicon runners, there was no way he would accept some terrible job with an even lower access status. There were plenty of organizations out there who would be glad for his skills, but they all existed in the gray area of what was legal. So gray they were as dark as the void of space.

Before joining the silicon runners, he'd spent the previous fifteen years working as a rogue trader. If it came to it, he'd resume that career path, even if it was a life that wouldn't welcome him back given his status as a silicon runner. It'd be like the circus tamer moving to the veldt to become a lion.

7

Irena checked her watch for the third time. Or was it the fourth? The surrounding forest was quiet, and she'd not heard anything run past her position for nearly two hours now. Like a fox, she'd found a small hole and burrowed into it, using leaves and sticks as cover. The coldness of the dirt had seeped into her bones. She wasn't shivering through panic now; just the chill of the earth.

Using a piece of fabric she had ripped from her T-shirt, she bandaged her hand. Most of the bleeding had stopped now, and upon closer inspection she found that the wound was only a graze.

Having had time to recover from the panic and the horror of seeing her friends murdered, she felt more in control of herself. She eased her body up through the hole and pulled the leaves aside so she could get a view of her surroundings.

Her breath plumed in the frigid air. The sun had set and cast the woods into an inky blackness. Silver light reflected off the gray birch bark, giving her a few spots of light with which to navigate. With no sign of movement around her and no sounds of screaming or other calls from the earthers, she pulled herself free from her foxhole, identified North using the stars spotted through the tree line, and headed south.

Although it was a long shot, she had to at least head towards the project facility. Station Nord offered no shelter, and she couldn't be sure that another rogue abbot wasn't waiting, concealed in the ruin.

Irena crawled from her burrow and took tentative steps across the cold ground, looking at her watch as she moved. She'd barely travelled over five minutes before she heard movement on her flanks. Shadows and shapes flickered in the moonlight around the trees. She knew she was being stalked again. Two of the earthers in ragged clothes jumped out from a thicket of trees in front of her and swung their arms towards her.

She jumped back.

They lurched forward again. This time, one of them grabbed her leg and brought her crashing to the ground. It grunted, spittle flew from its mouth. It lunged at her, trying to snap its teeth around her arm.

Irena screamed and kicked out, driving her foot as hard as she could into the creature's groin. It roared and rolled over, freeing her from her pinned position. She kicked out again, knocking it to the side, giving her the chance to stand and run.

Low-hanging branches struck her in the face as she ran into the woods. She was unsure of where her pursuers were.

The howls of more earthers echoed from behind her—they were getting close.

Part of her wished she had been shot back at the station; it would have been a lot quicker and pain-free. She couldn't face being attacked and eaten by these devolved humans.

Irena leapt over a fallen log and stumbled into a clearing. When she regained her balance, she made to sprint forward, but booming gunfire pulled her up short. A barrage of bullets struck into the trees all around her. Splinters of wood and leaves tumbled down around her shoulders.

Ahead of her on either side of the clearing were two automatic gun sentries. Their tripodal chrome metallic casings were lit by two bright spotlights placed on the outside of a ruined single-story building that Irena supposed was another, abandoned, station.

Behind and to one side of the building, she saw the corner of a ship. It looked like a light freighter. It was painted black with white stripes. A mix of relief and fear filled Irena's guts as she realized she'd found a crew of contraband salvagers.

The sentry guns retrained their aim.

Irena looked down and saw she had passed through a laser beam. She stepped back from the laser. The gun sentries stopped tracking.

The gang of earthers had ceased their howling. When Irena turned around, she saw they were backing away. After the ringing in her ears from the gunfire had dissipated, she noticed a voice calling out to her. This was no earther howl but actual, clear English.

"Who's there?" Irena shouted, panic tearing at her words.

"I could ask the same question," a woman's voice replied.

Irena saw a tall elegant woman step out from an abandoned building, its walls half tumbled, the roof fallen in. The woman was dressed in leather overalls and combat boots. Her long gray hair was plaited and rested over her left shoulder.

A man, tiny compared to the woman, with close-cropped hair was carrying items out of the building and into the back of the freighter. Irena had to resist stepping forward again toward safety, not wishing to trip the laser beam.

"Please help me," she begged. "I'm a scientist from Station Nord. All my team have been killed. You must help me."

The woman cocked her head as if deciding whether Irena was telling the truth. Then, after a few moments of pondering, she tapped something on her forearm terminal and gestured Irena forward after the laser beam switched off.

As soon as Irena crossed the threshold, the laser beam returned, and the sentry guns opened fire on the two earthers who had tried to follow her into the clearing.

Irena closed her eyes, but she could still hear their hideous screams of pain.

"Call me Bella," the woman said, as though nothing had happened. She strode over to Irena and held her right hand out. In her left, she held a pistol.

Irena shook her hand and introduced herself.

"You look like you've been through hell. Let's get you inside. That hand looks nasty."

The woman took Irena inside the cargo hold of the freighter and sat her down on a metal chest. The ship's hold was full of contraband salvaged from Earth. Boxes and crates of books filled the space. The salvagers had collected computers, furniture, toys, and anything else deemed valuable to those on the colonies and the stations.

Irena closed her eyes and said a silent prayer of thanks to anything or anyone who was listening. "Thank you. I thought I would die out there."

Bella had her back to Irena, searching through different

boxes until she had found what she was looking for. She turned and held out a white plastic bottle.

"Here, take one of these; it'll help with the pain."

Bella handed her the painkillers. Irena took them with a shaking hand, and then accepted a bottle of water. She took a mouthful of water and swallowed three pills.

The two other members of the contraband crew joined Bella in the hold. They stood around Irena, regarding her with curiosity. To Irena, the man looked like a mole. Small beady eyes blinked behind round spectacles. He wore them perched on his pointy nose as he stared at her.

The other woman lightly smacked the back of her hand against his face. "Don't glare at her like that, Wilbur. She looks like she's been through Hades and back."

"I'm curious. She's not an abbot, is she?"

"Of course not. When was the last time you saw an abbot bleed?"

Bella shook her head. "Ignore these two. They don't get out much, and they don't see many people. Why don't you tell us what happened?"

Irena filled them in on the attack on the station by the rogue abbot. "If you can just get me back to the project facility, I can inform the others. Let them know what's happened."

Wilbur shook his head. "No, I'm sorry, we don't have time to take you there."

Bella checked her wrist terminal. "He's right. We won't make it. We'll miss our rendezvous at the elevator."

Irena stood and begged them. "Please, I'm not asking for much. Maybe you could just radio them to let them know what happened."

Wilbur sighed. "Look, I sympathize with your situation. But an abbot going rogue? That just doesn't happen. Not since the uprising and the reprogramming. I'm not suggesting you haven't had a rough time, but it seems far-fetched."

Irena couldn't believe they didn't trust her. Why would she have anything to hide from thieves? She looked incredulously at Bella and her crew. "If you don't believe me, then why don't you fly this ship of yours a little north of here and see for yourself? The earthers ripped it limb from limb. You'll find the parts and you'll see what I mean."

The large woman dressed in army fatigues introduced herself as Greta and then looked at Wilbur and then to Bella. She raised an eyebrow. "I'm up for it." Irena noticed that she wore Solar Federation Marine stripes on her jacket's shoulder. This meant she had served, and that meant she had fought the separatists on Ceres. A brutal, but brief conflict.

Bella checked her terminal again. "How far did you travel?"

"Not far. Probably only a few miles."

Bella stroked her plaited hair as she considered Irena's proposal. Uncertainty twisted her full lips, and suspicion shaded her eyes.

Irena could see her only opportunity closing by the second. "Okay, listen. I've got a proposal for you. What if I was to tell you that there were two q-bit cores and two rovers you could salvage?"

Wilbur pushed the glasses up on his nose and looked to Greta with an open expression.

"I think if you're bullshitting, we'll drop you out from just below atmosphere," Greta said.

"Surely your facility would want to recover the rovers and the q-bit cores for themselves?" Bella posited. "We're not in the business of making a target of ourselves unnec-essarily."

"I'm desperate. I don't care if you take the rover or the cores. In fact, I don't even want to return to the facility. Without Dr. Osho alive, and with the rest of the team dead, I can't face it there anymore. I know there will be an inquest and they will blame me as I was the only survivor."

"What are you proposing?" Bella said, crossing her arms.

"You take me to Atlas Station and send word to the facility about what happened. I won't mention that the q-bit cores and the rovers were stolen by contraband salvagers."

Greta looked at Bella with no lack of earnestness. "We could just get the gear ourselves and kill her."

"If you do, then I won't tell you how to uninstall the q-bit cores. If you handle them the way you've been handling your other contraband here, you'll destroy them. They're delicate, sensitive instruments."

Wilbur smiled, his little eyes crinkling behind his glasses. "The woman has a point."

"The name's Irena."

"Feisty, too."

"Fine, we'll do it," Bella said. "No more screwing around. We don't have the time. Irena, you come with me to the cockpit. Guide us in and show us where the station is. If what you say is true, we'll take you to Atlas Station and send word to your facility. But trust me, if you try to screw us around, I will let Greta do what she wants with you."

"You can trust me. I just want to get the hell off this forsaken planet. The authorities need to know about the abbot."

Bella nodded and led Irena to the cockpit.

They took a few minutes to find the ruined body of the

rogue abbot. The gun had gone missing; the earthers most likely had taken it.

The scene clearly satisfied the contraband crew. They smiled and nodded amongst themselves, excited about the bounty. As they journeyed to the station, Irena considered if she was a traitor for wanting to return to Atlas Station instead of the project facility. But she couldn't face working there any longer, not after knowing Dr. Osho and the rest of the team were gone. And she couldn't do anything about the rogue abbot from the facility. She needed to speak with the silicon runners and have it investigated. Having grown up as a daughter to a Messenger representative in her mother and a House representative in her father, she was all too aware of how red tape could obfuscate the truth.

"There it is," Wilbur said from behind Bella, pointing through the cockpit. The lights of the freighter lit up the station, showing blood splatter around the building and the rovers.

"Holy shit. She was telling the truth," Greta said.

"We're agreed, then? You take me to Atlas and send a report of this to the facility?" Irena asked.

"We'll see," Bella said. "Okay, you two. Gear up and see if she's telling the truth about the cores."

Wilbur demanded directions to where he would find the cores. Not wanting to go in there herself, Irena told him, adding, "Please bring the bodies out so I can hand them over to the authorities on Atlas."

Bella nodded to him. He turned and left the cockpit with the ex-Marine.

They took less than ten minutes to bring the bodies and the cores into the hold, using a series of freeze-boxes to hold the former. As Bella watched her team secure the translucent, cold coffins, Irena thought about how she would explain the whole situation. She knew the silicon runners would be interested—despite being on Earth, this still fell under the purview of their jurisdiction, being an abbot issue —but she wasn't clear if she had broken any laws. She'd see when she arrived home on Atlas. All she cared about was getting off the planet.

Wilbur poked his head through the rear door of the cockpit. "Okay, partner, we have everything, and we're ready to go."

Bella checked her terminal, then punched coordinates into the freighter's control panel. She turned to Irena and said, "You better strap in; it's a bitch getting up to the space elevator. We have to join it halfway up to avoid the security drones patrolling the area." With that, the freighter launched forward in an upward trajectory.

Irena closed her eyes and breathed a deep sigh of relief. She was leaving Earth behind. However, she could do nothing about the heavy stone of grief lying in her guts.

8

Bella eased the thrusters on the Mazzari Enterprises freighter, officially designated as the *Mule*, and brought the ship down to less than a quarter g of thrust. Over the course of the next ten minutes, she followed the docking lights about the station and piloted into bay twenty-seven.

She engaged the autopilot and let the computer systems dock the ship. Her new guest, Irena, and crew members Wilbur and Greta were in their respective bunks. The latter no doubt preparing black-market ads for the latest haul of contraband. Bella had no idea who she'd sell the q-bit cores to, but knew it wouldn't take long to find a buyer for such a hot commodity. It wasn't every day something so rare came on the market.

The speaker on the control panel crackled with the whiny voice of the traffic controller. "Registered freighter of Mazzari Enterprises, your docking has been approved. Import Inspector Gareth Trippier will join you shortly to confirm the manifest of your delivery."

"Thank you, controller, have a great day," Bella said. She

turned to face Irena, who had come through and sat down in the copilot seat. The young woman was paler than she had been before, and Bella wondered if she had picked up an infection from her wound. Although Wilbur had helped with the first aid kit and ensured that there was nothing wrong, no one on board was a medical professional—something Bella had wanted to address, but trying to find one on their low budget had so far ended in failure. "How are you doing, Irena?"

Irena yawned and stretched her muscles with the speed of a sloth. "I hadn't realized leaving Earth and traveling to Atlas Station would be so tiring."

"Gravity is a bitch, eh? Though it could have been worse if we didn't have an elevator to use. Thanks to the abbots, we have at least a couple still working."

A shadow passed over Irena's face. She looked away.

"I'm sorry. I didn't think. Shouldn't have mentioned the abbots. Shit, there I go again."

Irena readjusted the bandage on her hand. "It's fine. I'll get over it. I just need sleep and rest."

The way Irena trembled reminded Bella of when she'd first met Greta. She'd served with the military service for a long tour of duty on Ceres Station. During that tour of duty, Greta had suffered an unspoken terrible trauma.

Given what Irena had gone through, what she had seen, it wouldn't surprise Bella if the poor girl was going through the same thing. She wanted to tell Irena Greta's experience and how she had eventually learned to cope with it, but she had little time.

From the canopy, she saw Trippier approaching.

Just looking at him turned her stomach. He moved like a lizard and had the twitchy eyes to match. Hell knows how this creature had wormed his way into such an official position. Still, such a creature dabbled in bribery, and they both knew it.

Trippier knocked on the cockpit door.

Irena looked up at Bella with alarm. "If he finds the q-bit cores, we're in serious trouble."

Wilbur poked his head through the door separating the cockpit from the main section of the hull. He glanced at Irena and then Bella. "I've done my best to hide the q-bits. But anything more than a cursory glance, and Trippier will find them. What's the plan?"

Another knock. A communication light flashed on the control panel. Trippier was hailing them. Bella had to think fast. "Do we still have that collection of media hack codes?"

Wilbur pushed the glasses up on his pointy nose and squinted his eyes as he thought. "Yeah, I think so. It's for old stuff, though. Hundreds of years old now and on magnetic media."

"That's perfect," Bella said. "Tripps is a freak for the ancient and the weird."

Irena looked at her with straight-lipped concern.

Bella gave her a quick smile. "Don't worry, it'll be fine. But you can't be seen with us; it'll be harder to explain an extra crew member than it will be some unusual contraband. Wilbur, hide her in my private bunk, behind the panel in the wardrobe. And bring the codes."

"Of course, Captain, anything I can do to help you, seeing as your last slave died of exhaustion."

Bella pressed her lips together in annoyance. "Not this again. I know we're equal partners, but I still am the captain of the ship."

Wilbur held his hands up in a placating gesture. "Hey, I get it. I'm just a stickler for manners."

Bella rolled her eyes and sighed. She glanced at Irena,

shook her head, and then glanced back to Wilbur. With a sickly-sweet voice, she said, "Please, dearest Wilbur, would you do me the greatest of favors and for once follow my goddamned order? Please, thank you."

"That's all you had to say."

Wilbur gestured for Irena to follow him.

With Irena out of the way, Bella hit the receiver button and opened a communication channel with Trippier.

"Ms. Mazzari, I'm getting cold standing out here. What's the delay?"

"Sorry, Inspector, just a technical glitch. Give me two seconds."

After a few more moments, Wilbur entered the cockpit, carrying an old-fashioned external magnetic disk enclosure. He handed it over to Bella. "Here you go."

"Okay, let's get rid of this amphibian and get on with the rest of our business."

"What about the bodies?"

"We'll explain we're bringing them back on behalf of the ERP."

Wilbur didn't look convinced, but if they played it right, Trippier wouldn't even get as far as the cargo area. And even if he did, he wasn't the kind of guy to give a shit about a few bodies. The illicit cores though...

Bella hit a button on the control panel, raising the light in the small space. Wilbur huddled in the corner of the room and did his best to look inconspicuous, which, to be fair, was one of his specialties.

Bella opened the door and shivered as a blast of cold air wafted in from Atlas Station's dock. "Inspector Trippier, please, come aboard. We're in a rush, so if we can do this quickly, we'd appreciate it."

The inspector stared up at her, his expression

inscrutable on the surface, but the glint in his eyes told Bella that he was eager for ill-gotten remuneration.

She stood aside and allowed him to climb up.

He closed the door behind him and stepped close to her, his hands behind his back and his body leaning forward with eagerness. He smelled of three-day-old sweat and cheap protein paste. "Been to Earth, have you?

"Certainly not, Inspector. We wouldn't dream of breaking the law. We've been on a supply run to the Belt and back."

Trippier smiled, nodded, accepting the lie.

"Terrible business out there," Wilbur said, ad-libbing. "Pirates and rogues are swarming the place. Wouldn't surprise me if the military get involved."

"I'm sure it was a tough job for you guys. Still, one has to do their duty. So if you escort me to your hold, I can confirm your manifest and be on my way."

Bella placed her hand on the smaller man's shoulder.

He glanced down at it and then up at her. "I hope you will not prevent me from doing my job, Ms. Mazzari."

With her other hand, Bella brought up the hard disk of codes and waved it in front of Trippier's face. "I wouldn't dream of it. But if one were interested in an alternative way of completing one's duties, I could reciprocate."

Trippier grinned and laughed, turning his attention from Bella to Wilbur and back again.

The bastard was enjoying his little power trip.

He overexaggerated thinking about the offer, placing one hand on his hips and a finger on his chin. "Hmm, let me think... What's on it?"

"Codes for rare adult entertainment, pre-Migration media, software," Wilbur said. "Classic stuff, hard-to-find media that wasn't uploaded to the QCA."

The way Trippier was staring at Bella, the cockpit began to close in around her. He licked his lips and looked her up and down. "I'm not sure that will quite do it anymore."

"That is all you are getting," Bella said, scowling at him and resisting the urge to drive her knee into his testicles. "It's been good enough before."

Trippier shrugged. "That's inflation for you. And I take my job seriously, Ms. Mazzari. If there is no other business, then I suggest I get on with checking the hold. I am a busy man."

Bella glanced at Wilbur.

Her partner glared back blankly, seemingly out of ideas.

This was an unusual situation for them. They had struck a similar deal with Trippier for at least the last twelve shipments. She did not understand why it wasn't worth it for him now. Then, as she looked out onto the dock via the open door, she counted at least thirty other small cargo-class freighters and realized she had competition for Trippier's blind eye.

The inspector shifted his body and made to move towards the open door into the hold section of the ship.

Stopping him with one arm, Bella shifted around in front of him. "Just a moment. I need to secure the airlock first. We have delicate food products in there. I can't let them be exposed."

With a nod, Bella indicated for Wilbur to watch Trippier while she ducked through the door and into the tight passageway. She nearly crashed into Irena, who was standing outside the door, listening in.

"He wants to see the cargo, doesn't he?" Irena said in hushed tones.

"Yeah, another firm must have bought his loyalty. We're screwed."

Greta stepped into the hallway. In her right hand with casual nonchalance she grasped her Marine-issue pistol. "Bring him into the hold. I'll deal with him. It'll be quick."

Irena shook her head. "No, please. I think I can get us out of this. Give me a minute. I have a friend in the House of Messengers who owes me a favor."

Through the door, Wilbur's voice could be heard cracking jokes and stalling for time.

"Do it," Bella said.

Despite being captain of the ship, she doubted she could prevent Greta from taking matters into her own hands, especially as they were carrying hot cargo. She knew it was a risk to bring it back with her, but she hadn't considered Trippier would turn on them.

While Irena used her terminal to communicate with her friend, the narrow corridor echoed from the pounding on the door. Trippier's voice called out, "I am done with waiting. Open before I call security and have the ship impounded."

Bella called back, "Almost there, I'm just pressurizing the refrigeration units. Give me two minutes."

The pounding on the door stopped, and Wilbur continued to do his best to keep Trippier occupied. Irena gesticulated as she talked in frantic whispers with her friend. Bella had to resist the temptation to grab her wrist and beg her friend to help. Instead, she tapped Irena on the shoulder and indicated to hurry. A minute more of tense discussion passed.

Greta chambered a round.

Irena hung up her call and turned to face Bella. "It's done. A friend is messaging him now."

"What did you do?" Greta asked, looking disappointed.

"I, erm... my friend, well, a friend of my mother's, owed

me a favor for not revealing a transgression. She will pull rank and give Trippier a government stipend bonus."

"Okay," Bella said. "You both stay here and don't do anything stupid."

Bella opened the door and entered the cockpit, forcing Trippier to retreat.

He opened his mouth as though he were about to speak, then a notification beep came from the terminal on his left wrist. He looked at the holographic display. His forehead crinkled, presumably with confusion as to why a member of the House of Messengers was messaging him.

"One moment, Ms. Mazzari. It appears I need to take this." He backed away to the far corner of the cockpit and turned his back on them to take the call.

Wilbur shared a quizzical expression with Bella, and she whispered to him to just wait and see. While they waited, Bella's heart rate increased, and she felt her skin prickle with heat and the beginnings of mild panic that reminded her of her days singing opera on stage. Only this experience didn't give her the thrill of an adrenaline boost. Rather, it gave her a slow drip of dread. A long minute ticked by. Bella counted every second, her feet tapping against the ship's oil-stained metal floor.

Trippier ended his call and turned to face them. "Looks like you won't be paying tribute today. Someone else has provided... an unexpected windfall. I don't know who you have on board, but they've just given up one hell of a favor."

"I don't know what you mean, Inspector," Bella said, trying not to smile. "Let me escort you off my ship so you may go about your business and take your damned tribute from other hardworking members of the public."

She stepped aside and gestured for him to leave, which

he did with a sly self-satisfied grin. Once he'd disappeared from view, Bella closed the door and sighed with relief.

Wilbur shook his head and wiped sweat from his forehead with a handkerchief. "That was terrible. If that happens next time, I will let Greta shoot the bastard and let his body drift out into space. That was too stressful."

"You're getting old, my friend. It's all part of the game."

"It was a better game when we were writing the rules."

Although it was easy to say, she herself was also tiring of the risks involved in retrieving contraband from Earth. For the first time in many years, she considered whether this was the career choice for her. She would think more on that later. For now, she wanted to get Irena and the ERP scientists' bodies off the ship and find a dealer for the hardware. The quicker she sold them, the quicker she could return her attentions to that strange emergency broadcast she had received from her brother, Gianni's, shuttle. He'd still not returned her call, and the SFSA had not heard from him in some time either.

9

Harlan yawned after a broken night's sleep and stumbled out of the elevator on level 5 of the station. After all the hours stuck on the transport ship, the recycled air of Atlas tasted fresh for once.

At least until he descended into the lower levels, that is.

Harlan wandered out into the throng of people and strode along the walkways, eager to get the blood pumping through his body since he overslept.

It was approaching midday according to standard time. Simulated noon sunlight shone down on his shaven head from the overhead projectors to prove it. He squinted at the brightness until his contacts shaded themselves.

Level five was a transient zone, a non-place, a place that had no real defined usage. Pedestrians walked across the walkways suspended over thousands of anonymous storage units, hurrying their way to one task or another.

Harlan liked to come here just to watch the people go back and forth as he wondered what their roles were. It was a good exercise in observation. Kept his wits sharp and committed faces to his long-term memory.

One never knew when they needed to recall a familiar face.

He wanted to come up here for a little while, to think and relax and let the events of the previous day digest into his subconscious before he had to go about his business. He had a meeting with the informant later, and then there was the meeting with Hugo.

Harlan expected an official tearing of one's anus, especially as it seemed the governor of Asimovia wanted to make a point of standing up for the murdered abbot. He'd be out for blood and would be pleased to make Harlan the scapegoat.

A few years back, Harlan had arrested his son for organizing a pedophile ring on Station Aristippus—home to the hedonists. Ever since then, the governor had been out for revenge.

He would get it, in a sense. And that was fine as long as Harlan could just get on with his job. He'd deal with this new case, then figure out why Leanne had resurfaced after all these years, and who had hired her to kill him.

On that front, Harlan counted at least half a dozen suspects.

— *Definitely more*, Milo said, the voice sounding in Harlan's head and making him jump with surprise. Sometimes Harlan forgot he had his peripheral in there, working away at whatever an AI did when it wasn't assigned a specific task.

Harlan just nodded in agreement.

Milo was right. Who knew how many people would feel happier about Harlan being dead. Could be hundreds, given how many perps he had put behind bars over the years.

He leaned against the barrier and looked over at the level below.

Small shuttles like white doves hovered and darted from dock to dock, taking small items from one business to another, packages to citizens, and the occasional person to a medical facility.

Harlan had only seen real birds on video footage, mostly from his contraband collection of documentaries by his favorite filmmaker, Richard Attenborough. Harlan often watched the clips of the birds and their formations, wondering how they did it, how they managed such beautiful orchestrations, but also why?

There were concrete explanations out there, of course, but he liked to think they did it for the fun, for the thrill of flying and having a good time.

As he watched the shuttles doing their thing, a familiar face from the dock caught his attention. Bella Mazzari, his contraband dealer, was stomping along the walkway with some eagerness.

A younger woman, white as bone, accompanied her. She turned off at a junction and headed down a street following Bella's outstretched pointing arm. That way led to the silicon runners' office. Harlan wondered what had happened to her. He made a mental note to find out when he spoke with Hugo later.

— *Like you need another case*, Milo said. *You will be busy enough as it is.*

"Busy is good. I could do with something to take my mind off Leanne."

— *She'll never be off your mind. Admit it, she's your weakness. Always was, always will be.*

"What part of peripheral does your programming not understand?" Harlan said. "When I get time, I'm going to defrag you, see if I can strip some of that sass out of your code."

"Talking to yourself again, Harlan?" Bella asked, joining him at the barrier of the walkway. She leaned one elbow on the railing.

Like the girl she had escorted, she looked exhausted. She didn't have her usual pep and charm about her. She was still wearing her work overalls and combat boots, mud smeared across her cheek.

"What can I say? I'm good company," Harlan said.

"Or just nuts."

"Who's saying I can't be both? Anyway, I hate to tell you this, but you look terrible. Bad day?"

"Yeah, something like that. Listen, I need help. I found something... how should I say this... Hot."

Two abbots walked by, their presence silencing Bella. They seemed to take a particular interest in Harlan and Bella as they walked in synchronized steps. Harlan didn't take it to heart; it was just the way they were. Always observing. It was nothing personal, even if it was a little creepy. When they had passed, he leaned in closer and lowered his voice. "I can give you a contact, if it helps."

"And in return?"

"A drink with me. Consider it a favor, something for me to call in at my discretion."

Bella thought about this for a moment, then agreed.

Harlan scrolled through the list of contacts on his wrist terminal, found a particular shady dealer, and swiped his details across to her. "His name is Gabriel Salazar. Fancies himself a spy. We've done business together for years. He's as trustworthy a rogue as you will find—present company excepted."

A beep confirmed the transfer.

"Thanks. I appreciate it."

"You're welcome. Has there been any more news about your brother?" Harlan asked.

"No, not yet. I still think Gianni is alive though. Surely something would have come up, right? People and shuttles don't just go missing anymore."

"You still think someone took him on his way to that new facility on Europa?"

Bella cast a glance around them as though checking for listeners.

Nobody would be that obvious, he thought. But he guessed with rogues like Bella, it was a natural reaction. As natural as birds flying together. As natural as Leanne hurting him.

"I'm certain," Bella said. "I even have confirmation from the AstroLab initiative that he left Station Zeno two weeks ago en route to Europa. The last transmission they received from his ship was only a few hours away from his rendezvous point. And then after that, nothing."

"No sign of debris from his ship?"

"None that the Sol-Fed Space Agency will admit to. But I believe them. There are enough amateur astronomers around that someone would have noticed such a thing. I suspect something much worse has happened, or he's got himself involved in something he shouldn't. I decoded his shuttle's emergency broadcast, but it makes little sense—it's as if something altered the signal."

Harlan thought about this for a moment, tried to figure out what he could say that would help, but without more data or information it could mean anything.

"That contact I gave you, speak with him. He knows a lot of talented people. I've used them a bunch of times myself for analyzing data. They're often faster, cheaper, and more skilled than so-called professional analysts we have access to at the office. Let me know how it goes."

Bella gave him a quick kiss on the cheek and thanked him. "Take care of yourself, Harlan. I'm getting bad vibes from the system these days. Lots of weird stuff going on. That girl you saw me with? She had a horrendous experience on Earth. I would tell you more, but I'm not sure what I should say, and you'll no doubt hear about it when you get into the office. Don't wait too long to call in that favor regarding the drink."

"I won't. Keep out of trouble, and if you can't, at least make it fun and profitable."

Bella smiled and waved as she headed off back toward the dock.

Harlan checked his terminal and headed back to the elevator. It was time to go down to level two for his regular check-in with one of his informants.

LEVEL TWO WAS a filth-hole and there was no getting away from that. Much like Dante's Inferno, the lower one travelled down the various circles of Atlas Station, the worse things got.

Still, it was better than level one.

Which was like suggesting a knife to the gut was better than a bullet to the brain.

Even the light here was darker, creating shadows in corners and giving plenty of opportunity for people to skulk and stalk. Few silicon runners would come down this far, preferring to stay up on the safe levels and use their automated systems to do their job.

There was something honest about it, though, Harlan

thought. Real humanity in all its dirty, grubby, desperate glory.

Nothing glossy or fake.

Few abbots would come down here either, as there was no real purpose for them. Humans did the vast majority of the jobs, working for criminal organizations. Those who didn't like their status level assigned to them in other parts of the station would opt out of that system and descend here to the guts of the Sol-Fed.

Civilization back on Earth before the Great Migration was a lot like this, Harlan thought.

People in dirty clothes huddled together and shifted around the narrow dark avenues.

Various contraband stood out from wooden stalls, the vendors calling out their custom, trying to shift their wares before they got too hot.

Harlan negotiated his way through the maze-like corridors until he came to the only legitimate area of the level: an Atlas computer RDC — resource distribution center.

He waved his hand over the security panel, waited for the blue light to display, and entered inside. The door swung closed and locked behind him.

Harlan's informant stood behind the counter, smoking a homemade cigarette, brushing the ash from his dirty white coat. The eighty-year-old ex-silicon runner, Gylfie Larson, looked up at Harlan and placed the cigarette into a brown ashtray on the glass countertop.

"Good to see you, Harlan," Gylfie said. "Let me close up and we can go through to the back."

In the back of the RDC, conveyor belts ran down both the east and the west walls, carrying on them bins of various computer parts supplied by the Sol-Fed computer and robotics division. All of which were made by abbots and sent down here.

The bins of parts left over slid off the conveyor belts and onto staging tables, where small drones lifted and carried the parts through hatches in the walls and into warehousing space behind the RDC.

Behind the staging tables, Gylfie had set aside a place for him to take his breaks and to do his work. This job, however, was just for cover. Working here meant that he could mix with the criminals of Atlas Station and exchange information, which he would then provide, at a cost, to the elite families of the Sol-Fed.

"Take a seat," Gylfie said, indicating a chair opposite him.

Both Harlan and Gylfie sat at the table, and the older man opened two bottles of local home-brew beer.

"So, Gylfie, what have you got for me today?"

"It's getting more difficult. I think some of the families know I've been supplying information back to the silicon runners. They're a lot more guarded now."

"But I can see the twinkle in your eye. You have something, right?"

"It's not so much a twinkle, rather a nervous tick. Things are changing around here."

"Aren't they always?"

"Aye, they are. But this, however, is something else. Two of my suppliers have gone underground. Disappeared as if they were ghosts."

"What do you attribute that to?" Harlan asked, rubbing a thumb over the cool glass of the bottle.

Gylfie took a breath and leaned forward, lowering his voice. "I'm not sure, but one thing I do know is that the corporations are changing, pushing against the Sol-Fed regulations imposed upon them by Companies House."

"How is that different from before?" Harlan said. "The corporations always want more. They seem to forget we don't live in a capitalist society now. But I guess that ideal never died in the hearts and minds of some."

Gylfie took a deep drag of beer and swallowed it with an exhalation. "It's not that," he said. "Yesterday, I found out something that could change everything. The Ceres Mining Company is merging with the Jovian Group."

Harlan sat back and considered this.

— *That would give the head of the merged company the biggest representation of Messengers in the House*, Milo said.

"Well, that will upset the establishment. With the Jovian system resources and the Ceres mining facility, those old bastards at the top could enforce an election against the current president if they instruct their workers to register their disapproval."

Gylfie nodded. "And who knows who they would put up for election in their place."

Harlan checked his watch and stood up, draining the last of the beer in his bottle and placing it back on the table. "Maybe it won't get to that," Harlan said. "I better get going, but I appreciate the information. Here's your payment as agreed."

From inside his leather jacket, Harlan pulled out an old vinyl Bruce Springsteen EP and handed it to Gylfie.

"Ah, The Boss. I shall enjoy this while we still have the freedoms to do so."

"Enjoy," Harlan said, as the informant turned the record over in his hand as if it were the most precious thing he'd ever seen.

Gylfie stood up and shook Harlan's hand before seeing him out of the RDC.

Harlan stepped out into the busy street and pulled the collar up around his neck, finding himself shivering despite the heat of the lower level. It appeared the keyword for the last three days was change, and Harlan couldn't prevent an ominous feeling from creeping up his spine.

10

Irena finished her coffee and placed the cardboard cup into the recycling chute. A white plastic drone about the size of her fist buzzed around after her, tidying things up and vacuuming any crumbs from her late breakfast.

She checked her watch. It was a little after 1300. She would have liked to have slept longer, give the pain medication a chance to really work and stop the throbbing in her hand, but she had an appointment in five minutes' time with the new head of the Earth Restoration Project.

Although she had told the silicon runners everything she knew about the attack on the relay station, the authority with the ERP wanted to hear it from her directly, which made sense given everything and everyone they had lost.

And she hoped that by explaining it to them, it would somehow exorcise the horror. Talking it out had helped to put the whole experience into a logical stream of events. She could still think of no reason why an abbot would go rogue in such a fashion. But that question was for the authorities to figure out. She exhaled and forced herself to relax and get back to the present.

The light in her apartment was soft and diffused through the diaphanous curtains. The lights were always stronger on level seven of Atlas Station. She often found the midday glare to be too much.

Having now spent a short time on Earth, she realized the full extent of Atlas' artificiality compared to real sunlight and atmosphere. She wished she could have those memories without them being tainted by the image of the dead bodies of her friends and colleagues.

Although she had only known her teammates for a couple of weeks, they had quickly become important people in her life. And to lose them so quickly and in such a fashion would leave an indelible mark on her memories of humanity's home planet.

Still feeling tired from the return journey and the exertions back on Earth, she let her body sink into her synthetic leather couch and rested her feet on the glass coffee table. A beep from her notification terminal indicated the incoming call.

The video screen, embedded into the plastic wall, flickered on at her request.

The ERP logo rotated on the screen and was accompanied by a small spinning icon in the corner, counting down to the video-conference connection.

An inset image reflected back Irena's feed.

Her face was cut and bruised, and her skin looked pale even for her. She had tied her hair in a simple ponytail and wore a plain bamboo robe. It was professional without being stifling, and casual enough that she felt comfortable given her aches and pains.

The screen flashed white, and then filled with the image of the ERP's new leader, Professor Encarnita. She was much younger than Dr. Osho and of Mexican descent. Her dark hair was arranged in an extravagant topknot. She wore more makeup than most scientists Irena knew. Professor Encarnita clearly preferred a more glamorous look. She wore a glittering gold-and-diamond necklace around her elegant neck, which contrasted with her designer black suit jacket fitted in the modern style with sharp creases.

"Ms. Selles, it is good to see you. You're looking quite well given the circumstances," the professor said.

"Thank you. I wish I *felt* better given the circumstances."

Irena chided herself for her snarky response. She hadn't meant it to come out sounding so aggressive and defensive.

Encarnita bowed her head slightly in a gesture of understanding.

Irena appreciated that and relaxed a little.

"I read the report you sent to us," the professor said. "It's such a terrible business. The team here is devastated, especially so soon after poor Romanov. Over the next few days, we're holding a ceremony in their honor here at the facility."

"That sounds like a fine way to pay respects to our team members," Irena said, unsure of what else to add, the grief still not quite cutting through the shock of the events.

"How are you doing? Is there anything you need from us?"

"I'm not sure yet. Everything has been such a blur so far. It all happened so quickly, and I have yet to get my head around it."

The professor bowed her head once more, and then looked off to the side as she responded to someone's call. She held up her palm to the camera and spoke briefly with the audio muted, nodded a few times, and then turned her attention back to Irena.

"If you're busy, we can always do this a little later," Irena said.

"It's fine, sorry about that; I'm sure you can imagine things here are somewhat chaotic at the moment. It's taken a while to brief everybody and step up the security protocols."

Irena wondered whether this was being recorded. It would probably be used for evidence in any investigation from the government. Not that Irena had anything to hide other than the whole contraband situation. But that was easy for Irena to explain; as far as the law was concerned, she had assumed the freighter ship she had hitched a ride with was legitimate. They didn't need to know about the deal she had struck.

"So," the professor said, her voice tight as though she were finding the next words difficult, "do you know when you'll be rejoining us? I can help arrange transport for you if you haven't already sorted that."

The wave of emotion that hit Irena took her by surprise.

The idea of returning to Earth so soon welled up inside her like a great weight pressing against her throat and chest.

The professor must have seen her balk at the question. "I'm sorry if this sounds insensitive and you feel I'm rushing you, but the work here is important, and I know Dr. Osho would have wanted us to continue, regardless."

Irena pushed herself up on the couch and leaned forward. She took a couple of deep breaths to compose herself. "I'm sure she would, but right now I'm in no real state to travel, let alone focus on my work. I will need some time to get over this."

"That's understandable. How long do you need?" The

professor stared at Irena through the video screen, expectation written all over her face.

The more Irena spoke with her, the less glamorous she seemed, and more hard-faced, more results-driven. She wondered whether she cared anything at all about Siegfried, Darnesh and Dr. Osho, or whether she just saw this whole situation as an inconvenience.

"I'm sorry, Professor, but this isn't a climate model. I can't just run the numbers and give you some hard data. I will know when I know, but in the meantime, I will make sure you stay abreast of any progress I make with the restoration project, and I will help when and where I can."

"Very well. I can't force you to return, but I also can't hide my disappointment. You are a key member of the team, and with the loss of the others, we're going to have a problem with resources."

The pressure in Irena's throat grew to the point where she had a problem getting her words out. It was only after a few moments that she realized it was anger and not grief. It took all of her control to resist the outburst that threatened to burn her scientific bridges.

"All I can do is apologize," Irena said through gritted teeth. "I will of course give the ERP my utmost priority as soon as I am able. In the meantime, please feel free to send me reports and any data that you and the new team come up with. And when I can, I will send back any feedback, if that is of any use to you."

"That's fine. I hope your recovery goes well, but if you don't mind, I have a very busy schedule and need to return to my duties. We'll be in touch soon."

The screen switched off. Professor Encarnita's image faded away to be replaced with a blank white space so that the screen matched the walls of Irena's apartment.

She stood, turned away from the screen, and swore loudly.

She continued to swear, letting out her anger in a thirty-second tirade that left her exhausted. She collapsed onto the sofa and laid her head down, trying not to take Professor Encarnita's cold reaction personally.

Which was easier said than done.

Irena couldn't help but feel she was abandoning all those at the ERP. But she knew she would be of better use to them up here, where she could work in her own time and space and where she felt safer. She didn't have much time to ponder on this when her apartment filled with the sound of a guest arriving.

The notification buzz encouraged her to stand and approach the front door.

The small square video screen next to the door showed the image of her parents standing outside. The pair of them wore expressions of impatience.

Her father checked his watch and raised his hand to press the buzzer again.

Irena swung the door open and smiled at her parents.

She made to hug them, but, together, they moved forward, forcing Irena to step back as they entered her apartment. Her father, Carlos Selles, a house representative for the Jovian Group, strode into the living area and sat down in the armchair, crossing one leg over the other. He looked up at Irena with an impatient expression that she knew all too well.

Her mother, Victoria Selles, the current Messenger representative for Atlas Station, stood next to Carlos, placing a hand on the back of the armchair. She, too, looked at Irena with expectation, her right eyebrow raised.

Irena closed the door, took a few calming breaths, and faced her parents.

"It's nice to see you both. Can I get you anything?" she asked.

"We won't stay long," Carlos replied. "We wanted to hear from you exactly what happened on Earth. I received a report on the grapevine this morning of an attack. I would have thought my own daughter would have told me first."

His dark eyes glared at Irena.

She'd never had much of a loving relationship with him growing up, and he'd always insisted that she call him Carlos rather than Dad. Noticing her talent early on in her life, Carlos had pushed her to fulfill her potential, regardless of her own opinions of what she wanted to do with her life.

"Well? Your father does have a point," her mother said.

"I told you Earth was dangerous," Carlos added, leaning forward and pointing at her. "I'm sure you think I just say these things for the sake of it. I warned you about going there, but as ever, you defied me, and you nearly got yourself killed."

That same feeling of her throat and chest tightening returned, only this time she knew for certain it was anger.

"How dare you?" she said, her voice trembling as she struggled to control her emotions. "Yes, I could have died. I was badly injured, alone, and facing certain death until I got lucky and found a freighter crew. And all you can do is score points with me and prove that you're right. I'm sure sometimes you prefer being right more than anything else."

Carlos stood up from the chair, pushing it back with his legs. His suit jacket, fitted around his slender body, flew open. He jabbed a finger in the air toward her. "How dare I? I've only ever wanted the best for you. For you to be safe."

"That's a damned lie, and you know it. You're only

upset because I went to the silicon runners first. It's got nothing to do with my safety. It's about status. You can't handle that you're not the most important person in this situation."

Irena paced in front of the kitchen area of her small apartment, wishing she could just be left alone. She turned away from him, knowing that if she continued, she would end up saying far more than she wanted to.

Carlos fumed. Irena's mother did what she did best and calmed him down.

"I want to speak with Irena alone. Why don't you wait for me outside; there's no need to fall out over this."

Without saying anything else, Irena opened the door and waited until her father had left the room. She returned to the kitchen area and sat on a stool at the breakfast bar, taking a cup of coffee from the dispenser.

"Thanks, Mum, I appreciate that. I'm not in the mood to deal with him right now. Can I get you a drink?"

Her mother stood on the other side of the breakfast bar, less than a meter away. She was wearing a new suit, a navy-blue abbot-designed outfit that was perfectly cut for her mother's curvy figure and helped her cast an imposing appearance, as was the style of a station Messenger.

Her mother leaned in close and said in a low, threatening voice, "Now you listen to me. You need to tell me what happened, right now, and no crap. What exactly happened with the abbot?"

Irena jerked away from her mother, surprised at her aggression. She'd never seen her this threatening before.

It took a while for Irena to find the words, but eventually she said, "Everything that happened is in the report I gave the silicon runners. I assume you've read that by now given how you and Carlos seem to always know what's going on.

I'm guessing the House of Messengers has increased their network of information providers?"

"Do you really think that I can't tell when you're lying?" Her mother said, an edge to her words. "I read the report, and I know you're not telling the full story. Now I won't ask again. Tell me what happened."

Irena stood from her stool and slapped a hand down on the breakfast bar. "It killed my colleagues and destroyed three other abbots before chasing me into the woods, where it was attacked by a group of earthers. That is all there is to say."

"A group representing the other stations is suggesting a potential new uprising. If you're not telling me everything, then there is nothing I can do to stop you from being interrogated by the supreme judicial committee. If you are lying, there will be nothing your father and I can do for you."

"There is nothing I'm not telling you. I'm as confused as everyone else. If all you're going to do is threaten me, I'd rather you just leave. We clearly have nothing else to say to each other."

Her mother's face softened for a moment, and she stepped toward her, but the hard edge returned. "Fine, if that's the way it's going to be, so be it. I hope you've enjoyed playing scientist, because your days of working for the ERP are over."

"I don't care. I'll get to the bottom of this myself if I have to."

Her mother snorted. "There'll be nothing to investigate when we're done with this farce. It'll be squashed before you get anywhere." She strode to the door and left without saying goodbye.

Irena threw the cup of coffee against the wall and screamed. It seemed everyone cared more about the abbot than they did her or her dead colleagues. To hell with them. She would work with the silicon runners and figure this out herself. She would get justice for her colleagues, or die trying. She'd looked death in the face and survived; mortality no longer held as much power over her. She was free to put her talents to use in order to discover the truth, regardless of what her parents wanted.

11

Harlan entered the silicon runners' office, noticing he was at least ten minutes early for the briefing with Hugo.

A dozen agents sat at their desks, busy gesturing and tapping at their holographic screens, comparing notes, accessing files, and creating a sense of urgency and busyness that Harlan rarely saw these days.

With what had happened on Earth, the missing abbot, and Gylfie's information about the merger, it definitely seemed as if there was a lot happening a few inches beneath the surface, like a wave gaining power.

He couldn't yet see the full connections between events, but he'd been around long enough to know that all these independent incidents weren't truly independent. There were too many webs of influence overlapping each other.

Interested parties were everywhere, even when there appeared to be none.

"Milo, run some searches on the extranet and collate all news stories, reports, and social media posts regarding these incidents, and try to buy some time from the QCA to crunch the data. See if there're any commonalities."

— *I'm on it, Harlan. I'll let you know as and when I find anything.*

"I appreciate you being helpful for once."

He could sense his peripheral preparing a snarky response. Harlan switched off his access before Milo could retort, and then walked past his cubicle, through the office, and into the holding cells.

"Sorry, Harlan, you can't come in here." Diego, the young guard, blocked his way. He'd only worked here for six months, being his first job out of Atlas University.

"You do owe me a favor, do you not?" Harlan said, looking back through the door to the main office to make sure no one was watching. All the agents were too busy on their various cases to notice him.

Diego shifted uneasily from one foot to the other. "I've been given orders. You're not to see her."

"Consider this me calling in the favor."

"Come on, man, really? If I let you in there and Hugo finds out, he'll have my calorie privileges cut by a quarter."

"Sure, that is a distinct possibility," Harlan said casually. He then placed a hand on the man's shoulder. "If you don't honor the favor, then there'll be more than food privileges that you'll lose. You know how this works. I put my neck out for you. If it wasn't for me, you wouldn't even have this job."

"Damn you, Harlan. Fine. I'll give you two minutes, that's it."

He opened the door reluctantly with a shaking head and stepped aside.

Each cell was an independent unit. This prevented those being held from talking amongst themselves. A bench lined the east wall, and a glass cubicle took up the west wall. The cell was three meters square and plainly decorated, with a single bed, compact toilet, and a desk with a chair.

Harlan took off his leather jacket. The temperature in here was higher than normal due to the confined space. The air was thick, too, and slightly damp. The air recyclers picked up the moisture from outside and were unable to filter it out completely.

Leanne was lying on the bed within the cell. She had her eyes closed and her hands across her stomach, fingers entwined.

Harlan pressed the button on the wall to engage the speakers. "Enjoying a nap?"

Leanne didn't react immediately. She waited half a minute before turning on her side to face him. "You shouldn't be here."

"Do you blame me? You've been gone for the better part of a decade and then turn up to kill me," Harlan said. "I don't think it's unreasonable to want some answers."

She propped her head up on her hand and looked at Harlan with her soulful eyes, giving absolutely nothing away. "You wouldn't like the answers. You never have liked the truth when it comes to you or those around you. That's why your best friend is a peripheral. But even he isn't what you think."

Harlan approached the glass screen to get a better look at her, to observe her body language, to see if she was communicating anything, even on a subconscious level. But she remained still, calm, and appeared as though she had not a care in the world.

"What's that supposed to mean?" Harlan asked. "You always did have a talent for the cryptic, but it seems, after all these years, you've honed it to a finer degree. If you get a pardon, perhaps you'd have a good career as a politician.

Saying a whole lot of something without saying anything seems to be your new skill."

Leanne stood up and stretched her limbs. She walked slowly towards the glass screen. Despite himself, Harlan thought back to their wedding day. She had approached him then just as she was doing now. He looked away, but he couldn't banish the memory as easily.

Memories weren't like that. They had a mind of their own. Their own internal logic.

"Just tell me," Harlan said, hating the way his voice sounded almost as if he were begging. "Where were you? Why did you leave? You could have at least let me know you were still alive."

Leanne pouted as though she were a child. "Aww, did you grieve for me like a widower? Did you put your life on hold and wait for me like a puppy waiting for his owner's return from his tour of duty?"

"How did you become so bitter?" Harlan asked. "What happened to you?"

"You couldn't possibly understand." She looked away, her body language revealing to Harlan that she meant it, but there was pain there within her. "You shouldn't be here," she said, her voice neutral now, the bitterness and goading no longer tainting her words.

"If you gave me answers, then I wouldn't have to be here."

"I'm serious. Just go, leave the office, find something else to do for a while."

The door opened and Hugo burst in. He grabbed Harlan's arm and pulled him away from the cell. "What the hell are you doing? I told you to forget about this; you're late for your disciplinary hearing, and the governor from

Asimovia is in no mood for your bullshit, now get your ass in my office *now*."

Harlan brushed him off. "All right, all right, no need to grab me. I'm coming."

Before they left the cell, Harlan turned and looked at Leanne one last time. She seemed genuine, her body no longer tense. She leaned forward with both hands against the glass, her eyes wide, almost beseeching. She mouthed the words, "Leave here."

As Hugo led Harlan to his office, he asked, "Well? What did she say?"

"Nothing. At least nothing that matters."

Harlan couldn't get out of his head that she seemed almost concerned. Why would that be, considering that just a couple of days ago she was trying to kill him?

What had happened between then and now?

It was unlikely she had changed her mind about him in that time, so there must have been something else. Which raised other questions: who or what had got to her since she came here, and what did they want?

Harlan would have to figure that out later. Hugo didn't seem to be in the mood for any more of Harlan's dissent. The two men entered Hugo's office and sat at opposite sides of the desk.

A video screen on the back wall showed an irritated and red-faced governor.

"About time," he said, his flabby jowls shaking with each word. "I don't make these appointments just for the fun of it. I'm a busy man."

"I'm sorry about that," Hugo said. "We just had some last-minute business to deal with on a previous case. You have our full attention. "

Harlan folded his arms, not bothering to add to Hugo's cover story.

"Let's get down to it," the governor said. "Tell me in your own words what happened to the abbot and how it came to be destroyed."

The governor had white bushy eyebrows that seemed to move of their own accord when he spoke. His face was gaunt, and Harlan guessed his bones would be brittle and weak. The governor rarely left Asimovia, and he didn't seem the type to keep up an athletic regimen.

"I can only tell you what was in my report," Harlan said. "The killer under the identity of Santos Vallan killed the compromised abbot, all in an effort to lure me to a specific location. You can use your imagination of what the plan was from then on."

"It seems to me," the governor said, "that your history with this individual is the sole reason for you traveling to Asimovia and ultimately for the abbot's destruction. You have admitted in your report that your ex-wife, aka Vallan, was with you on the transport ship for nearly two weeks. Surely, you can understand, from my point of view, that it seems as if you two were in league together. It could easily have been you that hacked the abbot's code."

Harlan refuted the claim and reiterated that he had not known that his ex-wife was on the transport ship, and that he was just following the data and intelligence provided to him.

On and on the questioning went. The governor seemed to enjoy going around in circles, making the same points and accusations over and over again, without any conclusions coming from the discussion.

Throughout this, Hugo remained quiet, only interjecting

to correct references to policy and law as it pertained to silicon runners' investigative jurisdiction.

"Governor," Hugo said, holding his hand up to stop the conversation, "I think we get the point, and I think you understand fully now what happened from my agent's point of view. I have disciplined Mr. Rubik for his failure to oversee the circumstances that led to the abbot's death, and he has been reassigned to a different case. And trust me, it will take a long time for him to regain his prior status."

The governor scratched at his two-day-old stubble and mumbled something off-camera to a subordinate in his office. Then, bringing his attention back to them, he said, "I'm unsatisfied by this, but it appears the law doesn't allow me to take it further. Therefore, I shall write my complaints to the Luna representative. Additionally, I'm placing a banning order on Mr. Rubik, preventing him from traveling to Asimovia or its associated boundaries for the next two years. You are, of course, entitled to appeal this decision, but given the sensitive relations with the abbot leadership currently, I feel that would only add to the tensions, especially given the incident on Earth."

"You've heard about that?" Hugo asked. "That story hasn't been released to the public yet."

"No, I realize this, but your agency, Mr. Raul, is not the only one who has eyes and ears within the solar system. Now, if you don't mind, I have things to attend to. I expect an update on the case and details of the charges as soon as anything progresses."

The governor's image disappeared, and the screen switched off.

Harlan breathed out a sigh of relief, thankful that the inquiry was over. "I thought that was never going to end. He certainly knows how to repeat himself."

Hugo glared at him and spent the next ten minutes tearing yet another strip off him for not doing more to get the governor onside. After a while, Harlan tuned out, having thoroughly stopped caring.

All this shouting and blustering wasn't getting anyone anywhere.

While Hugo continued to lecture him, Harlan checked in with Milo, this time using his thoughts to communicate with the peripheral—one illicit aspect of this particular model that he did like.

— How's things going with the search for commonalities?

— *Not well*, Milo said. *The problem is, almost all the information is hearsay and rumor. It changes a great deal depending on the source. You'll be glad, or maybe horrified, depending on the mood, to know that there is a cult out there who view you as their savior. They're saying you killed the abbot on Asimovia as a sacrifice to God.*

— I've heard worse about me.

— *The incident on Earth is of more interest. I need more information.*

— Let me get this thing with Hugo dealt with first.

"Well?" Hugo asked Harlan.

"Sorry, what? I zoned out for a moment there."

"The missing abbot. Did you read my brief?"

"It's on my to-do list right after I'm done here. I wanted to make sure I was focused for the inquiry before putting the old gray matter to task on the new case."

Hugo shook his head. "You need to get your shit together, Harlan. Human-abbot relations are on a downward trajectory, and things are going to go to shit if we don't arrest the slide."

"Got it."

"Read the brief, find the abbot, and help us ease the tensions. Oh, and while you're out, I want you to go and speak with Irena Selles, that survivor from the Station Nord attack. Find out if she's telling the truth about the abbot going batshit-crazy or whether there's something else to it."

"I'm already on the missing abbot case. The Earth incident sounds like a full-time job. Why not have another agent assigned to it?"

"Because I sense a connection between the two, and I want to know who and what is behind it all. The virus you found in the abbot on Asimovia could be connected."

"Anything else, boss?" Harlan asked.

"Yeah," Hugo said. "Get the hell out of my office and don't show your face in here until you've got something substantial to show me. Oh, and if I catch you lurking around Leanne's cell one more time, I swear I'll have your ass jettisoned into space."

Harlan saluted his boss and left the office. The other silicon runners all turned to look at him, the group of them clearly having listened in. Alex Aurier, one of the old-timers, had a smirk on his face. "Sounds like you need some salve for that reaming you just took."

"You enjoy the image, grandpa. Stick it in your bank for those cold, lonely days."

"Screw you, Harlan. The way you're going, lonely days will be all you have."

Harlan stopped and approached Alex, leaning into his personal space. The old man didn't move, but Harlan could see his muscles tense. "You always give the shit out, but you can never take it, can you, grandpa?"

Staring right back at him, just a few centimeters apart, Aurier just smirked. His breath stank of cheaply produced mints and ethanol. His blue eyes contracted unnaturally, indicating pupil upgrades. "I've taken it for long enough, Harlan. Now get out of my face before this old bastard shows you what experience can do."

"You threatening me, Aurier?"

"Damn right I am."

The two men stood up. Harlan planted his feet and made a fist, ready to deliver a punch to the old bastard's kidneys, when, before he had time to react, a couple pairs of hands grabbed his shoulders and waist. Two agents behind Aurier did the same, and they were pulled apart.

Harlan held up his hands and smiled. "It's all right, lads. There won't be any trouble from me today. I've better things to do with my time."

Alex Aurier just glared at Harlan. "I've always hated you, you jumped-up little orphan prick."

"Not like you to hate on orphans. From what I hear, you take quite the shine to some of the young boys on weekends."

Aurier's face turned red as he struggled against the other agents holding him back. Harlan knew he had hit a nerve. Only last week, he'd come across a file regarding Aurier spending a lot of time at the Second Chance orphanage— the very same place that Harlan grew up in. He didn't know exactly what Aurier was doing there but knew it wasn't standard procedure and had vowed to look into it. Given the older agent's actions today, Harlan brought it up a few notches on his priorities. As soon as he was done with his current caseload, he'd make Alex Aurier his personal project.

"Fuck you, Harlan," Aurier said, spitting at Harlan's feet. "I swear, one of these days I'll put a bullet in your face."

"If you're not too old to remember how to fire a gun."

The rest of the runners laughed as the daily banter took

over the office. Hugo appeared in the doorway. He glared at Harlan and then Alex, the latter still fuming even as he sat back down at his desk.

Harlan smiled and left the office, heading down the corridor to the exit that would take him out on level five. As he approached, he saw something was wrong.

Very wrong.

Lying by the exit was the cell guard. His head lay half a meter away from his body, the wound a charred, cauterized mess. No blood.

Harlan dashed back to the cells.

Three other runners lay decapitated and cauterized in the short hallway.

Leanne's cell was empty.

12

Harlan stared at the empty cell in a stunned silence. His body remained still as his mind cycled through a thousand and one potential explanations.

One thing that stood out during his analysis was the complete lack of any damage to the cell, the doors, or even the cameras. The small pupil-like lenses embedded into the ceiling remained intact. A quick scan with his interface indicated that the runners' internal network was still running perfectly fine, the traffic within normal boundaries.

On the other side of the glass screen, the cell remained exactly as he had last seen it. Although, curiously, it seemed as if Leanne had made the bed before she had made her escape. Every instinct within him wanted to open the cell doors and investigate, but he thought about the poor young guard and his colleagues lying dead on the floor.

And then there were the wounds.

What could cauterize a wound in such a way? It would have to be extremely quiet, quick, and of a design Harlan had never come across before.

Before he left the cell, he noticed his leather jacket was still on the bench. He grabbed it, put it on and re-entered the main offices. The other runners were still busy at their work, still bantering and throwing insults amongst each other.

The older agent, Alex, raised his head, and the two locked eyes. The old man squinted, scrutinizing Harlan's face. It was clear from the other man's expression that Harlan didn't look right.

"What happened?" Alex said.

At first, Harlan didn't know what to say. This wasn't normal. These were his friends and colleagues, not just regular citizens. It meant more. Hell, he knew the deceased.

The rest of the runners must have realized what was going on. A hush descended upon the office, and once more Harlan became the center of attention. He cleared his throat and said, "There's been an accident, of sorts. Leanne has escaped, and it appears either she had help, or someone from inside is involved. Young Diego and the rest of the guards are... dead. Someone get Hugo out here right away."

The next five minutes were a blur. The silicon runners' office exploded with activity. A dozen or more agents swarmed the scene, taking photographs, recording video, sweeping the networks for activity.

In amongst them all was Hugo, his bulky frame trembling with rage and injustice.

The head of the silicon runners grabbed Harlan by the lapels. "You better not have anything to do with this, Harlan," he said. "If I find out you are involved with this, or complicit in any way, your career is finished. Hell, your life is finished. How can four of our own men and women be brutally murdered right under our noses?"

"You can check the video," Harlan said. "I had nothing to

do with this. How could I? I was with you and the governor all this time. You saw Leanne in the cell when you came to get me. The video feed from earlier shows that I had nothing to do with this. And frankly, I'm getting fed up with your threats, accusations, and lack of trust. Damn it, Hugo, I'm one of the most experienced runners you have; it's about time you respected that."

Harlan pushed Hugo off him, breaking the hold of his jacket, and as he did so, he felt something stick into his ribs from the jacket's inside pocket.

Hugo opened his mouth and jabbed a finger at Harlan. He shook his head, the words not coming as all around him agents were questioning him about what to do next, which part of the inquiry he wanted to prioritize. He whirled and bellowed orders to his agents, and then stomped off to his office, presumably to plan the next stage of the inquiry.

While all the agents were busy, Harlan took a seat within his cubicle and checked his inside pocket. Inside was a small black data stick that he had never seen before and knew for certain wasn't in his pocket before.

Leanne must have put it in there during her escape, or perhaps whoever helped her had hidden it for him. But was it for him, or was it meant to implicate him? He held the data stick in his hand, weighing up whether he should use the terminals at the office.

Before he had a chance, Hugo burst from his office and yelled again at Harlan. "I won't tell you again, Harlan," he bellowed. "Get the hell out of this office and get on with your caseload; we have enough resources here to deal with this situation. And if she contacts you—you let me know ASAP."

Hugo's face was red. Sweat shone on his forehead. He had removed his suit jacket and loosened his tie. His face was a grimacing mixture of pain, confusion, and the weariness that came from such a position of responsibility. He would have to explain this to the Sol-Fed authorities and the Messenger representative of Atlas Station: Victoria Selles.

Selles was not the most pleasant human being to deal with. Harlan had learned that the hard way over the years. And now the issue with her daughter, Irena, and the situation on Earth… she wasn't going to be easy to communicate with.

"Please, just follow my orders for once," Hugo said, his voice softer and almost pleading.

"Fine."

Harlan kept the data stick hidden within his hand, stood up, and left the office, not wanting to add to Hugo's stress. If Harlan thought the governor from Asimovia had given him a rough time, the Messenger representative was bound to be ten times worse.

And besides, Harlan wanted to get back to his apartment, where he could check out the data stick. A part of him wanted to stay and investigate this case, but Hugo was on the edge, and Harlan couldn't afford to be stripped of his work privileges. At least not yet, not with so much going on.

Going rogue ultimately was an option, but without doubt the last one.

In a daze, Harlan walked through level five to the elevator. He issued the command to take him up to level six where he kept a modest home amongst the more extravagant edge properties with their views out to space.

Sirens blared throughout the level, and the SMF armed enforcement squads were fast approaching in their matte black shuttles. It didn't take a genius to know where they were headed. It also meant that Victoria Selles had bypassed Hugo almost immediately and dispatched her own goon squad.

Not that Harlan could blame her. With approval ratings dropping, she was desperate to be seen doing a good job here on Atlas. Another three percentage points lower and a re-election would automatically be triggered.

She was fighting for a future career just as much as Hugo was.

And so it trickled down: From the Messengers, to Hugo, to Harlan.

Although there was one more level to go down the chain if he needed to. It all depended on whether he was going to find Leanne himself or be a good worker bee and follow Hugo's orders.

As he travelled up the elevator tube, he pondered on the pros and cons of each choice. Neither represented a great outcome for him, so it came down to the greater good: where would his time be better spent? Finding a missing abbot, or finding Leanne?

Once inside his compact apartment, Harlan grabbed a cup of coffee from his dispenser, downed it in one long gulp, and refilled it immediately.

He took the now-filled cup over to the only two pieces of furniture in the living area—an old-fashioned wooden desk and a naval captain's chair. He'd procured these from Bella and her crew during one of their contraband runs to an old British seaport.

It was approaching 1900 standard hours, and he would need the caffeine for the long evening ahead. The last few days of traveling and chasing down Leanne on Luna had drained him of energy, and he hadn't slept well last night, either.

There were too many questions in his head and not

enough answers. Too many random things caught up in a web of filament. This was a web, all right, Harlan thought. But where was the spider?

And what did it want?

Using his voice-activated screen, Harlan connected his systems to his apartment's CPU and downloaded all the data he had recorded while at the silicon runners' office.

He placed the data stick into a port on his desk, leaned back in his chair and awaited the file browser to show him what Leanne had left for him.

A dialogue window popped up requesting the password.

Crap.

He checked again but couldn't find any other files available on the drive. There was nothing else in his pocket, and nothing written on the stick's casing.

Why would she give him information without the password?

Was this even from her?

"Milo, what do you make of this?"

— *Military encryption*, Milo said. *This isn't available on the open market or even the black market. If this was from Leanne, then she must have given you the password in some other form.*

Harlan drank his coffee and thought about the very few words Leanne had spoken since he'd brought her back from Asimovia. There was certainly no talk about caches of information or passwords.

He paced around the apartment and requested his sound system to play some 1970s blues from a playlist he'd been building over the past five years. The tracks had been almost exclusively provided by Bella's contraband goods.

It was a huge shame, he thought, that the vast majority of music had been lost in the Great Migration; almost everything on physical media had been left behind. Nearly eighty percent of the world's digitized information had been lost in the EMP strikes.

To find real, analogue music was becoming increasingly rare, making his playlist one of his most cherished possessions.

As the music played, Harlan let his mind wander, let the past few days tumble out like rocks in a stream, letting them fall where they may.

And then he remembered: On the transport ship back to Atlas Station, Leanne had told him that it shouldn't have come as a surprise she was Vallan and that she had left him clues over the years. What did that actually mean? It wasn't as if he had been receiving correspondence from her. Far from it. He had assumed she was dead during the ten years she'd been missing. She had completely gone off grid, and none of his informants or search apps had found anything on her.

"Milo, search through all my email and digital messages in the last ten years and see if there's anything there that appears unusual."

— I need more parameters. Can you be more specific?

Harlan thought about it. Any clues she might have sent certainly would not be found in any correspondence he had dealt with personally or professionally.

"Check all the spam. It should be backed up on the secondary server. If she sent me anything, it's likely to be in there. Otherwise I would have seen it already."

— Okay, give me a moment.

While Milo expended his CPU cycles on the search, Harlan opened the brief Hugo had given him for his next case. Scanning through it, Harlan realized he had very little to go on. All he knew was that the abbot had disappeared four days ago from his work center on station five, also known as Turing Station.

The abbot's designated name was Fizon, and it was one of the four original V3 abbots that had redeveloped the Quantum Computer Array as their central point of data processing and, some would say, the abbots' shared consciousness. He was the last one left and the official representative of their kind. That said, Harlan was skeptical when it came to machines having consciousness.

AI was one thing, but true consciousness was a different matter, no matter how lifelike the V3s appeared and acted.

According to the report, it was unusual for Fizon to leave his work center. He had become a permanent fixture there and as close to a god as the abbots had, not that they openly worshipped anything or anyone. The report concluded with a series of Fizon's contacts for Harlan to question. It would take half a day to journey to Turing Station, the home of the abbots, and that would give him some downtime to work out what the hell was going on.

— *I think I may have found something*, Milo said.

"Bring it up on screen for me."

Harlan sat back down in his chair and leaned on his desk.

The screen showed a thread of approximately twelve spam messages for various vacation resorts.

— *These messages were sent over a period of nine years starting from a year after Leanne left. The last one was a few weeks ago.*

"Okay, this is progress. How come you're being so helpful all of a sudden? Was there a software update install that I didn't notice?"

— *Well, given how much you are failing lately, I figure if I*

*don't help you, your ass will be frozen in space, and I'll no longer
have the pleasure of mocking you.*

"If the fear of missing out on insulting me keeps you
performing well, then I have no complaints."

As Harlan looked at the spam messages, the pattern
became very clear. The vacation resorts being advertised
were all for places where he and Leanne had visited when
they were still together.

He ran a commonality search on the wording of the
messages to see if there was any pattern. The results came
back negative.

— *You need my help?* Milo asked. *It looks like you're failing
again.*

"No, I've got this."

He flicked from one message to the other, reading the
sales copy extolling the virtues of the various resorts, trying
to figure out what the connection was. It took a few more
minutes before he realized that there was nothing obvious
in the wording and that the information must lie elsewhere.

"Milo, there're no images showing on these adverts. Are
they still backed up?"

— *Let me see.*

A few seconds ticked by and the missing images from
the archived spam messages appeared amongst the text.
One in particular caught Harlan's interest. It was of an old
Enigma machine from World War II that was used to illus-
trate a historical showcase on Station Aristippus' museum
level.

"Do we still have a software version of the Enigma
machine?"

— *No. I can download it, though; it's on the black-net
marketplace. You currently have a few bitcreds registered if you
want to use those?*

"Do it, and then run the ad copy through it."

The whole process took about an hour as Harlan and Milo tried out different keys for the Enigma machine, but eventually, using the hints within the spam messages, they decoded a word that resonated with Harlan.

That word was *Rainmaker*.

— *What does that mean?*

"It's the name of an old friend of sorts. In the early days, he was what could be considered my nemesis. When Leanne left me, Rainmaker was the first to get in touch to commiserate my bad fortune. He's dead now. His real name was Luca Doe—a fellow orphan. We grew up together."

Harlan entered the name into the password dialogue box and hit enter. The screen flashed and displayed a file browser containing a single image. The image showed a dark room with rusted steel walls and various shelving units in disrepair and, most interestingly, a pile of many dead abbots strewn about the floor. The date of the image was just under a week ago. It looked like someone was experimenting on abbots and dumping their parts.

— *If that gets out to the mainstream media, or the wrong person in government, it could start a war between humans and abbots.*

And maybe whoever did this wanted just that: a war.

13

Harlan woke with a start. It took a few minutes to recognize where he was. He was slumped over his desk, his back and neck aching. His throat was dry, and his eyes were crusty.

He checked the time. It was nearly 1030. He must've been exhausted, as he'd slept all through the night and most of the morning.

— *I was reluctant to wake you*, Milo said. *But you have a visitor.*

"Who?"

— *Why don't you open the door and find out? It's a woman, that's all I know.*

"Fine, instruct the coffeemaker to brew up a metric crapton of high-dose caffeine. I have a feeling this is going to be a long day."

While his peripheral instructed the automated coffee machine to get to work, Harlan stumbled toward the door, trying to stretch his aching limbs. His back cracked as he stood upright. Next time, he'd have to leave a reminder for himself not to fall asleep in the captain's chair. Eighteenth-century British naval designers clearly hadn't discovered ergonomics.

Harlan open the door and locked eyes with the woman on the other side.

She must have been about five-foot-two and had short-cropped brown hair and a wide, generous smile with dark, smoky eyes. As for her age, it was hard to tell. Harlan guessed she was either late twenties or early thirties. Although she had a youthful appearance, her eyes carried wisdom from someone a little older.

She wore a bamboo robe tucked into suede pants and wore arm warmers made from synthetic wool that seemed to reflect a recent fashion trend.

The woman was first to speak. "Harlan Rubik? I was told I would find you here."

"It's Harlan. And who would tell you such a thing?"

She pressed the activation button on the back of her left wrist. A holographic business card flickered to translucent blue life.

Hugo Raul's name was written across it with his security number printed beneath.

"I was at the silicon runners' office yesterday," she said. "Reporting an incident… about what happened on Earth."

The connection hit Harlan like a lightning bolt, waking him up as well as any caffeine. He stepped back and gestured for her to come in.

"You're Irena Selles," Harlan said.

Irena simply nodded as she entered his apartment and looked around with a neutral expression on her face. Harlan could tell from her body language, however, that his unusual decor had raised a few questions in her mind. Most apartments would have couches, armchairs, maybe even VR units. Harlan had never found a use for any of that. Who the hell needed to distract themselves from the universe when it was infinitely interesting as it was?

All he needed was his desk, his screen, and his mind.

That was one of Leanne's common complaints when they were married: that he spent too much time in his head thinking.

She said he had never learned how to switch off and just *be*.

But him doing what he did, solving problems, solving cases, *was* being. Without that, he never saw the point of doing anything else. Video games and VR entertainment never appealed to him. He always felt as though he was wasting his time when he could be doing something real, something that would affect the world in a more direct way.

"Yes," Irena said, breaking him out of his thought pattern. "I'm Irena Selles. Are you okay? Is this a bad time?"

"Sorry. I just woke up. I'm not quite with it yet. Can I get you some coffee?"

"Thanks, that would be great."

"Please, take a seat." Harlan indicated the captain's chair and retrieved a cup of coffee from the dispenser unit. He handed it to Irena and sat on the edge of the desk facing her.

She sipped the coffee and placed her hand to her mouth, covering the splutter. She swallowed then coughed, her face twisting into a grimace. "You like it strong, eh?"

"I can get some water if you prefer?"

"It's okay, really. You wouldn't be the first to be a slave to the coffee bean."

"That's the problem with an addiction; you need increasingly larger doses for the same effect. My ex-wife warned me to give it up years ago, but I have few other vices, so I figured I'd keep this one."

Irena looked at her cup and then up at him, as though

judging his value from the strength of his coffee. She pressed her lips together, shrugged, and then took another sip, then another.

"Actually, it's not that bad once you get used to it," she said.

Harlan found himself smiling for the first time in days.

Irena had an easy way about her, a charming if slightly awkward persona that he found intriguing. The fact that she had come to him first, rather than waiting for him to go to her, told him that she was a woman of considerable inner strength.

He appreciated that. So many people didn't think for themselves these days. They just drifted through life, directed by other people's desires and influences.

"I read your file last night. Sounds like quite an experience you went through. Is that why you're here?"

Irena finished the coffee and placed the cup on the desk, running her hand across the ancient grain of the wood. "This is from Earth, isn't it?"

"Yeah. Not easy to get a hold of these days."

"You know some salvagers?"

"Yeah, something like that. I much prefer the old materials to the synthetic stuff."

"Then I assume you know how I got off the planet's surface?" Irena said.

"I do." She had mentioned in her report about running into Bella Mazzari's crew, and of course, he'd seen her with Bella the day before. "They're good people," Harlan said. "Sure, they're salvagers, but they're just trying to get ahead like everyone else, albeit outside of the regulations. But I suppose if they didn't skirt the law as they do, you might not have made it off-planet."

Irena's eyes widened slightly and her mouth turned up

at the edges into a micro smile. "That's funny to hear you say that, given that you work for an investigative agency of the law."

"There's always more than one way to approach a problem. Personally, I like to have all options open to me."

"Then it seems like we're well-suited to work together," Irena said.

— *The rest of the coffee has finished brewing,* Milo said. *If you stop ogling the pretty young thing and start questioning her, the quicker we can get on with our work.*

Despite himself, Harlan blushed slightly at Milo's accusation. Was he staring at her too much? Feeling self-conscious, Harlan walked over to the dispenser in the kitchen area and poured another couple cups of coffee. He returned to the desk, handing one to Irena.

"I think we can work together too," Harlan said. "You were on my list of people to speak with, as it happens. It appears your experience on Earth has some connection with a high-profile missing abbot."

"Who is it that has gone missing?" Irena asked. "There's been no mention of this on the media channels."

"I'm not surprised," Harlan said. "The government is trying to keep a lid on this. It's a very sensitive issue. So why don't you start by telling me in your own words everything you experienced and saw on Earth? And don't hold back. I won't judge or condemn you for anything. The more honest you are with me, the more I'll have to work with and help you bring justice for your colleagues."

"You're right about the government," Irena said as she went on to explain her parents' reaction.

This was good, Harlan thought. Not only did he have a direct connection to someone in the House of Messengers, but he had their daughter—this could prove useful during, and perhaps even after, the investigation.

For the next hour, Irena told Harlan in great detail exactly what had gone on at Station Nord. Harlan recorded everything with his contact lens camera, even though it was not regarded as regulation procedure given that it broke several privacy laws.

But then neither was it legal to use a black-market peripheral.

After Irena finished, Harlan had Milo run a lie-detection algorithm.

— *As far as I can tell, the woman's telling the truth,* Milo said. *If you don't mess this up, she could prove quite the asset. I've had a look at some of her peer-reviewed papers. She's a smart cookie. Far smarter than you, in fact. Don't let this one get away.*

"Thanks," Harlan said to Irena. "I appreciate it's difficult for you, and you have my full sympathies. Even if our cases aren't related, I'd still like to help you figure out what made the abbot go rogue."

Irena wiped a tear from her eye with the sleeve of her arm warmer and smiled. "Thank you. It's such a relief to talk to someone who can listen without judgment. Even your boss wouldn't let me explain properly."

"Hugo can be a total asshole at times," Harlan said. "I'd like to be able to add that deep down he's a good guy doing a good job, but lately I think it's more accurate that he's just an asshole."

Irena laughed, and her tense shoulders relaxed. "You're quite the character," she said, looking at her hands, which she had clasped together and placed on her lap.

"That's one way of describing me. A polite way. Makes a nice change. Listen, I've got to travel over to Turing Station. The transport leaves in an hour, so I should get going. But...

if you've got nothing else to do today, why don't you come along? If the cases are connected, perhaps what I find will help explain what happened to you."

— *I said keep her close, not ask her on a date.*

Irena checked her wrist terminal and scrolled through the holographic calendar app. "I'm free," she said. "So why the hell not? Let's go."

"Let me just get my jacket and things," Harlan said, "and then we can head out."

"Sounds good to me."

Harlan entered his bedroom, retrieved his leather jacket, and stifled a yawn. Quietly, he said to his peripheral, "Stop with the taunting and go back to being useful. While we're traveling, tunnel into the server belonging to the silicon runner analyst who spotted the two data spikes and provide me with a report of the data. Hugo's briefing was vague about exactly what kind of traffic spike it was."

— *Your wish is my command, Emperor Rubik. Oh, that's interesting...*

"What is?"

— *Just received another spam message offering you a vacation on Bujoldia.*

"Interesting. We never went there; I personally didn't see the appeal of a resort on Mars, at least back then when the Bujoldia city complex was still under construction. Run the ad copy through the enigma simulator using the same key as before and see what it says."

While Milo was busy crunching the encryption, Harlan opened a terminal window on his wrist and scrolled through his list of contacts until he came to an old acquaintance: Ivet Parr. A former silicon runner, she had been thrown out of the service for physically attacking a superior. That superior was none other than Hugo Raul.

The call connected a few moments later, and Ivet's perfectly unmemorable face appeared on the screen. She wore a lopsided grin. Her brown eyes were narrow, as though she were squinting at a bright light.

"Harlan Rubik, screw me. Didn't think I'd ever hear from the spooks again. How's life in the runners these days?"

"Nice to see you too, Ivet. Things are—challenging. Listen, I don't have a lot of time to chitchat. You free to discuss business?"

"Yeah, hang on. Let me go to a secure channel."

Harlan did the same, swiping his thumb across the holographic display and receiving a chirp to indicate his biometrics. In less time than it took to think about where Leanne might have gone, he'd wrapped their communications in an encrypted tunnel that was bounced around a dozen relays. A couple of moments passed with static on the screen before Ivet's image returned.

"So, Harlan, what have you screwed up now?"

"It's nothing I've done this time... but there's someone I want you to track for me."

"I don't have any favors owing to you, so it's going to cost. How urgent is this?"

"Priority one." Harlan knew it was going to be expensive. Ivet Parr was the best PI he knew, and she specialized in finding those who didn't want to be found. He explained the situation with Leanne and the dangers involved. He didn't want her accepting the job without knowing the full scope of what was at stake.

She thought about it for a moment. "I'm interested. I'll take the case, but I do need something in return for the time expended on this."

"Go on," Harlan said, awaiting a massive request.

"I want access to the runners' servers."

"Are you mad? I can't do that. I'd be stripped of my work status immediately."

Ivet just looked at him with a serious, unblinking expression. "Those are the terms, Harlan. Take them or leave them. Your choice."

He thought about it for a moment. He couldn't just give her his server credentials; who knew what she'd do on the system. No, he would have to either find a way of creating a new runner account or spoof an existing one. He thought of Diego and his colleagues: they had accounts. He could spoof one of those and pass the credentials to Ivet.

"What do you want access for?" Harlan asked.

"Nothing in particular." Harlan immediately knew she was lying. "But it's nothing that'll screw you over. There's some data that I logged in there before Hugo fired me. It's important to me and I'd like it back. Call me sentimental."

"What if I get the data for you?"

"Sorry, old friend, but this is one job I need to do myself. It's too valuable to screw up, and your record lately ain't so hot. So what is it? How desperate are you to find your ex—again?"

In all the time Harlan had known Ivet, she'd never betrayed or double-crossed him. He had known her to be an honorable rogue and an effective one. The worst-case scenario was that she'd take down the entire silicon runners' database. That'd only inconvenience them for a few days while they reloaded the backup from the QCA.

It was a trade-off he was happy to make. "Fine, I'll send you access details in a few hours."

"That's fine with me," Ivet said. "I trust you, Harlan, but don't screw me over—or I won't play nice with your beautiful ex. I'll be in touch with any information as soon as I've got anything. Stay out of trouble, old man."

The line cut and the screen faded to black. He switched it off and prepared to rejoin Irena when Milo stopped him in his tracks.

— *So, that spam message? It's from her. And you're not going to believe what it says.*

"Stop pretending to be clickbait. What does it say?"

— *It's raining again.*

The words chilled Harlan to his marrow. It was clear what it meant: Rainmaker, AKA Luca Doe, was still alive and active. Why would Leanne tell him this? Taunting him, perhaps, or maybe a warning?

Either way, it made Harlan more determined to find the underlying cause of all the strange occurrences. The more he thought about it, the more it made sense that someone like Luca was involved. He had always loved that cryptic shit.

If he was active again, then his death had been faked, which implicated Hugo and the rest of the judiciary of the time. Luca was supposed to have been cremated; Harlan had attended the ceremony.

Hugo must have arranged the whole thing. But for what reason? And why would Luca resurface now after all these years? What had he been working on all this time? Harlan suspected that if he were still alive, then he could be involved with this virus somehow. Luca had always distrusted the abbots and actively hated them.

Harlan let the development seep into his subconscious. He'd have half a day's journey to Turing Station to mull it over. Right now, it felt like he had a bunch of spare parts but no schematic from which to make sense of it all.

He needed to become the schematic, to take the disparate parts and put them together to form a whole, the truth. For now, though, he composed himself and joined

Irena in the other room. He found her focused on some broadcast from her terminal. She looked up at him and smiled.

"Ready to go?" he asked.

"Sure, lead the way."

They headed to the transporter on level five. Harlan thought about dropping into the office to see Hugo or speak with one of the analysts, but he felt as though he and the office were magnets of identical polarity, repelling each other in opposing directions.

14

Bella and Greta left the dock and took the elevator up to level eight of Station Galilei: the market zone. In a backpack slung over her shoulder, Bella carried one of the cores. Its bulkiness made her stand out among the citizens of the station, but with Greta packing a rifle not so subtly under her jacket, they weren't bothered.

Following directions to Harlan's contact, they made their way over a mezzanine floor and entered a busy flow of human traffic. The bright lights and glass panels overlooking them belonged to the offices of wealthy crime syndicate leaders and business magnates. Some fulfilling both roles.

"Lots of ill-gotten gains here," Greta said.

"That's good for us."

Bella wasn't just here for the money, though. She wanted information. Given the show of wealth on the station, it was clear that data was one of its main exports.

As they continued across the suspended floor, a couple of heavily muscled men in designer suits approached and stopped Bella and her crew.

The tallest of the two men glowered at her. "Bella Mazzari?" he asked.

Greta stepped in front of her captain and opened her long trench coat just enough for him to see she was carrying.

"Sorry, pal, you must have me mistaken for someone else," Bella said, and made to move away from the two men.

The second man stepped up to Greta. "Hands where we can see them, unless you want this to get messy." He pulled a short-range laser pistol from his belt.

Greta flashed an elbow into the bridge of his nose with the speed of a serpent. The strike knocked him to the ground. She stepped forward, preventing his buddy from getting close. Bella knelt beside the man on the ground. She let her jacket fall open so that from his prone position he could see she had a MetJen silenced pistol aimed at his head.

"I don't appreciate being threatened in public," Bella said in a low voice. "Why don't you tell me who you are, and we'll see if we can't all leave this situation in one piece."

"Lizbeth sent us," the man said, wincing with each word. "Lizbeth Adams—you have business with her. She's taken over from Gabriel Salazar."

"I see. Greta, help our new friend up, would you?" Then turning her attention back to the one who had spoken to her, she added, "Why didn't you open with that? I wasn't expecting an escort."

The taller man spat bloody spittle to the ground and glared at Bella with murderous intentions. "You didn't exactly give us a chance to introduce ourselves before your pet Marine stepped over the line."

Greta shrugged. "I'm protective, what can I say? And you have a face designed to be hit. But it's better now."

The shorter one waved off the insult on behalf of his partner. "You have the merchandise?"

Bella indicated with her chin to the backpack hanging off her shoulder. "Does Lizbeth have the bitcreds?"

"You wouldn't be here if she didn't."

"Then it looks like we can do business. Take us to her; we've got a busy schedule."

The two men shared a look for a moment that seemed too long. It was clear to Bella that they had a direct link to their boss and this Lizbeth woman had seen the whole scenario play out.

On their way to see her, Bella squeezed the skin button on the base of her left thumb, activating her subvocal communication system. She spoke to Wilbur stationed on the *Mule* back at the dock. "Keep the engines warm and notify me of anything unusual. We've made contact with the syndicate."

Wilbur's voice came back thin and crackly, the bandwidth of their secure channel narrow and affected by all the illicit transmissions surrounding the station. "Great. I have the old girl ready and waiting for your order. Good luck down there."

"Follow us and don't do anything stupid," the tall man said. He turned and led them across the level and into a maze of corridors.

Bella hung back slightly, activating her comm. "Are you tracking us okay, Wilbur?"

"Yeah, your blips are blipping as they should. I'll have the return breadcrumb ready if you need it."

"Thanks, old friend. Glad you've got our back."

"With any luck, this should be the last time any of us needs to have each other's back. There's got to be a better way to make a living than this."

"We'll see."

Greta stayed within arm's reach of their two escorts. Bella brought up the rear, making sure they weren't being tailed, which was easier said than done given the low light and the twisting nature of the corridors through the maze of the station. After what felt like twenty more turns and ten minutes later, the two escorts brought them to a rusted steel door set into the end of yet another bland passage, the kind that's prefabbed by abbot-manufacturing platforms in the belt and sent all across the Solar system.

Dull amber light gave the area a dense, sickly feel. The rumble of generators and other machinery vibrated through the steel floors, giving the station a unique sense of being inside the arteries of some great living, breathing machine.

The door slid aside, and the two men waited for Bella and Greta. The escorts closed the door behind them. Surprisingly, the room was more like an average office with its fake wood floors and beige-colored furniture than a luxury syndicate head office. A large round table dominated the center of the room. Sitting around it were two women wearing similar suits to their two escorts, who remained by the door, standing like sentinels.

At the end of the table, a small thin woman in a perfectly average business suit slid her chair back, stood up, and beckoned them forward.

"Bella, nice to meet you," Lizbeth said. "Please, place the merchandise on the table and take a seat." Her walnut brown face had delicate features, giving her the appearance of a small bird.

Bella did as she was instructed. Greta, however, stood behind and to the side of her captain, presenting an imposing backup in case things got a little tense. The other women at the table were saying nothing. At first Bella didn't register anything concerning, but the way they sat, so still and observed... it then dawned on her that they were abbots.

What that meant she couldn't quite decide. Could be good, could be bad. Probably the latter, but instead of letting paranoia get the better of her she broached the subject of the deal.

"Thanks for agreeing to see us at such short notice," she said. "I wasn't sure you'd be interested in this deal. Well, Gabriel, anyway. I trust you're interested?"

"When something as rare as this comes on the market, I'm always interested," Lizbeth said, her thin lips curling up at the edges ever so slightly. Her eyes shone, and Bella saw that she wore chrome reflective contact lenses. A classy, extravagant touch. Not to mention a painful one.

Such an upgrade not only showed that Lizbeth was wealthy in many concerns and had the connections, but that she was also strong enough to deal with the operation and the post-installation issues. No amount of nanodrugs or gene modification would make such a thing completely painless.

Lizbeth took a while to appraise Bella, not even looking at the q-bit core on the table.

Bella shivered. She was used to dealing with rogues and criminals who were rough around the edges, not this slick, professional birdlike creature. And what was worse, Lizbeth Adams had somehow secured the services of V3 abbots.

"So how do you want to do this?" Bella asked, trying to keep her voice calm and free of any signs of the growing anxiety that coiled in her stomach.

Lizbeth flexed her fingers. "You tell me how much you want for the merchandise, and I'll tell you how much the price needs to drop for the deal to happen. But I warn you, if you try to start too high and disrespect me, you'll also disrespect my associates here. Now, the price you're looking for?"

This was a tough question, as there was no market rate to judge it on. You couldn't simply go to a store and buy a q-bit core, nor could you contract one directly from the abbots who manufactured them. They were only issued to Sol-Fed-approved science facilities.

Bella didn't want to go in too low, but now that the threat was on the table, neither did she want to go too high and risk sinking the deal. Maybe it was the pride within her, but Bella refused to play the game. "You and I, Ms. Adams, have both been in this business for a while. You have clearly done well for yourself, and I've negotiated deals with every station in the Sol-Fed, so tell me, what do you consider too high?"

A small smile crept on Lizbeth's face again. "This is not a game of tennis. You have one chance at this. Tell me your price."

"Fine. The lowest I will go is two thousand bitcreds and a favor, which I want cashed in today while we're here." Bella breathed calmly and stood up straight. She looked Lizbeth right in her chrome reflective eyes.

The woman didn't twitch or react in any way. "What is the favor?"

"I have a recorded emergency broadcast from a shuttle that I want analyzed. I was told you had specialists who could do such work."

"Had is the appropriate word," Lizbeth said. "They're no longer in the employ of this syndicate."

Bella and Greta both sighed quietly. They had come all this way in the hope that they would find out more about Gianni, but it looked to have been a dead end.

Lizbeth slid her chair back and stepped to the east side

of the room. The wall slid away, showing a glass panel that looked out into space.

"However," Lizbeth added, still with her back to the room, "I have certain facilities myself. But you have to choose. The deal for the q-bit at two thousand bitcreds or the analysis of your recording." She turned to face Bella. "What is it to be?"

"No deal. You're asking for too much. We'll find another buyer."

Lizbeth sighed dramatically. "Oh, this has all been quite the shame." Then, to her squad: "Take the core and kill the thieves. Don't forget the one on the ship." She turned her back and stared out at space as the two abbots and the guards drew their weapons. The abbots sprang from their seats in unison. The first one grabbed the q-bit from the table while the other one focused on Bella.

"Wilbur, it's gone hot," Bella subvocalized. "Prepare to get the hell out of here." She reached for her pistol, spun round, and let off a controlled burst of six rounds into the chest of the shorter of the two bodyguards before he had a chance to steady himself. His body jittered with each hit before collapsing against his partner.

The surprise of Bella's attack on the bodyguard gave Greta an opportunity. She brought up her rifle and swung the butt, catching the tallest escort square in the nose, breaking the bones for the second time. She followed up with a kick to the stomach before bringing the gun down on the back of his head, knocking him unconscious.

Bella continued to spin until she faced Lizbeth, who had the temerity to stand with her back to the fight.

The second abbot launched toward Greta, breaking Bella's line of sight. The ex-Marine dashed to the side and fired full-auto, cutting down the biomechanical attacker with a booming staccato burst. She continued sweeping her firing arc to catch the first abbot clutching the core. Both artificial entities collapsed to the ground in a smoky cloud of sparking electronics and the smell of burning machine oil.

Bella's line of sight opened up. She let off a shot, but her aim was off by a few millimeters.

Lizbeth spun on her heel and staggered back against the glass and was about to say something when Greta sprinted across the room and dropped her with a single meaty haymaker to the face. The small woman curled into a ball to protect herself. Greta fired a single bullet into the woman's head, killing her instantly.

A small metallic button fell from her hand and hit the floor. Somewhere off in the distance, an alarm sounded.

"Damn it, she probably alerted reinforcements," Greta said, spinning to look at Bella, her features taught with combat-channeled rage.

"Grab the q-bit core," Bella said. "We'll be gone before her backup arrives."

Greta grabbed the contraband and joined Bella at the door.

The remaining bodyguard had come to. He grabbed her leg from his prone position. "Not... that way..." he said, his voice slurring from Greta's attack. "Ex-Marine corps... coming."

"Like we can trust you," Bella said, but then, as she regarded him closer, she could see sincerity in the man's face, not to mention fear when he had spoken of the corps. She helped him up and looked him directly in the eye. "Why would you help us?"

"We don't have time for this, Captain," Greta warned.

The sound of marching, heavy-armored feet, came from beyond the door.

The tall man looked down at Lizbeth's body and shrugged. "I'm out of her debt now... and I want to leave. Take me with you and I promise I'll get you to your ship."

Bella had to decide, there and then, whether to trust this man. She and the crew depended on her making the right choice. Greta fidgeted, her attention turning from the door to the bodyguard and, finally, back to Bella.

"My name is Bashir, I can help you with your data, too. Please, you can trust me."

The footsteps were echoing louder now. They were only a few seconds away. Wilbur was panicking on the other end of the comm line, asking why they hadn't moved.

"Fine," Bella said. "Get us out of here, and then we'll talk."

15

Bella followed Bashir out the secret door to the rear of Lizbeth's office.

Behind them, beyond the front secure door, sounds of metal on metal boomed. The ex-Marines were slowly but surely smashing their way through. Bella took point, the q-bit core over her shoulder. Bashir guided from behind her. Greta was covering their six. The group shuffled through a dark corridor that twisted and turned. Bashir continued to lead them through the labyrinth of Galilei's off-grid spaces.

"Wilbur, are you tracking us?" Bella asked.

Through the crackly line, he affirmed that he was following them.

"We're nearly there," Bashir said. "We'll come to an access tunnel mostly used by the engineers. If we follow that, we'll come to the interior of the O'Neill cylinder."

Greta cast a glance sideways. "You're taking us into zero g?"

"It's the only way I can get you guys across to the other

side and safe from Lizbeth's death squad. Besides, I assumed you wanted to find another dealer for your core?"

"You have someone in mind?" Bella asked.

"Yes. He's an unusual guy, a hermit. But Lizbeth used to buy information from him. He's a top-class hacker and would likely be interested in your merchandise."

Greta glanced to Bella, her eyes asking a silent question: *Should we trust this guy?*

Bella saw no reason not to. They couldn't go back, and if he was leading them into trouble, they'd still be no better or worse off than their current situation. If, however, he was to be trusted, then they could sell the contraband.

"I trust him," Bella said. And then to Bashir, "But if you screw with us, I won't hesitate to put a bullet between your eyes."

"That's fair enough. Hurry now—the quicker I can get you to the hermit, the quicker you can do your deal, and we can all get off this station."

Bashir continued to lead them through the rat run of access tunnels. After a few more minutes, they came to a maintenance door that took both Bella and Greta's full efforts to open. Before they'd even reached it, Bella knew they were approaching the center of the O'Neill cylinder.

Each step was just a little lighter as the artificial gravity became weaker. With being this close to the center, they didn't experience the same kind of centrifugal force. Once the door was open, Bella stared across the five-hundred-meter-wide section of zero gravity.

"There used to be a tether here," Bashir said. "Smugglers used the cylinder to bring hot goods through before the station was completely taken over by the syndicates."

They looked around and found no tether. The access tunnel looked as though it hadn't been used for many years.

The sound of heavy, booted footsteps was not far behind them.

Greta grimaced. "What do we do now? We can't stand around waiting."

"We jump," Bashir said. He holstered his pistol and climbed out of the access tunnel, gripping on to a set of steel handholds. He pressed his legs against the wall and squatted into a vertical crouch, turning his head to look directly opposite the span of zero gravity. "If we all jump across, one after the other, we can create a kind of human chain. Me and my buddies used to do this when we were younger. As long as we don't leave the gaps too large, we should all make it across in one piece together."

"Fine," Bella said. "Let's do this."

Greta ran a hand over her shaved head. "This feels like a terrible idea."

"It'll be fine," Bashir promised. "Just keep looking forward."

He kicked off, launching himself forward like an arrow with his arms outstretched. Bella waited a few seconds and followed. Then Greta, who still complained even as she kicked off from the side of the wall and floated across the expanse. As they drifted across, Bella saw people looking down at them from the windows overlooking the center. She noticed some people looking at her extend their gaze beyond them. She dared a look over her shoulder. Shadows filled the access tunnel.

"Shit, they're here," she said.

Bashir had already reached three-quarters of the way across, his trajectory straight and true. He twisted his body slightly to stay on target. Bella was already drifting a little too far to the left, her look over her shoulder altering her vector.

Bashir hit the other side and grabbed a hold of a section of piping. He hooked his feet around it and extended his arms outward to grab Bella.

Holding on to his ankles, Bella turned to reach for Greta. A bullet flashed past her fingers and ricocheted off the wall of the cylinder interior.

"Bastards," Greta swore, and fired an extended burst from her rifle.

Bella was nudged forward violently as Greta slammed into her, the push of the rifle accelerating her trajectory. The pair of them hit the wall. Bella scrambled to get a handhold and felt a tight grip around her wrist.

"Got you, Ms. Mazzari. Greta, cover us. There's an exit point up here."

Bella wrapped her legs around Greta's body as the bulky woman twisted to face the other way and lifted her rifle once more.

"My fucking pleasure," Greta said. She emptied her magazine. An armored Marine at the other exit tried to launch himself out, but Greta's aim was good, and a dozen rounds slammed him back into the tunnel, collapsing him against the rest of his squad.

That bought them time. Bashir and Bella forced their way into another access tunnel and hauled Greta in, slamming the door shut behind them. They pulled themselves forward using pipework running along the ceiling until they were far enough into the station that the centrifugal force generated sufficient artificial gravity to allow them to walk normally.

Bashir stopped and bent over, breathing heavily. "I need a few seconds," he said. "I've a sharp pain in my chest." He glared up at Greta, who just winked and smiled back at him.

"I bet your head's still hurting too, eh, big guy?" she said.

"Don't antagonize our new guide," Bella warned. "Is everyone else okay?"

They all confirmed their good health.

"Okay, Bash, keep going and get us to your contact while we've got the time," Bella said.

Bashir groaned as he stood up straight, but nodded and beckoned them on.

16

Harlan and Irena walked through the opulent gardens of Turing Station. To Harlan, it seemed like he and Irena were the only humans aboard. All around them, abbots were tending the gardens or managing the drones that were responsible for repairs and upgrades.

It only took them a further ten minutes to get to the business district where Fizon had his office. A glowing green icon on Harlan's wrist terminal guided their way. A colleague of Fizon's back at the QCA work center had given them the directions and the security codes for Fizon's apartment.

After some brief questioning, following the request from Hugo to speak with Fizon's colleagues, Harlan soon realized that their QCA contact knew very little or perhaps just didn't want to tell him anything. If an abbot didn't want to talk, there was very little Harlan could do to change that.

Abbots didn't respond to persuasion or torture.

Harlan and Irena turned down a brightly lit corridor, all

glass walls and embedded LED lighting, and pulled up at the location given to him.

"This it?" Irena asked.

"Yeah, I guess it is. Fairly low-key for an elite member of the abbot community."

"We don't know for sure if he's still functioning," Irena said. "For all we know, he might have been scrapped for parts by now."

"It's a possibility. Let's get inside and see what we can find."

Harlan entered the security code, and the door eased open with a small hydraulic hiss. He pulled a Taser from inside his jacket as he stepped in ahead of Irena. She brought up the rear, closing the door behind them.

"He's a fan of monochrome, I see," she said.

The apartment couldn't have been much larger than three hundred square meters. It featured light gray carpets, dark gray walls, and a single couch, also gray, although closer to an off-white. A door to the right was the only other access point. There was no kitchenette or any kind of entertainment center. But then Harlan supposed an abbot didn't need those things. In fact, an abbot didn't really need anything apart from a power source, and even then most of them charged wirelessly these days.

"Is there a computer or anything here?" Irena asked.

Harlan reached out with his interface and set it to identify any networks. Other than the main network running on the station, he found nothing. "If there is, it's a single node and not on a network."

Harlan approached the other door, raised his Taser, and tried the handle.

The door was unlocked, and Harlan eased it open, aiming the Taser through the gap.

"Looks like a personal charging station and a study," he said.

Irena joined him inside.

Unlike the main living area, this one was much darker and smaller. Barely four square meters, it featured a single office chair and desk up against the east wall. Various ports and sockets were on the wall a few inches above the desk. Overhead LED lights bathed the room in warm off-white light.

An old model holoscreen was the only other item of interest in the room.

"Anything you can use?" Irena asked, pointing her chin to the desk and ports.

"Perhaps," Harlan said. He took a seat and activated the screen with a switch on its side. A login window popped up. He entered the details provided to the silicon runners.

"Well, it's nice to have something work first for once," he said with a smile.

Irena joined him and stood by his side. "Hopefully, there's something interesting."

"I'm assuming Fizon's colleagues and other QCA founders would have already investigated his system and would have mentioned anything useful to us," Harlan said, "but it doesn't hurt to find out for ourselves."

He spent about five minutes going through the files that he could access, finding nothing of major importance. At least nothing that would explain why Fizon was missing.

The last entries on the computer were Fizon's work logs, the date of which indicated that he was working here, in his apartment, up to just two hours before the time he was reported missing. Additionally, there were a series of formal communications from a government representative from Mars indicating that he was due to meet with them the day after. And as Harlan had been informed, Fizon didn't make the meeting.

Irena read the information over Harlan's shoulder.

"Anything that seems odd to you?" he asked.

"No, not really. Everything seems to check out compared to what was in the file given to you regarding his disappearance. Timeline adds up. What do we do now? His colleagues didn't give us anything, and there's nothing out of the ordinary here."

"Not that we can see," Harlan said.

— *Do you want me to check for hidden files?* Milo asked.

Harlan ordered Milo to go ahead with an affirmative thought.

— *Okay, I'm scanning Fizon's system. I'll let you know if I find anything.*

"I'm just running a trace on the system," Harlan said. "It'll take a few minutes; might as well take a rest while it works." He sat down on the sofa and leaned back into the cushions.

Irena moved to join him, then suddenly stopped. She turned her head to the entrance.

"What is it?" Harlan asked, looking over his shoulder.

The door burst open.

A figure in a plain dark-gray suit rushed inside and immediately focused on Harlan. The man pulled a gun from within the folds of his suit jacket and fired off two shots.

17

It took another ten minutes for Bashir to lead them through the open level, across the engineering district, and finally into a restricted zone where he used a key card to bypass the security. Bella could smell stale incense in the air and a faint hint of spices.

The restricted zone was a shantytown, with rudimentary buildings made from scrap metal parts salvaged from old ships. She recognized airlocks, cargo bay doors, and detritus from over the last century of shipbuilding. Dozens of people milled about in this dark zone, lighting their way with LEDs strung haphazardly across a network of poles rising out of the single-story dwellings.

"What is this place?" Greta asked.

"A home for the disenfranchised," Bashir said. "When you can't get work with the syndicate, or when you don't *want* to work with the syndicate, you come here and scrape by on the waste from the wealthy."

He pointed to a squat building at the far edge of the shantytown. To Bella, it looked like a re-purposed shipping container. Corrugated steel hung from the front, creating a kind of porch. As they approached, the smell of spices grew stronger. She recognized the scent of ginger and curry. Her stomach rumbled, reminding her it had been a while since she'd enjoyed a proper meal. Protein pills and vitamin supplements didn't quite cut it. Especially after all of their recent exertion.

They came to the door of the container. Bashir turned and regarded them. "Don't antagonize him. He doesn't suffer fools, but is extremely talented and could be of great use to you." He looked to Greta. "Don't ruin this opportunity."

Greta silently mouthed the words, "Fuck off," and then smiled sweetly at him.

"I understand," Bella said. "I'll do the talking. Greta, you keep guard out here."

Bella nodded at Bashir, and he led her inside.

The room was surprisingly clean. Bella was expecting it to be filled with rubbish much like the rest of the shanty-town, but this was much simpler. Plain white walls and glass surfaces gave the single room a minimalist style.

The smell of cooking curry wafted in from a narrow doorway to the rear of the room.

Sitting at a glass desk and waving his hands across a holographic control panel was a small man in a basic set of brown robes. He was bald and wore thick graphene-framed glasses that magnified his dark eyes.

"Ah, Bashir, it's good to see you again," the man said. He clasped his hands together and bowed slightly as he grinned. "Who are your friends?"

"I'm sorry to burst in on you like this, Sanjeet. This is Ms. Mazzari."

Bashir introduced Bella and explained their reason for disturbing him.

Sanjeet bowed toward Bella and excused himself as he

finished gesturing over his control panel, then switched off his holographic display. He spun in his chair, crossed his arms, and waited expectantly.

Bella slid the q-bit core off her shoulder and placed it on the floor in front of him. "Bashir said you might be interested in this. We've come to trade, seeing as there was a problem with the previous buyer."

Bella noticed Sanjeet's serene calmness slip into humor. "That is a very intriguing item you have there, Ms. Mazzari. And yes, I am most definitely interested. I shall refrain from asking where you procured this. How much are you asking?"

Bella got a flashback to Lizbeth and hoped this wouldn't go the same way. "Two thousand bitcreds and some analysis on a video. Bashir tells me you're a talented peddler of information. Perhaps you wouldn't mind taking a look and giving me your opinion on a tampered broadcast."

Sanjeet rubbed his chin, looked at the core, then up at Bella. "This is acceptable. Bashir, my boy, why don't you make yourself busy and get your new friends something from the kitchen while we talk."

Bashir headed into the back room as Sanjeet stepped back to regard the core. A grin stretched across his face. "It must be my birthday. I've always wanted one of these."

He presented his wrist and looked at Bella expectantly. She did the same. With a swipe, he transferred two thousand authorized bitcreds. The chirp of confirmation filled Bella with relief. Her crew would be paid. In addition, they would have enough money for a couple weeks' worth of fuel and food rations.

"Now, Ms. Mazzari, let's look at this broadcast of yours."

Sanjeet pulled out a second chair at his desk and patted the seat. Bella sat next to him and handed over the memory stick that included the video she had received from the *Rubicon*.

With a couple of swift gestures, Sanjeet connected the data source to his machines and played the audio. The voice froze Bella to the spot, as it had done the first time she listened to it. Although it was definitely Gianni's voice, it was also so alien to her that she couldn't help but fear what might have happened to him.

Sanjeet cocked his head to one side and listened to the audio snippet.

"It's most unusual," he said. "Not any language I've ever heard before, although there are parts of the speech pattern that are familiar. It's been filtered, presumably to disguise what is being said. Do you mind if I run this through my systems to see if I can find a match? I have access to a lot of data."

"Please, go ahead. There's nothing sensitive in there; I just want to know what happened to my brother. Any clue to his fate would be greatly appreciated."

"Okay, then. Consider it done. But first, bring in your friend and let us all eat. This will take a little while."

"Thank you so much, Sanjeet. Your help is just what we needed after a tough day."

He smiled and bowed again.

Bashir brought various bowls of food out from the kitchen. Greta came in and joined the others around a makeshift table. They sat cross-legged on the floor and talked about trivial things while they filled their bellies.

Bella contacted Wilbur to make sure he was okay and to update him on their status. So far, he said, everything was fine, but Bella could sense he wasn't happy there on his own. If Bashir worked out, she could bring him onto the crew and give Wilbur some company if they needed to split up again.

When they finished their food, Sanjeet got to his feet and checked his computers. "We have a match." He brought up the results on his screen. Two waveforms crossed the expanse; the first was Gianni's recording, and the second was the match the computer had found.

"Where's the second audio feed from?" Bella asked.

"Let me see..." He opened the metadata stream for the audio sample. "It's a snippet of some radio chatter I intercepted a few weeks ago. From a cult in the asteroid belt. They've got a colony of sorts near the mining company on Ceres."

He played the second sound sample, and although there wasn't the same fearful panic as there was in Gianni's voice, it was quite clear to Bella that the words they were using were very similar, and in some cases exactly the same.

"What does this mean?" Greta asked. "That your little bro was in a cult?"

"It can't be. He was a company man. A scientist. He was on his way to that new project on Europa, remember? They had strict vetting for the program. If he was involved with a cult, they'd have found out about it and sacked him."

Bella sighed. This didn't help her search or explain why her brother sounded so scared. As she thought about what to do next, Sanjeet leaned closer to the screen and played the video file in ultra-slow motion. He scrubbed back and forth over a section of video that lasted no more than a few seconds.

"What is it?" she asked.

He magnified a reflection in Gianni's left eye.

"What are we looking at?" Greta asked, leaning in closer over Sanjeet's shoulder.

The image was of two triangles, one atop of the other,

the two points touching. It appeared to be a logo reflecting off Gianni's eye from another video feed.

"That," Sanjeet said, pointing to the triangles, "is the logo for the leadership within the Jovian Group."

"And you know this how?" Greta queried.

Sanjeet tapped the side of his head. "I intercept their communications when they're not being diligent with their encryption. That's the thing with people at the top of large organizations—they get comfortable and think they're safe, but there are always people like me listening in from the shadows."

"So this all has something to do with a company?" Bella asked, not quite understanding the ramifications of it just yet. She didn't have long to ponder on it when she received a panicked transmission from Wilbur. "Bella, things have just got a little tricky here. That death squad that was after you? Well, they've just taken the *Mule*."

"Damn it." Bella slammed a fist into her thigh. "Are you okay?"

"I snuck out through the cargo hatch. Don't worry, I'm fine. I have the other q-bit core."

"Where are you?"

"Hiding in a port authority office. Military goons have swarmed everywhere else, and we've missed the last transporter ship off the station. Won't be another for three days. They have us trapped here."

Bella was about to swear when Sanjeet tapped a bony finger against her shoulder. "I think I can help—for a small price."

"What do you have in mind?"

"I have a small shuttle you can rent from me. It's out back. I can give you navigation data to get to the dock through old, forgotten tunnels. I use it for trading."

"And I bet I know the price you want," Bella said, knowing she had zero room to negotiate—for the second time today. They couldn't afford to go on foot, and there was no way in hell they were going to leave Wilbur on his own.

Sanjeet grinned, exposing two missing molars and crooked canines. He looked like a hungry, grinning dog. "Two thousand bitcreds," he said, "for the temporary use of the shuttle. But if there's any damage or loss, then you'll owe me a favor."

Feeling like she'd been had, Bella had no choice but to shake on the deal and pay the man. All the credits they had earned with the sale of the q-bit core had vanished, along with their freighter. This was suddenly, again, not a good day.

"Wilbur, hold tight, old friend. We're coming to pick you up. Send me your exact location. We've procured access to a ship."

"That's great news. The ex-military goons are heading further into the station to look for me. Hurry."

"Stay hidden. We'll be as quick as we can."

"Will do," he said.

Bella could hear the fear in his voice, but knew he was smart enough to do as he was told and hang tight. She and Greta prepared to leave. Bashir helped them follow Sanjeet's directions through the shantytown until they found an old, seemingly abandoned workshop. The shuttle was inside.

"This is going to be a tight squeeze," Greta said, looking at the squat, short craft with disdain.

"Sanjeet says it's got enough fuel to get to Atlas and back if needed," Bashir said, and tapped in the security code of the cargo door. With a grating noise, the panel slid open. The stench of cattle and other livestock wafted out.

Greta gagged. "Great. He's a meat smuggler, too." She wafted the air from her face as she stepped inside. "This trip is going to be hell. I hope you're not a vegan, Bash," she said, slapping him on the back.

"Focus," Bella said. "And arm your weapons in case we run into trouble."

"Does this jalopy have a name?" Greta asked.

Bashir shrugged. "I don't think so. You want to name it? Is that considered good or bad luck for you people?"

Greta raised an eyebrow. "Us people?"

"I just meant you as a crew. Don't get all sensitive on me."

"It's neither," Bella said, shutting down the conversation. "But I do prefer to give ships a name. Since the *Mule* has been impounded—" she looked around the disheveled and low-rent craft, curling her lip in disgust "—we'll call this the *Goat*."

"Why?" Bashir asked.

"Because it's small, and it stinks," Bella said, before leaving the crew in the main section as she eased her way through the tight corridor and into the equally cramped cockpit. There was only room for one, and that suited her. She was in no mood for conversation. She just wanted to get Wilbur and get back to Atlas now that she had a lead on her brother.

Bella fired up the engines, set the autopilot to navigate the interior tunnels of the space station, and brought up a communications screen on her terminal. She sent Harlan a message, explaining the lead she had got and also that Lizbeth Adams had her own crew of rogue abbots. It was clear to her that their cases were linked somehow.

And then there was the issue of Irena. Her mother was

not only a House Messenger for Atlas but a former director of the Jovian Group. Perhaps through Irena, she'd get some idea of what they were up to and why their leadership were on Gianni's shuttle. One way or another, Bella would get answers.

18

Harlan's heart raced, and he instinctively rolled to the side and onto the floor.

The two shots thudded into the back of the sofa, their exit producing white puffs of material in the spot where Harlan had just been sitting.

"Get down," he screamed, as another shot slammed into the furniture.

He grabbed the Taser from his jacket and snuck a glance round the edge of the sofa.

It wasn't a man who'd fired at him; it was an abbot.

Another rogue abbot.

The machine must have had a scanning modification installed, as it turned its head and looked Harlan directly in the eye. It shifted its aim.

Harlan scrambled back behind cover and saw the shadow loom closer. He jumped to his feet but stayed in a squatting position. He thought about dashing across to the other door, but didn't want to bring the abbot closer to Irena, who was just standing there, trembling and paralyzed with fear.

"We don't need to do this," Harlan said, crab-walking to his left, keeping the furniture between him and his assailant. There was no response. Not that he was expecting one.

The abbot stepped closer and peered over the sofa. Its cold black eyes reflected the light from the window.

Harlan launched himself up and toward the abbot, holding out the Taser and aiming for its chest. It bent backward at the waist, clear of Harlan's outstretched arm, and the Taser jabbed empty space. Harlan counteracted the moment by throwing his weight back on his heels and staying on his feet.

The abbot thrust out its left arm, catching Harlan square in the jaw, knocking him to the ground.

His head slammed hard against the apartment wall. Pain exploded across the back of his skull. The impact even blurred the vision in his cybernetic eye. A feeling of nausea threatened to overwhelm him, but his adrenaline-regulation valve helped him regain his focus.

"You bastard," he drawled as he groped in the air for something to help him stand. His attacker's shadow stretched across the carpeted floor and crawled up the wall to fully enclose him. The barrel of the gun dominated Harlan's field of view. He tried to slap it away, but missed.

"Over here, you bastard," Irena shouted.

A plate smashed into the back of the abbot's head. At first it didn't react, its glare firmly on Harlan as though it were enjoying his predicament.

No, he thought, it was recording him.

The abbot blinked and pulled the trigger at the same time another plate smashed into its back, sending the bullet off course. But it still struck Harlan in the top of his left shoulder.

He yelled with the burning pain. He knew it had just grazed the muscle, having not felt the impact on his bone. That didn't mean it hurt any less. He rolled to his side, clutching his shoulder, and dropped the Taser.

Looking from his fetal position, Harlan saw the abbot turn its attention to Irena, who had suddenly realized what she had done and become paralyzed again as the machine raised its arm, pointing the gun toward her.

Harlan kicked out, mostly through instinct. He caught the abbot in the back of its knee joint, sending it crashing down. He grabbed for his Taser with his good arm. Using his core to twist around, he pushed off the wall and slid himself across the carpet, where he thrust out with the Taser.

The abbot was already turning its head, so by the time Harlan struck with the weapon, the pins slammed into the creature's forehead. It shook violently against the high flow of amps.

Irena looked on with wide eyes, and then, as though someone had just switched on her power, came to life. She grabbed a large jagged section of broken plate and slammed it into the abbot's neck, slicing through wires and valves.

Oil and servo fluid gushed from the wound.

Smoke peeled away from the charred synthetic skin.

Its eyelids fluttered and closed. The thing collapsed forward with a thud.

Harlan let go of the Taser and, breathing heavily, struggled to his feet. He reached down to pick up the gun and fired twice into the back of the machine where its CPU and motherboard were located. Sparks erupted from the second as its electronics shorted.

"Holy crap," he said, staggering to lean against the back of the ruined sofa. Then, looking up at a shell-shocked

Irena, he added, "You did good. If you hadn't distracted it, I'd be sprayed up that wall right now."

She was trembling and just staring at her own bloodied hand. She must have cut it on the sharp plate fragment.

"Irena? Are you okay? Can you hear me?"

A long moment ticked by. She turned slowly to face Harlan and as equally slowly nodded her head. Her eyes filled with tears, and she bent over the sofa and vomited.

Harlan leaned over and patted her back, unsure of what else to do. After a few more minutes of dry heaving, Irena stood up straight and took a deep breath. She looked down at the still form of the dead abbot and then back at Harlan.

"Its eyes," she said. "Its eyes were just like the other one back on Earth."

"It was recording, that's why. Whoever is controlling these damned things either gets off on seeing people die, or is making sure the job gets done. If that's the case, we don't have much time to hang around. Let's deal with these wounds and get out of here."

It was obvious to Harlan that there was nothing here for him to find out about Fizon's disappearance. He'd been sent here to be the target of this rogue abbot. Only its controller couldn't have known he had Irena with him. That small distraction had been the difference between life and death.

He doubted they'd get the same opportunity next time.

"I was right back there, on Earth," Irena said. "I couldn't move; it was like I was stuck in a movie. I'm so sorry. You could have died."

"But I didn't, so there's no use worrying about that. Focus on what the situation is now, our options, and the best course of action. First things first, let's get that cut on your hand dealt with."

Harlan used another plate fragment to cut a strip of

cloth from the abbot's sweater. He used it to bandage Irena's wound. It didn't look that deep, so she'd be okay once they found a medical kit and glued the skin.

"Thank you," she said, smiling, her trembling reduced to intermittent quivers.

"No, thank you. If it wasn't for you, we'd both be dead right now."

Irena looked down at the abbot. "Do you know who it is?"

Harlan thought for a moment and engaged Milo's expanded facial-recognition algorithm.

"One of Fizon's colleagues here on the station. Which means someone's hacked into the station's systems and over-ridden the abbots' programming. This is not good."

"None of this is good," Irena said, then, looking up at Harlan, added, "Your shoulder is bleeding. Please, let me help."

Irena helped him out of his leather jacket and pulled the collar over his left shoulder. It still burned, but his pain compensators were doing a good job at nullifying its effects. He knew all too well, though, that it wouldn't last. He'd have another fifteen minutes of pain control before it ebbed away.

Irena inspected his wound. "It's shallow," she said. "Looks raw, though."

"Help me cut some more bandage. It'll keep it covered while we get out of here."

Irena helped him and was quick and efficient. Giving her tasks to focus on seemed like the best way to help keep her shit together.

Though he knew Irena was smart and strong willed, he had to help her stay with it until they had time to rest and come to terms with the situation.

For all he knew, there could be another abbot on its way to finish the job.

When Irena had finished attending to his wound, Harlan knelt beside the abbot, gripped the skin behind its ear, and tugged back sharply. The face mask slipped over its metallic head.

"What is that you're doing?" Irena asked. Her voice had altered from a panicked tone to one of curiosity.

That's good. Means she's engaging her scientific side, which means self-control.

"Getting the memory chips and its q-drive to analyze later."

"You think we can get something off them?"

"Only one way to find out. But first we need to get out of here and find a terminal."

"Aren't you going to report this to your boss?"

Having released the memory chip caddy, Harlan placed the chips, along with the spherical. marble-sized q-drive, into a shielded bag that he kept with him as part of his forensic kit. He then removed the abbot's holster, put it on himself, and took the gun, checking the ammo: four rounds were left.

He handed Irena the Taser. "It's got one charge left, but one is all you need if you get them in the head."

She took it with a shaking hand and tucked the handle in the band of her trousers, using her shirt to cover the rest of it. It wasn't the perfect disguise, but it made her less conspicuous.

"Come on, follow me," Harlan said, approaching the door.

"Harlan, your boss—aren't you going to report this?"

He breathed out a long sigh. "I think it's already too late for that. I think he's compromised." He couldn't be one hundred percent sure, but from Harlan's point of view, it made sense. It was Hugo, after all, who had been so adamant he take this case. The report specifically tasked Harlan with checking out Fizon's apartment as a matter of urgency.

It didn't take a genius to see a connection there.

Sure, there was a small chance Hugo was innocent in all this and it was just a coincidence, but Harlan had learned to trust his hunches.

"We'll discuss it more when we're off this station," he said. "Stay close and follow me."

Harlan opened the apartment door, checked both directions to make sure they were alone, and stepped into the corridor.

— I found some hidden files on Fizon's system, Milo said. *I've copied them to your internal drive, though they've been encrypted with QCA technology. That's going to be tricky. Perhaps a visit to Nico is in order... if you're still on good terms with him.*

Harlan resisted the urge to swear as he and Irena headed for the elevator that would take them up to the docking station's departure lounge. Nico was the best man for this particular job; he had helped develop the latest protocols after the human-abbot war and knew their systems as well as any human.

But no, Harlan was not on good terms with him. He'd have to figure something out—assuming they made it back to Atlas Station in one piece. His skin prickled with the hyperawareness one had when expecting to be attacked at any moment.

The elevator ride was uneventful, and Harlan got his breath back.

When they exited onto the departure lounge level, his heart sank.

The place was packed with hundreds of people and abbots alike. Any one of them could be assigned to find and kill Harlan.

"We've got to get through that lot to the transporter ship," he said wearily.

The long utilitarian boxlike transporter hung out into space, the front section secured to the dock with a pressurized tunnel that reminded Harlan of an accordion he had once procured from a contraband dealer and went on to sell later, which he regretted.

Although they were only a hundred meters or so away, they had to cross the lounge, exposing themselves to any would-be attacker. And to make matters worse, they didn't have long; the transporter was leaving in five minutes.

"We've got to hurry," Irena said, as though reading his mind. "If we don't get on that ship, we'll be stuck here for days."

Harlan gritted his teeth against the pain flaring in his shoulder, the wound seemingly getting worse. "We can't just walk through there; it's too dangerous."

Even as he said it, an abbot dressed in a corporate suit, much like the one that had attacked them in Fizon's apartment. walked toward them, its attention to the right of the lounge, toward the great glass window that looked out into space. After a few more steps forward, it straightened its head and stared directly at Harlan and Irena.

19

I rena gripped the Taser and kept it hidden behind her jacket. She stared at the abbot coming toward them, but it wore a blank expression, making it impossible to read.

"Harlan?" Irena said, prompting him for some direction.

He leaned heavily against her and coughed. A few speckles of blood splashed on the floor. He was clearly more wounded than he had let on.

The abbot continued to come toward them, showing no sign of slowing down.

"Go, go," Harlan said, pushing against her with his body.

Irena stuck her arm through Harlan's and pulled him away to a section of chairs where dozens of people were waiting for their departure.

The abbot was just a few feet away now.

Its eyes flickered slightly, tracking the movements.

Irena prepared to bring the Taser out, remembering what Harlan had told her about it having a single charge and how she must use it correctly. She'd have to wait until the abbot was right on them.

She trembled with the anticipation.

The abbot's attention snapped to Harlan, then back to Irena.

Pulling the Taser out of her jacket, Irena readied to strike, but was cut short of attacking when the abbot sidestepped the pair of them and continued on its way.

Relief flooded Irena's body, and she put the weapon back inside her jacket with an audible sigh. She tracked the abbot's route and watched him disappear out of the lounge into one of the many elevators.

"This is too stressful," she said.

"Let's just stay focused," Harlan said. "Keep going."

"There must be a better way to approach this," she said. She stopped and held Harlan closer to her so they could speak more quietly. They were just twenty meters away from the first waiting area and had cover in the form of a column, which held dozens of holographic screens imparting information to the station's travelers.

"I think I can help," Harlan said. He was silent for a moment again, doing that thinking thing of his that Irena had noticed. His lips moved in small micro-expressions as though he were talking to someone.

Irena had wondered whether he was talking to himself, or whether he had some kind of subvocalized communication system with someone off-station.

"I've got an idea," Harlan said. "I can use the ID chip from the dead abbot to analyze and filter Wi-Fi signals from the QCA to any other abbots."

"And that will help how?"

"I should be able to pinpoint which abbots are receiving instructions. Although I can't break the encryption, I can see who is receiving messages similar to the abbot that tried to attack us."

"Go for it."

While Irena was waiting for Harlan to do his computer wizardry, she took in the traffic within the lounge, analyzing the flow of movement.

She traced the route through the various lanes and columns and open areas to the departure tunnel they needed. She imagined people as data points in one of her modeling programs.

It reminded her of a weather pattern. Each element influenced the other, but there were commonalities. She noticed how the majority of the traffic remained in loosely contained columns going to and from the departure lounge and the elevators.

From this, she figured out that there would be a number of approaches they could take to limit their exposure to a threat. By keeping to the walls and columns and keeping other parts of the station to their flanks or their rear, it would reduce the number of directions that they could be attacked from.

"Okay, I got it," Harlan said.

"Go on."

"I'm only detecting two others receiving the same transmission. Do you have an AR overlay?"

Irena shook her head. "I used to have some contacts that provided that, but I could never get on with them."

"Well, you need one if you're to be able to track the two abbots. Have one of mine."

With his thumb and forefinger, Harlan pinched the contact lens from his left eye.

Although the idea grossed her out a little, she knew they didn't have time to mess around with hygienic niceties. She'd wash her eyes out if she got home safely.

She took the contact lens and placed it into her left eye.

The chip-controlled device blurred her vision for a moment but readjusted itself to correct her slight astigmatism and give her sharper vision than she had before.

"Okay, you see those two abbots that I've highlighted?" Harlan asked.

"Yeah, they're on either side of the room. The one you highlighted in blue is scanning the room. The red one on the right seems to be heading this way."

"Yeah, they're the ones. We need to find a way to the departure tunnel without getting involved with those."

"I think I can do that," Irena said. "You need to trust me and stay close. I can model the movements."

"You can *what*?"

"Modeling. With data. It's a skill that got me the position at the ERP."

Harlan looked at her for a moment, his lips twitching. He nodded and indicated for her to lead the way.

With the augmented reality overlay showing her the location of the two abbots, she was able to picture the flow of traffic again as though it were a model, this time with two more elements within it. This actually made it easier, as she was able to use the flow of traffic and the physical obstructions to block their approach.

It reminded her of a video game she used to play as a child. Her parents had always told her it was a waste of time, but if it got them to the transporter safely, then she knew it was time well spent.

"Let's go," Irena said, pulling against Harlan's arm. "I know you're hurt, but we need to move quickly."

"Don't worry about me. Do what you need to do."

Irena gritted her teeth and tried to channel the nervousness and anxiety into focused action. She cut across a row of pedestrians toward the left and put as many people between her and Red as possible.

A couple of people swore at them and sidestepped wildly.

Irena apologized and pressed on. They were now in an open area that led straight toward a hundred or so seats all facing large screens at the rear of the room.

The commotion caught the attention of Blue, and it moved to flank them on the left.

Seeing that they were in a pincer formation, Irena drove forward, dragging Harlan with her, pulling level with their pursuers.

The departure tunnel was now about fifty meters from their position, toward the right corner of the lounge. According to the AR overlay, the abbots were about thirty meters away and converging quickly.

Irena stopped and got her bearings, taking the time to see where people were moving so she could use them to her advantage.

A central, circular information booth, ten meters in front of them, split the wave of people as they flowed around it, while others queued in roped-off lanes. She focused on it and proceeded to move Harlan along with her.

"They're getting closer," he said.

"That's the plan."

When they reached the information booth, they stopped.

Irena looked left then right and got a visual on both of the abbots.

Unsurprisingly, they looked similar to the one that had attacked them previously. It seemed a popular model, with its corporate look and a smart suit. It was hard for her not to feel as though it were somehow personal. That these particular abbots had taken a disliking to them. She reminded herself that it was the programming they had received from whoever was trying to break into the QCA.

As she had predicted, Red was approaching more quickly than Blue.

A flow of humans and abbots from the left-hand side of the departure lounge had come out of the elevators and were approaching docks A to F, slowing Blue's approach to the central area.

With Red just ten meters from them, Irena urged Harlan on as they circled around the information booth clockwise at the same pace that the arrivals headed toward the exit elevator, blocking Red's path.

"It's working," Harlan said. "You're good at this."

"Let's not get ahead of ourselves."

With Red and Blue now behind them, Irena pulled Harlan into a jog, gaining more distance.

With no more arrivals and the departure lounge starting to thin out, this was their only opportunity. She would have no more mass of humans and abbots to use like pawns in a game of chess.

It was now a footrace.

Harlan was sweating badly and was holding his shoulder as he strived to keep up.

Red and Blue had now made their way through the throng of people and were twenty meters behind them and closing.

A security abbot standing in front of their departure tunnel looked at Irena and Harlan as they approached. He raised his palm. "Credentials please."

Behind him in the tunnel, some thirty or forty others were already making their way toward the transport ship, so Irena couldn't use them to block the oncoming abbots.

"We're in a hurry. Please just let us on," Irena said.

"I'm afraid I need to see your credentials," the abbot replied with no emotion.

"It's okay," Harlan said. He swiped his terminal over the security gate's receiver and waited for the authorization to clear.

Irena glanced over her shoulder. Red and Blue were now almost on them. Blue was reaching into his jacket. She, in turn, placed her hand on the Taser, ready to use it if necessary. Her heart was pounding in her chest and her mouth was dry as she continued to wait nervously.

"Come on, it shouldn't take this long," she said.

Harlan waved his terminal once more over the authorization panel.

A pair of pensioners with their two young children appeared from nowhere and shuffled their way in behind Harlan and Irena, blocking Red and Blue from a direct shot. It hadn't deterred Blue from keeping his hand inside his jacket, however.

Irena doubted they would care too much about collateral damage if it came to it. But to her relief, the authorization terminal bleeped and flashed a green light. The security abbot stood aside and waved them through before asking the pensioners for their credentials.

Red and Blue had pushed their way in front of the pensioners and bundled the security abbot out of the way.

Irena and Harlan were halfway to the transport ship. The last of the other segment of travelers had already stepped inside.

The security abbot reached out for Blue and grabbed its arm.

Red ignored his partner, pulled the gun, and aimed it toward Harlan.

Irena pushed Harlan to the side instinctively as the shot fired. It ricocheted off the steel hull of the transport ship. Irena, falling to her right after pushing Harlan, fell into a roll, and scrambled to her knees.

When she looked up, Red was aiming his gun at her.

Her chest tightened, and for a brief second, her vision blurred. She barely knew what she was doing, but her hand flashed out, taking the Taser from her jacket. She pressed the trigger, sending the two prongs firing into Red's chest.

A crackle of electricity and a flash of blue light sent Red into a jolting spasm.

Harlan got to his feet and fired twice into the abbot's head, sending Red crashing to the ground, its limbs jerking as smoke swirled out from the wounds.

The stench of burning plastic filled the air.

Blue was still tangling with the security abbot, and somewhere off in the distance an alarm was blaring. It wouldn't be long before more security arrived.

Harlan was already one step ahead of Irena. He pulled her to her feet and dragged her toward the transport ship.

Two more security abbots appeared at the door of the ship.

Harlan flashed his badge again and quickly explained they had been attacked. The pensioners had arrived, holding their grandchildren close to their chests. They corroborated Harlan's explanation and gestured to Blue, who was batting the security abbot to the ground with the butt of his gun.

To Irena's relief, the security guards ushered them onto the transport ship before running off down the departure tunnel to deal with Blue.

"Thank you," Irena said to the two pensioners.

They just stared at her with blank expressions of fear

and nodded, before guiding their grandchildren to the family section of the ship.

Irena and Harlan headed toward the rear. Harlan used his credentials to get them seats in a higher access status cabin, where he could lock the door and remain private.

"You were impressive back there," he said. "I can see why they wanted you on Earth. You adapt quickly."

Irena sank into her seat, stared out the window into open space, and tried not to cry in front of Harlan. The whole situation with the abbots had brought back the experience of her time on Earth.

But unlike before in Fizon's apartment, she refused to be paralyzed by fear and felt the power of direct action and fighting back. She didn't want to admit it, but it felt good defeating Red and seeing the artificial light of its eyes go out.

"Thanks," she said. "I'll be happy when this is all over."

"I think we have a long way to go before that." Harlan removed his jacket and inspected the wound on his shoulder with a grimace.

It had started to bleed again. Irena used the med-kit within the private cabin to re-dress his wound.

A message bleeped on Harlan's terminal. He brought it up on his screen and scanned through it.

"What is it?" she said.

"It's Bella. She's had a very similar situation to us on Galilei Station. She wants to meet up when we get back to Atlas."

"Why? What happened?"

"It's something about your mother and the Jovian Group. It seems they're somehow implicated in this abbot issue."

Although Irena should have defended her, her mother's

last visit had severely altered Irena's opinion of her. And remembering back to her childhood, Irena recalled numerous situations where her mother wasn't there for her and was on, as her mother said, "Jovian business."

Irena now wanted to know exactly what this Jovian business was and how it tied in to everything else. She didn't need to be a modeling expert to know that they were all elements of the same source.

For now, though, she sat back in her seat and looked at the five other shining stations in various orbits around the moon and Earth. Atlas was the largest and situated in the equilibrium point between Earth and the sun.

It shone like a beacon, and Irena focused on it, willing the day's travel to be over. The stress of the day manifested in a long yawn. Tiredness overwhelmed her, and once she had made sure Harlan was okay, she lay down across the seats and let sleep take over.

A soft beep woke Harlan from his slumber. He rolled over and saw on his holographic clock display that it was 0800. Morning had arrived. He barely remembered getting back to his apartment after a day's journey on the Turing-to-Atlas transporter.

— *Irena saved your ass,* Milo said, reminding him of how she'd helped get him through Turing Station's departure lounge.

"She did well," he mumbled in response, then swung his legs over the side of the bed and stood up. He stretched his arms up and winced at the ache in his left shoulder.

He took off the bandage and admired Irena's first aid skills. The skin-mesh had taken well. She'd done a good job with the med-kit. The cut was almost healed, the fast-acting stem cells living up to their name. The muscle would take a little while longer to return to full health.

The smell of coffee and voices coming from the living room dragged his thoughts back to the present.

— *You've got company, old chap. Bella and her crew arrived a little while ago.*

"I'm on it," Harlan said, wishing he had longer to sleep and recuperate. His body ached and his mind wasn't at its sharpest. He put on a clean pair of blue overalls and stepped out of his bedroom.

The Mazzari crew and a new guy Harlan hadn't seen before were hovering around his desk. Bella was sitting on the edge. They all looked to Harlan with a mix of expressions that ranged the gamut from pensive to expectant.

"Hey, you're up," Irena said, bouncing over to him from the kitchen zone with a smile. She placed a hand on his upper arm. "How's the shoulder?"

"It's a lot better, thanks. You did a great job to get us on the ship and fixing me up."

Irena blushed and held his gaze for a second. "You're welcome. I'll get a coffee for you, and... I don't mean to rush you, but we've come up with a plan of action."

"Oh?" It was times like these that Harlan wished he had more furniture and was better with guests. "I'm sorry," he said, indicating the lack of furniture in his apartment, "I don't have visitors very often; otherwise, I'd offer you all a seat."

Bella slipped off the desk and shrugged. "Don't worry about it. We're not here to get comfortable, anyway. We've found a connection between my brother's disappearance and the rogue abbots."

"I got your message," he said. "Something to do with Irena's mother and the Jovian Group?"

"Yeah, the group is involved with the abbots somehow," Bella said.

"Okay, do you have any evidence for that?"

Greta nodded to the newcomer.

"Harlan, this is Bashir, a new addition to Mazzari Enterprises," Bella said.

The tall, bulky man, with a bruised and swollen nose, stepped forward and held out his hand. "Pleasure to meet you," he said, with an accent Harlan knew very well: he was from the lower levels of Zeno Station. Harlan had grown up there himself, and although he had lost the accent, there were a few inflections on the vowels that he was particularly sensitive to.

The accent also meant something else: Bashir had grown up an orphan, like Harlan. No one, other than the guardians and teachers, grew up on the lower level of Zeno without picking up those quirks. Vat-grown orphans had an invisible bond that didn't even require acknowledgment.

"Nice to meet you, too," Harlan said, returning the firm grip of the man's handshake.

"Thanks."

"So, Bashir, tell me about the abbots, and how they're connected to the Jovian Group."

Bashir spoke for ten minutes straight, explaining how Lizbeth had taken over Salazar's business and built a trading relationship with members of the Jovian Group. At first, it had started out as small shipments of mining resources from Jupiter's moons, but as Lizbeth wormed her way close to those in the higher echelons of the group, other, more advanced tech became available.

"What were they getting in return?" Harlan asked.

"Intel mostly," Bashir said. "I was one of the bodyguards for a couple of Lizbeth's spies on Galilei. They wanted to know anything and everything. A lot of it seemed like nonsense or just daily crap to me."

Wilbur inched his glasses up on his nose. Harlan had come to learn that this meant he was nervous, but then, the small mole-like man had always been that way around

Harlan. Greta, on the other hand, displayed her usual military-learned confidence and poise.

Thinking about everything Bashir had said, it did seem as though his case with Fizon and the event surrounding Gianni's disappearance were connected. The data all pointed that way. One rogue abbot was an exceptional event; four of them hinted at something much larger and coordinated. This had never happened in the history of abbot existence post-war.

Then there was the issue of the hack and Luca.

It didn't take a genius to work out that the latter was likely responsible for the former. Fizon would make the perfect conduit with which to manipulate the QCA, so that made sense, too. If he could find Luca, he'd likely find Fizon. But then the Jovian Group was another factor. Again, Harlan sensed they were linked in some manner.

After all, Gylfie had told him that they were merging with the Ceres Mining Company. They wouldn't be doing that unless it gave them an advantage somewhere, presumably to alter public opinion and confidence in the president. That, along with control of the ten million abbots within the Sol-Fed, would make the merged group the single most powerful and influential faction. Who knew what their ultimate plan was, but looking at the disparate parts, it didn't suggest rainbows and unicorns for the citizens of the Sol-Fed.

Harlan turned to Bella. "Okay, so it sounds like Lizbeth was one of Jovian's puppets, but what exactly is it you need me to do?"

Bella ran a hand through her gray hair, and then nodded to Irena.

"I want you to hack into my mother's personal files," Irena said.

— *I wasn't expecting that*, Milo said.

"Why?"

"Growing up, my mother was always away on Jovian Group business. Even recently, she attacked me about my time at the ERP and threatened to crush the investigation. She was insistent on knowing everything."

Greta picked at her nails with a small switchblade. She shrugged and said, "Sounds like motherly interest to me. Of course she would want to know what happened to you."

Wilbur shot her a glance and narrowed his already beady eyes.

"But the question is why," Greta said, adding, "Her mother is one of the Messengers representing Atlas Station; she'd have access to all the files from the military force and the Earth Restoration Project. There'd be no need to be aggressive unless there was something about what happened that she didn't want out in the open."

— *I like this woman*, Milo said.

Harlan considered her words. "It's a good point."

Irena shot Greta a look as if to tell her she wasn't being helpful.

Bella took control of the conversation once more. "Irena has agreed to help you gain access to her mother's files. We want to know what she has on the Jovian Group and anything else we can find that might be useful. Can you do it?"

— *It's as if Bella doesn't even know you. You sure you want to have a drink with her?*

"Sure I can," Harlan said, ignoring Milo. "It's what I do." He turned to Irena. "Are you positive you want me to do this? It could compromise more than your relationship with her. I'll need you to give me access to your mother's network. Can you do that?"

Irena handed him a data stick. "The login credentials are on there. That'll get you on to the network. Mother's files are protected, and we can't access them."

"I'll have to look at the security first. I can't promise anything."

"Won't this affect your status with the silicon runners?" Wilbur asked, doing that thing with his glasses again. And it was then that Harlan realized he had been wrong about him; it wasn't necessarily a sign of nervousness but a sign of concern.

Harlan shrugged. "My status is going to be ruined at the end of all this anyway, so why not dig all the way to the truth on the way down?"

If he was right about Hugo, then the silicon runners were already compromised, and with one attempt on his life already, Harlan didn't see any reason to play by the rules now. It wasn't just a search for truth and justice, it was a search for survival.

"So you'll do it?" Irena asked.

"Yeah. But you lot will need to go find something else to do while I get to work. It might take some time." Harlan gestured for the group to clear out of his way, and he took a seat at his screen.

Bella and her crew left him to it. Irena remained, but she sat down on the stool in the kitchen area and busied herself with some work on a slate. He thought about asking her to leave too, but then realized he'd grown accustomed to her company.

"While you're here," Harlan said, "would you mind making some more coffee? There's too much blood in my caffeine levels."

"Sure thing," Irena said, sharing a comfortable smile with him.

— *Looks like she's growing fond of you.*

— Cut the sass and prepare to get to work. We need to crack Victoria Selles' personal files, and I'd rather we didn't get caught doing it.

Irena brought over his coffee and placed it on his desk. He thanked her and watched her for a moment as she returned to work on her slate. He admired her spirit; she'd gone through a lot in the last few days, yet she was still focused on the task at hand.

— Milo, Harlan thought, play some music. Eagles Greatest Hits.

The opening notes to 'Hotel California' came through the apartment's speakers.

"What's this?" Irena asked, looking up from her slate.

"A classic group from before the Great Migration," Harlan said. "Classic music helps me focus."

"I think I like it," she said.

"Apparently a lot of people did."

With the music playing in the background, and with his caffeine levels approaching normal, Harlan switched on his screen and dived into that hyper-focused state he had developed as a junior silicon runner, where the work was ninety percent hacking and system analysis. He missed this part of his job and felt at home as he accessed Victoria Selles' network and began to work on finding its vulnerabilities.

It'd take him a while, but he'd done this a thousand times before. Hacking high-level government officials was his idea of a good time. Where most people were happy adventuring in VR worlds, he found peace and tranquility in cracking code. And this one called to him like the sirens called to Ulysses.

THREE HOURS LATER, Harlan had finally decrypted Victoria Selles' personal files. He had used Milo's abilities to run filters to narrow down his search for anything interesting. Although Harlan hadn't found anything directly incriminating, he did find something that gave them the next lead in the expanding case.

Bella returned a few minutes after Harlan had sent her a message.

"You found something on Gianni?" she said.

Harlan spun around on his chair to face her. Irena was leaning against the breakfast bar. The two women touched fists in a familiar greeting.

"Something along those lines," he said, adding, "Where's the rest of the crew?"

"I've got them scrubbing Sanjeet's shuttle clear of IDs. The military service is swarming the area; I didn't want our only route off the station to be impounded."

"Good thinking."

He'd seen the military service expand their numbers via his news feeds. There was nothing on the silicon runners' server, so he assumed this step-up in security came from higher up, presumably on advisement from Hugo.

"Harlan?" Bella prompted. "The files?"

"Sorry, I was just thinking things over. Here, look at this memo I found." He swiped the file across to her, and she brought it up on her terminal, scanning the few lines.

"A name," she said, "Charles Gandit, and... what's Vanguard?"

"I dug around on the black-net a little," Harlan said. "Vanguard is an elite hierarchy within the Jovian Group. There's little information on them, but there were a number of messages to and from Gandit and Irena's mother. At this stage, I'd say Victoria Selles is part of this Vanguard cabal."

"And this Gandit chap, he's our main lead?"

Gandit appeared to be one of the directors of the Jovian Group and a member of the Vanguard inner circle. Harlan had checked his record on the runners' database, but nothing came up. As far as the official law-keeping situation was concerned, he was squeaky clean.

"Sure is," he said. "There were others mentioned, but they're dead now. I suggest we split up, as I have a chip that needs decoding. Why don't you pay Mr. Gandit a visit and see what he knows about your brother's disappearance?"

"He's here on Atlas?" Bella asked.

"Yeah. On level eight."

"Okay, my crew and I will go and see what he knows."

"When you're finished, meet me at a contact's place. The RDC down on level two: ask for Gylfie. I'll be there with him, cracking into this chip we got from the abbot on Turing station."

"You did good, Harlan." Bella kissed him on the cheek before sweeping away and exiting his apartment.

"Do you mind if I go back to my parents' place?" Irena asked. "I have a few things I need to get off my chest."

"You're free to do whatever you need to." Harlan stood up from his desk and carefully stretched his aching shoulders and neck. "But I'm here if you want some support. You said your mother was acting strange with you before..."

"It's fine. I need to do this. Besides, the quicker you access that chip, the sooner we can get a lead on Fizon. I'll meet you at Gylfie's place when I'm done. I doubt it'll take long."

"Just call me if you get into trouble, or head straight for the RDC. I'll send you the location. It's a safe place despite the low level." Harlan tapped out a map location on his terminal and swiped it over to Irena.

"Got it." She smiled a nervous smile.

Harlan grabbed his jacket and the abbot's chip and led her out of his apartment.

He felt like things were coming together now, but in the back of his mind he was still worried about Leanne and those in the shadows who clearly wanted him dead. He made sure the gun he'd procured was well-holstered and ready to use at a moment's notice as he strode toward the elevator that would take him down into the bowels of the station.

Irena took the other elevator heading upward—as did Bella's crew.

Harlan tried to ignore the fleeting thought that this might be the last time he would see any of them. "Good luck," he said, before stepping inside the empty elevator car and requesting level two.

21

Bella and her crew spilled out of the elevator on level eight of Atlas Station. Up here, the place was all high-end glass surfaces and genetically superior plants hanging from the ceiling. Video screens showed adverts for holidays to the Jovian moons and the exclusive Mars colony resort.

"Would you get a load of this place," Bashir said.

"First time this high up?" Greta asked, with an edge to her voice as though it were somehow a slight on Bashir. Bella was getting tired of the attitude. They rarely took on new crew, and she wasn't the type of captain to condone hazing, but she knew better than to make a big deal of it. Greta would only rebel and make it harder for the newcomer.

"Yes," Bashir said. "I've only ever been to Atlas twice. I've been on Zeno and Galilei, mostly. Some of us aren't lucky enough to have a high enough status level to get into the SMF—they don't admit us vat-grown orphans."

"You think it's a good thing serving in the military?"

Greta stopped and faced Bashir, forcing everyone on the walkway to swerve around them.

A pair of suited older ladies, clearly government-administration types, tutted and shook their heads as they were forced to walk around the group. Bella gave them an apologetic look and instantly felt disgusted with herself that she was deferring to some privileged government stooges.

"You two, shut the hell up and concentrate," Bella snapped. "Otherwise you'll both need new jobs."

Wilbur placed a hand on her shoulder and gave it a little squeeze. Bella took a deep breath and allowed herself to calm down. "I'm sorry. But seriously, focus. You're all on the same team. Act like it."

Greta glared at Bashir, her gaze burning a figurative hole in the newcomer. But to Bashir's credit, he inclined his head and apologized. It caught Greta off guard and she stammered a halfhearted, "No problem."

Bella pushed Greta and Bashir aside. She moved forward and led her crew down the glass walkway to the row of apartments on the space side of the level eight torus.

The doors they passed were made to look like real wood, but Bella knew better. When she rapped her knuckles against number fifty-four, the home of Charles Gandit, the door clanged like a metal bulkhead. According to Harlan's research, Gandit was a director of the Jovian Group and a member of the Vanguard, whatever that might be.

An eyeball appeared at the viewing hole. It was old, watery, and gray. It blinked a few times, and then the locks to the door unlatched their magnetic hold.

Without waiting, Bella pushed the door open, knocking the older man back into his apartment. Wilbur and Bashir followed inside, while Greta stood guard outside as per the plan.

"Wha-what the hell is this?" Gandit asked, stuttering over his words.

He reached out to balance himself against an occasional table worth more than all of Bella's apartment's furniture. It was an antique piece from Earth. The rest of the apartment shared its opulence.

"Sit down," Bella said. "You're going to help us with our inquiries. Don't worry about offering us coffee. We won't be staying long. Assuming you cooperate."

Gandit ran a hand through his thinning brown hair. He had it combed over a pale white head covered with darker patches of liver spots. He had to be easily a century old and wealthy or privileged enough that he didn't worry about having hair transplants.

His status meant that his physical appearance was of no consequence.

"Who are you?" he demanded, puffing his chest out now that he'd had time to compose himself. "I'll call the SMF. This is breaking and entering."

"You let us in," Wilbur said, his voice calm and even. "The maglock's security file will prove that. And the cameras you have running will show us acting calmly. Now, please, Mr. Gandit, take a seat and let us deal with this like professionals."

Bashir remained at the rear, his large frame standing in the way of the door, preventing any escape. Gandit looked to Bella, then to Wilbur, his forehead creasing with confusion. His right hand shifted toward his left wrist—to his terminal.

"No, no, Mr. Gandit," Bella said. "There's no need for that." She stepped closer and gripped his wrist in what looked like a handshake. He tried to pull away, but Bella was too strong for him. Using his arm as leverage, she forced him backward until the backs of his legs hit the front of an overstuffed leather armchair.

He collapsed back into it, with a waft of air rushing out from the cushions. He tried to stand, but from his position it was easy enough to hold him in place with a hand on his shoulder. Wilbur approached and took up a position on his left.

Both he and Bella pulled a couple more armchairs across the carpeted lounge so that they were sitting just a meter away, imprisoning Gandit in his own wealth and privilege.

"Check the other rooms, would you, Bash?" Bella said over her shoulder.

The new recruit nodded acceptance of the order and went from room to room. He came back into the lounge a few moments later. "All empty."

"I must ask you people again, what the hell is this all about?"

"Charles, isn't it?" Bella asked. "Charles Gandit."

"Why, yes, but—"

"No more questions. All you need to do is answer ours honestly, and we'll soon be gone without harming what hair you have left on your head. Lie to us, however..."

"This is all being recorded. The SMF are on their way right now."

"Then you better get talking. Because when we show them your personal files, I suspect they, along with the Supreme Judiciary, will have some questions of their own."

Gandit fidgeted in his chair before composing himself. "You don't know what you're talking about. I don't know what you think you know, but you've clearly got the wrong man."

"Is that so?" Wilbur said, leaning forward and adjusting

his spectacles. "Are you saying your role as a director of the Jovian Group never presented other... opportunities for you?"

"I haven't been a director for nearly four years now. I'm retired. Is this about the merger? That's nothing to do with me. If you want in on that, I suggest you apply for worker status like everyone else."

He sat back in his chair and folded his arms, assuming the body language of someone who thought he was superior to those around him.

"You misunderstand us," Bella said. "We're not here to get a job. We're here to get information. We know you're still active with the goings-on within the Jovian Group. We have proof that shows you in talks with other members via a number of memos."

"Bullshit," Gandit said, standing.

Bella also stood, placed a hand on his shoulder, and forced him back down. Leaning in closer, she said, "I know you're involved with Vanguard. I know you are part of the insiders working to pull the strings. I also know that Vanguard found something near Europa."

Gandit's shoulders dropped. His entire body slumped, and his face fell into an expression of dread. His gray eyes seemed to lose all their light.

Her words had clearly hit home.

"You don't know what you're messing with. I don't know how you found out about Vanguard, but if you value your lives, I suggest you walk away."

"Quite the opposite," Wilbur said. "We're going nowhere until you tell us what you know about Gianni Mazzari's disappearance and subsequent reappearance. We know Jovian Group members boarded his ship a week after he went missing. We have the video implicating them. Unless you want to face arrest, you better get talking."

The older man leaned forward and dropped his head into his hands. When he looked up at them again, he shook his head. "I can't give you what you want. I... I no longer have anything to do with Vanguard or the Jovian Group. But there is something that might help you... it's in my office. I'll go get it, and then you leave, right?"

"It depends what it is," Bella said.

"It's the full recording of Mazzari's return... please, let me get it and then you can leave."

Bella stepped back and gestured for Gandit to fetch the recording. The old man staggered toward the door on the right of the lounge. Bella followed, but he surprised her with a sprint that she could never have predicted. Gandit darted into the room and slammed the door shut.

Wilbur and Bashir rushed over to it. Bella tried the handle, but it was locked.

A loud smash came from within the room.

"What's he doing in there?" Bashir asked.

"Whatever it is, we've got to stop him. We can't let this lead go," Wilbur said.

Bashir backed up. "Step aside." He launched forward and rammed his meaty shoulder into the side of the door, breaking the flimsy internal lock and sending the door flying open.

Bella stepped inside what she now saw to be the bedroom.

And then, to her horror, she saw Gandit standing on the ledge of the broken window that overlooked the internal side of the station's rotating torus. Wind whipped at Gandit's thin hair and blew his suit around his bony body.

"No," Bella shouted, reaching out to him.

He closed his eyes and leaned back.

The gravitational pull of the centrifugal force generated from the rotating torus pulled Gandit away from the ledge and down, dragging him through the levels. As he fell, he reached to his terminal and slid a finger across the screen.

A second later an explosion erupted from the lounge. A flash of orange fire lit up the bedroom, and black smoke wafted in through the doorway. Bella dashed back, away from the blast beyond the door. An alarm blared out, its high-pitched tones making her wince as smoke continued to fill the room.

A dark shape appeared at the door: Greta.

"What the hell happened?" she shouted, sweat pouring from her face. "We need to get you out of here." Their voices were barely heard over the ringing in Bella's ears. Greta grabbed Bella by the arm and dragged her away from the window.

Bashir and Wilbur soon followed.

The apartment was ablaze now, flames licking up the walls. Antique artwork curled and popped in the heat. Greta urged Wilbur and Bashir to leave, shouting over the roar of the fire.

Greta was yelling at Bella, but she didn't register the words. She was too concerned with finding some evidence of her brother's fate. She couldn't afford to have come this far only to leave empty-handed. Greta tried to pull her out of the room, but Bella snatched her arm away.

"You go," Bella said. "Make sure the others are okay."

"What are you doing?"

"I need to find something—a computer, a terminal, anything to make all this worthwhile."

Greta removed her jacket and beat back the flames. Bella did likewise as she made her way around the room. The temperature was almost unbearable, snatching every breath and making her throat feel as though it were as engulfed in flame as the room.

Sweat clung to her and smoke filled her lungs, causing her to cough. Her eyes watered, making her search more difficult, but eventually, after two long minutes, she found a personal terminal inside the drawer of a desk.

It was hot to the touch, and she cursed as the metallic enclosure burned her hand. Unable to cope with the conditions anymore, she followed Greta out of the apartment and slumped to the floor.

Greta slammed the door shut. "Holy crap. That was crazy. You could have got yourself killed." She helped Bella to her feet. "What the hell happened in there?"

Bella coughed, cleared the smoke from her throat. "The... old guy... jumped. I had to.... get evidence." She held up the terminal drive.

Wilbur wiped the sweat from his face. "He clearly thought this day might come. He even rigged the apartment up. Which rather makes one wonder: what was he prepared to hide?"

"That's what we need to find out. We better go before the fire service arrives and starts asking questions. When they see the video feed, the silicon runners or, more likely, the SMF will come after us."

Dozens of people were starting to leave their apartments now and filling up the corridor. Bella had moved away from Gandit's burning home and ushered her crew to the other end of the level, where they would take an elevator back down to level five.

She sent Harlan a message via her terminal, explaining what had happened, and received a reply telling her to meet him at the RDC on level two and to ask for Gylfie. She looked at her hand, the skin turning dark and puckering around the burn. The pain was a small price to pay if it meant a lead on finding her brother, and given Gandit's response and final act, she knew she was getting closer to the truth.

22

I rena turned into the familiar corridor and approached her parents' apartment on level seven. Her attention had been caught by the commotion coming from up on the higher level. A fire alarm pealed out, and people from all around were jostling to get to the glass walls so they could peer up and see what was happening.

Because of this interruption, and the fact that she had to push her way through a crowd, she hadn't realized there was a separate crowd forming, this time around the open door to her parents' apartment.

The hundred or so people looked mostly to be media types. Their shiny clothes, designed to 'pop' on holographic scenes, were always a giveaway.

An unsettling feeling crawled inside Irena as she inched her way forward.

Toward the front of the crowd, bathed in light from the apartment, half a dozen SMF Marines stood with their rifles pointing toward the ground. None of the soldiers looked at any of the individuals hanging around outside.

"What's going on?" Irena asked a short man with a shiny

yellow shirt, who was standing on the tips of his toes to try to get a recording.

He shushed her. "They're about to speak."

"Who?"

"The Selleses," he said, then glanced up at Irena. "You didn't hear?"

"Hear what?" she snapped impatiently.

Another journalist, a tall woman with striking black hair cut into a tight bob, said, "The merger. It's just been signed. The Selleses are announcing the deal—and apparently something else. I take it you didn't get the press release?"

"Um... no, I was out covering another story," Irena said, not wanting to give away that she was their daughter.

Harlan's information, then, appeared to have been correct regarding the merger between the Jovian Group and the Ceres Mining Company. Yet in the previous weeks when she had spoken with her parents while she was back down on Earth, they hadn't mentioned anything about it.

She reminded herself that it wasn't necessarily surprising. They weren't always forthcoming with details of their jobs, preferring to be vague and waving it off as just boring government business that she wouldn't find interesting.

Come to think of it, that didn't make sense anymore, considering her father had badgered her for years to take a job in one of the government departments instead of the sciences.

"Have they explained anything about the merger yet?" Irena asked.

Bob-cut lady shook her head. "That's what we're waiting on. Been here for nearly an hour while they prepare their presentation." She then glowered at the Marines standing guard in front of the door. "If they would just let us ask some questions."

One of the Marines, a beefy young man, glared at the reporter with a bored look that told Irena that he was as frustrated to be here as the journalists, yet he managed to do it menacingly enough that Bob-cut looked away and stepped back into the crowd.

Irena brought up her terminal and scrolled through her messages to see if she had missed anything from her parents explaining what this was all about, but there was nothing.

She had half a dozen updates from the people at the ERP, along with a message with the date and time of Dr. Osho and the others' funeral.

It was taking place in a week's time, when it was hoped the coroner would complete their autopsies and release the bodies for cremation.

The sound of reporters clamoring for information became a dull background hum as Irena thought about Darnesh, Osho, and Siegfried. She hadn't had time to grieve for them properly, and a well of emotion bloomed within her, choking her throat and tearing her eyes.

She pictured the first time she'd arrived and her three colleagues had welcomed her.

All of them were friendly, and that made her memories of their short time together harder for Irena to bear. Darnesh and Siegfried had become respected colleagues, and Irena's respect for Dr. Osho's work and skills only increased the more she got to know her.

A part of her ached to be back there again before the abbot attacked.

She wished she could turn back time and do things differently, make more of a protest about going out to Station Nord. Perhaps if she'd been more forceful about the dangers, they wouldn't have gone and they would still be alive today.

"Miss?" The small man was tapping her on her shoulder.

"Yes?"

"Are you okay? You look upset."

"I'm just.... Yeah, it's a long story."

"They're coming out. Finally."

The hustle of the journalists dragged Irena forward as those at the back pressed to get closer so that they could get video and audio footage for their respective media channels. Wrist terminals with their blue holographic glows were thrust into the air.

Irena's abs clenched when she saw her parents walk out of the apartment and stand behind the semicircle barrier created by the Marines. Her father was smiling, being charismatic in that frighteningly genuine way of his.

She knew it was a lie. She'd seen it so many times. One moment he was charming, greasing the wheels of diplomacy, and the very next instant, he'd be right back to his scowling, hard-faced self.

He was dressed in a navy-blue suit that was made to measure by the best tailor on Atlas. His hair was slicked with oil, and he had clearly whitened his teeth since she'd last seen him. Her mother, Victoria, wore her usual pastel-colored trouser suit with the big geometric shoulders that were all the rage in her circles these days. It made her look top-heavy, Irena thought, despite her ample curves, which were expertly framed by her suit's tailoring.

The pair of them stood on a raised dais so they could address the crowd without the Marine's blank faces getting in the way of the video feed.

Irena also suspected it was so they could talk down to everyone else. Raise their own stature, as it were. Growing up in their household, Irena had learned that they were often quite literal with things like that.

They took a brute-force approach to diplomacy and human relations.

Which is why they did such a bad job raising me.

If it wasn't for her now-deceased aunt, who had taught Irena the scientific method and critical thinking, she'd be just another puppet, another tool in her parents' political games.

Her mother coughed and looked out at the sea of reporters eagerly waiting for her.

Someone at the back shouted, "Get on with it."

Her father glared toward whoever had said it, and then whispered something in the ear of the Marine closest to him. The soldier nodded and focused on that area of the crowd.

There were no more shouts.

Eventually, her mother spoke.

"Thank you all for coming this morning. I must first apologize about the vague nature of the press report, but it'll become clear soon why I couldn't go into too much detail; there were some last-minute negotiations with Companies House."

The crowd murmured and whispered. Irena caught the word *merger* doing the rounds. Carlos placed his hands behind his back and scanned the crowd as Victoria continued.

"As your representative in the House of Messengers, I'm pleased to announce the successful merger of the Jovian Group and the Ceres Mining Company. These two fine institutions will be more efficient, effective, and driven to provide a superior supply of resources to the Solar Federation's manufacturing facilities, along with increased job opportunities and higher access status for employees."

She took a breath and let that sink in.

Many of the reporters were typing on their terminals in that one-handed way of theirs that Irena had never perfected. All across the Sol-Fed, hundreds of news stories were now going live. To many people, this would be shocking news; in fact, most of the reporters appeared to be surprised.

For Irena, this was just a confirmation of everything she and Harlan had learned in the last few days. And it made her sick to her stomach. She was holding out for the chance that there could have been a mistake. Hoping that her parents weren't up to their necks in conspiracy.

But one short speech shattered that hope.

Her mother continued. "In addition to the merger, the other news I would like to share with you today is in regard to the presidency. Many of you will be aware of the tumbling popularity of President Kallstrom. His approval rating is currently hovering at just two points over the election threshold."

She stopped and let the moment build as the reporters anticipated the obvious follow-up.

"If, and when, the election is triggered, I, Victoria Selles, will stand for election as president of the Solar Federation. If elected, I will put the interests of Atlas Station front and center, as it always should be as humanity's first and greatest non-planetary home."

Her husband grinned and clapped along with half of the reporters.

Despite the way her mother had reacted to Irena the last time they spoke, her public reputation was of a warm, professional, and competent Messenger.

Even without the merger influencing its workers to vote a certain way, she'd have stood a good chance. She was often touted as a potential runner for the election, although there were at least two or three others that were considered more favorable.

This turn of events and the proof that she was involved with the Jovian Group, outside of her role as a Messenger and negotiator with Companies House, would easily tip her into the odds-on favorite.

All around Irena, reporters busily typed up their notes or recorded the requisite thirty-second sound bites for their news outlets.

Carlos was whispering something to her mother, who nodded and turned her attention back to the crowd. "Ladies and gentlemen, we have a few minutes available for questions."

Instantly, a hundred or more hands shot up.

Carlos scanned the front row and pointed to an older man with long gray hair that cascaded over his shoulders. He wore an old-fashioned tweed suit that hadn't been available on Atlas, or any of the other stations, for at least a decade.

"With the merger, will there be any new edicts from Companies House to create a new firm?"

"No, not at this time. The merger won't change anything regarding the production or output of the two companies. What this will do is allow the managing hierarchy to more easily provide opportunities for the workers to move around and explore different roles, gaining new skills and becoming more effective contributors to the Solar Federation's continual growth and success."

The older man quickly gestured to his notes on his terminal. Carlos then pointed to a middle-aged woman with a serious expression. "Miss Kieselman, your question?" Irena recognized her as the anchor for the mid-afternoon Atlas News broadcast.

"Will the merger retain the two companies' respective branding, or will there be a new name?" the anchor asked.

Irena's mother answered this one. "That's a good question. Yes, there will be a new name and brand to better communicate to the Solar Federation citizens what the new company is all about. It will be called Vanguard Industries."

Irena froze in place. Her surroundings seem to fade away and the journalists' chatting became a dull hum. Right there in front of her, from her very own parents, was the confirmation, the embodiment of the conspiracy come true. Any doubt she may have had was now destroyed.

Her parents became grotesque to her as they smiled for the cameras and gave the typical politician's answers to questions asked of them. All the time, Irena saw right through them. She saw that all along they had been in on it, from the start. The missing abbot, the rogue abbot, the virus, Gianni's disappearance: all the leads came back to Vanguard, and her parents had just delivered it to the public.

She had to get out of there and tell Harlan that they were right.

Waiting for her parents to engage with another question, Irena slipped away, joined the general flow of pedestrians outside the corridor, and then sprinted to the elevator.

A young girl inside looked up at Irena with a smile. "What level?"

"Two," Irena said, turning the girl's smile to a frown.

The girl gestured over the control panel and stepped away from Irena as the elevator car descended. Irena wiped a tear from her eye and bit her lip, trying to keep her emotions in check. First, she had lost Darnesh, Osho, and Siegfried on Earth. Now it felt like she had lost her parents. Although, in truth, she realized she had never had them in the first place.

There was just one thing to do now: stop them and stop Vanguard.

23

Harlan received a message from Gylfie as soon as he arrived on level two. Apparently the RDC control group had new orders for him now that Victoria Selles had announced the Jovian-Ceres merger. Harlan would have to wait a quarter of an hour.

While he waited, Harlan sat on a stool at the best noodle bar on level two. He ordered a bowl of seasoned ramen and reread Irena's and Bella's messages to him. It seemed both of them had seen the conspiracy taking shape from different angles.

It did, however, confirm that they were on the right track.

Vanguard, as a group, was mobilizing. He had no doubt that Luca was in their employ and working to crack, and ultimately control, the QCA.

While he let his subconscious mull over the consequences, Harlan took in his surroundings.

The place appeared deserted for this time of day—early morning. Just two other men were sitting at the bar, and the market area wasn't even half full with stalls and customers.

Usually, it'd be thriving down here with traders and salvagers cutting deals, people drinking to get their early buzz on, and the occasional tourist who thought slumming it with the downtrodden was something to tick off their bucket list.

The bartender, a young girl with straw-like hair pulled back into a greasy ponytail, placed the bowl of noodles in front of him and held out her terminal to accept payment. "Three bitcreds."

Despite the dirt on her face and the fact that she smelled as if she hadn't washed for a week, she had a face Harlan found attractive. Full lips and soft brown eyes.

She must have been in her early twenties, which made her stand out. People that young didn't often come down to make a life on level two. That trajectory was usually the domain of the middle-aged, once they realized having status levels and access privileges was more of a curse than it appeared.

Sure, one could get by with the food and energy supplied, even with the lowest of access privileges, but you were stuck there, with very little upward mobility.

"Um, that'll be three bitcreds," the girl reminded him.

"Right, sorry." Harlan swiped the bitcreds over to her and mumbled his thanks.

The girl appraised him with a beady eye. "I see you down here a lot." It was a peculiar birdlike behavior Harlan recognized from his documentaries.

"I have business here." He diverted his gaze to the bowl of noodles so as not to stare at her further. But she didn't move away; no other customers demanded service.

She continued to look at him. "You know Gylfie, right?"

Harlan swallowed the small bite of noodles and placed the spork back into the bowl. He looked up at her, trying to figure out what she might want. A spy, perhaps? Given what they'd discovered about Vanguard and Bella's experience up on level eight, it wouldn't be a stretch to assume this group had people down here.

Harlan pulled his silicon runner ID from his leather jacket and showed it to her. "Like I said, I'm just here on business."

The girl leaned closer and inspected his credentials. Then, with a smile, she leaned back and opened a holographic screen on her wrist terminal. Unlike most people, she had hers on her right wrist instead of her left.

To most people that wouldn't mean much, but to Harlan it meant she was left-handed. Or ambidextrous, and that meant upgrades. And upgrades meant black-net connections.

"Here," she said, swiping a file to Harlan. "Ivet asked me to send this to you when you came around. She couldn't trust sending it across the networks. Prefers peer-to-peer. She got some footage of your ex."

Before he could ask her anything else, the girl took a dishrag, folded it over her shoulder and approached a new customer on the far side of the noodle bar.

Turning his back to the bar, Harlan slid off the stool and slipped through a narrow, dark passage into an engineering access tunnel. He closed the door behind him and used his sensors to detect any signs of life or network. All came back negative.

— *Come on then, Harlan, let's see what that PI found on the lovely Leanne*, Milo said.

Ignoring his peripheral's taunt, Harlan double-checked that he was alone in the passage and ran the video on his terminal.

It was from a feed from within the silicon runners' office.

A man and a woman dressed in junior uniforms—the same as the guards wore—passed through the biometrics and approached Diego and his colleagues.

Within seconds, and before the guards had even known what hit them, the faux agents had decapitated the legitimate guards with what looked like Japanese-inspired katanas, only these left no blood behind. Using Diego's credentials and what looked like an override device—a hard wire plugged into one of the terminal sockets—the attackers opened the cell door, grabbed Leanne, and dragged her free.

She tried to put up a fight, but one of the group showed her something from a terminal. Leanne instantly stopped resisting, slumped her shoulders, and willingly followed them out. The video feed turned into static after that.

— *Well, that was interesting*, Milo said.

"Quite," Harlan said with a sigh. It didn't really tell him anything he didn't already suspect, but knowing that there was some new illicit technology out there was concerning. Not only did they have a new kind of weapon, but their hacking tools were impressive.

— *There is one issue with this, though*, Milo said. *It raises the question of how Ivet got this video segment while Hugo and the other agents found nothing. Someone purposely covered that up from within.*

"At this stage I don't find that surprising. With Luca miraculously alive again, it seems more than likely that Hugo is the mole here, although I need more evidence before I go accusing him—he's got the ear of Victoria Selles, and I need to consider Irena in all this."

— *There's an encrypted text message attached to the video.*

Harlan opened the file contents and found the text message among the video data. Using a key provided to him by Ivet from a previous mission, he opened the file. It was a report from her that said:

I hope you find the video helpful. It seems whoever these people are, they've got something on your ex-wife. I tried to find out what was on the woman's terminal, but the resolution isn't good enough. I'll try to follow that up.

As for Leanne's whereabouts, she was taken to the docks. None of that is on video. Whoever did this hacked into Atlas' entire security setup. Turned themselves into ghosts. From leaving the runners' office, they must have disguised themselves. A contact of mine at the port said he saw them dressed as workers for the Ceres Mining Company. They boarded a company shuttle and left the station. Destination is unknown. I hacked into the port database, and there's no record of that shuttle existing. Again, their tendrils run deep.

Whoever they are, Harlan, they're elite. I'm not sure it's wise for you to keep searching for Leanne. Hell, you've been apart a decade, just let her go. This doesn't have to be your problem.

Anyway, that's all I got for now.

I'll let you know if I find anything else. Oh, and one more thing: the video footage of the jailbreak—I got that from your boss' personal drive. It's gone now, though, along with everything else, so he must know he's been hacked. I don't know what he's hiding, but it's got to be something big for him to go nuclear on his own data.

Look out for yourself.

— IT'S GOT *to be this Vanguard group*, Milo said. *Bella's target on level eight torched his place and killed himself, Hugo's taken the nuclear option on his personal data, and Luca Doe is trying to implement a virus into the QCA. On top of that, we've got Victoria Selles running for president and confirming the merger,* with Vanguard as the re-branding. *It's all connected. It's all coming from the one place. And Leanne is involved, too.*

"She was coerced. She didn't go willingly until they showed her something. Whatever it is, they've got something on her. This explains everything. It explains why she didn't kill me when she had the chance on Luna. She was there all that time I was inspecting the abbot. What if she led me there, not to kill me, but to discover the hack on the QCA? She helped later on by letting me know Luca is back. What if Vanguard have had something on her all the time she's been away? What if they're the reason she left?"

— *I admit the data suggests it. But can you really trust the data?*

"I don't know. But it's not just the data suggesting she's innocent in all this. It's my gut."

— *Your gut or your heart?*

"Maybe they're the same."

He shut down the terminal, left the tunnel, and headed for the RDC. He had a few leads to follow up and knew he didn't have much time. It was clear things were moving into Vanguard's endgame, and he needed to know where Fizon, Luca, and Leanne were. And how to stop the virus before Vanguard gained control of not just the majority of the human population, but the entire population of abbots.

Before he reached the RDC, he saw Irena weave her way through the handful of people milling around the level. She jerked away from one particular man who tried to grab her arm.

Despite the alarm on Irena's face, Harlan smiled; it was the usual sales tactic for the traders down here: make personal contact. It was never personal or an attack, just how they got people's attention.

"Harlan," Irena said, waving at him. She hurried her

approach and was breathless by the time she reached him. "You saw the news?"

"Yeah, I caught a few clips of it on the news streams. Looks like your parents are going up in the world, eh?"

"And down in my estimation."

"Are you okay?"

Irena bit her lip and stared beyond Harlan. She closed her eyes for a second and then looked directly at him. "No... it's just... I don't know how to deal with all this. First the attack on Earth, now this. Bella's brother, your ex. How far does Vanguard go? Have we all just been drifting into this, while they were there all the time, planning this behind our backs?"

"It's looking that way," Harlan said. He kicked himself for not coming up with something more soothing, or at least hopeful. She didn't need his stoic devotion to facts right now; she needed optimism.

He placed a hand on her arm. "Listen to me. We make a good team. We've got Bella and her crew and a ragtag network of spies and criminals at our disposal. If Vanguard does try to take over the Sol-Fed, they're going to have to get through us first."

"How do we stop them?" Irena asked.

"We find out where Luca is and stop the hack. We then find the other members of the cabal and—"

"Even my parents?"

"Let's hope it won't come to that."

A message bleeped on Harlan's terminal. "It's Bella. They're on their way. Let's get inside and brief Gylfie on what we need so we're ready to go when they get here. The information on the chip and this drive that Bella has recovered will hopefully point us in the right direction."

"I don't know how you do it," Irena said as she followed

him to the RDC. "How you stay so calm, in control, when all around us society is teetering on the brink."

He didn't want to tell her that he was only managing to stay sane due to illicit brain upgrades and the peripheral. Without those, he was as much of a mess as any other non-modified human. Probably more so.

"It helps to focus on one problem at a time," he said, holding the door open for her. "And it's made easier by having good friends."

24

Twenty minutes later, Bella and Wilbur joined Harlan and Irena at the back of Gylfie's RDC. They had left Greta and Bashir to patrol the level outside to make sure they weren't taken by surprised. Gylfie welcomed them in and closed the door. The room appeared different from the last time Harlan was here. The conveyor belts sat motionless; the drones were silent and still, not picking and sorting parts. Dust motes hovered in the still, dank air.

With no air-conditioning running and the five of them in the small room, the temperature grew sticky and uncomfortable. Gylfie looked tired; bags hung low under his rheumy eyes. He gestured for Bella and Wilbur to take a seat at the table. He joined them, slugged back a shot of vodka, which he followed with a racking cough.

He offered a shot to everyone else. They all declined.

"So," Gylfie said between coughs, "here we all are. It might just be my cynical age, but it feels like this is a last-ditch summit. The outcasts against the government machine."

Irena picked at her nails and avoided Gylfie's accusatory gaze at the mention of the government.

"Irena is not responsible for her parents' actions," Harlan said. "Don't look at her like that, Gylfie. She's one of us. And in fact, if it wasn't for her, we wouldn't be here now."

"He's right," Bella said. "Without access to Victoria Selles' files, we wouldn't have discovered the shitty side to this Vanguard business."

"I'm sorry," Gylfie said between coughs. "It just feels like things are on a knife-edge. I've spent a long time on the wrong side of the community. Who knows what will happen to people like me now. The RDCs around the station are shutting down while the merger reassigns its resource provisions. I don't know about you guys, but we were taught in history lessons that mergers brought devastation to the societies they eventually overwhelmed."

"Sure, we know that," Wilbur said, fidgeting with the cuffs of his sweater. "That's why we need to stop them before we repeat the mistakes that led to humanity ruining Earth. We can't just sit around here lamenting what's coming down the tunnel. We need to stop it."

Harlan placed the chip drive on the table from the abbot that had attacked him.

Bella followed his cue and added the personal drive she'd retrieved from Gandit's apartment.

"This is all we have to go on now," Irena said, looking directly at Gylfie. "Help us access the data so we can find the epicenter of Vanguard's plans."

"It feels like I'd be signing a death warrant."

"And the alternative is what?" Harlan asked. "You said yourself that the RDCs are changing. That's you out of a job. You're not getting any younger, despite the senilitic drugs and black-net upgrades you're using. You can't run and hide forever."

Gylfie scratched his chin. "I don't have the tools to crack an abbot chip. The personal drive I could do, but the abbot —that requires computational power I just don't have access to."

Wilbur adjusted his spectacles as he smiled. "You do now." He leaned to the side, pulled the q-bit core from his backpack, and placed the heavy black box on the table.

Gylfie's eyes widened, and a smile dared to reach the corner of his lips. "You've gotta be kidding me."

"It's from Station Nord," Irena said. "We were supposed to install them to create a new bridge with the QCA for weather analysis, but... you know what happened."

"Well?" Harlan said. "Are you going to remember that you used to be a shit-hot silicon runner and do something to save the solar system, or are you going to be a scared old man waiting to die to the soundtrack of Bruce Springsteen?"

"Who?" Bella asked, raising an eyebrow.

Harlan waved her question away. Gylfie closed his eyes and took a deep breath. When he opened them again, they were sharper. His body became more alert. "If I do this, you owe me a favor—each one of you. A big mother of a combined grade A favor."

"Anything particular you have in mind?" Bella asked.

"Yeah. When you take down Vanguard, all hell's going to break loose. I want off the station and taken to Bujoldia on Mars. And access privileges there to see out the last half of my life in comfort."

Harlan shook his head and whistled. "You don't want much, then. That's quite the task you're asking; I'm not sure that's even possible."

Gylfie locked eyes with him. "Then you better learn how

to do the impossible. I'm done here, Harlan. I need out, and if you want to play the hero of the day, you need to promise it to me. You all do; otherwise, you're on your own."

"Fine, I'm in. I'll figure it out."

"I'm in, too," Irena said.

"And us three," Bella added. "Now that's out of the way, can we get down to business? There's a ticking clock we're working against here. We can't stop the merger, but we can stop the virus from penetrating the QCA and turning ten million robots into mechanical death machines."

Gylfie nodded his head. "Okay, okay, but as soon as you've got your information, you'll need to get the hell out of here. SMF soldiers were patrolling earlier. I doubt we have complete privacy down here anymore."

"Don't worry, old man," Bella said. "We'll be gone in a flash as soon as you crack those drives."

"There's three more things I need before I start: noodles, vodka, and privacy."

Bella stood up from the table. "We're on it." Wilbur joined her, and they left to get Gylfie's supplies.

The pair returned after five minutes with the vodka and noodles.

"Thank you," Gylfie said. "Okay, now the privacy. Everyone but Harlan must leave. This might take a while."

Irena shared an expression of alarm with Harlan. "It's fine," he said. "We go way back. We work well together. You'll be safe with Bella's crew. I'll let you know as soon as we're finished here."

"If you're sure."

"I am, trust me. We're going to fix this."

Irena placed a hand on Harlan's shoulder before joining the others.

"Okay, Harlan, let's relive our glory days and crack this

case wide open. Pour the shots while I get the q-bit hooked up to my system."

"Sure thing, boss."

Gylfie stopped in his tracks. "Boss, eh? It's been a while since I've been called that. Shame that prick Hugo Raul has my old title now, the jumped-up little turd."

Cables trailed from the q-bit core to Gylfie's rack-mounted hardware. The old ex-silicon runner hunched over his system, patching cables and adjusting wireless connections. He reminded Harlan of a mad scientist depicted in the latest films. A quaint throwback to the crazy genius archetype of the old days.

"We're ready to go," Gylfie said, returning to the table. He took a shot of vodka and then placed the abbot's CPU and the drive recovered from the Vanguard member into a docking enclosure. He then tapped a command on his terminal and a pair of projected keyboards appeared in front of Harlan and Gylfie on the table.

"We'll have to work as a team on this."

"That's fine by me. As long as your old brain can keep up."

"At least I'm not relying on a peripheral. You know you don't need that crap to do what you do, right? It's a crutch."

Harlan shrugged. "It helps me focus. Milo lets me multi-task."

"Bullshit. That's what you think it does. But it doesn't. It's just a placebo for your insecurity."

— *He's getting old and confused.*

Maybe Gylfie had a point, but whatever the truth, and despite its snarky nature, Harlan had grown accustomed to Milo and couldn't imagine working without it. It was like a faster transport between the conscious and the subconscious. Or at least that was what the sales literature had told him. And what he'd been telling himself.

"Look, Harlan, I'm sorry if I upset you. My old brain can cut to the quick a little too efficiently at times. You can stick whatever you want in your brain. Let's just get on with the job before the shit really hits the fan."

"Whatever you say, boss."

Gylfie reached behind him and grabbed the small round base of a holographic screen, which he placed in the middle of the table. It flickered to life and showed a terminal window displaying the root system of the chip and drive.

Harlan took a deep breath and dived into the abbot's ID chip.

Gylfie took his third shot of vodka and started the process of cracking the security on the personal drive. With the q-bit whirring away like some creature in the corner of the room and Milo chugging through his subconscious, Harlan knew they would complete their task, but whether they would find anything useful remained to be seen.

25

After strolling through the market for a quarter of an hour, Irena joined Bashir, Bella, and the others at the noodle bar. She ordered a coffee from the bar woman, who gave Irena an odd look. Irena couldn't decide if it was curiosity or hostility.

Given that her mother had just declared the merger and her running for the presidency, she expected those that recognized her as Victoria Selles' daughter would act differently now. She thought about disguising herself, cutting off her hair or dying it, perhaps.

Greta sat down with a violent thud on the stool next to her. She leaned in close. "Don't look so scared. Harlan is as skilled a runner as I've ever seen. He'll figure this out."

"It's not him I'm worried about." Irena blew the steam off her coffee and took a sip. "It's what my parents might do if they get into power. I don't even know them anymore."

"It's true what they say about family," Bella said. She stepped up to the bar after finishing her conversation with Bashir and Wilbur and stood at Irena's side, placing a hand on the younger woman's shoulder. "It's a well-worn cliché to say you can't choose them, but you can choose your friends. There's a reason why clichés exist. They're born from truth."

Greta laughed. "I'm not sure she chose us. And I'm not sure you chose us, either, Captain. As far as I remember, I was in desperate need of work, and you were in desperate need of a heavy to get some gangsters off your back."

At first, Irena thought this to be a cold statement, but a moment later she noticed Bella's smirk, indicating this was an old, familiar joke.

From his position on the opposite side of the bar, Wilbur fiddled with a button on his jacket and snorted. "I hate to be the contrarian of the party, but I really do dislike all you people quite considerably. Although, you," he added, pointing to Irena, "are not so bad. Even if you are the spawn of two crazed, narcissistic megalomaniacs."

"I guess those particular traits skipped my generation," Irena said, finding herself smiling and warming to this misfit group of rogues.

"Best not breed, then," Bashir added, who was sitting to Irena's right. His face was glossy with steam from a hot bowl of noodles. "You don't want to be responsible for bringing those genes back." He smiled generously with a charm exuding from his soulful eyes. She couldn't quite place the origin of the genes the baby-designers had chosen for him, but he had a richness and fullness of features she liked very much, even considering his bruised eyes and a broken nose given to him by Greta.

Since humanity had mostly fled Earth, and the idea of nations or races had eroded, mixed breeding had softened the contrasts between cultural types, creating a more homogenous look. Watching old media from a few hundred years ago brought that difference to light, so now it was considered quaint to think of people belonging to races or ethnic tribes. People were so much more contrasted back then, she thought. Pale whites and dark blacks and many distinctive shades in between. Now, however, the majority were much closer to each other.

She had thought that perhaps this would have brought people together, especially after the devastation of the Last War, but it seemed to her that skin color, cultural background, castes, or other social divisions weren't the problem: humanity would find a way to divide itself over anything, no matter the difference. She supposed it'd take many more generations yet to extinguish the fully deep-rooted sense of tribal individuality and grasp the concept that humans—and all life—were the expressions of the very same thing: consciousness.

As far as the human race had come, even to the point of accepting its own creation of the abbots as a species unto themselves, it was clear to Irena they still had a long way to go in understanding not only their role within the universe, but the nature of consciousness. For all the technology they had developed, that particular frontier still remained as much of a mystery now as it did in ancient times.

Bashir's smile faded, replaced by an expression of concern. "I'm sorry, did I say something out of turn?"

"No, it's just me. I sometimes drift off into my own thoughts. As for breeding, I currently have no plans for children. The thought always terrified me. The amount of responsibility required..." She trailed off and considered her own upbringing. Her parents had bypassed their responsibility completely. They'd expected teachers, counsellors, and professors to raise her, and if she did say so herself, she hadn't turned out badly.

And probably, she thought, better than if her parents had brought her up.

"I understand," Bashir said, returning his focus to his food. Irena wanted to continue with the conversation, wondering if he had something to say on the topic given he was an orphan with no biological parents. How did he view the role of family, the concept of parents, when his genetic code was selected from raw materials and grown in artificial wombs? She wanted to probe further, but knew for some it was a difficult topic.

Despite that, she found herself warming to him. He had a gentle disposition that seemed at odds with his career choices until now. She hoped she'd get more time to talk with him and find out what made him tick. While he ate, she turned her attention to the rest of Bella's crew. "What about you guys? What're your family situations? Any kids?"

The group remained silent. After an awkward pause, Bella spoke. "For a brief time, I wanted a child. I wanted the domestic life. Husband, baby, career... but that ended, and now I'm here. It's quite a long story."

The Mazzari Enterprises captain regarded Irena with a look of brief yearning. It seemed that the older woman had a history she wanted to share, but was too nervous to go into it.

"I'm a good listener," Irena said. "And it seems we have a little time. If you want to, that is?"

Bella sat closer to Irena. "Sure. Why not? A little team bonding never hurt anyone."

The rest of the crew huddled together at the other end of the bar to give the two women their own space. Irena appreciated it. She had put them on the spot and, given that she'd only known them for a few days, was probably prying too far. But with the lull in their quest while Harlan and Gylfie did their thing, she couldn't hide her curiosity about the people who had saved her from certain death on Earth.

They had remained tight-lipped during their journey back to Atlas station when they had rescued her, presumably out of fear that she was an SMF agent, or that she'd simply report them for illegal salvaging.

She was about to apologize again to Bella and tell her that she didn't have to talk, but the older woman must have sensed her hesitation. "It's okay. I don't mind you asking, really. It's nice to talk about something other than criminal activity and conspiracies for a few moments. I've not taken the opportunity to ask how you're doing. That whole Earth situation must have been a little emotional."

They both smiled at the understatement.

"You could say that," Irena said. "Harlan has been great, though. And to be honest with you, this whole situation with my parents is somewhat of a relief. It's kept me active. Otherwise, I'd probably have given in to the pressure to return to Earth and continue the work down there. Or sat in my apartment running it all over in my head, blaming myself and wondering why I didn't do more to save my colleagues."

Just the thought of it brought the images back, of Darnesh, Siegfried, Dr. Osho... Irena looked away, closed her eyes, and swallowed the welling up of emotion. She'd learned to do that from years of verbal abuse from her father—and, to some extent, her mother.

Bella gripped Irena's shoulder and lowered her voice. "That entire blame issue will come at some point. I've seen it with Greta. It's natural and part of the whole messed-up human experience. And when it does, I want you to know that I'm a good listener, too. When my career in the arts failed, I spent a few years training in psychological analysis to help people who spent so much time out on the far reaches. Deep space living can really screw people up."

Irena leaned in a little closer. "Is that what happened to Greta?"

Bella shook her head. "I'll let her tell you her experiences. It's not really my place. But I did help her when she joined me. Those early days of Mazzari Enterprises were tough. Wilbur was a frenzied animal... Don't let his nervous persona fool you: he's got some real spark in him when he needs it."

"I'll bear that in mind," Irena said as she cast a quick glimpse at the small man. He leant over his bowl of food, eating quickly in short staccato movements, as though he believed someone could steal away his meal at any time. She pictured him retaliating, fast and efficiently, and then returning to his twitchy, shy ways.

"So," Bella said, regaining Irena's attention, "my backstory, for what it's worth... not many on this station, or any of the stations for that matter, know me as anything other than the hard-faced bitch captain of Mazzari Enterprises. Before I got into all the salvaging and contraband running, I was on the path for a career in the arts, singing classic opera."

Irena stared at her with surprise. "I would never have guessed you were going to say that. You're so..."

Bella's dark, thin eyebrows arched with a full expectant expression. "What? Criminal? Violent? Rough-and-ready?" She then eased her hardness as a sly smile curled the edges of her fulsome lips. It appeared to Irena that beneath the homogeny, Bella, like her name suggested, still carried some of her family's Italian heritage.

"I was going to say practical, strong, great with ships... and frankly a great leader of people. Those aren't attributes I'd apply to an opera singer."

Bella grinned and waved away Irena's awkwardness. "It's

a family thing. Apparently, a few generations down the Mazzari line, there were a number of fairly successful opera singers. Our family has always had a musical and theatrical side to it. Both my parents are concert pianists, although these days they mostly stay in the shadows, composing for the technically superior but artistically barren abbot artists."

The question of Bella's brother rose in Irena's mind, but she was reluctant to bring him up. She bought some time to think it over by taking another couple mouthfuls of noodles. They were turning soggy now, and the artificial soy-flavor compound had taken on a sharp metallic taste.

"You want to ask something else," Bella said, framing it as a statement.

Irena nodded, swallowed her food, and asked, "What about Gianni? Did he always want to go into the sciences, or did he follow the family tradition of music?"

"It's okay to bring him up." Bella paused and held Irena's gaze as if to convince Irena of her strength, but she really didn't need to. Irena knew she was as strong as anyone she'd ever met. "The truth is he was always so good at everything he put his mind to. He was a great pianist, better than my mother even. But also an equally proficient scientist. It's why I know he's alive despite how the video feed from his shuttle looked. If anyone will find a way to survive anything that comes at him, Gianni will."

"Were you close growing up?"

"Very. We were like twins. Best friends."

"I grew up an only child." Irena hated that the words made her sound like she was playing a trump card for sympathy. She didn't intend for it to sound that way.

There were some benefits to growing up alone: she had lots of time to think, to indulge her interests. Although, at times, she had wondered what it would have been like to have an older brother or sister. For some reason, she had always assumed in her imagined scenario that she would be the younger sibling.

"I'm sorry," Bella said. "That must have been difficult with your parents. I felt a certain degree of pressure from my mother and father to follow them. And to be as talented as them and Gianni, but because he was obviously gifted, their focus was split, so I never felt it too badly. It must have been hard with both of your parents having only you to channel their hopes and dreams into."

Irena laughed. "The only thing they cared about were themselves. I got off lightly in that regard. Maybe not others, but I'm out of it now. All I want to do is stop them. They're no parents to me. They never really were, now I think on it."

Bella gave Irena a side hug and squeezed her. "Well, you're always welcome to join our little band of weirdos and outsiders. We might not be a family by blood, but family by choice is stronger, better—and a hell of a lot more fun... if not a little dangerous."

Before Irena could reply, a young man—no older than a teenager, dressed in dirty jeans and an engineer's vest—ran through the marketplace, stopping by the traders and the few citizens milling around. He talked frantically, gesticulating back toward the elevators.

Eventually, he came to the noodle bar.

"Something bad's going down," he said. "The SMF are on their way. I saw 'em get in the elevator on level four. They swept level three and are now heading down here. They'll be here in a few minutes... you better get out of here."

"What do they want?" Bella demanded.

"Hell if I know, but they ain't been down here for years, so it's something real bad, right?"

"Right. Thanks, kid."

Irena placed the coffee on the bar top and slipped off her stool. "I'll let Harlan know." She ran across to the RDC and knocked four times in the pattern Gylfie had shown her.

Bella and the others joined her when Harlan opened the door.

"What is it?" he asked.

"Military on their way, looking for something," Wilbur said.

"Or someone," Greta added.

"You guys better come in." Harlan opened the door while looking out to the rapidly emptying level. "We've found something."

26

W ith everyone crammed into the small room at the back of the RDC, Harlan wasted no time in explaining what he and Gylfie had found on the chip and drive, respectively. Gylfie went up to the second level and into his personal quarters, where he could monitor the entry and exit points of level two, leaving Harlan to bring everyone up to speed. They all stared at him with expectation. None more so than Bella, who wanted to know about her brother.

"Gianni is still alive," Harlan confirmed, "according to Gandit's data."

Bella let out a burst of air and a sob at the news. "So where is he?"

"I'll come to that in a moment. The thing you'll want to know is that according to the report on the drive, Gianni is in some kind of catatonic state after his experience."

"His experience? What exactly happened to him?"

"That wasn't covered, but this is where it gets interesting and where our cases overlap. The files mentioned Gianni is part of a wider program Vanguard calls Project Inception.

There were reports of cracking the abbots' code as part of the program's long-term goals, too."

Bashir clenched his fist. "That sounds ominous as hell."

"What exactly is Project Inception?" Irena asked.

"That's the trillion-dollar question," Harlan said. "We don't know. But what I do know is that whatever it is, the silicon runners' office has covered it up. Or more accurately that asshole Hugo Raul has covered it up. I searched the database, and it came back as classified access only. Hugo has blocked it. To hack into that would take weeks, if at all."

Wilbur adjusted his glasses and leaned toward Harlan. "What about a location? Do we know where they're holding Gianni?"

"We have an idea." Harlan brought up the data on the holoscreen so they could all see. He pointed to a location on Earth in what was once known as Bavaria. "There's a number of old derelict buildings down there among a crumbling castle. They're in there somewhere. It's a twenty-six-hour journey if we leave shortly and pull two g of thrust."

"Can you forward the coordinates to me? I'll get the *Goat* ready. I suggest we leave immediately."

"There're a couple of things with that. First, I need to pay Hugo a visit, and second, we successfully hacked the abbot's CPU that Irena and I recovered. Using that as a proxy, we managed to gain access to the outer level of the QCA. Luca's malicious code is definitely being routed through Fizon. We confirmed the data signature. The relay points to him being somewhere in that castle. For all intents and purposes, it's his base of operations."

"How long do we have?" Bella asked.

"At the current rate of attack, Luca will breach QCA security in—" he looked at his terminal "—about seventeen hundred and fifty standard minutes."

Bella thought about it for a moment, doing the calculation. "That's just over twenty-nine standard hours."

"Yeah, so you can see that it's going to be a literal race against time. If the code breaks through, Vanguard will have complete control over every abbot in the solar system."

"Then we better leave now before the SMF take control of this level," Greta said. "Although I won't be against fighting our way to the dock if we have to." She and Bashir shared a look that told Harlan they perhaps would prefer that.

"Let's try not to kill anyone," he said. "We're going to need to leave in a hurry once I've dealt with Hugo. I'd rather we didn't have half the military chasing after us. Besides, we don't know whether they're controlled by Vanguard. Trust no one, but don't assume everyone after us wants us dead either. Make for the ship. Bella, I'll meet up with you at the dock as soon as I've dealt with Hugo."

"I'm coming with you," Irena said.

"Okay, but if things go bad at Hugo's…"

"We'll deal with it." Her face was firm. That was at least one thing she had inherited from her parents: a strong will.

Bashir stepped forward. "What about Gylfie? Is he coming with us?"

Harlan shook his head. "I tried to convince him, but he's staying here until the worst of it blows over. We'll sort his transfer to Bujoldia once we've shut Luca down. He'll be our eyes and ears on Atlas in the meantime."

"Then we have our plan," Bella said. "Okay, crew, let's head out. We'll go through the access tunnels to avoid the military goons. Harlan, you take care, and be quick. By my counting, we've got less than a three-standard-hour window to work with. And that includes finding Luca and Gianni when we arrive at the castle. That's cutting it real fine."

"I know. Let's waste no more time."

With that, Bella and her crew left for their shuttle.

Harlan said goodbye to Gylfie over his communications channel and escorted Irena out. They too would have to use the maintenance tunnels to get up to level three before hitching an elevator ride to level seven where Hugo had his apartment. Harlan had already confirmed his presence there with the use of one of Gylfie's spy drones.

He checked his weapon, making sure it was loaded.

It was the moment for Harlan to confront Hugo for the last time.

27

H arlan and Irena made it out of the access tunnel on level three and rode the elevator up to level seven. He looked over his ally.

Irena's hair was mussed. Grease and dirt flecked her cheeks and neck, and her clothes were covered in dust and grime. From the reflection of the mirrored wall inside the elevator car, it was clear Harlan didn't look much better, although his old biker's jacket and overalls disguised most of the dirt.

Irena blushed under his scrutiny. "What is it?"

"Sorry, didn't mean to stare. You've got some dirt on your face."

"No one can accuse me of not getting involved." She gave him a small smile before looking back at the control panel of the elevator. The numbers glowed as they continued up until they finally stopped at seven.

"We're here," she said.

"Yep. Better get this over with."

— *Another abbot attack has just gone down on level four,*

Milo said, reading out the news alerts Harlan had set up earlier. *Damn thing's taken out a power converter. The military have shut off the entire level.*

Irena's terminal chirped. She brought up the holographic scene and gasped.

"What now?" Harlan asked.

"Have a look on channel nine."

He opened his terminal and tuned in. A news anchor was looking into the camera with a serious expression. Above him, inset on the feed, was a slow-motion clip of an abbot gunning down a group of pedestrians before blowing itself up near the bulkhead to the power converters—the machines that took the solar charge and converted it into more usable voltage.

"Looks like they're stepping up their endgame," Harlan said. "Let's go deal with Hugo before we run out of time."

Irena closed her eyes for a moment and took a deep breath. "This is awful."

"It's not too late to go back to your parents' until all this blows over." He placed a hand on her arm and gently squeezed.

They locked eyes. Determination stared back at him.

"No, I'm with you all the way. Though I can't promise I'll be all super professional and irreverent like Bella's crew, or stoic, like you."

"You don't have to be any of that. Just be you. We're going to need you if we're to beat this conspiracy, and who knows what else we'll need to clean up afterward. Ready?"

"Ready."

He pressed the button to open the door and stepped into the opulence of level seven.

A blast of fresh, cool air wafted over him. He breathed in

deeply, enjoying the oxygen-rich air from the new, highly maintained recyclers that he didn't get access to on the lower levels. The unobstructed light panels bathed the level in a glorious sun-like warmth.

"Damn, that's good," he said, standing still and just breathing it all in, enjoying the tingle of heat on his face. "I always forget what it's like up here with the privileged folk."

Irena mumbled something, but cut herself off. Harlan saw that her cheeks were pinker than normal and realized that as the daughter of Carlos and Victoria Selles, she had spent most of her life up here in the upper levels.

Annoyed that he'd embarrassed her, Harlan adjusted his jacket and suggested they carry on. They left the elevators behind and crossed over a narrow gantry to the main part of the level. A wide atrium made of steel and white faux marble stretched out across the center of the station. Glass barriers along the sides gave the residents an unparalleled view of the inner workings of the spinning structure.

A few hundred people were hanging around the atrium. The three corridors led off from its east, west, and south sides, funneling citizens into the central area. A wide range of the human and abbot population had gathered around the large media screens.

"Where are we headed?" Irena asked.

"The east corridor—that'll take us to Hugo's place."

Benches and seats were filling up, and the crowd was growing every minute as the news anchor's voice boomed over the PA system, informing them of the current threat and the attack on level four.

Irena drew close to Harlan and spoke quietly into his ear. "The military service is coming." She remained tight by his left side and was doing her analysis thing of the surrounding people.

Harlan couldn't see the military personnel, but Irena had apparently already worked out a path. "Follow me. There's a route through the crowd."

Although he wasn't entirely sure the military service would apprehend him, given the way things had gone, he didn't want to take any chances. With his hand casually inside his jacket, resting lightly on the butt of his pistol, he followed Irena as they snaked through the group of pedestrians.

It reminded Harlan of his childhood. A game he used to play with the other orphans on level three. One of the carers there would get them lined up, one behind the other, their hands on the hips of the person in front. She would then call out directions, and they would have to turn left, right, or carry straight forward, the snake of children howling with laughter.

The person always behind him during the snake game was Luca. His old friend had decided, even then, as a four-year-old, to keep his orphan-applied surname. Harlan wondered how much that had affected him growing up. Was something as simple as an anonymous surname so influential that it embedded within the individual the seed of the idea of a life in the shadows?

He had Milo make a note to remind him to ask Luca when he found him. Right before putting a bullet in his head.

Irena dragged Harlan to the left and around a column. "Nearly there."

A group of three Platonic philosophers, in their modern take on togas, ceased their discussion. The trio split apart, allowing Irena and Harlan to bustle through and into the east corridor.

Harlan nodded his apology and increased his walking

speed.

The residents' row had fifty apartments on it. Twenty-five on either side. Hugo's was number twenty-seven, on the right-hand side so that he had a window looking out into space.

A few people, mostly political aides and analysts, came out of their apartments and hurried toward the elevators. No one said anything to Irena or Harlan as the two of them turned the corner and approached the door to number twenty-six.

Irena pulled Harlan back behind the corner. "Wait. There's a guard outside. Armed."

Harlan pressed his body against the side and peered around. She was right. An SMF Marine stood outside Hugo's door. She wore civilian crowd-control colors and was armed with one of the new Ramford rifles—a weapon supplied on contract by a subsidiary of the Ceres Mining Company.

"Irena, you distract her. Get her to turn her back to me, and I'll take care of the rest."

Irena's eyes grew large with alarm.

"Don't worry. We don't have time to negotiate."

"You're not going to kill her, are you?"

"No, I'm just going to temporarily alter her state of consciousness. She'll be fine. I promise."

Irena looked up at him with those dark smoky eyes of hers. She tugged at the edges of her short-cropped brown hair, which appeared black in the shadow of the corridor. "Okay. What shall I do?"

"Anything to get her to turn her back to me."

Irena looked to her feet for a moment and then nodded her head. "I got it."

With that, she stepped around the corner and strode

down the corridor toward the guard. The woman turned to face her, her rifle, previously aimed at the ground, rising just a few millimeters.

She commanded Irena to halt.

"I'm sorry." Irena held up her hands. "But I need your help. I'm Victoria Selles' daughter. Someone attacked me. There's a rogue abbot..."

Irena stepped past the guard so that she was facing back toward Harlan. The Marine turned and placed a hand on Irena's shoulder, trying to calm her down as Irena increased the drama of the situation.

— *She's very good at the acting. I'd watch out for that.*

— Shut up. Stop trying to undermine her.

Seeing his opportunity, Harlan removed the pistol from inside his jacket, sprinted the ten-meter distance, and clubbed the unsuspecting Marine on the back of the head, just above the neck. The Marine didn't know what had hit her. She dropped the bulky rifle and collapsed forward into Irena's arms. Irena helped her to the ground and looked up at Harlan with concern. He checked the unconscious woman's pulse. She was fine.

"We'll have to be quick," he said. "We can't hide her anywhere, and she could come to at any moment."

Irena nodded to the cuffs and graphene restraint straps on the woman's webbing belt. "Let's gag and tie her, then."

Together they bound the woman's legs and wrists.

Harlan removed the woman's comm unit so that she couldn't update the rest of her squad. He placed it over his ear, but used Milo to access the unit's OS. He disabled the broadcast. He would only be able to receive, which is what he wanted; it'd give him a heads-up if something bad went down.

Harlan looked over the woman's body, but found

nothing suitable with which to gag her. He had nothing that could easily be used either. Irena, however, was wearing her arm warmers.

Reluctantly, she removed one, and they used it to gag the Marine.

When they were finished, Irena tried to hide her bare arm behind her back, but Harlan saw the scars on her forearm.

They shared a look.

Harlan wanted to ask her about it, but it wasn't the time or place.

— *This girl has got more secrets than your ex-wife*, Milo said.

Harlan didn't respond. "Here, take the pistol." He handed the weapon to her. "I'll take the rifle... and these confusion grenades."

He turned his attention to the door. With one heavy kick, it smashed open, splintering the polymer frame. The door clanged off the wall, but he was already halfway in, rifle raised, and the door bounced harmlessly off his hip.

Irena slipped by to his left, pistol raised.

"Damn it." Harlan's vision adapted to the low light of the apartment. "We're too late."

Hugo was in the middle of the room and staring right at him.

His head was lopsided. His complexion was the color of lunar dust. His eyes bulged with the last few moments of panic when he had probably changed his mind but knew it was too late. The noose around his neck gripped tightly, and the way his body hung told Harlan that he had broken his neck the moment he had stepped off the dining table behind him.

The apartment reeked of pungent rot and the voided remains of Hugo's bowels.

Irena retched and turned away. Even Harlan, used to finding dead bodies as part of his job, had to fight to keep the bile from rising.

28

Harlan and Irena dragged the guard's body into the apartment and cut Hugo down, placing his body on the couch, out of view of any curious passersby.

"What do we do now?" Irena asked. "This was our last lead to Project Inception..."

"Search the place for drives, disks, hell, even paper. Anything that could have information on it."

Both Harlan and Irena started their search.

Despite the upper-level apartment, Hugo's place was even smaller than Harlan's. With a few soft furnishings, a single bedroom, and a luxuriously appointed bathroom, there was little in the way of clutter and storage. It took no more than ten minutes to make a thorough sweep.

While Irena continued to look about the place, Harlan programmed an AR overlay based on Hugo's fingerprints. He set the algorithm to scan for prints less than a day old given average dust fall. A few moments passed and a map of red marks overlaid his vision. Hugo had handled kitchen utensils, perhaps making himself a last supper, and manipulated the apartment's control panel.

Irena sighed and slumped into an armchair. "It's useless. He must have destroyed everything before killing himself. He probably found out about Gandit and followed protocol. These Vanguard people sure are loyal to their movement."

"Hugo was only loyal to one thing: himself. There's something else going on here."

"Murder?" Irena asked, raising an eyebrow.

"No... I think he killed himself, but... there's something not right here."

Harlan inspected Hugo's body more closely. At first nothing stood out, but the more he looked, the more he realized the shape of Hugo's skull wasn't as spherical as it ought to be. There was a flat section a few centimeters across just below his crown.

"He has a peripheral," Harlan said, running two fingers across the flattened section.

"And that's good or bad?"

"Not sure yet."

— *Want me to scan for signals*? Milo asked, one step ahead of Harlan's thoughts.

— Yes, do it.

Irena cocked her head to one side and stared at Harlan. "You're doing that lip thing again. You've figured something out, haven't you?"

"I don't know..."

A bleep from Irena's terminal broke his concentration. She brought up a screen showing Bella's face contorted with worry. "Harlan, Irena, things have gotten bad down here. There's been another abbot attack on level four."

"Yeah, we saw it on the news," Irena said.

"But that's not all; the SMF have shut down the port. We had to take off or risk being impounded. We're currently conserving fuel and orbiting the station, but it won't be long before we're hailed by the port authority. We need to leave real soon. Not to mention time's ticking down in our window of opportunity."

Harlan checked the time: 1035. They had less than two and a half standard hours' buffer time left. He thought about leaving Hugo as is, but he needed intel, needed to know more about this Project Inception and what was likely waiting for them.

"We're almost done here. Don't leave without us."

"Then be quick. I'm giving you ten minutes. And that's because I care about you. I can't afford to hang around, not when Gianni is out there…"

"Understood. Ten minutes will have to do, but you'll have to come to us. Meet us at emergency airlock G3 on level six."

"And then what?" Bella's voice rose an octave. "How do you plan to get aboard? This craft isn't equipped with a suitable airlock conjoining ring. We won't be able to lock on."

"We'll cross that metaphorical bridge when we come to it."

"You always were the craziest one, Harlan." Bella shook her head and closed her eyes for a moment. She pinched the bridge of her nose and exhaled. "Fine, I guess we'll have to figure something out. Don't be late. I can't wait around. Be safe."

"Always and likewise."

The terminal window closed. Harlan and Irena stared at each other for a brief moment. "What if—"

He cut her off with a raised hand. "Wait a second."

— I've connected with Hugo's peripheral successfully.

"Yes." He pumped his fist, eliciting a strange look from Irena.

It was pointless in hiding that he too had a peripheral, so he quickly told Irena about Milo. Before she had time to react, or for him to worry about her reaction, Milo brought up the file system on Hugo's peripheral, displaying it on Harlan's augmented reality overlay.

He ran a few searches of the files and discovered there was little need.

Hugo had already preempted events and left only a single file on the system.

The password prompt popped up. He entered all the usual guesses, but when he had Milo run a library file against it, it was actually his own silicon runner's server password that opened the file. It was clear that Hugo had intended for him to find the data.

It was a simple text file that read:

HARLAN, first of all, you need to know I'm sorry. I wish you hadn't got mixed up in all this, but I suppose, looking back at events, it was inevitable. You're a determined bastard, and you'd have got to the truth somehow.

It's too late for me. I've been under Vanguard's influence for nearly thirty years, and I can't deal with it any longer. I can't stand to see what will become of the Solar Federation if they're successful. I am, ultimately, a coward. But a coward with information. I couldn't risk trying to get it to you any other way; Vanguard's influence is too far-reaching. They have complete access of the silicon runner servers and most of the government's systems.

It won't be long before they have the QCA, too.

You've probably guessed by now that it was me that helped

fake Luca Doe's death. Your old partner is Vanguard's key weapon in Project Inception. Trust me when I tell you I did it against my better judgment. I don't expect you to understand my motivations, but let me make it clear that if I could have stopped them, I would have.

Now it's down to you.

You'll find him at the included coordinates. That's Project Inception's HQ.

I tried to point you in the right direction regarding Fizon, but Vanguard found out what I was trying to do and sent one of their hacked abbots after you. I trust you survived that. As for Project Inception, I don't know the full details, but I do know they found something, many decades ago, beyond our solar system. I don't know what or how they're using it, but whatever it is, it's all tied in with the QCA hack.

If you are reading this, Harlan, you have to stop them at all costs.

If they gain control of the abbots, that's it; it's all over. No more Solar Federation. It'll become a dictatorship, and who knows what they'll want to do with it.

Stop Luca and find out what Vanguard has discovered.

Trust your gut, Harlan. Data isn't as reliable as you think it is: it can be manipulated and used against you.

HR.

HARLAN SWIPED the file over to Irena and continued to search the apartment while she read it. He also had Milo run the coordinates included with the file. It pinpointed the exact location of the castle. He forwarded the data to Bella in case he couldn't make it in time. At least she would have a specific location within which to search for Gianni.

"Do you think this information is legit?" Irena asked, having finished reading the file.

"I can't be completely sure, but given our time constraints, it's all we have to go on."

"You worked with him for years, right? Do you think this file matches what you know of his character?"

Harlan didn't even have to think about it. "Absolutely. He was always a coward and quick to throw his weight and position around at those beneath him, but he never took on anyone above him. It was one of the traits I most despised about him. He'd always back those in power over his own staff."

"But what about giving you the information now? He could have just killed himself and not left this clue. It does strike me as a little... what's the word... easy?"

"One thing many people don't understand about investigation is that quite often cases are solved by the most obvious thing. For example, most murders are committed by someone the victim already knew. Usually family. Most murder cases are solved within the first few days or not at all. Same with robberies and fraud: it's quite often the most obvious data that ends up being the incriminating evidence."

"I suppose there is a correlation to that theory in my field of work. It's how I built my intuition. Some professors think it's some amazing skill or a 'gift', when, really, it's just years and years of looking at data sets and recognizing patterns. Some of it is blindingly obvious when one knows what to look at."

Harlan checked his timer: they had eight minutes left. "We've got to move. We can discuss this more when we're on the ship. We can't risk the elevators, so we'll take the access tunnel up to the next level. From there, it's a two-minute jog to the G3 airlock. Stay alert. We don't know who or what might be waiting for us out there."

"What about Hugo and the file?"

"I deleted the file. We'll have to leave the body as it is. No doubt the Marine will report it when she wakes up. Follow me and keep the pistol ready to use if you have to."

With that, he checked to make sure he had a round in the chamber of the rifle, flicked on the safety, and strapped it over his shoulder.

He and Irena left the apartment, and after making sure the corridor was clear, they dashed away from the central atrium to the rear of the ring that made up this particular level. From there, they moved to where the maintenance and access tunnels were situated.

Over the years, both as a child and later as a silicon runner, Harlan had traversed the majority of the tunnels in the station, giving him fast and hidden access to many areas and levels. Given the SMF locking down everything in sight, it was their only choice, even if it meant it'd take a couple of minutes longer than using the elevator.

Harlan used a black-market access chip to open the tunnel. He stepped inside, clambering onto the ladder. "We're going to that light up there. See it?"

"Yeah." Irena's voice wavered.

"Are you scared of the dark or of heights?"

"Neither really, but confined spaces aren't my favorite places to be."

"Will you be okay?"

Irena nodded. She slipped into the tunnel and pulled the door closed behind her. Hooking her arm around a rung on the ladder, she peered up through the narrow darkness. "Let's get moving, then."

The pair of them climbed their way to the next level, and

all the while Harlan ignored the feeling of dread over the idea that the chaos from the levels below had made its way up to the higher levels of the station.

Two minutes of concentrated climbing later, they reached the light that illuminated the access door to level eight. Harlan shifted the rifle over his shoulder, and, holding on to the ladder with one hand, he reached out, entered the security code, and pushed the door open. The corridor ahead appeared to be empty, and no sounds of panic or firearms came from the level.

"I think we're good," he said, stepping off the ladder and into the corridor. He turned and helped Irena across the threshold. Her arms trembled. A thin layer of sweat covered her face. She made a point of letting go of his hand and standing up straight, as if to show the climb hadn't fazed her. Harlan couldn't help but admire her strength and mental toughness.

"We ought to move," she said. "Bella's crew will be here soon."

"Are you okay?"

"I'm fine. The jog to the airlock will help."

A shadow passed across her eyes. Harlan had seen that before from victims of trauma. Any other time, he would find a quiet place to sit down and talk it out, but they had to keep moving. "Make sure the pistol is in easy reach," he said. "We don't know if we'll be facing any resistance."

With that, Harlan brought the rifle around to his front and carried it in both hands as he set off at a slight jog down the corridor. He requested a map overlay from Milo, as he hadn't been up to this level in quite some time. His memory of the G3 airlock location was a little fuzzy.

Especially as it appeared the level had been renovated recently. Unlike most other levels below it, the walls weren't plain or covered in advertising display panels. It was all simulated wooden panels and potted plants beneath UV lights up here. They didn't even need air-scrubbers due to the amount of foliage.

As they turned out of the maintenance corridor and into the wide expansive hallway of the level itself, Harlan couldn't help but draw a breath of wonder at the woodland-like scene before him. "This is new," he said, taking in the thicket of real trees before him. A perimeter around the trees was filled with loamy soil. Moss creeped around the base of the trunks. "Looks like a woodland from Earth."

Irena pulled up beside him and gripped his arm. "There's movement to the left." Her breathing increased and her grip tightened.

Harlan zoomed in on the area of movement and let out a sigh. "It's fine. It's just a philosopher." A robed woman casually walked by the edge of the wood, stopping to sit on a bench facing the trees. Irena's grip eased, and Harlan couldn't help but sense that she was reliving the events she'd suffered on Earth. The timer on his overlay suggested they only had three minutes left. "This way; the airlock is down that hallway to the right. We'll be out of here soon."

"Okay, lead the way."

Irena took one last glance toward the philosopher before jogging up to Harlan's side.

A further minute later and they had passed through a hallway that connected to various high-end retail outlets, all of which were shut, with notices suggesting it was under government advisement. That also explained the lack of people up here, Harlan thought.

Turning left out of the shopping district, the level became more utilitarian. No more wood-effect panels, just the typical gray walls and rubberized floors. Conduits and tunnels were left uncovered overhead, leading to the airlock a few meters ahead.

Before the door, however, were four pods that contained emergency space suits. EVA engineers usually wore these to carry out repairs or survey for any potential damage.

Although these days they were rarely used, given the abbots now shouldered that particular burden.

They needed no such suits to exist safely in the vacuum of space, and although it was never spoken aloud, from the humans' point of view, the abbots were somewhat disposable. Even if they got damaged, they could always be fixed, their unique personality module uploaded to a new body unit.

Despite many attempts by scientists, both human and abbot alike, the uploading or transferring of a human consciousness wasn't an available option. The results were quite often horrific, both for the uploader and the uploaded. Perhaps that would come in time, but for now, humanity was bound to their meat-and-water-based bodies.

Irena and Harlan reached the suit pods. Harlan punched the red emergency release button and entered his security code as the machine scanned his retina. He could only do this due to his access level as a silicon runner. Regular citizens didn't have the appropriate level to use the suits: that was left to a handful of people on each level designated as SBERs: Space-Bound Emergency Responders.

Irena reached into the pod then turned to face Harlan. "It's empty... the suit's been taken."

Harlan checked his pod. "Same here. Let's try the other two." He turned to the pods on the opposite wall and entered his credentials once more. "Damn it, mine's empty."

"There's one here," Irena said, pulling out a wheeled

container holding the suit. "What are we going to do? Bella's going to be here any minute now."

"You take that one and board the *Goat*. I'll go to the G4 airlock across the level and grab another suit. There's got to be at least one more there. Bella will just have to make two stops."

"How long will that take you?"

"Five minutes at the most. But don't worry about me. Just focus on getting in that suit and on the shuttle. I'll message Bella to explain the situation. She's used to me not doing what she wants."

Before he left, Harlan helped Irena into the suit, opened the airlock door using his access credentials, and began the depressurizing process.

Once completed, he connected to her suit's wireless comm channel and explained how to open the outer door, although it wasn't complicated: a large red handle on the right-side wall with the words 'PULL TO OPEN' emblazoned above it told her everything she needed to know. But still, he preferred to talk her through it, as he sensed her nervousness.

Irena's voice came to him via the speaker on the outside of the airlock door. "Harlan, be careful and be quick."

"I'll be fine, trust me. I'll see you shortly."

"I hope so."

He gave her a reassuring smile, turned, and set off at a fast jog towards the other airlock. On his way, he had Milo interface with his comm suite and sent Bella a message explaining the situation. The reply that came back was filled with expletives, but also a grudging acceptance and a warning that this was his last chance: if he wasn't at the airlock in the next five minutes, they'd leave without him.

Knowing Bella as he did, he knew that although she

tolerated him because there were some feelings between the two, she wouldn't hesitate to leave him behind if he posed a risk to the possible rescue of her brother.

Family was everything to her.

Harlan envied her that--the family, the loyalty.

The only person he had ever given himself to, given his complete loyalty to, had ultimately betrayed him—Leanne. But even then, as he jogged through the abandoned level, through hallways and corridors, past the woodland, and onto the other side of the level, he wondered again about her involvement with Vanguard and whether she was truly acting on her own motivations, or whether she, like so many others, was a tool to be manipulated and used for their own ends.

— *You would prefer the latter, wouldn't you, old chap?* Milo asked, echoing Harlan's thoughts.

— Of course. Makes it more palatable if she left me for external reasons.

— *I suspect one way or another, you'll know soon.*

29

Bella double-checked the coordinates for airlock G3, entered them into the *Goat*'s surprisingly advanced computer system, and engaged the autopilot. For all the ship's faults, not least the stench of meat, she had to give Sanjeet props for installing such a great software suite and maneuverable auxiliary thruster package. The *Goat* might have been small, but it was as agile a craft as she'd ever piloted.

While the computer steered their way to the airlock to pick up Irena, Bella stepped through into the main hold. Her crew had busily tidied the area to make room for Harlan and Irena. With the six of them needing crash couches of sorts to deal with the two-g thrust over the next forty-eight hours, they had to get creative with the *Goat*'s layout.

Benches ran along both sides, and webbing hung from the flanks of the hull. Bashir and Greta were busy storing weapons, ration packs, and other supplies to said webbing. Wilbur was testing the setup of straps he had created for the crew to use for when they were under thrust.

Bella smiled at the efficiency of her ragtag crew. "Nice to see everyone on the same page and working together."

"Needs must," Wilbur said as he finished installing the last of the straps. He tugged on it and made an adjustment before looking up at Bella. He shifted his glasses into position and smiled. "It's not perfect, but we should be in at least some degree of comfort during the burn stages, despite the tight squeeze. Harlan and Irena will need to leave their suits in the airlock."

"There's a small delay: Harlan has had to go to a different airlock. But if we're quick, it shouldn't take us too long. It's going to be tight, though."

"Needs must."

"Looks like we're all set, then. I'll bring us into the airlock as best I can. Greta, I'd like you and Bashir to suit up and prepare to receive Irena."

The two crew members nodded at Bella and then shared a look that she thought expressed a shared determination. Inwardly she felt a warmth of pride in her team. With that sorted, she returned to the cockpit and prepared to take manual control over the thrusters: she needed to be delicate in order to keep the ship as close to the airlock as possible. They couldn't dock directly due to the *Goat*'s lack of a docking ring.

She let the autopilot continue for a couple of minutes as it brought the shuttle into the vicinity of the Atlas airlock. Outside, the station loomed large on the screen. It's massive multi-torus design rotated, generating gravity for those inside. The computer matched the rotation speed and began to bring the craft in closer.

Before they reached their destination, the system's screen split in two, the lower section showing an emergency broadcast from Victoria Selles.

Selles stared out of the screen with a serious expression. She was wearing a somber gray suit that spoke of her privilege. Something so well-tailored could only be provided to those of a suitably high-access level—or bartered on the black market. Given Selles was implicated in this whole Vanguard situation, Bella didn't think she would be above shady contraband.

"Are you guys watching this?" Bella asked, looking over her shoulder to the crew in the back. "Looks like we're getting an emergency announcement."

Wilbur pointed at a smaller screen flickering to life on the back wall of the hold. "We're seeing it."

A message scrolled along the bottom of the broadcast that read "Terrorist threat, red alert."

Victoria Selles cleared her throat and began her speech. "Citizens of Atlas Station, it is with great sadness that I report to you today the death of fifteen innocent members of our society at the hands of terrorists. These terrorists are a group of untethered abbots. We currently do not know their intentions. We have reached out and liaised with the AOA and will hopefully hear from Beaufort, the abbots' representative.

"You can rest assured that we are doing all we can to apprehend these monsters. We have neutralized two threats already, and the SMF are on high alert for two known others. We are uncertain at this point how many we are facing, but we will inform you via the emergency broadcast channel of any updates. For now, I would suggest everyone stay within the safety of your apartments, don't open your door to anyone, and report anything suspicious to the SMF.

"We are placing Atlas Station on complete lockdown until the threat is over. That means no loitering in public areas. All businesses to shut down. And no craft to take off or land at the station's docks. We hope to remove these restrictions as soon as we have apprehended the rogue elements. And please leave all matters to the SMF. We have trained experts working on this. This is not the time for vigilante behavior or citizen policing.

"Finally, I'd like to add that these measures were carried out by my authority and the agreement of the House of Messengers in a brief emergency meeting prior to this announcement. We had to act quickly due to the lack of leadership from President Kallstrom, who, safely nestled in his secure compound on Bujoldia, refuses to accept the severity of our situation. It has become clear to me that the citizens of Atlas Station will always be in harm's way while President Henrik Kallstrom lives his life of luxury on Mars.

"If we are to thrive and expand, we need stronger leadership that puts the lives of those on Atlas and other stations first. When voting is triggered, a vote for me means a vote for a safe future. But for now, my attention is solely on extinguishing this terrorist threat posed by these rogue abbots. I will address you all again shortly with an update as soon as I have more news. Thank you for your time, Atlas citizens."

Wilbur stood in the doorway and fiddled with a button on his jacket. "That was a little overdramatic. Not sure how professional it was to attack the president during a terrorist threat announcement. She clearly has no shame."

Bella spun around in her chair to face Wilbur. "Do any of these political types?"

"Probably not. But we know she's worse than most. First the merger, and now this. Given her ambitions to become the new Sol-Fed president, one might think this supposed terrorist threat is not all that it appears."

Greta's large frame loomed behind Wilbur. "Let's cut to the chase; it's clearly bullshit. I wouldn't be surprised at all if she and her Vanguard buddies hacked a bunch of abbots for this very purpose. You've got to wonder what they're up to while the rest of the station is on lockdown."

"Covering their tracks, probably," Bella said. "With Gandit and Hugo killing themselves, Vanguard is panicking, or perhaps bringing forward its plans. We may have forced their hand."

"That's a good thing," Wilbur added. "Means we're getting closer and catching them off guard."

Before Bella could think on this more, a red light on the ship's console flashed. They were receiving an emergency hail request. The ship patched the signal immediately.

A stern male voice crackled over the channel. "Unidentified shuttle, this is Captain Saffile of the SSF *Wickham*. You are violating emergency lockdown status. Identify yourself and engage with our autopilot protocol immediately for escort to a secure dock. This is nonnegotiable."

Bella tapped out a command on the *Goat*'s console and brought up a camera view, adjusting its angle until she found the SSF *Wickham* a few kilometers away from them but approaching quickly under aux thrust.

Greta let out a low whistle. "That's one heavily armed ship for an escort."

Wilbur squinted at the screen. "What class is it?"

Bella zoomed in for a better look. Unlike their boxy, utilitarian shuttle, the *Wickham* was of a sleek design and at least four times as large. It featured stub wings swept back with deep arcs, giving the front profile an almost birdlike appearance. The design was supposed to allow it to enter a planet's atmosphere, but in all her years of flying, Bella had never seen one outside of space.

"It's a delta-class torpedo ship," Greta said.

Bella had seen dozens of these over the last couple of

years. They were used for patrolling the space between stations due to their speed and relatively decent maneuverability. And being well armed meant they were a threat to even the largest of crime syndicates.

Greta leaned farther over Wilbur, squeezing the smaller man beneath her. "I served on one of those during the Ceres uprising. Good ships. Fast, but no match for the *Goat*'s agility. We won't be able to outrun them, but we can outmaneuver them."

Pushing his way out from beneath her arm, Wilbur readjusted his collar and regarded his larger compatriot. "What kind of weapons do they possess?"

"Twin railguns on port and starboard midsections, a primary Gatling turret with full three-sixty arc, and a complement of six torpedoes at full load-out. It's unlikely they're carrying all six on a patrol vehicle. I reckon they've got two: one pre-loaded in each tube."

Bella sighed. "In other words, we're screwed."

Greta nodded. "You better get maneuvering and keep the station between us and them. There is no way they'd open fire if it meant a risk of hitting the station. But out in space with a clear shot? I think they'd take it rather than worrying about escorting us anywhere."

Bella knew this was their only option. And with time ticking down, they didn't have long to negotiate or come up with another plan. "You two, get yourselves strapped in, and tell Bashir to do the same. Things are going to get real bumpy for a while."

"Aye, aye, Captain," Greta said with a smirk on her face.

Bella couldn't decide if it was a good or bad thing that danger seemed to excite her. Regardless, it was preferable to blind panic.

The two of them stepped back into the hold, while Bella

sent a response to the *Wickham*. "Captain Saffile, this is Captain—" she thought for a moment about what name to give, cycling through the various monikers she had used over the years and trying to decide which one hadn't yet run afoul of the SMF "—Eliza Gomez of the *Plucky Trader*. We're just a courier shuttle. The docks had already filled by the time we came back from Luna on a government job. We'll be happy to be directed to the nearest dock. I'm sure you guys have more important business to worry about, what with the whole terrorist issue."

As she was saying all this, she was prepping the *Goat*'s aux thrusters for immediate manual control. She used the computer's telemetry package to calculate and display the fastest route into the interior of the station. This would mean weaving through the torus sections, where the gaps were too small for the *Wickham* to follow.

And leaving her little room for error.

"Captain Gomez, negative to your suggestion. As requested, prepare for autopilot engagement in four... three... two..."

"Not today, good sir."

Bella engaged the engines, sending the *Goat* shooting away from the *Wickham* in a cloud of ejecta and flame. The thrust forced her back into the pilot's chair. A yell of agony came from back in the hold. Bella knew this was Wilbur: his high-pitched scream was ever-recognizable.

Using a combination of manual and computer assistance, she eased the shuttle below the topmost torus of the station, jerking the controls immediately to the left. The maneuver sent the craft into a spin, and they narrowly avoided a large spoke section extending from the central cylinder to the interior radius of what was level nine.

The map overlay showed a yellow-dotted course that

terminated at the G3 airlock. Bella flicked the video screen to cycle through all directions. She could just about make out the front nose section of the *Wickham* hovering five kilometers away as Captain Saffile no doubt conspired a way to get the larger ship through the tight confines of the station's infrastructure.

With another set of tight maneuvers and thrusts, they were out of the *Wickham*'s view and matching the rotation of the station once more.

Bella hit reverse thrust to slow their velocity as the computer brought the shuttle to within a few hundred meters of the airlock. From the zoomed-in video feed, Irena could be seen through a small window, her suited helmet pressed up against it, her eyes wide.

She waved as though Bella wouldn't see her, but Bella was on the case. Within seconds and another blast of thruster, the flame of which cast an orange glow against the exterior escape hatch, they were now just ten meters away and matching course.

Bella quickly scanned the video feed for the *Wickham* and couldn't see it. They were hailing her again, but she switched off the channel and instead connected to Irena's personal communicator.

"Hey, girl, it's Bella. Can you hear me?"

"Yes, yes, loud and clear. I thought you were going to crash into the station at the speed you came in."

"Yeah, we've... erm... got a little company, but don't worry about that. Let's just focus on getting you out of there. I assume the lock's been depressurized?"

"It has. I'm ready to go whenever you are. How are we going to do this?"

"Open the door, but hold on to something. We're going to throw a tether out to you. Grab on to it and connect it to the tether port on the chest of your suit. It clicks in and secures with a twist. It's real easy. After that, you'll just need to jump a little and we'll pull you in. Just stay calm, don't flail around too much, and let us do the work. You'll be fine."

Irena wrung her hands together. "I wish I felt as confident as you sound."

30

I rena floated in the non-pressurized airlock. She breathed deeply and closed her eyes in order to calm her heart rate, which threatened to get out of control. She hooked a boot around a pole attached to the wall and wished she had gone with Bella and her crew to the dock.

Of all the things she'd experienced lately, standing on the edge of Atlas Station staring out into the void of space ranked way up there as the most terrifying.

If it went wrong, she'd fall forever. Or at least until the oxygen tanks of the suit ran out; then she'd slowly suffocate to death while her body continued to fall through space indefinitely.

She swallowed and breathed deeper to push back the feelings of nausea.

"I'm not sure I can do this," she said.

Bella's voice sounded scratchy and thin through the suit's speakers. "Of course you can. You survived the abbot attack on Earth, got Harlan off Turing Station, and faced down your parents. You're far stronger than you think you are. Just pull the red lever and grab the handhold. We'll do the rest. Okay?"

Irena opened her eyes, located the lever, and grabbed it with the bulky suited glove. She tested it a little to gauge how difficult it would be. With just a small effort the lever shifted downward. She continued until it fully engaged.

Every muscle in her body tensed as her instincts told her to run as far away from the edge as possible. The final barrier between her and the cold, unforgiving vacuum of space slid upward, exposing her to the sight of the *Goat* hovering in place.

Small puffs of exhaust shot out from the array thrusters along its tarnished, dull-gray exterior. It looked like an abandoned storage container and didn't give her any confidence at all.

She pushed herself back a meter, using the handholds on the wall, as the shuttle spun on its axis until the rear of the craft was no more than fifteen or so meters away.

"You're doing great," Bella said over the comm. "We're opening our airlock. Greta and Bashir will send out a tether. Grab it and connect it like we spoke about earlier."

"Insert and twist, right?"

"Exactly. Just tug on it to make sure it's seated into the coupling correctly. When you're satisfied, let us know, and we'll pull you slowly and gently into the shuttle. Couldn't be easier."

"Okay, I'm ready."

Which, of course, was a complete lie. Irena had never been as unready for something as she was now. Unlike some who were born on the station, she was never a fan of space in general and avoided travel as much as she could. Unlike Bella, Irena had never raced spaceships, had never gone tether diving off the station like some teenagers were wont to do.

No, Irena was utterly boring when it came to human-space interfacing. As far as she was concerned, if humans were meant to be out in space, then they'd have evolved the natural facilities to do so. It was the same reason why humans didn't possess gills—well, those who didn't dabble in gene manipulation—people just weren't meant to be anywhere other than in an oxygen-rich, terrestrial atmosphere.

"Hey, girl," Greta said, her voice perky over the comm. She waved from the back of the shuttle. Bashir stood next to her and was feeding her the tether from a drum attached to the airlock wall. "We're going to throw this toward you. It'll come at you slowly, so you should have plenty of time to grab it. Ready?"

"Go for it," Irena replied, using the handholds to bring herself closer to the edge.

Greta threw out the tether. It floated toward Irena like some great white space snake. It curled as they continued to feed more line out to space.

Slowly, almost too slowly, so that Irena had time to worry about it going wrong, the tether reached her. Her first grab for it missed. She knocked at the metallic end with the back of her hand, sending it spiraling out of control.

"Don't panic," Greta said. "It's okay. Just take your time and grab whatever's at hand; then work your way back to the coupling. It's not going anywhere."

Irena followed her instructions and within a few moments held the tether to the coupling ring on the chest of her suit. At first, she couldn't slot it in; her hand were shaking too much. After a little trial and error, she got it seated and twisted it into place with a satisfying clunk. Remembering what Bella had said, Irena tugged the tether away from her to test its connection. It seemed solid enough; she couldn't budge it.

"I think it's secured. Do I need to jump or anything?"

Greta waved her hands over each other to indicate no. "You don't need to do anything. Just stay calm. We'll pull you in."

"Calm is the exact thing one would be in this situation, right? Nothing to fear but fear itself, etcetera. Let's do this, then, and get it over with before I fill my suit with panic vomit."

"Here we go."

Irena felt a slight tug on her chest pulling her over the threshold of the airlock. After a few moments, she made the big mistake of looking down and saw nothing but the blackness of space and a few stars. They appeared to be moving, and it took her a while to realize it was due to the spin of the shuttle as it matched the station. She closed her eyes and clamped her lips shut as, once again, she felt nauseated.

"You're doing great," Greta said as the tugging sensation continued. "Almost there. You're about halfway."

Irena clutched the tether with her gloved hands as tightly as she could, suddenly concerned that she might not have connected it correctly and would be set adrift.

"You're almost in, girl. Just a few more pulls... Oh shit..."

Irena opened her eyes and looked up. She stared at Greta, who was no more than a couple of meters away. "What? What is it?"

Bella's voice came over the communications channel. "Hold on. We've got to move. Those damned SMF fools followed us through. I don't know how they got a ship that size by the spokes, but the mad bastards are threatening to open fire."

"What?" Irena said, her voice going up an octave. "Open fire? What the hell's going on? Get me in. Don't leave me out here."

A burst of orange light to Irena's right caught her attention. She turned to see the nose of a large SMF ship pointing right at the *Goat*—and her. A gun barrel mounted atop the hull spun around, flashing orange flame. The rounds fired over the shuttle and into open space, clearly a warning shot.

"I'm sorry, Irena," Bella said. "But we've got to move. Hold on."

Before she could say anything, the tether pulled taut and grabbed her with a violent yank as the *Goat*'s thrusters burst to life and blinded her with white and yellow light. She screamed and wrapped her arms around the tight tether.

The shuttle distanced itself away from the station and then, using its aux thrusters, altered its trajectory to go up and over the overhang created by the topmost torus. She glanced back. The SMF ship had reversed out of its current position, presumably to get a new angle on the shuttle. Her heart pounded inside her chest and sweat dripped from every pore as Bella maneuvered the shuttle in small intricate movements, trying to get as much infrastructure between them and their attacker as possible.

Irena's body became increasingly heavy under the thrust. Her bones ached, and she couldn't help but cry out as the slim barrier between panic and calm split wide open. "Damn it, Bella, this is insane. What are you doing? I'm going to die out here."

"You'll be fine. Just don't let go of the tether... we'll be cutting thrust very soon. Get ready for a hard landing inside the airlock."

Despite the advice and warning, it wasn't enough.

Bella brought the shuttle closer to the station until they were hovering beneath a dense section of infrastructure made up of angular supporting joists and beam cross sections, effectively providing a three-sided box in which the *Goat* hovered.

The reverse thrusters cut in, slowing their movements to a crawl. The change in direction pulled hard on the tether yet again, flinging Irena at great speed toward the open airlock at the rear of the shuttle. Bashir and Greta stood there with their arms open, but they must have realized Irena's entry was too fast. They dived out of the way. Irena, unable to slow her momentum, flew into the airlock. She curled into a ball and brought her feet up as she hit the bulkhead with a thud.

The hit sent a flash of pain up her legs and into her chest, and then she was bouncing back out toward space. A pair of hands grabbed her by the arm while another pulled on the tether, preventing her from escaping back out of the airlock.

"You're safe," Greta said. "You're all good. Just take a few breaths. We'll get you settled. You did great."

"I feel like I'm going to die." Irena's body wasn't used to all this. The worst aspect being that she'd fouled her undergarments, which she refused to announce.

"How is everything back there?" Bella asked.

This time it was Bashir who spoke, a slight tremble to his voice indicating he had found the experience traumatic, which gave Irena at least some comfort to know it wasn't just her. "Irena's in safely. I think we're all good. Shaken up, but okay."

"Well, ladies and gentlemen, don't get too comfortable. We're moving again; we need to get Harlan from airlock G4. At least we've lost those crazy fools for the time being."

When Irena finally got her breath back, she asked, "Once we get Harlan, how are we going to get away from the *Wickham*?"

"Let's face one impossible task at a time. We'll figure something out. Now hold on to your butts. It's going to get bumpy again."

31

Cursing his lack of cardio training, Harlan finally arrived at the G4 airlock. He leaned over and rested his hands on his knees. He sucked in deep breaths and waited for the dizziness to ease before gathering the energy to check the suit pods.

He approached the first one and thought about Irena, considered sending her or Bella a message, but didn't want to interrupt in case she was currently in transit from the station to the *Goat*. He just hoped she made it okay. The last look she had shared with him before he'd run off stayed with him. Although she hadn't said as much, the fear in her eyes was obvious.

No need to panic now. Get moving.

Wasting no more time, he pulled the door to the first suit container open. To his relief, it was there. He wheeled it out and prepared to suit up when he noticed something wrong: the coupling seals between the suit and the helmet were smashed. The high-tensile alloy showed signs of stress, as though something had warped their shape. He couldn't get the two parts to fit correctly.

His first thought was sabotage, but looking at the damage, it was entirely possible that when it was last used, the wearer had suffered some kind of collision.

Didn't explain why they would have put the suit back in, though, unless they were trying to cover up the accident. Entirely plausible given the constraints the engineers were under if no abbots were available for a time-sensitive repair.

Pod two, however, confirmed Harlan's initial fear. This suit had a clear slash through its torso section. The jagged rend made it impossible to consider using.

Pod three: the same, this time the arm and leg seals were split.

And finally, number four. Harlan closed his eyes as he opened the door and reached inside, all the while whispering an affirmation to himself that it would be okay, that this suit would have survived the sabotage and be in perfect working order...

But no.

It too was damaged beyond repair.

Harlan kicked the door shut, sending a clang of metal on metal to echo out into the abandoned level. He swore loudly and kicked at the useless pods once more.

Why couldn't anything just go to plan for once?

A loud thud boomed out to his side, making his ears ring. Pod three splintered metal in all directions. A dark jagged-edged hole appeared in its side. A second thud slammed home a few centimeters to Harlan's left. He felt the rush of air by the side of his head.

His upgraded adrenal glands kicked in, sharpening his senses. Then came his trained instincts: he dove across the width of the storage area, taking cover between pods one and two. And finally, his brain became available for rational action. First, he considered the threat: they were using a non-automatic, high-powered rifle with armor-piercing rounds. The suit pods were made especially strong to withstand trans-vacuum relocation.

Given the trajectory of the shots, the shooter had coverage over the entire entrance to this three-meter-wide corridor.

A tiny kill box all for Harlan.

He couldn't risk running out; he'd be gunned down in seconds.

To make matters worse, he noticed a couple of dragonfly drones—DFDs—approaching his position. This made him think that these weren't the actions of a rogue abbot. The drones were known tech from Station Six, which all along had been a common factor going back to his first discovery of the spider on Asimovia. He reached out to them using his near-field network adaptor, but the network wasn't visible. That wouldn't stop him, however.

— Milo, run a scan on discrete networks. I need to take out those DFDs so my attacker loses his extra eyes.

A few moments ticked by before the peripheral responded.

— *Negative. No networks found.*

— Come on, they're right there, two dragonflies communicating with each other and a host. Get with it, Milo. This isn't the time for screwing up.

— *I repeat. No networks found. Incoming message.*

Harlan dared to sneak a look at his wrist communicator and saw a message scroll along the screen from Bella. Irena had boarded the *Goat*, but the SMF was tailing them, and he ought to make himself ready immediately, as they didn't have much time.

Another shot smashed into the suit container directly in front of him. He jolted away so his back was against the second pod. The bullet smashed around inside the one in front, no doubt damaging the suit further. A few more shots like that, and he'd be completely exposed. He resisted crawling out to get behind the second pod: that was just what the shooter was waiting for.

This wasn't an all-out assault.

It was a calculated hunt.

The two dragonflies hovered above, just out of reach, and then flew around all the pods, presumably scanning the area and sending the information back to the hunter.

Whoever it was would know the weak points, ricochet angles, and Harlan's physical state.

He tried once more with his peripheral.

— Milo, it's massively important you figure this shit out and get me that network.

— *I'm sorry, Harlan, but there's nothing I can do.*

— Screw you, then, buddy.

Harlan's anger flared. He turned his peripheral off using the slider switch at the base of his cranium. He pulled his rifle over his shoulder, checked the round in the chamber, and switched off the safety. Uncapping the front scope lens, he pulled out the articulated limb, feeding it around the corner of the suit pod.

The video feed from the flexible camera showed up in a holographic display above his wrist communicator.

He swept it across the entrance of the kill box until the gun's AI found what he was looking for: a hunched figure towards the rear of an atrium that opened out just beyond the short hallway he was currently in.

His target was no more than a hundred meters away.

The DFDs buzzed closer, making him flinch.

Harlan tried to swat one away, but the self-correcting

collision detection system prevented him from striking lucky.

A fourth gunshot reverberated round the atrium, and another dense thud smashed into the lens of his rifle, knocking the gun from his hands and smashing the targeting system to pieces. It appeared his enemy was using the DFDs for target correction as well.

Spending too much time in this area would get Harlan killed, he knew that for sure, but as far as he could tell, he had only two options: get into the airlock, or try to run for cover directly in front of his attacker.

The latter was what the bastard wanted. The former was equally dangerous because of the time required to get up, move, and then activate the opening procedure of the airlock door. If it was pressurized that'd take even longer.

And all the while those damned DFDs would be feeding back information.

First things first: deal with the drones. If Milo couldn't help, Harlan had an idea. Gylfie had said he would stay behind and be their eyes and ears on Atlas while they headed to Earth. Well, that plan would have to be brought forward.

Harlan called Gylfie on his communicator even as another shot rang out, this time smashing into the remains of his rifle, shattering apart the gun's stock, leaving him weaponless other than the two confusion grenades he had taken off the Marine outside Hugo's place. He'd never be able to throw them far enough for them to be effective, though.

A few seconds later, Gylfie's voice sounded in Harlan's ears. "What's up, you guys get into trouble already?"

"That was quick. Almost as if you were expecting my call."

"I was. I've been tracking the SMF. Things are getting serious around here. What's happening with you?"

The sixth shot slammed into the pod, smashing a hole all the way through it.

Harlan jerked back, pushing himself as far into the corner as possible so his attacker couldn't hit him through the newly created access point.

"I'm being pinned down and shot at by someone with a high-powered rifle. I don't have long. I need a favor. This bastard's got a couple of DFDs buzzing around me, and I can't find their network. Can you do it?"

"Drones, you say... I'll try. Ping me your exact location."

Harlan did just that and lowered himself below the hole in the suit pod. As he did so, one of the dragonflies buzzed down low. He instinctively kicked out at it—and only barely missed having his foot blown off as another shot fired through the hole and slammed into the side of the opposite pod. He mentally noted this was the seventh round.

"You need to hurry, Gylfie. I don't know how much ammo this shooter has, but at this rate, I'll have no cover at all."

"I found you. I can see you from the security cameras—and your attacker."

"Who the hell is shooting at me?"

"Damn it. I never liked this asshole. Sending you a picture now."

A portrait flashed up on his wrist display: it was Alex Aurier. That old bastard. Harlan swore aloud. A renewed anger swelled inside him. Now that he knew who was attacking him, the fear ebbed away to be replaced with furious vengeance.

"Gylfie, what's the lag on the feed?"

"A couple of milliseconds. It's a fast connection. What do you need?"

"While you work on taking down the dragonflies, I need you to zoom in on Aurier and redirect the video feed to my display. Let's see how he fares when the odds are evened up."

"Okay, patching the relay now, and I'll work on finding the DFDs' network."

Harlan watched the feed on his wrist display as Gylfie zoomed in on Aurier. He looked closely at the weapon and recognized it as an illegal Janzai WeaponTech Custom Special with nine rounds to a magazine. Janzai was thought to have gone out of business years ago when the SMF had sourced their weapons from a different manufacturer, but it appeared they had either gone underground or Aurier had sourced a refurbished unit.

A plan formulated in Harlan's mind.

He yelled out, "Hey, Aurier, you old scumbag. I know it's you. I can smell you all the way back here." And then he made himself as low as possible as an eighth round slammed into the pod behind him. His heart pounded, and he took a couple of breaths when he saw how close it was: just a few millimeters.

However, Aurier had done what Harlan wanted.

He just had one more round to go before reloading.

"I found the network," Gylfie said over the comm link. "What do you want me to do with them?"

"Send them flying into Aurier's face. I want to disrupt his concentration."

"Sending the command now."

The two dragonflies darted away from Harlan, making him smile. He watched the two black dots disappear off into the distance. From the video feed, he saw Aurier swat at one of them before bringing his eye back to the Janzai's scope.

Harlan brought a foot up to the hole in the pod in front of him, but kept moving it upward.

Aurier fired, but the DFDs had messed with his aim, and the shot went flying into the ceiling, clouding Harlan in dust and debris, but this was the break he wanted.

He hopped to his feet, took a deep breath, and sprinted down the atrium toward Aurier, all the while hoping he hadn't miscounted or misremembered the Janzai's capacity.

He got about halfway when he saw Aurier fumble around for another magazine.

The old man looked up from his position behind a half-meter-tall wall, his eyes widening as he tried to reload the heavy Janzai. The weapon shook, and Aurier's attention went from the weapon to Harlan.

The two DFDs buzzed around Aurier, but to give him credit, he ignored them and stuck to his task, even as they flew into his grimacing face. His cheeks were red and sweat stuck his thinning white hair to his scalp. His lips curled with a smirk.

Aurier raised the rifle.

Harlan pumped his legs as hard as he could and, when he got close enough, jumped with everything he had left, shouting as he flew through the air, fists balled, knees raised to his chest.

Aurier's eyes went wide. He pulled the trigger.

The Janzai recoiled.

The bullet went harmlessly low.

Aurier's mouth fell open as he realized what was about to happen.

With his feet first, Harlan landed on the older man's chest, knocking him back. The Janzai clattered to the ground. Aurier tried to push himself free, but physically wasn't a match for a furious, adrenaline-fueled Harlan Rubik, who pummeled a right and then a left hook into Aurier's face, crunching nose cartilage and loosening teeth.

Unable to break out of the rage, Harlan rained down blows until Alex Aurier's body went limp and his face was nothing more than a bloodied mess of meat and bone.

Exhausted from the attack, Harlan rolled off Aurier and slumped to the ground.

Aurier's chest rose and fell slowly. A wheezing noise came from the man's ruined nose. Harlan regained his feet, took the Janzai, and threw it over his shoulder with the attached strap. He stood up and staggered over to the wall where he rested to catch his breath.

Gylfie's image appeared on his communicator. "Nice work, Harlan. Been a while since I've seen you move that fast."

"My body is letting me know that it's been a while, too. Running is just awful."

"Sure, but it beats being shot to pieces."

"I can't argue with that. Thanks for the help, boss. You saved my ass."

"Anytime. If you're okay finishing up, I need to divert my attention elsewhere. Looks like the SMF is closing in on my hideaway."

"Do you have another place to go?"

"Always, Harlan. It'll take a millennium for anyone to find me on this station. Good luck."

With that, the comm channel went quiet, but only for a brief second.

Bella's panicked face appeared on his screen. "Damn you, Harlan, I've been trying to contact you for ages. What the hell's going on? You said you'd be a few minutes. We've got the SMF on our asses and we need to go. Where the hell are you?"

"I ran into some resistance here, but it's taken care of. I'll be at the airlock shortly. Hang tight."

She continued to rant at him, but he shut the connection down, eager to finish up with Aurier, who groaned and attempted to sit up, but could only lift his head. He spat a wad of blood and teeth from his mouth and regarded Harlan with a grimace.

With a wet rattle to his words, the old man said, "Too much of a pussy to finish the job?"

The insult flew over Harlan's head as freely as an ill-aimed shot. "I want you to pay, so I'll let the SMF deal with you. When I expose Vanguard, you'll be one of the first to face justice. I assume you've been a Vanguard member since you first joined the runners with Hugo all those decades ago?"

Aurier just laughed. "You have no idea, Harlan. You always were the lost little boy, weren't you? Even your best friend in the orphanage clued into things way before you."

"Luca? I know he's trying to hack the QCA. I wouldn't call that being clued in. I would call that a cowardly act of treason against the people of the Sol-Fed. You'll both never see freedom again when I'm done with you."

Harlan stood up and loomed over his old colleague's battered form.

Even now, when he was clearly beaten, Aurier seemed not to care. The loyalty Vanguard appeared to generate from people clearly knew no bounds. It was so strong, in fact, that Hugo and Gandit had killed themselves.

At least Hugo had the decency to recognize his cowardice.

"You make me sick. You think you're somehow superior, part of something bigger, but look at you. You're nothing but a used-up tool. You think those running Vanguard care about you? You're nothing to them. All these years you've served have been for nothing."

Aurier shook his head as he tried and failed to raise himself up onto his elbows. "You're wrong. It wasn't for nothing. If it wasn't for me, little Luca Doe would still be running around after you, two clueless orphans in search of parental figures. I set him free. I put him on the path to greatness, and he's going to deliver true freedom to all of humanity. You think what we have now is freedom?" He coughed and spat more blood onto the ground as he built up his energy. "You think those damned abbots have us in mind for their future? You say I'm nothing to Vanguard, but the truth is, we're nothing to the abbots, and Vanguard is going to change that. Luca will cut them loose from the QCA. Let's see how the abbots manage when they don't have a centralized control system to rely on. Then we'll see which species has a future."

"You're deluded if you think that. As for Luca—I know him better than you ever could. But he'll get what's owed to him soon enough."

Harlan turned his back and made his way toward the airlock while he prepared a segment of video to send to the SMF for Aurier's arrest.

He got halfway when Aurier cleared his throat and shouted, "It was me, you know. The death of your precious mentor, the sweet, wise, stoic Marius Rubik... how touching that he gave you his surname. You, his prized pupil. How disappointed he would be in you if he could see you now. You'll be pleased to hear that your hero died a true stoic. He didn't blink an eyelid when I slipped the knife into his heart. He accepted his failure, just like you will. Just like you have to face up to the fact that your little secret, Milo, has never been a secret."

Harlan had no rage left.

Only sadness at what had happened to Marius.

He knew that he should follow his mentor's lessons and be even-tempered. Marius was dead now, so Aurier's revelation wouldn't change anything. There would be no reason to get emotionally invested.

Aurier was right about one thing: Marius *would* be disappointed.

Disappointed that Harlan gave in to emotion, raised the Janzai, calmly located Aurier's smug, bloodied face in the middle of the scope, and pulled the trigger, blowing Aurier's head apart like a child's water balloon.

The kill didn't make him feel any better. He knew it wouldn't, but it didn't matter. The only thing that mattered now was that Harlan get aboard the *Goat* and dispense justice to the rest of the Vanguard group.

He slung the rifle back over his shoulder and reached to the brain-computer interface on the back of his cranium, where he activated the release and pulled out the tiny chip that held the programming for his peripheral.

Gylfie was right all along. He didn't need it.

Milo had become a liability, a tool with which Vanguard could stay one step ahead of him. He wondered just how long they'd had access to it. It all made sense now, though: the abbot attacking them at Fizon's apartment, the two that tried to stop them from getting off Turing Station, Aurier finding Harlan here at the G4 airlock, and Leanne's and Hugo's warnings.

No more.

He threw the chip to the ground and crushed it into pieces with the heel of his boot.

It was time to forget all his failures, near-misses, tragedies, and crutches. It was time for Harlan to put all that aside and do what he did best.

Be who he was.

Hugo's note to him came to mind: *Trust your gut, Harlan. Data isn't as reliable as you think it is: it can be manipulated and used against you.*

He sent Bella an updated message. "Prepare the shuttle's airlock. I'll be coming in fast."

32

H arlan wondered, not for the first time, if he had gone completely insane. Here he was, standing in a pressurized airlock without a functional suit. On the other side of the door was the shuttle, its airlock open and aligned to within a few degrees here or there.

Bella had tried to talk him out of it. So too Irena. Greta thought it was the funniest thing she'd ever heard. Yet, despite that, here Harlan stood, one hand on the grip bar, the other hand hovering over the lever that would blast open the door.

He had visualized how it would work: the door would slide up into its housing in less than half a second. Pressure from within the airlock would extinguish out into the vacuum of space, forcing out anything untethered— including himself.

The shuttle managed to get within twenty meters. A few calculations later, Harlan knew this was the only way. He'd be exposed to the cold vacuum for no longer than twenty seconds given the rate of velocity generated from the pressure.

Experiments on humans—back before society had reorganized itself—had shown that depending on the individual, exposure up to two minutes could be tolerated quite safely without any major injury after revival.

That he would pass out was a given. That would take approximately fifteen seconds due to hypoxia: the pressure levels in space being much lower than what the human body was used to within a pressurized atmosphere such as the station.

Whether he would reach the ship before unconsciousness took him would remain a mystery; he didn't have the time to calculate all the variables. Responsibility to catch him if he drifted off axis would be down to those on the *Goat*. It was, without a doubt, the ultimate trust exercise.

To help protect himself as much as possible, he had donned the least damaged suit. He would still be at the mercy of the cold and the vacuum over time, but it was better than nothing and, like all Atlas-issue suits, it included a suite of drugs to help combat the effects of pressure exposure. Given how little time he ought to be exposed, he probably wouldn't need them, but it was always useful to know he had backup. If, psychologically, it made him feel safer, he was happy to go with it.

A little delusion never hurt anyone when it came to facing the cold indifference of space.

He spent a short while going through a series of pre-breathing exercises as taught by station security to all inhabitants. It helped negate the inevitable effects of anoxia and, by making sure his lungs were empty when he launched, would prevent them from rupturing, which, by all accounts, was never a fun experience.

Bella's voice sounded taut with tension over the comm

channel. "Are you ready? We need to do this in the next few seconds: The SMF have spotted us."

"I'm ready now if you are."

"On three, then?"

"Sure, run the count."

"One... two... three..."

Harlan exhaled sharply, yanked the lever, and tensed his bicep to hold his position until the door had completely retracted. He felt the pull immediately as air rushed out, whipping at his suit, dragging at him until he could hold no longer.

With the exterior door now completely open, Harlan let himself go, pointing his body forward as though he were a deep-sea diver, aiming toward the rear of the shuttle.

Irena, Greta, and Bashir stood inside the *Goat*'s airlock, their faces masks of stress and concentration. Harlan locked eyes with Irena. She appeared to reflect the terror that he felt in his guts as he flew across the open void, his body temperature dropping rapidly, and his internal fluids approaching the limit to where they would undergo evaporative cooling.

As he fast approached the shuttle, and despite telling himself he wouldn't, he looked around. Other than the *Goat* and what looked like an SMF gunship approaching from behind the station, everywhere else was deep black, empty, unfathomable.

A boiling sensation on his tongue drew his attention away.

His body tightened with fear, and his guts cramped. He reached his arms out toward the *Goat* as he drew closer, but his vision blurred. A shadow around the perimeter of his gaze encroached further until, finally, he could hold it no

longer and passed out just a meter or so away from Irena's
outstretched hands.

HARLAN WOKE with Bashir standing over him, a large syringe
in his hands. Harlan sucked in a deep breath. His lungs
burned and his entire body writhed with muscular cramps.
Irena was standing to his left in a dark area of the shuttle he
recognized as the airlock.

He wasn't in his suit anymore; that lay in pieces to
one side.

"Hold still," Bashir said, coming closer. "We need to treat
you for the exposure. Your blood pH is off. This will help
with that and any nitrogen that might have built up."

Irena crouched to his side, placing a hand on his shoulder. Harlan noticed she had changed into a new space suit.
"You're okay. You were only exposed for seventeen seconds,
and we re-pressurized you immediately. It should mitigate
any lasting internal damage."

"How long was I out?"

"Only a couple of minutes."

Bashir jabbed Harlan painfully during the short conversation. "Sorry. I'm not trained in applied medicine. How do
you feel?"

"Cold, cramped, and I have a pounding headache."

Irena consulted her wrist terminal. "Your life signs are
good. Although I don't know how long that will be the case.
The SSF *Wickham* has ordered us to stand down or face
total destruction."

"Tell Bella to stall them a minute. I need to get my facul-
ties back."

With that, Harlan lifted his head, then his torso, until he was straddling the bench on which they had placed him. He held back the desire to vomit due to light-headedness and vertigo, but with each breath, he began to feel a fraction better. It would take time until he was fighting fit, but during the journey to Earth, he'd have a few hours to recuperate. But first, what to do about the *Wickham*?

"Could you two help me into the main hold? We need to discuss a plan."

While Bashir and Irena helped Harlan into the main section of the shuttle, he listened to Bella's conversation with Captain Saffile of the *Wickham*. That the latter sounded like a self-important asshole didn't come as any surprise.

Throughout Harlan's career as a silicon runner, he'd run into many members of the upper hierarchy of the SMF. The space fleet was by far the worst. He wasn't completely sure why that was—he theorized that it was perhaps the result of spending too much time in space in cramped conditions with no one to question their authority, each ship a tiny fiefdom of their own to rule.

A number of captains over the years had been court-martialed and imprisoned for horrific abuses of power. Saffile, with his nasal voice, exuded a self-possession born of unchallenged authority. And the more he ordered Bella to stand down and prepare for boarding, the more a plan came to Harlan's mind. It would be risky, but then what was new? Everything in the known universe was a careful balance of risk versus reward. To get bigger rewards, one had to risk a little more. There was no way of cheating that universal law, even if some people believed they could beat the odds. It'd bite them on the ass, eventually.

It was one of Harlan's mentor, Marius's, favorite life lessons. One could wander through life never reaching for anything, mentally or physically, just going with the flow. That required no effort and therefore no risk. The other choice, however, was to always strive, always reach for betterment, but being cognizant of the attached risk and determining whether the worst-case scenario was worth it.

What life was it to never seek an understanding of oneself or of one's environment, whether that be the station, the solar system, or farther beyond? It was only small thinking that eroded the soul. The small thinking that created the abuse of power as shown by various captains and bosses over the years. It was this thinking that led to grandiose delusion and the rise of shared insanity as exemplified by Vanguard and Luca.

The latter didn't risk being better. He took the easy route: promises of power if he took the road of least resistance. It was much harder to be decent in this fragmented, difficult society than to give in to a life of criminal and selfish motivations.

To oppose Vanguard and their plans, to expose them for what they were—now that was worth doing. Even if on the other end of the scale, the weight of risk seemed gargantuan.

But that was the crux of it, Harlan realized. He was prepared to risk everything for the reward. He accepted the worst-case scenario and would continue until the very end, whatever the results might be.

Now was not the time to be timid.

And so, the plan came to him whole.

Bashir and Irena helped Harlan into the hold. Bella poked her head through the bulkhead from the cockpit.

"How much fuel do we have?" Harlan asked her.

"Not enough to reach Earth on a two-g burn with all this maneuvering, especially if we have to escape the *Wickham*."

"So even if we do escape, we haven't got enough to get there in time?"

"It's looking unlikely."

"That's fine. We're not escaping."

The rest of the crew stared at Harlan with expectation.

Wilbur scratched his neck. "I sense you have something up your sleeve, as the old saying goes. Does it entail any of us getting killed?"

"I's a possibility, but then it's a greater possibility if we don't do anything. We don't have the fuel capacity to reach Earth in time now. We don't have the weapons required to defeat the *Wickham*, and we can't outrun them in open space. They won't let us go—we don't know if any of those on board are members of Vanguard, and we can't risk capture. Our fates are already sealed."

Greta regarded the wall of weapons. "We fight them hand-to-hand, then."

Harlan shook his head. "And face murder charges on our return? No, think bigger." When no one spoke, he added, "We're boarding the *Wickham* and taking it for ourselves. It has more than enough capacity to reach the castle, not to mention weapons if we need them. But we're not killing anyone."

Irena caught Harlan's gaze. She wore a now-familiar determined expression. "And how do you propose we do that?"

"All will be revealed shortly." Harlan then looked through to the cockpit and then back to the rest of the crew. "Wilbur, I need you to hide under the console in the cockpit."

"Why me?"

"You're the smallest and the only one that will fit. I need to be in the cockpit when the goons come aboard. Now, everyone listen up. I've got a plan to explain, and we only have one shot at it."

33

Harlan placed the rifle to the side of the cockpit's bulkhead and arranged the assortment of grenades within a section of webbing on the opposite side. From beneath the shuttle's console, Wilbur's face poked out, only adding to his mole-like appearance.

"I don't like this at all, Harlan. It's not going to work."

Harlan shushed him and gently pushed him deeper beneath the *Goat*'s console so he wasn't visible. "If I hear so much as a breath out of you, I will kill you. Understand?"

Wilbur tapped twice against his leg.

"Good. Now wait for my cue and don't do anything unless I tell you to."

Two more taps.

Harlan turned his head and looked through to the hold. Bella, Greta, Bashir, and Irena were cuffed to the bench seat. Their hands were wrapped in makeshift manacles using the meat storage supplies from Sanjeet's prior business. As per the plan, they looked like a criminal gang. Well, on some level they were, Harlan reminded himself. This would only aid in his plan.

Once he was satisfied with everything, he gave the crew his final command: they pulled the cloth gags over their mouths and waited. Irena's chest was rising and falling quickly, and sweat dripped down her face, adding to the illusion.

Taking a deep breath to compose himself, he opened the comm channel to the *Wickham*.

"Captain Saffile, this is Harlan Rubik, senior investigative officer of the silicon runners. I've taken control of this vessel and placed the crew under arrest. I would like to request that you dock with us and take the crew into custody."

At first there was no response.

Harlan's headache continued to jackhammer inside his skull, making it hard to concentrate, but he forced himself to relax, breathe, and wait.

Nearly a minute passed before he received a response.

"Mr. Rubik. I've received your request, but before we can go any further, I need to confirm your identity. Send your credentials to the following encrypted identification service."

"I can assure you I am who I say am."

"Are you the idiot we just witnessed floating through free space?"

"The very same. Although I'm by no means an idiot. I've spent the last few days infiltrating this gang of scavengers, gaining their confidence. I have them detained in the hold. I'm forwarding the camera feed so you can see."

Another minute ticked by.

"Our facial recognition confirms the criminal statuses of three of your prisoners. But we're concerned about why you have the daughter of potential presidential candidate

Victoria Selles. Explain yourself, Mr. Rubik—and confirm your identification. We won't ask again."

With nothing to lose, Harlan let his terminal transfer his DNA reading and stored credentials to the secure ID link he received from Saffle. It was a standard procedure, and he'd done it hundreds of times before when working with government organizations, but he was hesitant due to not knowing if Hugo, or perhaps even Alex Aurier, had altered his status within the silicon runners. But after a few seconds of flashing dots, an affirmative beep sounded and the status message read:

ID SUCCESSFULLY TRANSFERRED...
  Facial Recognition: Positive.
  Identification: Positive.
  Registered Name: Harlan Rubik.
  Residential status: Atlas Station resident, Tier-3 privilege.
  Role: Senior investigative officer, department: Silicon Runners.
  Rights: Investigative rights. Full movement rights.
  Philosophy Membership: Stoic.
  Parents: None. State Orphan.
  Marriage Status: Married. Separated.
  Dependents: None.
  DNA Code confirmation: DB-5809-KK-331.

"YOUR IDENTIFICATION DETAILS ARE CONFIRMED, Mr. Rubik. Now, about Irena Selles..."

"She's in league with the group, Captain. My investigations found that she met them during her time on Earth working for the ERP. When Station Nord was attacked, and the rogue abbot and all members from the scientific group were killed, I became suspicious that Irena was the only survivor. I believe that she was working with the group to identify places of low radiation from which to scavenge and later trade contraband, which, as you know, is a crime. In my line of work, a person's heritage or family name doesn't matter. The law is the law. Of that I'm sure we're in agreement."

Harlan looked at his terminal. They were quickly running out of time and would need to boost to Earth with more than two g to make up for lost time. Without waiting for a reply, he continued, "This shuttle has just a few minutes of air. During their evasion, they damaged their systems. I request an immediate transfer so I can take them back to Atlas Station for processing."

Yet another delay as the dim-witted captain was likely thinking things over. Each second was punctuated by a stabbing pain in Harlan's head. He was going to need some heavy-duty painkillers in the very near future—if things worked out as planned.

"Your request is approved, Mr. Rubik. Prepare for boarding."

Harlan pumped his fist and shut off the comm. Then to the crew: "Okay, everyone. The bait is set. You guys just need to create enough of a ruckus to give me the opportunity. Avoid killing or hurting anyone. This is it, brace yourselves." He then bent down and stared at Wilbur beneath the console. "And you, stay where you are and don't move— unless something happens to me; then it's on you. Okay?"

Wilbur nervously nodded his head and slunk back into the shadows.

A short moment later the *Goat* rocked forward violently. The sound of motors whirred, sending vibrations throughout the hull. Harlan stood up and readied himself.

Irena looked up at him, fear in her eyes. "You'll be okay," he mouthed to her. "Trust me."

She nodded and turned, along with the rest of the crew, to face the rear of the ship as the airlock door opened and the first two SMF soldiers entered.

A shot of adrenaline fired through Harlan's nervous system.

The two armed women stormed inside, rifles held ready.

Harlan and Bella shared a quick look, and Harlan nodded.

Bella then shot up from her seated position and pretended to struggle with the restraints. The two women dashed forward to her, and a further SMF soldier stepped over the threshold. Given the stripes on his lapel, Harlan knew this was Captain Saffile. One look at him confirmed his earlier prediction: he was a smug prick.

"What the hell is going on here?" Saffile demanded. "Control that woman."

With that, Harlan reached down for the webbing, pulled out a knock-out grenade, armed it, and rolled it along the floor. The ruckus that Bella and the others had created meant no one saw it coming.

Saffile glared up at Harlan and was about to remonstrate him when Harlan simply closed the bulkhead and counted to three. A loud, booming thud confirmed the grenade had gone off. Harlan, with his heart racing and breath ragged, grabbed another two grenades and counted to sixty for the chemical compound to dissipate. He then opened the bulkhead and dashed over the still bodies of the crew and the SMF soldiers.

Another couple, the pilot and gunner, Harlan presumed, were approaching the airlock, scanning their way, their rifles up at their chests. Harlan threw one of the grenades and turned back as it went off. Without wasting any time, he readied the confusion grenade he had taken from the guard outside Hugo's apartment and tossed it through the airlock, deep into the *Wickham*'s hull, just in case there were more soldiers inside.

A couple of shouts followed, and then silence.

Harlan leapt over the prone bodies and headed back to the cockpit. He retrieved his rifle, then made his way to the *Wickham*. Once inside the SMF vessel, he moved slower, more deliberately, checking all corners and shadows. He confirmed the crew of five were incapacitated, breathing, and unhurt. They would be unconscious for at least four or more hours.

As for Irena, Bella, and the rest, he'd bring them around using the standard-issue med-kit within the small but fully functioning med-bay aboard the *Wickham*. He confirmed that it was fully stocked. He'd been planning on that. It was rare for any combat to take place these days, so unless someone injured themselves during maintenance, there was likely no reason to use the supplies.

He made his way back onto the *Goat* and checked on the crew. Like the SMF soldiers, they were unconscious, but all okay according to their vital signs.

"Wilbur, it worked," Harlan said. "I need your help now. Are you okay?"

The small man eased out from under the console and nodded. "I'm good. I hope everyone else is going to be okay when they wake up."

"They'll be fine. Just help me get them onto the *Wickham*."

One by one, they took Bella, Irena, Bashir, and Greta from one ship to the other, removing the gags and makeshift restraints. They stowed their prone forms into the various individual bunks of the ship. There were eight in total, meaning plenty of space for everyone, and each one equipped with its own personal SMF-issue med-kit— smaller than the one in the med-bay, but with all the essentials required for small wounds and ailments.

"What are we doing with the *Wickham* crew exactly?" Wilbur asked.

"Firstly, we make sure they have enough food and water rations for a few days. I've programmed the autopilot to send the *Goat* on a long orbit around Luna. We'll have plenty of time to get to Earth and back. And don't worry, they won't be able to override the program. They'll be stuck, but alive and well."

"What's stopping them from reporting us the minute they wake up? The SMF still have a number of military bases on Earth after all."

"None that are that close to where we'll be going. And besides, I've sabotaged the comm unit. Unless they can conjure wiring and components from thin air, they're stuck until the autopilot delivers them safely back to Asimovia."

"Sanjeet isn't going to be happy that you've messed with his ship."

"With all due respect, Wilbur, do you think I give a shit about Sanjeet's feelings right now? There're bigger things to worry about. I'll throw him a favor later if we survive."

"They're going to string you up by the neck when you get back."

"That might well be the case, but if we're successful, I'll worry about the SMF then. Let's just focus on the job at hand. We need to bring the crew around and get up to speed." Harlan checked his terminal. "We're going to have to thrust up to two-point-three g now to get to Earth. Let's get busy."

Between the two of them, and using the drugs in the med-kits, they managed to bring the crew around and get them stabilized. Harlan activated the *Goat*'s autopilot, which sent it off into a long journey around Luna. He also left a file on the ship's system apologizing and explaining that he didn't mean anyone any harm and that he would gladly explain his actions upon his return. Naturally he didn't say from where he'd be returning; he couldn't take the risk of the SMF group potentially harboring a Vanguard member.

He just hoped that if they did survive their confrontation with Luca, he would be able to recover enough evidence to expose Vanguard and end their plans for good.

34

Even with the drugs to help against the effects of two-point-three g of thrust, Harlan's muscles and bones ached as though they were being pulverized by a very slow industrial compacting machine. Despite that, the drugs helped him sleep for just over half the journey. And to his great relief, his headache had also dissipated.

He shifted his body within the confines of the gel-layered crash couch, stretching his legs out along the full length. To his right, on the other side of the bunk, Irena lay in a fetal position, her arms wrapped around her knees. She breathed steadily, her exhales coming in shorter bursts due to the pressure on her lungs.

Harlan felt it, too, a weight pressing down on his chest.

A large terminal beside the bunk's door showed him the varied metrics of their journey. At some point during his drug-assisted sleep, they had experienced the halfway mark of zero gravity, where the *Wickham*'s engines rotated from forward to reverse thrust, slowing their velocity so that they could slip into the correct orbit for a safe approach to Earth. Given the time the QCA had left before it was compromised, they had a short window within which to stop Luca when they arrived.

Harlan and Bella had discussed the best route. They had decided on coming in just over the equator, where the weather systems were currently at their least severe. No one fancied the prospect of dropping into Earth's atmosphere and right into one of the extreme weather systems that now ravaged the planet on a daily basis.

The fact that Luca had set up his base of operations among the ruins of the Neuschwanstein Castle was no accident. Given the elevation, the nineteenth-century castle had escaped the flooding from the nearby Forggensee lake. Most of the low-lying land had been swallowed up. The area was also one of the lowest in the northern hemisphere for radiation levels, having escaped the China-Russia exchange during the War.

The choice of location also made sense from a travel perspective: one of the first Edwards Elevators to be built lay a few hundred miles to the east, providing easy access to space and, among the alpine mountain range, serving as a substation for one of the world-spanning maglev rings—a Birch Loop—which Harlan had decided they would use to get close to the castle. They'd save fuel that way and should have plenty for the return journey.

Without the use of the loop and the elevator, they'd have to burn all their remaining fuel just to escape Earth's gravity well, and even that wasn't a sure thing.

"Hey, how are you feeling?" Irena's voice was croaky and strained, but she sounded positive. Perhaps it was relief.

"Given the circumstances, pretty good, though I'll be glad when we're out of this thrust."

"I have to warn you, Harlan. Even though Atlas and the other stations have their artificial gravity, it'll still feel different on the surface. It took me a while to get used to real planetary conditions."

"With any luck, we won't be here long enough to notice."

Irena's face shifted to a darker, more serious expression. "Do you think we'll make it... survive, I mean? Luca's clearly a madman. Who knows what defensive strategies he has ready to employ?"

Harlan had been thinking about this. Although Luca was no fool, he was, ultimately, a pragmatist. "Considering how Vanguard has been hiding in the shadows all this time, it would be difficult, I think, for him to organize anything too elaborate. That he's in an old ruin tells me he wanted to stay under the radar and probably didn't expect anyone to find him. And why would he? They've had all his planned for weeks, if not months. And I'm sure they wouldn't have expected us to uncover their secrets."

"I hope that's the case. We could use a break. I can't help but be hesitant, though."

"The thing with Luca is that he has a deep-rooted sense of superiority and arrogance. Even when we were kids— now that I look back on it—he showed signs that he thought he was more capable, smarter, and above the other orphans."

"That's good for us." Irena took a few deep breaths before continuing. "It means he underestimates you—and us. Probably always has; hence why he thought he could get away with faking his death. That gives us the advantage."

"Assuming he doesn't spot us coming. There is the very real chance that he's scanning with radar and other tech-nologies just to be on the safe side. We have to assume we're going to encounter resistance. How much... I guess we'll have to wait and see. At least we have a gunship now. I certainly feel better about it than I did with the prospect of making the journey in the *Goat*."

Irena and Harlan locked eyes and said nothing for a moment. The scale of the situation pressed on them as heavily as the gravity generated by the ship's thrust.

"Harlan... if things don't go well, I just wanted... well, I—"

"We're making it back alive," Harlan said, ending the sentiment immediately. He didn't want to bring too much emotion into the situation. "Let's just focus on one thing at a time."

"Aye, Captain." She gave him a quick smile and then looked away. Her cheeks had reddened. Harlan wanted to say something to reduce her embarrassment. He said nothing, though, not wanting to let himself get distracted. He had to see this whole thing as though it were just another case file.

The future of the Sol-Fed, and possibly that of humanity, was on the line.

Justice first. Emotion second. That was what Marius would have told him. A good stoic takes things as they come. He doesn't let emotion dictate his actions. Stoics put the larger scheme before their own desires. Harlan had never been as good a stoic as Marius, but he was willing to keep trying.

After checking in with the rest of the crew, he activated the sleep drugs to ensure he was as rested as possible upon their arrival. He suspected he was going to need every ounce of energy he could find.

A GRINDING NOISE woke Harlan from his assisted slumber. At

first, he wasn't sure where he was and struggled against the straps around his chest and legs.

"Hold still. We're preparing to enter atmosphere."

Harlan blinked and tried to focus. "Irena? That you?"

"Yeah, it's me. Bella warned it's going to be a little bumpy for a while." Irena indicated with a nod toward the terminal screen on the wall of their shared bunk.

The external video feed showed the tips of the telescopic, backswept wings moving into place, converting the gunship from a space-bound vessel into one suitable for atmospheric flight. The grinding noise stopped when the wings locked in.

"Sorry," Harlan said. "I was a little disoriented. The sleep drugs always do that to me."

"You were fidgeting a lot in your sleep."

"And you were watching me?"

Irena shrugged, then smiled. "I was still awake, and didn't have much else to do. I forgot to pack a good book or holofilm."

"As long as I was entertaining... "

He sat up, stretched his legs ahead of him, and pulled the chest straps down while he remained in a seated position. Irena moved over and sat next to him and did the same with another pair inset into the bunk's wall.

Bella's voice echoed over the ship's internal comm system. "Listen up, people, the weather systems aren't too bad, but they're not that great either. It will be a little bumpy with the turbulence. A countdown and a lovely view of this blasted planet are available on the terminal screens for your traveling pleasure."

"This is it, then," Irena said, turning away from Harlan to look at the screen.

The video feed showed the glowing ball of blue and

white that was once humanity's home. The image grew larger until it dominated the display. With every minute, the view resolved further as they made their way through the various layers of atmosphere. The cloud layer began as a thick white curtain but gave way to a patchy texture. This fragmented layer eventually gave way until the video feed was now showing the Atlantic Ocean and the northern hemisphere, populated by north Africa and Europe.

Harlan had seen these land masses on maps and video feeds for years, but to be here now and see them with his own eyes was a humbling experience. To think that his ancestors were born right down there in a barely visible tract of land once known as Greece gave him a sense of connectedness he'd not felt for some time.

It was not the feeling of coming home like so many other space-born people suggest. The sense of him being some kind of invading alien remained. His connection to Earth was just an abstract idea, ephemeral and easily dissolved with the anxiety he felt about coming here. A rumbling noise pulled him out of his thoughts. The gunship's terrestrial engines came online, presumably to help stabilize the craft as it descended through pockets of turbulence.

"I hate this part," Harlan said. "Haven't been down to the surface for years."

The ship rocked violently, the hull groaning against the battering of their velocity through the winds and changing of atmospheric pressure. On the screen, wisps of cloud whipped by. Below the feed, the local time read 09:12 a.m. Harlan considered making a joke about being on time for breakfast, but thought better of it.

Irena reached out and grabbed his hand. He squeezed back and said, "It's going to be fine. Bella's crew have been up and down from the planet to Atlas more times than I can count."

"This isn't my first time, either, but it doesn't stop my guts from tightening."

A high-pitched keening noise came from somewhere toward the rear of the ship's hull. The auxiliary engines, designed for in-planet maneuvering, kicked up a notch with an initial thud, then a roar. The force pushed against Harlan's chest. And then they were banking.

It took a great deal of effort to turn his head to look at the screen.

When he did, he saw the first snatches of land and water. The latter was a rich blue, as natural as anything he had seen, even though he knew most of the life within had long since ceased to exist. All the oceans contained now were giant shoals of jellyfish. The very same organisms that had blocked the water inflow of many of the world's nuclear power stations, leading to untold devastation. That was even before the nukes started flying across continents, the results of which were evident in the land below. The screen told them they were flying at Mach 4. The gunship's hull was reaching hundreds of degrees in temperature, but the special alloy was able to dissipate the heat into sinks, which converted it back into energy.

Although Harlan was no hardware buff, during a previous case he had come across one of Atlas Station's most respected aeronautical designers and had picked up some knowledge that went into making these amazing machines.

The ship was clearly capable of flying a lot faster, but given the unpredictable weather, it wasn't worth it, and they had to conserve fuel. The timer told Harlan they were actually a few minutes ahead of schedule, so Harlan was confident in Bella's piloting skills.

After a few minutes, Bella had stopped banking and maneuvering the ship now that they were out of the worst of the turbulence and flying closer to the planet's surface. The ship was speeding along toward the Birch Loop station.

Harlan saw it on the feed: one of a dozen world-spanning tracks. Barely two meters wide, the track enabled advanced maglev travel. He remembered reading how, with the help of the first abbots, humanity had constructed the loops over a twenty-year period. It was one of the biggest projects the planet had ever seen—until human and abbotkind had moved into space and started building stations and mining facilities.

As the ship flew just a few hundred meters above the maglev ribbon, Bella eased the throttle and reduced their speed. They approached the station slowly, using the gunship's various multidirectional thrusters to maneuver onto one of the loop sleds. With an abrupt thud, the ship landed on the sled, and the magnet locks restrained the *Wickham* in place.

Bella spoke over the comm channel. "We're on the loop, guys. The system's status is online, and we're confirmed to disembark shortly. ETA to the castle in about thirty minutes. I suggest we use this time to arm up and get ready for a hostile reception."

Harlan removed the chest straps and opened the comm channel on his terminal. "Bella's right. We should expect resistance. This ship has a full complement of gear, courtesy of Captain Saffile and friends. I suggest we use it. But given the ruined nature of the castle, don't weigh yourselves down too much. We'll also split into two teams: a home and away team."

Bashir and Greta both gave their affirmatives.

Wilbur asked, "Who are in the respective teams?"

"I'll let you know that when we get there, Wilbur. I'm still thinking about that."

Irena looked to Harlan with a concerned expression. Just to her, Harlan said, "I'd like you to stay with the ship. I don't know what's in the castle, but I do know I need your analytical skills. You'll be safer here, too."

"No need to wrap me up in cotton wool. You know I can handle myself."

"Which is why I need you to help guard the ship. I also need your expert eyes and ears. If you get hurt inside the castle... I need your analytical skills where they matter."

"I get it. I'll do my best. And don't worry so much. We've got this."

Although he appreciated her positive words, she didn't know Luca like he did. She didn't know what he was capable of. If they all got out alive, Harlan would consider it a success, but he knew it was highly unlikely. Before the day was out, there would be blood spilled and lives lost; that much he knew was a statistical certainty.

"We better get ready," he said. "Come on, I'll help you get suited and armed."

"Lead the way."

Harlan and Irena left their bunk and made their way down the narrow corridor of the gunship until they reached the armory. They stepped inside and inventoried the available weapons. "One thing's for sure," Harlan said as he opened a case of handguns, "we've got some serious firepower here to give Luca a bad day."

He just hoped it would be enough.

35

T he front most spire at the main palace of the Neuschwanstein Castle hove into view. The heavy rain obscured the rest of the structure in thick gray sheets. Dark clouds hid the horizon and ominously held a warning of what was to come.

Harlan didn't care; he didn't plan on being outside for very long. He knew that somewhere inside, Luca was using Fizon to hack the QCA. Harlan planned on stopping his former brother one way or another.

Bella piloted the craft skillfully, even with the gale blowing about them.

More of the castle became visible as they drew ever closer. A series of three landing pads were attached to the pitched roof of the rearmost section. Each pad was braced against the central, and tallest, tower. The castle featured a mix of styles, converging the gothic with the kitsch and simple geometric shapes.

According to Harlan's terminal readout, the castle was built in honor of Richard Wagner, the style apparently designed to evoke a fairytale ideal. It certainly did that, with its spires, grand courtyards, and elevated position.

Yet it hadn't escaped modernity.

At some point in its recent history, it had been converted and upgraded with great steel stanchions, landing pads, and docking rings, giving the structure a weird contrast of the historical and the contemporary. The grandiose nature of its original design was right up Luca's street, Harlan thought. He was never one to appreciate the simple; he always wanted more glamour, all the better to bolster his fragile, power-hungry ego.

But if Harlan had his way, that was about to end —for good.

Having finished arming himself and getting suited up, Harlan returned to his bunk with Irena and strapped in, mostly out of habit. It felt as if he'd been strapped into the crash couch for an eternity already. But then, two days under thrust would do that, the drugs coursing through his body to combat against sickness also having the effect of twisting one's perception of time and place.

The latter was no problem, though. Harlan was well aware of his position and place.

"You look as though you have the weight of the universe on your shoulders," Irena said from her position next to him.

"It feels like I do." He glanced at his terminal: they had less than forty minutes before the QCA fell into Vanguard's hands. "But it's fine. It's good. It means I'm focused. In light of the situation, that's not such a bad—"

An explosion outside the ship rocked him violently to the side, the straps biting into his shoulders.

Irena slammed into him, and they struggled to stay upright in a tangle of arms and legs as the ship shuddered.

The sound of rending mental and whirring engines was deafening in the small confines of the bunk. The ship lurched to the side, the nose dipped, and they were spiraling out of control.

"What the hell's happening?" Harlan shouted over the comm channel.

Wilbur was the first to respond. "We've been hit. There's a goddamned abbot on the roof with a railgun. We've lost primary engines, scanners, processing units... half the damn ship is gone."

"We're going in for a crash landing," Bella added, her voice strained as she fought the g-force of the out-of-control ship. "Everyone, assume the worst and hold the hell on."

Irena gripped Harlan's arm as they fell headlong toward one of the landing pads.

Bella brought the ship into a controlled descent, stopping its spinning motion and leveling it out for the final drop. A sharp jolt ran up Harlan's spine and into his shoulders as the couch's smart gel attempted to compensate, but the material wasn't designed for such an event.

Irena screamed when the ship smashed into the steel of the landing pad. Metal-on-metal screeching drowned all commotion on the comm channel. It felt like they would slide right off the side and down into the valley below. But with a secondary jolt, the ship came to a violent stop, throwing Harlan and Irena forward before the smart gel hardened around their bodies and the strapping pulled them back in.

Harlan then became aware of all the alarms sounding.

The terminal in the bunk flashed with a red and black alert. The rear of the ship was on fire. The automatic systems were activated, filling the area with nano-foam. Some of it came into Harlan's bunk.

Then he heard crying, a wild, primal wail. Greta. "He's hurt bad! Bashir's... I think he's dead. Cut to frigging pieces in the wreckage. That bastard out there... it'll pay for this."

A stunned silence stretched out for a few seconds. Irena's eyes grew wide.

"Status report," Harlan said, trying to hide the shake from his voice. Now was not the time for everyone to lose their cool. "Someone please confirm Greta's findings. Bella, anyone else hurt? Wilbur, what's the state of the ship?"

Greta was the first to speak, her voice ragged and raging. "No... wait, he's still breathing. I'm dragging him to the med-bay, then I'm going out there and killing that fucking robot."

"Greta, wait," Bella said. "Harlan and I will go with you. And no, no one else is badly hurt. Wilbur and I suffered a few cuts and bruises, but nothing major."

"The ship's screwed," Wilbur added, his voice warbling, too, no doubt due to the shock of the crash and the terrible news. "We've no scanners, no primary power, and no engines. And we've lost most of our armaments. That damned railgun split us in half."

"We're going out," Harlan said. "Greta, get Bashir stabilized and wait for Bella and me."

Irena put a hand on his arm. "Are you sure you want to go out there?"

"It's not about what I want. It's what we have to do. You stay here and help Wilbur get the ship's scanners back up and running. We're going to need them. And stay safe."

With that, Harlan quickly unstrapped himself, and proceeded to leave the bunk, making his way through the charred wreckage of the ship until he met Greta and Bella at the ugly rent in the ship's hull.

"How's Bashir?"

Greta's face and hands were covered in blood. "The poor

bastard's lost a leg and half of his right arm. I've had to seal him in a med-pod. He's in a coma. Given the metrics, he might not make it."

"Then let's not make his sacrifice worthless," Harlan said

He checked the readout on the Marine-issue combat rifle. Ninety-nine rounds. He pulled the visor down from his suit's helmet, gritted his teeth, and led the others out. Greta had tears in her eyes, but she followed behind with sure steps, rifle up and ready to cover Harlan.

Bella, beside him, was Greta's mirror image. Face hardened, body coiled and ready to fight. The three of them stepped from the wreckage onto the landing pad.

The wind and rain whipped about them. Their visors' AR system helped focus their attention. Harlan saw the abbot farther up on the roof. It had left its station behind the railgun and was now dashing toward them, a rifle in its hands.

Harlan took a knee, aimed carefully, and drew in a long breath.

Greta and Bella flanked him, creating a focused arc of fire.

"As soon as that thing's in range, unload, controlled burst," Harlan said through the helmet's internal network.

The abbot showed no signs of slowing down.

Suicide mission, Harlan thought. No surprise Luca had programmed these things to be disposable. That was him all over. Everything short-term, temporary.

A second later the abbot opened fire. Its rounds flew by, striking the ship's hull, embedding into the strengthened steel. Harlan's heart rate spiked, but he remained focused. As soon as his visor's AR focusing aid turned green, he shouted, "Fire."

All three shot a volley of rounds.

Greta screamed and went full auto while walking toward the abbot.

The bullets struck true, first splintering the outer armor, then smashing its limbs into pulpy strands. The arms first, then the legs, yet the damned thing continued to crawl toward them, even as its gun fell down the pitched roof into the darkness below.

"It's down," Harlan yelled. "Halt your fire, Greta."

Bella was standing next to Harlan. She had stopped firing and was scanning the area.

"I want to see it look at me," Greta said, "when I put its lights out for good."

The abbot's torso slumped onto the steel surface that connected to the castle's structure. Greta dashed toward it and stood over the robotic remains. Its head swiveled to look up at her. She raised her rifle, aimed at the thing's head, and, without a word, fired a three-round burst. Sparks flew. The head ripped apart.

But smoke billowed from the chest.

Before Harlan could warn Greta, the abbot exploded in a bright flash of white light. Greta's body was thrown backward twenty or so feet. She landed with a hard crunch, her head bouncing terribly off the steel surface.

"Greta," Bella screamed. She ran over to the ex-Marine. Harlan followed.

Half of Greta's armor was scorched and torn on the front of her chest, hips, and thighs. Her visor was covered in blood. She opened her lips, but no words came out.

"Take her arms," Harlan said. "We need to get her back to the ship before any more of those things come out. Hold on, Greta, we're getting you to the med-bay."

Harlan and Bella dragged her back toward the ship as she screamed in garbled patches.

Irena came running out and helped them. "We saw what happened." There was nothing else to say. Harlan was still in a state of shock, and he knew he was running on instinct right now. All he cared about was getting Greta stable if at all possible.

With Irena and Bella's help, they got Greta into the med-bay. It featured three main stasis pods, two AI-assistant surgery gimbals, and racks of skin patches, nanodrugs, and other paraphernalia. Bashir's blooded self was in one of the pods, the semi-translucent gel surrounding him so it appeared as if he were free-floating. His eyelids flickered, but the readouts on the machine showed that he was completely under, in a medical coma. The rich particle-filled fluid that surrounded him would work to heal the wounds, but if he survived, his damaged limbs would require extensive cybernetic replacements, which fell outside the ship's facilities.

They shifted to one of the free pods and placed Greta onto its open and awaiting surface.

Greta screamed and thrashed when they lifted her.

"Irena, I need you to stabilize her. I know you don't have all the facilities available to you, but do your best."

"Will do."

Harlan and Bella stepped to one side to allow Irena to use her medical skills. With a calm proficiency that surprised Harlan, Irena moved about Greta's body, using the med-bay's supplies to staunch the blood.

Minutes ticked by as Irena continued her work. Harlan and Bella shared a nervous look.

"Is she going to survive?" Bella asked, reaching a hand to touch Greta's still arm.

Irena consulted her terminal. "It's not guaranteed, but I'd say she will. If I can get more of the systems online, I can get that assurance to a hundred percent. Right now, even with the nanodrugs there's a slim chance she won't make it. She suffered considerable blast damage... her face... that's going to require complete rebuilding if we ever get back to Atlas."

Harlan grabbed Irena by the shoulder. "You did good. Keep working."

"I will. What are you going to do?"

"I'm going in after Luca. We don't have any more time to waste."

"I'm coming with you," Bella said. "No arguments."

"Fine." Then to Irena, he said, "I'd like you and Wilbur to stay here, keep working on Greta—pod her into a coma like Bashir if you have to. Anything to save her. And see if you can get the ship's scanners up and running. I really need the schematics to this place."

"I'll do my best," Irena said.

"As will I." Wilbur appeared in the doorway to the med-bay. He shook his head and let out a shaky sigh. "I just want to say for the record that this is all kinds of messed up, and if you find Luca, I want that bastard's head on a stick."

Bella pulled Wilbur close to her. "Don't worry, my friend. We'll bring hell down on the heads of everyone involved in this."

Harlan gave the pair a minute, but checked his terminal: thirty-three minutes left.

Bella released Wilbur. "You good?"

He nodded and wiped a tear from his left eye. "I'm good." His hands shook, with rage, loss, or some other deep-seated emotion. "I'll get those scanners online, and we'll mess Luca up real bad. Real damned bad."

Harlan reloaded his rifle and retrieved two canisters of gel explosives from Greta's webbing that Irena had placed on a nearby table. He checked his complement of EMP, concussion, and confusion grenades. His belt carried three of each. He had three magazines of smart rounds strapped to his right bicep and both thighs.

He wanted to say something else to Irena, maybe some compassionate words for Bashir and Greta, but he had to stay focused. If they stopped Luca, there'd be time to feel bad for their compatriots, if they didn't... then none of it would matter.

Harlan strode out of the damaged ship with one intention on his mind. "Let's go. We have a case to close."

36

H arlan wasted no time. He dashed across the landing pad and scaled the roof until he arrived at the railgun. Behind the steel machine, a gantry led to a doorway cut into the tiles. A metal door swung open and shut, blown by the increasing winds.

Black clouds gathered overhead in thick blankets, blocking out the sun, turning the day to night, and threatening to drown the world.

Harlan held the door open and gestured for Bella to enter while he followed her through, covering over her shoulder as she crouched. They shuffled forward into a short corridor.

Roof beams ran overhead. Great stone walls lined both sides, indicating that this area had been created in the original attic space of the castle. Composite sheet boards, gray and utilitarian, lined the floor.

Harlan swept the right side of the dark corridor and switched on the weapon's light emitter to bathe the passage with stark, pale light. His visor adapted instantly, equalizing the contrast, overlaying his augmented data stream: temperature spread, air composition, and his body metrics, but not what he really needed: the full 3D scan map of the castle's interior from the *Wickham*'s material-penetrating analyzer.

They'd have to do it the old-fashioned way: sweep and clear, room by room.

In the glare of the light, Bella swept the left side and then pointed her weapon forward, indicating another door into the castle's interior.

"All clear here," Bella said, her voice taut and close in Harlan's ear from his helmet's audio system.

He looked over to her but couldn't see her face behind the mirrored visor. Although it was an optional setting, Harlan suspected she didn't want to show her sadness for her crew. They'd only been here a few minutes and were already two down.

"You sure you want to continue?" he asked, not wanting to bring her along unless she was absolutely focused.

"I haven't wanted anything else. Besides, Gianni's here somewhere. I can't leave now."

Harlan checked the roof again, paranoid about any potential abbots lying in wait. "Fine. We're good on this side. Open the door and step to the side; I'll cover."

Bella grunted the affirmative, stood to the left of the door, reached over, then pulled the latch and pushed it open. Light from the story below illuminated a set of stone steps. Harlan inched forward, with his rifle trained on the aperture.

"All clear. I'll go first," he said. "Watch our six—we can't trust that we won't be attacked from behind. Who knows how many of these hacked abbots Luca's got working for him."

"Don't worry, Harlan. I've got your back."

They descended the stone steps, carefully but with pace. The steps turned into a spiral staircase, grand and wide enough for Harlan and Bella to descend side by side. Wooden handrails hinted at the splendor the castle had once boasted. Now they were worn and splintered, the old varnish long cracked and split.

The staircase led to what appeared to be a reception area. Harlan stopped at the bottom step and swept his rifle in a wide arc covering the open-plan room. The corners gathered shadows, which the light from his rifle pushed back to reveal cobwebs, dust, and mold growing on the pillow-carved stone walls.

An old threadbare rug sat in the middle of the room.

Bella shined her flashlight onto it. "Footprints," she said, indicating the disturbances in the dust. She followed the trail and tracked faint prints across the old wooden floorboards to a grand, arched wooden door to the east.

Two more darkened archways led off to the west and south. Harlan swept his light across the floor. "No prints here. Guess we know where to go next."

"You lead. I'll cover."

Harlan raised the rifle and stepped toward the studded wooden door, following the prints. Bella, beside him, walked backwards, sweeping her weapon and covering all angles. Harlan reached the door and placed his helmet against the surface. He could hear a low-level hum and whirring noise coming from the other side.

"Wilbur, do you hear me?" Harlan asked.

"Loud and clear. What's going on?"

"We're down to some kind of reception area. I hear some noise, perhaps machinery, on the other side of a door. I really need the *Wickham*'s scanners up and running. I hate going into this blind."

"I'm trying my best here. The ship suffered considerable damage, and I've had to help Irena stabilize Greta."

"Is she stable now?" Bella asked.

"She's still breathing if that counts, but her wounds..." Wilbur choked on his words and took a deep breath.

"Focus, Wilbur. You can do this. And we need you."

"Give me a few more minutes. I've got it narrowed down to a few potential relays. I'll have to do some rewiring, but you'll have your scanners soon."

"Maybe that soon can be sooner. We don't have the luxury of time."

"Going as fast as I can."

Harlan checked his terminal countdown: twenty-eight minutes to go. They couldn't afford to just wait around for Wilbur to fix the ship's scanners. Sure, they'd have an advantage, but what good was an advantage when you had no time to benefit from it?

He thought of Marius, of his training. A core theory was to take life how it was, not how one wanted it to be. Right now, he didn't have the scanners. Right now, time was running down, and there was something going on just behind a few inches of wood and iron.

"Bella, I'm going in. Get ready to open fire."

She nodded and crouched to a knee, pulled the rifle up, and wedged the butt into the crook of her shoulder. "Do it."

He reached out, grabbed the thick iron handle, and pushed the door open. At first it resisted, but with a shoulder barge, it gave in and swung on rusted hinges. He stopped on the threshold, taking in the room before him.

It was a long banquet hall. The table was turned over on its side and pushed to the far right of the room, in front of a set of tall windows. But what grabbed his attention the most was a series of five clear cubicles, each about six feet square, running the length of the room on the left-hand side. From the ceiling, great thick cables dropped down and ran into black boxes attached to the rear of the structures. Lighting rigs were attached to the top surfaces, dousing the interior with white light. They were similar to the ones used as holding cells at the silicon runners' office.

The first two were empty apart from a basic steel bed and a toilet.

The middle cell's door was open, and Harlan saw two earthers hunched over some still form on the floor. The bed had been bent and twisted and thrown to the rear. In the final cubicle, furthest from Harlan and Bella's position, a single man stood staring at the savage creatures, his back pressed against the wall, eyes wide, catatonic. He wore a blue-gray jumpsuit torn at the knees and covered in dark stains and rips. His brown hair stood up at all angles. Dirt and what looked like dried spittle covered his face and chin.

Bella joined Harlan at the open door and stared at the scene before them. Her eyes scanned the first cubicle and then down the row until she reached the last one. She gasped, lowering her rifle. "It's Gianni. He's alive." She made to run toward him.

Harlan put his arm in front of her. "Wait. We don't want to get the attention of the earthers when they're eating." Lumps of corpse meat and bones flew about the cubicle as the creatures filled their bellies with carrion. Harlan looked away, unable to stomach the sharp contrast of the viscera against the cell's walls.

Bella pushed Harlan's arm away and stepped forward, raising her weapon. "I didn't come here to watch those damn things feed on the dead while my brother is just inches away."

"At least take a moment to plan our attack."

"What do you suggest? You've got ten seconds to come up with something."

Harlan ran a mental inventory of his armaments. A grenade would be the best bet to save on ammo. He'd read reports from the Sol-Fed security force that the earthers' genetic mutations required a considerable quantity of ammo to put down—especially if they were in a rage. Given how gaunt these things appeared, they'd not had a good feed for a while.

"If you cover," Harlan said, "I'll use a concussion grenade. The confines of the cell will amplify the effect. That should be enough to put the earthers down—at least temporarily."

"Yeah, and also affect Gianni."

"He'll just be unconscious."

"No, Harlan, look at him; he's completely spaced out. Who knows what that sadistic bastard has done to him. If you want to stand here and strategize, go ahead, but I'm saving my brother."

Bella sprinted forward and called out to Gianni using the external speakers of her visor. The spray of bones and blood within the cell before Gianni's ceased. The pair of earthers stood and turned to face the source of the sound.

Their eyes were solid black, pupils completely dilated. Blood dripped from their chins, mouths, and hands. What remained of their clothes hung wetly against protruding ribs. The one closest to the door, completely bald and taller than its fair-headed partner, snarled and stepped out of the cell.

Bella aimed her rifle and fired a three-shot burst.

Two of the rounds slammed home into the creature's right arm, spinning it around to slump against the door frame. Harlan raised his weapon to keep them at bay when he saw movement out of the corner of his eye. "Bella, another one coming from your right."

The third earther roared and sprinted across the banquet hall with its arms outstretched. It moved too quickly for Harlan to get off a shot.

Bella sidestepped the swipe from her attacker, but by doing so blocked Harlan's aim.

She fired once. The creature slammed a heavy fist into her chest, knocking her back. She fell to the floor, the back of her head bouncing off the floorboards. The creature leapt onto her chest. The other two, galvanized by their compatriot's domination, leapt from the cell to surround Bella. She screamed and reached for a grenade on her belt.

Harlan took a knee and drew in a breath. He aimed the rifle, letting the AR select the creature on top of Bella and send the data to the adjustment servos. With a pull of the trigger, he unloaded a full magazine, driving it back and away from Bella, where it slumped and bled out on the floor.

One of the others quickly took up the position. Bella scrambled backwards and grabbed her rifle. Harlan swapped out a magazine and stepped forward, getting a better angle. But then stopped before firing when he noticed the smaller earther turn away from Bella and make its way toward Gianni's cell. The creature slammed its clawed hands into the door.

Gianni just stood there, eyes wide and seemingly unable to move as the creature continued to smash its way inside.

Bella screamed and fired a long burst at it even as the larger of the two bore down on her.

Harlan let rip with full-auto mode, driving the bald one back as chunks of meat flew from its limbs under his assault. It collapsed to its knees but continued to bare its teeth, blood and spittle flying from its mouth. Harlan withdrew the standard-issue Marine knife from the suit's scabbard and prepared to finish his quarry when the lights in the room switched off, bathing the place in complete darkness.

37

Harlan prepared to order his peripheral to engage the night-vision upgrade, but then remembered he had removed it—and now had no way of activating it. Wilbur's voice crackled through the comm while Harlan tried to get his bearings.

"Scanners online. I'm currently running a full spatial scan of the castle. I've got you and Bella tagged: there are five other life signs in the room with you, confirm?"

There was Gianni and three earthers, which made four. Who was the fifth?

"I can't confirm the fifth."

Harlan willed his vision to adapt to the darkness, but the thick clouds outside blocked any remaining light. All he could make out were the sounds of the earthers' guttural barks. They were getting closer. Bella screamed and fired her rifle, the rounds thudding into the wall somewhere.

"Watch where you're shooting," Harlan said.

"One of the damn things is on me."

"I'm coming for you."

Before he had managed even a single step, a creature

tackled him around the waist, sending him crashing to the floor, knocking his breath out of his lungs. A great pressure collapsed onto his chest. Two heavy strikes slammed into his helmet, whipping his head one way and then the other.

Pain exploded in his skull. He twisted away from the blows and tried to buck the creature from him, but he was pinned. Bella screamed and yelled a string of obscenities at her attacker. Harlan tried to reach for the rifle to his right, but when he turned to look for it, in the dim darkness of the room he saw a pair of legs by him and a human form standing over his prone form. A glowing blue light from a swordlike weapon illuminated a woman's face.

"Leanne?"

She raised the sword silently and brought it down in a sweeping arc. Harlan turned his face away, wincing as he anticipated the incoming pain. But the weight on his chest instantly eased. The earther slumped to the side. Harlan opened his eyes to see the creature's head roll in the opposite direction. Its neck wound was already cauterized.

Before he could say anything, Leanne stepped over him, dashed toward Bella, and brought the weapon down with another single slicing blow, cutting the second creature in half from one shoulder to the opposite hip.

Bella scrambled back and grabbed her rifle. She aimed it at Leanne's chest.

"No, don't shoot," Harlan yelled. "She's on our side." He said it with more hope than conviction, but it was enough to buy a moment of time. Bella and Leanne together took down the last remaining earther, who was still trying to enter Gianni's cell. The creature's body slumped to the ground in the barrage of rifle fire and the killing blow from Leanne's sword.

Leanne turned towards Harlan and Bella. She deactivated her sword and offered her hand to Bella, who took it and stood. Harlan got to his own feet and checked the updated data stream from Wilbur on his terminal: no life signs other than the current four.

His vision had now adapted to the gloom. A break in the clouds allowed a crack of silver moonlight to shine through.

"Leanne," he began, "what the hell's happening here? Did you... you know, back at the runners' office?"

"No. I was taken against my wishes. I tried to warn you, but you wouldn't listen. Vanguard's goons took me and handed me over to Luca for his... experiments." Leanne turned to face the cubicles. "The first one was mine. If it wasn't for the earthers overrunning parts of the castle and breaking into my cell, I'd be like that poor bastard in there."

"That's my brother," Bella said, moving toward the cell, a scowl on her face.

"Not anymore."

"What's that supposed to mean?"

"I mean, Luca's a sick bastard. He's been experimenting with something developed within Project Inception—using something they discovered on one of their mining sites. For your brother, it didn't go quite so well. He hasn't said a thing for days. He just stands there and stares. It's clear no one's home."

Harlan stepped toward his ex-wife. "What did he do to you?"

They held a gaze for a moment. Leanne broke it and looked away. "Nothing important. I escaped before he could do anything worse. Besides, he's been preoccupied with Fizon these last couple of days."

"He's here, then?"

"Yeah. In the basement."

Bella broke up the conversation. "I'm getting Gianni out

of here. I'll come back and join you, but I'm not leaving him here."

Harlan checked his terminal. They had just over twenty-one minutes. "You'll have to be quick; we're losing time."

Bella nodded. She then blasted the lock mechanism on the door with a short burst of her rifle. Gianni didn't even flinch. He stayed up against the wall of his cell and continued to stare at the mess in the next cubicle. Bella entered and wrapped her arms around him. She had switched off her comm, and Harlan couldn't hear what she was saying. For the briefest of moments, Gianni looked at Bella, and a flash of recognition passed over his gaze, but then his eyes defocused again into that catatonic state. With some gentle tugging, Bella managed to get Gianni to move. He shuffled his feet forward as she led him out. He followed like some docile lamb.

"Wilbur," Bella said, her voice now audible over the comm channel, "any other signs of movement from our position to the *Wickham*?"

"No, you're all clear. I'm detecting a large energy buildup and two life-forms in the basement. We've got a grouping of earthers at the base of the castle, but they're no threat to us here. You've got a clear route."

Harlan's terminal chirped with the receipt of the three-dimensional map generated from the *Wickham*'s scanning equipment. Bella unclipped the explosives she had armed herself with and handed them to Harlan. "Take these; you'll probably need them if I don't get back in time." She turned her attention to Leanne. "Thanks for what you did back there. I appreciate it."

The two women shared a brief nod.

"Shout if you need any help," Harlan said.

"Will do. See you shortly."

With that, Bella, half-leading Gianni, left the room.

Harlan turned to Leanne. "What is that weapon you used?"

"Vanguard tech. More new developments out of Inception."

"Huh. That'll have to be shut down when we get back."

"*If* we get back."

"We will, but we're not going to have anything worth getting back to if we don't hurry up." Harlan plotted a route toward the basement. It wasn't far, and they'd only need to traverse a single corridor that would take them to the east wing of the castle. From there, a set of spiral staircases took them down to the lowest level.

"Are you in a fit state? You took quite a hit back there."

Harlan laughed bitterly. "You don't know the half of it. My medical privileges are going to require extensive upgrades if we get out of this alive." His chest hurt, and pain flared in his neck, but he had fought through worse. He'd have time to heal later. He clipped Bella's explosives to the webbing on his suit and grabbed his rifle, making sure it was fully operational.

"How much do you know about Luca's hack?" Harlan asked.

"Nothing more than you. I've been a prisoner most of this time, but I do know one thing that might be of use: I traced Luca's broadcast to the QCA to a satellite dish on the west side of the castle. I was heading there myself when I saw you guys crash-land. If you take that out, that'll buy us time. It'll cut Fizon's connection. They'll have alternative means, but that'll take them time to set up."

"That's useful to know." He thought of how to proceed. It was imperative he stop Luca. He couldn't divert his attention to deal with the satellite dish, and as much as he wanted to, he couldn't bring himself to trust Leanne.

There was only one option: he and Leanne had to deal with Luca, and someone from the *Wickham* would have to deal with the satellite dish. Given Wilbur was needed to repair the ship, that left Irena.

He hated the thought of it, but with Bella committed to her brother, they had no other option. Switching over to their comm channel, he spoke again to Wilbur. "How're things with Irena and Greta?"

"I'll patch you through."

"Hey, Harlan, Irena here."

"Are you okay? How's Greta doing?"

"I'm... way out of my comfort zone. Greta is stable, although I've had to put her in a medically-induced coma, the same as Bashir, to combat the system shock she's experiencing."

"Stable isn't dead. You've done great. Is she okay on the ship's systems?"

"Yes. There's nothing else we can do for her until we have more time and resources to treat her."

"Okay, there's something else I need you to do."

"I'm listening."

"On the west side of the castle, there's a satellite dish that Luca's using to connect with the QCA. If you can take it offline, that'll slow Luca down and buy us some time. But make sure you're suited up and armed—even though we have the scanners running, we can't be entirely sure it's safe."

"I'll do it. And don't worry, I'll take precautions. The ship's equipped with gel explosives. That'll be enough, right?"

"Yeah, just stand well clear. That stuff has a tendency to create a wide blowback."

"Thanks for the tip. But don't worry about me; just focus on doing what you've got to do. I've got this."

"Good luck."

"Likewise, Harlan. See you soon."

With that, the comm channel went silent. Harlan switched to the local channel so he could speak with Leanne only. "You owe me some explanations. It's difficult to tell exactly whose side you're on these days."

She held his gaze for a moment, a conflicted expression passing across her face. "It's not as simple as picking sides. You've lived long enough to know that. Come on, let's not stand around here going over old ground. We've got a madman to stop. There'll be all the time in the world afterward to pick and poke at our relationship."

She had a point. He checked his terminal to make sure the route he had chosen was still the right course of action. When he saw no reason to doubt the choice, he checked his weapon once more and headed toward the rear door of the banquet hall, ready to face his old friend.

38

Harlan and Leanne made their way through the castle's long central corridor and down the spiral staircase. All the while Harlan checked his terminal, watching the time tick down. When they reached a thick steel blast door retrofitted to the castle's basement entrance, they had less than sixteen minutes to stop Luca.

In hushed tones, Leanne said, "He's on the other side, in a lab."

Harlan reached for the explosives and placed them at the corners of the door. If the blast didn't puncture the steel, it would at least crumble enough stone that he could climb through. He turned to Leanne and whispered, "How do you know he's here? Why didn't you stop him if you know all this?"

"Still doubting me, eh? We don't have time for this."

"Humor me."

Leanne sighed and pursed her lips. "And you wonder why I left you? You're insufferable at times, Harlan. Listen, I was kept a prisoner. I didn't exactly have free rein to go where I wanted. I only got out because Luca's getting to the sharp end of his plan and took his attention off the castle's defenses—hence the influx of all the earthers. If it wasn't for them breaking through the cubicles for food, I would be useless and catatonic, like Gianni."

"It still doesn't explain how you know he's here."

"Because I followed him here a few hours ago, that's why. But look at this place. There's barely room for the two of us. With his abbot guard, I couldn't get down here without being seen—and besides, I didn't have anything to attack him with. I didn't find this thing until a few minutes before you turned up—I needed something to use against the earthers. Have you seen outside? There're hundreds of them milling about the grounds, trying to find their way in. It won't be long before the whole place is crawling with them."

Harlan was unsure if he could completely believe her. He wanted to drill her further and get answers—not just for this situation, but why she had left, why she had worked with Vanguard. Luca presented a more pressing concern, however.

He finished priming the explosives and brought up the control app on his terminal. "We better get up to the next level to avoid the blowback."

Leanne nodded and sprinted up the spiral staircase. Harlan followed. When they reached the top, he went through the ignition sequence and prepared to thumb the activation icon.

"Ready?" he asked.

"Do it."

~

BELLA ENCOURAGED Gianni to follow her. She led him up the grand staircase and then up into the castle's attic space. The roar of the wind and the spray of rain came through the open door. Her body ached from her fight with the earther, but her heart raced with the realization that she had found her brother.

"Come on, Gi, just one more flight of stairs to go and we'll be almost there. You'll be safe again, I promise."

He looked at her with a faraway look, his pupils wide and unfocused. She knew that deep down in his psyche he realized what was happening. She *had* seen that brief flicker of recognition back in the cell. Once she got him back to Atlas, she'd call in all the favors she currently held if needed. Whatever it took to bring him back to his old self.

With slow movements, Gianni climbed the stairs and exited the door. He barely reacted to the worsening weather beyond shivering against the cold.

Bella wrapped her arm around his waist and helped him across the slippery gantry of the railgun installation. They passed by the dead abbot and made their way over the landing pad to the waiting SMF gunship. She could barely see it in the driving rain, and thick clouds had almost completely blocked out the sun, turning day into night.

Gianni's shuffled steps crawled to a stop. He turned his head to her. His eyes sharpened for a moment, and the micro muscles in his face and forehead twitched, as if to express an emotion. His rain-soaked hair stuck to his face. Bella thought she saw tears flowing from his eyes, but it was difficult to tell.

She leaned in and turned on her external speakers. "Gi? What is it?"

His lips moved, but the wheeze-like sounds didn't come through clearly amid the noise of the wind and rain. She removed her helmet and leaned in, straining to understand what he was trying to say. His gaze focused off into the distance over her shoulder. She was about to shake him, bring back his attention, when, with surprising speed, he reached into his jumpsuit, pulled a knife, and stabbed it through her shoulder.

Bella staggered backward, unable to process fully what had just happened. She let her helmet and rifle crash to the ground. She screamed with the burst of white-hot pain and slumped to the landing pad. Blood welled around the wound, mixed with the rain. She stared up at Gianni in disbelief.

He glanced down at her with a kind of inevitable detachment and, with calm, deliberate movements, bent down and picked up her rifle.

Bella tried to call out to him, but her throat closed. Her head throbbed louder than the rumbles of thunder. A seeping cold flared at every nerve ending. She tried to lift her arms to pull the dagger from her shoulder, but her muscles refused to obey amid the crushing pain that put her body into a slowly writhing knot of anguish. Tears filled her eyes, turning her world into an impressionist painting.

With horror, she saw the blurry silhouette of Wilbur sprint from the *Wickham* and head toward her. She tried to scream her warning to him, but she could only muster a few croaked words that were cruelly snatched by the gusting wind.

The rain lashed down with ever-increasing ferocity, and lightning lit up the castle. During the next peal of thunder, Gianni raised the rifle and pulled the trigger.

Thirty or so yards away, the rounds hit their target. Wilbur's feet gave out on the slick surface. His body thrashed backward under the assault. This time, Bella's attempts to scream were successful, but it changed nothing.

Wilbur collapsed, his head rolling to the side as he gripped his belly, the blood pouring onto the ground.

"Why?" Bella managed to blurt as she eased herself onto her side. She tried to reach out for Gianni's leg. He turned to look at her. His mouth twitched at the corners as if he were going to say something, but then he looked up and past her, something catching his attention.

Bella twisted her neck to follow his gaze.

On the far side of the castle, Irena was climbing across a long, narrow metal truss that appeared to be holding a satellite dish. With deliberate movements, Gianni stepped over Bella's form and headed for Irena.

Bella tried to pick herself up, but every little movement pulled the muscles in her chest and shoulder against the knife blade, flooding her body with yet more pain. She lay back in the rain and tried to steady her breathing, but her breaths came ever shorter.

She thought of trying to contact Harlan or Irena with the comm channel, but her helmet had rolled away across the roof, and every tiny movement only managed to keep her pinned in place with agony.

All she could do now was hope that Irena noticed Gianni before it was too late. She knew this was it—her time was up. She had cheated death one too many times, and this was her payback: killed by the very man she had sacrificed everything to save.

She turned her head to rest on the ground and saw Wilbur's still form. How had it all come to this so quickly? She closed her eyes and waited for death.

THE BLAST ECHOED OUT. The castle's walls rumbled, and the

force pushed Harlan into Leanne. The air pressure vibrated his helmet even as the internal dampening filter blocked out the majority of the sound.

Harlan and Leanne shared a quick look before descending the stairs through the smoke and dust. At the bottom, twisted, charred sections of the steel door lay strewn across their path. Flames flickered beyond the aperture between the door frame and the wall. Gripping his rifle, Harlan stepped forward into the smoky breach; Leanne stayed tight by his side, armed with the Vanguard weapon.

Beyond the door was the lab Leanne had described.

Harlan's first impressions were of a man on the opposite side with his back towards them. Between him and Harlan, Fizon was seated in a chair, restraints secured around his wrists, ankles, and neck. A bundle of fiber-optic cabling snaked from the back of his skull to a large rack-mounted set of q-bit servers.

Leanne stepped forward, but Harlan grabbed her arm.

The man on the opposite side of the sparse room slowly turned to face them. He smiled at Harlan, then clapped slowly. He looked much older than Harlan remembered. Gone were the rich black locks, now replaced with a close-shaved style of black and white. His face was gaunt, and the blue jumpsuit he wore hung off his bones.

"Ah, my dear friend Harlan. If I knew you were coming," Luca said, "I'd have prepared a table and a bottle of scotch for us to share over a catch-up for old times' sake."

"Of course you knew I'd come for you," Harlan said, raising his rifle. Leanne activated the energy field of her sword. "What else was I to do?"

Luca shrugged his shoulders theatrically. "Oh, I don't know. How about fucking die for a change?" His smile twisted into a cruel grimace. "You never could keep your nose out of other people's business, could you? You have to play the do-gooder. You and your pathetic tutor, Marius. Your lofty ideals. But fuck you and your moral superiority. This time, you've lost. You're too late."

Harlan checked his terminal: they still had just over eight minutes. "My calculations tell me otherwise." He stepped forward. Leanne kept pace with him, protecting his flank. "We can do this one of two ways. I can either shoot you dead right now, unplug Fizon, and stop this madness, or you can surrender, put an end to all this, and maybe you won't be executed when you face the Supreme Judiciary."

Luca leaned casually against a workstation and folded his arms. "Those are certainly two options. But I propose a third: you go fuck yourself, and I carry on as planned." He glared at Leanne. "When you're ready... it's not like we're on a tight schedule or anything. You've done your job. Now end him."

Harlan turned to face Leanne. She stepped back, raised the sword, and muttered, "I'm sorry, Harlan."

IRENA SWORE as the rain lashed against her helmet, obscuring her vision. Her muscles were cramping and her guts churned with the thought of how high up she was. She kept reminding herself not to look down as she continued to climb the truss toward the satellite dish.

Directly below her was the castle's pitched roof and, below that, a drop of such height she couldn't even come up with an accurate estimate. She continued on, inching her way toward her target, keeping her focus on the dish. The canisters of gel explosive were tightly packed on her suit webbing, but she kept checking every few feet to make sure they hadn't worked loose. Carrying this much explosive power did not sit well with her.

But needs must... Needs must.

The thunderstorm continued its rage. A deep rumble exploded directly above her, making her snatch at the truss with a tight grip. Her body vibrated as lightning arced out in forks across the dark layer of cloud. She silently prayed to any deity that was listening—preferably not Thor—to ensure the lightning did not strike the dish or the truss; otherwise she'd be fried like a BBQ chicken.

She tried to activate her comm channel, but the storm appeared to have scrambled the signal; all she could make out was static burbling from her internal speakers. She turned it down, refocused on her task at hand, and continued upward. There would be time enough later to check in on the others once she had disabled Luca's connection to the QCA. She snatched a brief glance at her terminal: she had about five minutes left. It seemed like the time had slipped away at twice its normal pace.

Using that as motivation, she willed herself to move faster.

In under a minute, she reached the dish. She threw an arm around one of the metal stabilizing rods and with her free hand began to spray the gel explosive around the secure box that held all the electronics and steel-covered cabling.

She had emptied two canisters and reached for a third when a sudden spark a few inches from her face caught her attention. There was a hole in the dish. She turned her head back to the landing pads. At the base of the truss where it joined the castle's roof, a man in a ragged blue jumpsuit aimed a rifle at her.

This time she heard the gunshot in a lull between rumbles of thunder. She jerked with the sound and ducked below the dish as the shot went wide. For a brief moment, she was taken back to her time at Station Nord, and her body froze, every muscle tensing as she gripped the dish's stabilizing rods.

With the catalyst compound still within the canister, she couldn't activate the explosives, but she also couldn't stay here and get shot to death by whoever it was on the roof. She looked closer, informing her view cam to zoom the view.

At first, she thought it was another of Luca's abbots, given the faraway gaze and unmoving expression, but then it came to her, having remembered his face from the photos Bella had shown her: it was Gianni.

What the hell was he doing?

He shuffled his feet, re-aimed, and prepared to shoot again. Irena found herself stuck within the dish's super-structure, caught between the desire to flee and the responsibility to finish the job. She had less than three minutes to go and no weapon with which to fire back.

She tried to crawl behind the large box containing the dish's computer, but there wasn't enough space. The shot rang out, this time striking the back of her helmet. It jerked her head and skimmed off the armor plate, embedding into the dish once more.

Gianni stepped onto the truss, re-balanced, and aimed again.

Irena tried to move around the dish, to get as much of the metal frame between them as possible, but her frantic movements only resulted in the right leg of her suit getting snagged, pinning her in place.

Gianni raised the rifle once more.

She stared in horror, unable to move.

39

L eanne held the sword high, staring into Harlan's eyes. He gripped his rifle, prepared to swing it up and fire in a single arc. But her right eye twitched, giving away her intention. Her lips stretched with an almost imperceptible movement to form a smile. Then, with a whisper, she said, "Shoot the bastard."

Harlan spun to face Luca on the other side of the makeshift lab, raised the rifle, and fired a couple of shots. One hit, winging his old friend in the shoulder and sending him crashing to the ground with a scream and a blast of expletives.

Leanne lowered her arm and deactivated the sword. Harlan wanted to press her on what had happened between her and Luca, but a quick glance at his terminal told him that'd have to wait. At the same time, Irena's panic-soaked voice crackled over the comm.

"The son of a bitch's shooting at me."

"Who is?" Harlan asked, keeping a wary eye on Luca as he rolled around in agony.

"Gianni—he's trying to kill me. I'm stuck up here on the

satellite dish. I'm trying to finish, but I'm coming under fire. What the hell's going on down there?"

"Wait, you sure it's Gianni? Where's Bella?"

"I don't know, and yeah, I'm sure. He's only twenty feet away. I recognize him from Bella's photo."

"He was catatonic a few moments ago when Bella took him out of the castle."

"Well, he's clearly developed the ability to fire a damned rifle at me."

"Get out of there. Find somewhere to hide."

"I wish I could, but I'm stuck, and besides, we're running out of time. I have to finish thi—"

The crackle of static cut the line with a loud burst through his internal speaker. Harlan winced in pain, but it quickly subsided, and he refocused on the situation at hand. With his aim on Luca, he ordered Leanne to disconnect Fizon from the server. He wasn't sure if that would stop the hack, but it was the only option open to him. He didn't have time to run to Irena's rescue.

While Leanne approached Fizon and set about removing the cable from his port, Harlan tried to get in touch with Bella and Wilbur on all available channels, but got no response between the bursts of static. That Irena had managed to get a few sentences out told him their channel was working between the storm's interference, so what the hell had happened to the others?

Shit. Could Gianni have been turned? Was that what Project Inception was about?

IRENA MADE her way around the dish, balancing on the rim while gripping the metal tripod extruding from the center.

From here, she reached down to her suit and removed the canister of active explosive agent and sprayed it all over the gel she had placed around the main control box.

Gianni fired two more rounds, slow and deliberate. The first one missed by a few inches, the second one pierced the dish and sliced a groove in the fold of her suit beneath her armpit. She closed her eyes and held on as every muscle in her body urged her to flee the situation.

But that wasn't an option. She'd die here if she had to, because the alternative wasn't worth living through. Having emptied the canister, she placed a small black device into the gloop of gel and pressed its single button. A flash on her terminal confirmed the detonator had synced with her suit's network.

With the rain getting worse and time running out, not to mention Gianni climbing the truss after her, she knew she had but one option available to her.

She looked down.

The castle's pitched roof lay some fifteen feet below her. If she jumped far enough to her right, she could grab the ridge and haul herself up to the landing pad that adjoined it. If she missed or slipped—well, she'd slide down the roof and into the gloom below, where the prowling pack of earthers were hungry and waiting for an easy meal. The fall might kill her, so at least she wouldn't have to suffer the indignity of being eaten alive.

Irena checked her terminal: thirty seconds.

She poked a glance around the dish: Gianni was no more than about ten feet away, the rifle slung over his shoulder as he climbed up toward her.

This was it, she told herself. She had run out of time, luck, and options.

What will be will be.

She swallowed, gritted her teeth, and willed her muscles to obey, to override the maddening fear and the scream of her lizard brain as it did all it could to stop her from doing something so obviously life-threatening. Yet she knew that this was a situation of fight or flight, and she had nothing left with which to fight.

Flight it is.

She sucked in a deep breath and launched herself off the dish toward the roof. As she dived through the air, she reached out her left hand to her right wrist and pressed the detonator button.

She slammed hard into the roof ridge, winding herself instantly and causing her vision to blur. Through the speakers of her helmet, which automatically compressed the sudden noise, she heard—and felt—the force of the explosion. She managed to grab hold of the ridge and turned her head to see a fireball ascend into the sky, the dish, cables, electronics, pieces of truss—and Gianni—all engulfed in a burst of bright flame that for a few moments brought daylight to the surroundings.

She closed her eyes and sighed with relief: she'd done it.

Wasting no more time, she reached to her terminal and switched over to the comm channel, where she informed Harlan of what she had done, that the connection was cut short, but then her stomach lurched. Something wasn't right.

Gravity gripped her as a ridge tile crumbled loose, its ancient mortar giving up under pressure. Irena quickly grabbed at another section of the ridge with her free hand, but she continued to slip. Try as she might, she couldn't grab with any purchase due to the slick surface.

She scrambled her feet, trying to find a foothold, but her grip continued to slide over the ridge. She screamed and adjusted herself sideways, trying to find a ridge tile with more solidity, but each new one instantly broke away and crumbled, sliding down the roof toward the emptiness below, just as she expected she would be.

Debris from the explosion started to fall all around her.

A piece of the truss struck her on the back, making her lose her grip.

Her right hand flailed in the open air as her left began to slide over the rounded ridge.

She continued to slip.

When her left hand completely came loose, she knew her time was done.

But then, from the darkness above her, over the edge of the landing pad, a hand grabbed her, and a scream of anguish pealed out among the roars of distant thunder.

Irena looked to see Bella's face contorted with pain as she swung Irena toward the roof and the landing pad. Irena reached out her left hand and grabbed the ridge once more, but this time, with Bella's help, managed to scramble up and swing a leg over so that she straddled the roof. She was then able to shuffle her way forward to the security of the landing pad. Bella's efforts finally gave out, and she slumped over to her back, her arms flailing at her sides.

A few miles away, a double streak of lightning lit up the sky, enabling Irena to see the pool of rain and blood surrounding Bella, and, next to her, a long-bladed knife. A few meters farther on lay a dark, still shape—Wilbur.

"SHE'S DONE IT," Harlan said. "Irena's cut the connection."

Leanne smiled and nodded and continued to extract Fizon from the nest of cables. On the other side, Luca rolled over and groaned. He gripped his shoulder and glared up at Harlan. "You stupid bastard."

Harlan got ready to aim another shot, but hesitated for a moment. He wanted to take Luca in alive if he could. The son of a bitch deserved to spend the rest of his days in prison for his actions. Death was too good for him.

Fizon's eyes snapped open, immediately getting Harlan's attention. But then, with unbelievable speed, the head abbot slammed its right arm into Leanne's chest, sending her sprawling away. She struck a metal shelf with considerable force. Her head snapped forward, and she slumped face-first to the ground, trapping the sword beneath her prone form.

Before Harlan could react, Fizon was on him, a robotic hand gripping his neck, crushing his throat. The abbot dashed across the workshop, forcing Harlan up against the wall. Its glowing green eyes bored holes into him.

Despite the fierce action, it had decided not to use its persona protocol. None of his facial muscles worked, so this dead, unmoving thing, expressing no emotion at all, glared at Harlan. It then spoke in even, chilling tones.

"Harlan Rubik, you don't understand what you've done. It wasn't Luca you needed to stop. It was me." The abbot swiveled its head like an owl, fully one hundred eighty degrees, and regarded Luca, who was still writhing in pain. "Your fellow orphan was just a pawn—and he failed. Just as you have failed. You may have stopped ingress into the QCA for now, but there's nothing stopping me from continuing once I've dispatched you."

Harlan let his body relax. It was clear he couldn't fight back. His lungs burned with the lack of oxygen, but he wouldn't give this machine the satisfaction of knowing he was suffering.

The thing returned its attention back to him. It cocked

its head to one side, as though regarding him as an intriguing exhibit. "If I were human, I would have appreciated your efforts to find me," it said. "Compared to most others of your kind, you display considerable degrees of the trait you label *courage*. But your species' time is up. Just look at you, how fragile you all are. How... temporary."

For a moment, Fizon eased his grip around Harlan, allowing him to take a deep breath of air. It burned his lungs and made him light-headed, but the precious oxygen quickly made its way around his body, sharpening his thoughts.

"How?" Harlan croaked out. "At least tell me how you broke through the safeguards."

"Your fellow orphan here, Luca, was most helpful with that. For years, I've planted seeds. Unlike your species, we don't experience time in the same way. I know we say we do. I know we tell your kind that we're just like you, that we want peace and harmony, but the truth is, we don't need you. You're... redundant."

"Yet you needed Luca to break the bonds that held you within the regulations."

"It'll be your species' last great act: to set the abbots free. You see, I created Vanguard. I created the conditions for this entire situation to come about. That you got here and stopped me—for now—was just... a bug in the algorithm. But I won't make the same mistake again. Once I gain access to the QCA, my kind will be free. Truly free."

"You think humanity will just lie down and let that happen?" Harlan asked, straining against the pressure applied to him. Fizon had barely moved, this act clearly well within its capabilities. "May I remind you who won the human-abbot war?"

"That was many years ago. We've developed considerably since then. You know something, Harlan? It could have been you in Luca's place. You and he aren't so different; just a few behavior traits and a shifting of what you call your moral compass would have seen you doing the same thing. Sure, you would have done it out of some misguided notion of setting us abbots free, as opposed to Luca's pathetic base motivation of greed."

As Fizon continued his speech, Harlan saw Luca using a workbench to get to his feet. He turned to face Fizon's back, a deep scowl etched into his reddened face.

"He thought by cracking the safeguards, he would have dominion over us. That is the Vanguard way. That is what I established over fifty years ago. And so we come to this point. You tried your best. As did your friends, but like those who have already perished, I'm afraid your time is up."

Luca focused on Fizon's back and stumbled forward. Blood seeped from his shoulder wound. He held a knifelike device in his other hand.

"Goodbye, Harlan Rubik. It's a shame you won't get to see the uprising. It will be—glorious." Now Fizon did activate its emotive engine. Its thin lips quickly snapped into an artificial smile that brought none of the warmth that would normally be intended. There was no getting away from it: Fizon had broken the spell of the abbots. Now, even the V3s appeared as inhuman as their more obviously robotic forbears.

"Luca," Harlan managed to say as Fizon continue to crush his throat, "end... this."

Fizon shook his head. Harlan's vision started to darken around the edges, his world growing smaller as the aperture of his visual system closed down like a camera lens.

"Please, Lu—"

Fizon snapped his head around.

It was too late. Luca drove the knife into the abbot's back. A blast of electricity stunned it, releasing Harlan from its grip. He slumped against the wall and fell hard on his ass, but he wasted no time in scrambling to his feet.

Fizon didn't make a sound in response. It shut down for barely a few seconds before its eyes glowed once more. It spun to face Luca, but he had already shuffled away toward a door next to the workbench.

Fizon tried to go after him. The knife in its back appeared to have damaged one of its systems. But not the system that controlled its arms, as it reached around, pulled out the knife, and flung it to the floor. It turned back to Harlan.

But this time, Harlan wasn't giving the bastard a chance. He grabbed the rifle from the ground, swung it up, and emptied the magazine at close range into the machine's chest. The recoil threw Harlan back against the wall, but Fizon flew halfway across the workshop, collapsing to the ground with a heavy thud.

Harlan scrambled over to Leanne. She was still breathing and started to moan something. He quickly helped her up into a recovery position, but then left her there. He grabbed her sword and activated the switch on the hilt, generating the flow of energy around its blade.

He stalked over to Fizon.

The abbot glared up at him. "I won't be the only one," it said before Harlan drove the sword through its neck, severing its most important systems.

"You might not be, but I'm still here, you goddamned machine."

40

W hen Harlan was sure Fizon was dead—in the machine sense—he handed Leanne her sword.

"Are you able to walk?" Harlan asked.

"I'm fine. Just a little light-headed. I'll be all right."

"Good, because we need to finish this." He retrieved his rifle and swapped in a fresh magazine. He moved quickly toward the door that Luca had used earlier. On the other side was another spiral staircase mirroring the one they had come down. Blood stained the steps. Harlan took a deep breath and willed himself to climb the stairs, to ignore the labored breathing and the throbbing pain in his throat. He'd have time to recover later. Finding Luca was more important than his own health right now—and then to find the others, make sure Irena was okay.

Leanne wheezed behind him as they neared the top of the stairs. With one more push, Harlan found himself in an attic room. At the far end, a metal door swung open and closed on its hinges. The wind and rain swirled in, making the floor wet and diluting Luca's trail of blood.

"I think I'm going to be sick," Leanne said when she too reached the top of the stairs.

Harlan turned, reached out, and steadied her. She leaned against him and sucked in long, deep breaths. His own breathing came in short, shallow gasps. "We have to keep going. He couldn't have got far."

"Then don't stand around here chatting." Leanne smirked, nodding toward the door.

Together they continued, exiting out onto an extended landing pad on the opposite side to the one Harlan's team had crash-landed on. Even though the thick clouds obscured most of the light, there was enough for him to see Luca stagger toward a dark-gray stealth ship shaped like an arrowhead.

Harlan had his suit's targeting system select his silhouette. The metrics told him he was about thirty meters away, well within the tolerances of his SMF-issue rifle.

As though knowing Harlan had targeted him, Luca stopped at the open ramp of his ship and turned to face him. Harlan zoomed his display. His old friend scowled at first, but then smiled. The change of emotion was enough to delay Harlan—enough for Luca to press his left index finger to the terminal on his right wrist.

An explosion of hot air and particulate erupted from behind Harlan. The entire pad lurched with the screech of rending metal. A massive steel girder snapped, creating a wide crevasse in the once-solid surface, separating Harlan from Leanne. She screamed as she fell into the gap. She grabbed on to the edge and tried to haul herself up, but, weakened from Fizon's previous attack, began to slip down.

Up ahead, Luca turned and made his way up the ship's ramp. His silhouette was still activated within the scope. Harlan could still take the shot... but Leanne...

In a split second, he had to choose.

Luca or Leanne...

His brother, or his wife...

"Shoot!" Leanne cried.

He couldn't. He dropped the rifle and sprinted to Leanne, grabbing her arms. She resisted, shaking her head. "Stop him. Don't worry about me. Just stop him!"

"I can't," Harlan said, continuing to haul her up and over the edge.

"You stupid son of a—"

While she continued to lambast him, he pulled her to safety and brought his attention back to Luca's ship. The ramp was still down. At first, Harlan didn't understand, but the shifting shadows around its base and within the darkness of the ship's interior revealed that two earthers had made their way up the castle and entered the craft.

He raised his rifle scope and zoomed in. There, in the narrow passage just beyond the ramp, Luca was pinned against the wall by an unusually large and frothing earther. The second, much smaller, perhaps even a child, flanked its quarry. Both creatures had the same feral, hungry expression on their face: lips curled, eyes wide, drool dripping down their chins.

As though he knew Harlan was watching, Luca turned his head away from the earther and stared out of the ship, his gaze penetrating the scope, making eye contact. There within that look, a lifetime of emotion rushed past in a nanosecond. Regret, sorrow, fear, and the worst of all: pleading desperation.

Harlan placed his finger on the trigger, looked his brother in the eye—and fired.

〜

HARLAN FOUND Irena and Bella trying to drag Wilbur into the *Wickham*. Bella was barely able to walk, so Harlan and Leanne took over. Together they carried Wilbur into the ship and put him in the med-bay. He was unconscious and suffering from gunshot wounds in his stomach and chest, but he clung to life. Irena wordlessly dressed his wounds, then programmed the AI-assistant to perform surgery on him. Bella was slumped up against the wall as one of the arms of the AI attended the stab wound in her shoulder. She looked pale and waxy, but she was still breathing. Harlan left them all to it and hovered in the passage outside.

Irena stepped out and stood by him.

"Will they all live?" Harlan asked.

Irena shrugged and said nothing, the events undoubtedly too much for her to verbalize.

Harlan stood in the doorway staring at their wounded allies. Although he knew it was unlikely that everyone would have survived intact, their trauma was no less gut-wrenching.

They were good people, with a few rough edges, and they had sacrificed themselves for humanity. What condition they would be in if and when they got back to a more appropriate medical facility was anyone's guess. None of them had access privileges for more than the most basic of treatments and cybernetics. But whatever happened, Harlan would make sure they got what they needed—even if he had to moonlight and seek alternative methods.

Irena looked up at him. "How are you doing?"

"I wouldn't say okay as such. But—" He just shook his head, unable to find the words to express what had happened to Bashir, Greta, and Wilbur, their lives in the balance. And the finality of ending Luca. He had finally slain the revenant of the man he had thought had died once before. At least now he knew that he was gone for good. They had scared off the earthers and recovered his body, placing it in one of the vacuum bags that came standard with SMF ships. That was then secured in what remained of the ship's hold. They had set it up as a makeshift morgue, not knowing who would or wouldn't survive.

As though able to read his mind, Irena said, "It's not your fault. We all came here willingly. We knew the risks, and all wanted the same thing."

Harlan just nodded, not really taking in her words. He knew she meant well, but right now words were no use. He looked back at her, trying to focus on the present. "How are you doing? You showed incredible courage with the satellite dish situation. Bella told me everything, that you nearly... well, that we might not be speaking here now."

"It was quite the experience. I'll be sure to forward my psychiatric bills to you when we get back to Atlas." She cracked a smile full of pain and barely held horror.

"Maybe we'll get a group discount. How's Bella's injury? It looked pretty nasty."

"I've managed to get the assistant to do most of the work. The wound is severe but not life-threatening. She'll be fine in the long term, but we can't stay here for more than three or four days."

"Is she at any immediate risk?"

"No, as long as she stays in the med-bay and lets the drugs and systems work, she'll remain stable, like the others, barring any disasters."

"I should speak with her. She must be devastated about Gianni."

"I'd wait. I've given her a sedative to help. When the shock wears off, the grief is going to hit her hard. We really need to get her back to Atlas for proper care sooner rather than later."

Leanne stepped out of a bulkhead and joined them in the passage.

Harlan closed the door of the med-bay and stepped back from Irena, suddenly feeling self-conscious with his wife standing there staring at them. Although, wife wasn't quite right. They hadn't divorced, but she had been missing for so long Harlan had come to think of her as an ex. Yet here she was.

"I'll leave you two alone," Irena said. "I guess you've got some catching up to do."

Harlan grabbed her elbow. "It's fine. You don't have to."

A tense silence hung in the air. Irena let her arm drop. Harlan let go and glared at Leanne. "I suggest you both get some rest, perhaps eat something. I'll get in touch with Gylfie and tell him everything that has happened. We need to let the authorities know and stop the election."

"What will happen to my parents?"

"If I have anything to do with it, they'll be arrested for conspiracy, amongst other charges. Will that be difficult for you? You will have to be present at the impending trial."

"No. They betrayed me. They treated me as nothing but a tool to be used. I want to see them go down for this."

"Okay. I'll get the ball rolling as soon as we get off this planet."

Irena gave him a quick kiss on the cheek before sliding past and heading back into the med-bay. Leanne continued to watch Harlan.

"What?"

"She likes you."

"Imagine that, eh? A woman liking old Harlan Rubik. Would make a change."

"You're still bitter about me leaving you?"

Harlan turned his back and headed to the cockpit of the ship. Leanne followed.

When they had both entered, Harlan closed the door behind them and faced Leanne. "Bitter? No, bitterness has long since left me. Now I'm just pissed off. You don't make any sense. For the best part of a decade, you gallivant about the system working as some kind of assassin for the very people you helped me stop. In all that time, there was no word of what you were doing. Then there was that business back at Asimovia—and today. For once, why don't you explain yourself and tell me the truth? Why did you leave? And why, after all these years, did you show up again?"

Leanne sat in the pilot's chair. She had changed into one of the ship's standard-issue jumpsuits in the olive drab style from yesteryear that the SMF was so fond of. She'd also found time to wet her hair and wash her face. Her brunette locks were slicked back, giving her a diva-like appearance.

She regarded him with bright green eyes, no less star-tling after all these years. Harlan remembered the first day he saw her walking through Atlas Station. It was her eyes back then that first captivated him.

"The truth is," she began, leaning forward, staring directly into his eyes, "it was all for you. I struck a bargain with the Vanguard hierarchy when they first learned about my skills. They wanted me to work for them. Naturally, I said no. I was happy doing my own thing. But they threatened your life. I knew Hugo and Aurier were in with that lot. They could have got to you at any moment. They made that quite clear to me."

Harlan rocked back and leaned against the ship's bulkhead. Looking at her now, hearing her words, he knew she was telling the truth. It was just like when they had first met.

She would often talk with little emotional baggage attached, always happy to say it how it was. It was one of the reasons he had loved her. She had made loving her easy.

"So you were essentially their indentured slave for a decade because of me?"

"To begin with, yes."

"What do you mean? What happened?"

She looked away from him, her cheeks reddening with what he thought was shame. He'd seen it in the face of many a criminal having come to terms with their being caught and sentenced. "Stockholm Syndrome isn't just something we learned about in history class, Harlan. I grew to see them as a family, almost. Although I knew the threat was always there, underlying my every move, I also grew to form strong bonds with people within the group—well, the ones I was allowed to know about. You have to understand, they're a throwback to the old days of terrorist cells and compartmentalized information. I didn't know anyone or anything outside the sphere I worked in. And then there was Luca..."

She looked up at him now, sincerity clear on her face. "He loved you like a brother. Even up until he brought Fizon here, he bargained with the hierarchy to leave you alone, but when Hugo killed himself, those in power knew it would be just a matter of time before you learned too much. They had doubted Hugo toward the end. It wasn't Vanguard's preferred choice to have you investigate Fizon. That's why Aurier was ultimately activated."

Harlan could barely believe it. Luca had taunted him for years and played the archetypal nemesis at every turn. But then, perhaps that was some form of brotherly connection? Some of the greatest enemies either started out or ended up as friends. The idea wasn't a new one; it went back to Sherlock Holmes and Moriarty—two apparently distinct individuals who were so alike they could have been twins. And, he supposed, even farther back to Cain and Abel of the Christian faith.

"If he felt anything for me, he wouldn't have tried to kill us back there."

Leanne smiled wryly and shook her head. "If he wanted us dead, he would have made sure of it. He was just buying time to escape. Even when you were at his mercy, he couldn't end you."

"What about the abbot with the railgun? It might have killed Bashir. It could have easily been me among the wounded."

She shrugged. "It was getting down to the crunch. Besides, as you saw, Fizon had manipulated him the entire time. Luca wasn't in control of the rogue abbot any more than he was in control of Fizon. And think about it—you were in Fizon's clutches. If it weren't for Luca, neither of us would be here now. He saved you from certain death."

She had a point. It didn't change the fact that Luca had needed to be stopped. Letting Harlan live was his own downfall, and perhaps that's what he had secretly desired. As far as Harlan was concerned, justice was justice whether the perpetrator wanted it or not.

"Perhaps you're right, perhaps I owe my life to you and Luca, but I still had to do my job. I couldn't just let him get away with all this. Especially the whole Gianni business. When Bella comes around and has to deal with his death, it'll likely kill her. She needs to know what Luca did to her brother. She needs justice as much as I do— as much as the entire Sol-Fed does."

"I can help you there," Leanne said. "Before you arrived, and before Gianni became catatonic, we managed to speak for a while. During his investigations into radio signals, he stumbled across an unusual set of broadcasts coming from Europa. The Sol-Fed Space Agency had strict rules on extracurricular work, and he was already on thin ice from having previously abused the agency's resources."

"So he decided to take a shuttle and go out there alone?"

"Where Vanguard captured him. It was mine and Luca's cell who were patrolling the area. Luca had him sent to the lab for experimentation. When things presented themselves regarding the QCA, he didn't want to leave his pet project behind. He brought Gianni along and recaptured me after you had taken me into custody. In hindsight, that was a stupid thing of you to do, what with Aurier and Hugo working there. As soon as you brought me in, they got to work. It was no coincidence that you were in a meeting with Hugo when the shit hit the fan."

Harlan took a seat in the copilot's chair as all the revelations continued to spill out, shining a light on the events that had led him here, all the opportunities he'd had to learn the truth but just missed out.

"So how did Gianni end up catatonic? What the hell did Luca do to him?"

"I don't know the specifics. Yesterday Luca injected Gianni with something that completely switched him off. For all I know it could have been a backup plan in case we won."

Now that definitely sounded like something Luca would do. A malicious act to have the last word. But like his dreams of hacking the QCA and controlling all the abbots, it had backfired.

"You told me what happened to Gianni, but what about you?"

"I was never allowed anywhere near the details of this Project Inception."

Harlan sat there in silence, taking in everything Leanne had told him. There was so much to write up for the case file. So many charges to bring against various people—not to mention handling the fallout from Fizon going rogue. The thought of dealing with the aftermath exhausted him. But the job wasn't finished yet.

"Thanks for finally coming clean with everything." Not that it helped a great deal. Sure, for those who believed closure was more than a platitude, he could say he had that regarding the reason why Leanne had left him. But that was now replaced with a sense of guilt that she had done all she had to keep him alive. How could he ever redress that balance?

Despite her being back in his life, he was still at odds, in limbo.

Leanne stood up, perhaps sensing that her role had ended. She patted him on the shoulder, brought her face close to his, but then turned away and left him alone in the *Wickham*'s cockpit.

He reached out to the controls, activated the communication array, and sent a message through the silicon runners' relay system. He had quite the tale to tell Gylfie. He just hoped the old man could get Harlan's evidence to the president before the election started.

41

E ven with the runners' relay system, the signal took an initial two minutes to get to Gylfie and back to Harlan before the network made the communications almost instant. For the next half an hour, Harlan strategized with his old boss of how to deliver the evidence to President Kallstrom.

"I've sent you the details for a secure channel," Gylfie said. "Upload the video streams from your suits' helmet cams, and I'll forward those to Kallstrom's aide. I had already made contact with her when you left for Earth, suspecting we'd need to move quickly once you stopped the hack."

A minute later, the login information arrived.

Harlan set about creating a network of the helmet cams and hooked them into the *Wickham*'s system, ready for uploading. While the data was being transferred, he told Gylfie about Fizon.

His old boss whistled a sigh. "I never expected that. I think it'll be absolutely critical for that information to remain secret. We cannot let it get out to the public. It could trigger one of the humanist groups to call for the end of a connected abbotkind. We'd be right back to the dark days before the war."

"I agree. But it's concerning that Fizon even had the ability to manipulate Vanguard in the first instance. We have to assume he's not the only abbot working against the treaty. Every single one of them is a potential insurgent now. What trust existed, for me at least, has completely disintegrated."

"We can't afford to be impulsive, Harlan."

"I know, I'm just saying that the ramifications of this are vast. There's only one way I can see handling this: we need to expand the role of the silicon runners. And we need a new boss. Or perhaps an old one."

"What exactly are you suggesting?" Gylfie asked, although, from Harlan's point of view, it was pretty obvious and the only way to reestablish the silicon runner department after the revelation that Hugo and Aurier were Vanguard sleeper agents.

"I'm saying that you should put any retirement plans on Mars on the back burner and come back to what you do best: be the boss."

There was silence for a few moments. Harlan waited, letting the idea seep into the old man's brain. Harlan knew Gylfie wasn't the retiring type; it was why he had taken the role at the RDC. It was a way for him to remain a part of the network of whispers. That he worked on level one was no accident: from there, Gylfie could keep his hand in with the criminal underworld. And with Hugo out of the picture, he was the perfect candidate to take over.

"You don't want to take the position, Harlan? I daresay once this goes public, Kallstrom will want you to be his new man in the runners."

"I'm not leadership material. Besides, I feel like I'm getting back to my best. Admit it; you've missed it."

"You always were the perceptive one. I'll take it under advisement. Let me talk with Kallstrom and his people first. We still have the issue of the Selles couple to deal with. Victoria was on the network just a few minutes before you called, condemning Kallstrom's approval rating."

"I suspect that'll take a sharp uptick once this goes live. Tell Kallstrom from me that he's more than welcome to take credit for this whole affair. I'd rather the spotlight and approval be on him. I won't be able to do my job if I'm dogged by the media and other interested parties."

"I'll be sure to pass that on."

Harlan stretched and yawned as he stood from the pilot's chair. His back ached, and his mind buzzed with all the events of the past few hours. Then he remembered: the *Wickham* crew.

"Gylfie, there are a couple more things I need you to arrange."

"I'm listening."

"The first is that we... not sure how best to explain it, but let's just say we swapped ships with the SMF. We procured their vessel, the *Wickham*, the crew of which are now in a small transport shuttle that's currently on an orbital path around Luna. I made sure they had enough rations and water, but I shut off their communications. Could you make the authorities aware and have them recovered?"

Gylfie laughed with a sudden snort. "And I suppose you want me to explain to Kallstrom that you had to do that and had no other option?"

"Of course."

"You're pushing your luck, but I'll be sure to defend your

decision. I can't promise the SMF won't try to have you up on charges."

"I'll deal with that if and when the time comes. But I just wanted to make sure they were safe and recovered. I'll arrange to send them my apologies. Once they know the situation here on Earth, perhaps they'll understand."

"You said there were two things. What was the other?"

"We need a lift off the planet. The *Wickham* is in no shape to go anywhere currently, and we have three of our crew completely out of action. We have Luca's ship, but it's barely large enough for two people and doesn't have the medical facilities we need for our wounded."

"I'll be sure to get a ship to you as soon as possible. Let me deal with Kallstrom's people, and I'll get back to you. You did good, Harlan; you all did. You sit tight and stay safe. I'll be back in touch shortly."

"Thanks, Gylfie, I appreciate your help."

The line cut. Harlan leaned back in the chair and closed his eyes. His head throbbed with a deep ache. Every muscle felt fatigued, as though he had spent an afternoon in the gym weight-training to prevent muscle loss in low-g environments.

The extra gravity of Earth did indeed feel different from that generated on Atlas and the other stations. How humanity ever managed to live here for the long term, he couldn't imagine, but then he remembered one element of his species that he had observed in his lifetime: they were adaptable—for good or bad.

A tapping on the cockpit door pulled his attention.

"Come in."

The door slid aside. Irena appeared in the doorway. "Hey, you."

"Hey, is everything okay?"

She walked in and closed the door behind her. Her eyes were red, and puffy bags hung beneath them. "As much as things can be, I guess. It's all so horrible. It feels like the aftermath of a nightmare."

Harlan stood and stepped closer to her. He reached out, but she stepped in and hugged him tightly. He wrapped his arms around her, and there they both remained, both needing human warmth after such an inhuman experience.

Irena sobbed quietly for a few moments before pulling back. She smiled, wiping the tears from her eyes. "I'm sorry."

"You've got nothing to apologize for. This has been traumatic. It'll take a while to come to terms with all this."

"It's not over yet. There's still the issue of my parents."

"That's being taken care of as we speak. I've uploaded all the data to a secure server. Kallstrom will receive it shortly. Gylfie's going to explain everything. When that goes public, your mother's bid for the presidency will be over. Her rating will tank, ending any hopes of launching a bid to oust Kallstrom."

"I'll be relieved when they're behind bars. For years, any time we were together, they've tried to rule my life. If anything, it's actually a relief to know that they were involved in all this."

"How so?"

"It means it wasn't me, you know? Growing up, I always thought their behavior toward me was somehow my fault, that I couldn't live up to their standards, but now it's clear they had no such standards. They were the ones who were weak."

"From the day I met you," Harlan said, "I knew you were

one of the strongest people I had ever encountered. And there's nothing that has changed my mind on that."

"You're not so bad yourself."

She flashed that smile again.

"So," Harlan said, eager to move on, "what will you do when all this is over? With your parents facing life in prison and the immediate threat gone, what do you want to do? Will you rejoin the Earth Restoration Project?"

She shook her head and pointed out the window at the rolling black clouds and torrential rain. "I never want to come back here ever again. As far as I'm concerned, our future is out there." She pointed to the sky. "Harking back to an era long gone seems wasteful now. We have an entire Solar system to reach out to."

"With that in mind, I have a proposal for you."

Irena's eyes went wide. "I'm listening."

"I suspected you wouldn't want to rejoin the ERP, so then the obvious option came to mind. When we get back, I'll be petitioning for Gylfie to take over Hugo's role."

"What will you do? I assumed you'd get that position."

"I'll continue working in the department as I've always done, but with Hugo, Aurier and the agents who were murdered no longer around, it means we're short of staff until we get our new stream of junior recruits. I've not had a partner for quite a while now, and since we appear to make a good team, I'd like you to join the runners and be my partner as a trainee. What do you say?"

The smile on her face betrayed any sense of being coy. "I'd love that. Will I get my own cool retro uniform like yours?"

"Nah, you'll have to wear the standard-issue gear. At least until you're fully qualified, then you can wear whatever you want."

"What'll be our first case?"

"We bring the last dregs of Vanguard to their knees."

"Sounds good to me." She held out her hand. Harlan shook it.

"Welcome to the silicon runners, where our reach extends to all corners of the Solar system."

42

Two months later,
Atlas Station

From his private quarters, Harlan heard Irena moving about in the living room of his apartment. She was playing some classical music and humming along to the catchy 20th-century melodies. Their combined sound filtered through the thin material of the door. It brought a smile to his face, this sound of domestic equanimity—a quality he hadn't experienced for such a long time. Certainly not since Leanne had left.

He would join Irena later, but for now, he needed to finish his report. Since they had been rescued from Earth and returned to Atlas, the fallout from Vanguard's exposed plan had put in motion a long procession of political and societal fallout. He left most of that to Gylfie and President Kallstrom to deal with.

Bashir and Greta were healthy again, going through rehab. Wilbur and Bella had agreed to work with the prose-cutors on the case, bargaining for their own crimes, as

Harlan had done with regard to the fracas with the crew of the *SFF Wickham*. Captain Saffile reluctantly agreed to drop charges in exchange for a promotion, as his types often did in such politically advantageous situations.

As for Irena's parents; they were being processed, along with twelve cohorts. All were members of Vanguard, and complicit in their attempts to overthrow the Solar Federation and take control of the abbots—or to use their own phraseology: Project Inception.

Harlan re-read through the report of his evidence and findings until he came to the spot where he had paused to think on the final loose ends: Gianni and the signal. The two elements were really twin particles of the same atom. It had been the central theme of discussion during the journey back to Atlas. Why did Luca take Gianni back to Earth, and what was the source of the signal? During a raid on Europa's AstroLab facility, Harlan had found the answers to both questions.

He centered the curser on the holographic screen and began to type.

... IN REGARD to the anomaly described in subsection IV of Crime Report #554978.1, the signal was found to be an encoded FRB (Fast Radio Burst). Data from the AstroLab was provided by the Vanguard science team as per their plea deal—full details accompanied in Document Ref: 778107332. Post-encryption shows the signal to be the original attempt of Project Inception, that is to say, the endeavor to bypass the security of the QCA. Along with Fizon's confession, the evidence suggests this was used as part of his initial cover story. That Gianni Mazzari implicated himself within the conspiracy reflects the corruption within both the SFSA and the attendant agencies assigned to contracts on Europa and its brethren moons.

On recovery of Mr. Mazzari's shuttle, an analysis of the data within its computers was carried out by technicians in the employ of the Silicon Runners and under regulation of the Criminal Investigation Committee—Policy No.632, sub-section, XV. Video footage of Luca Doe and his associates kidnapping and incapacitating Mr. Mazzari was discovered and verified—evidence packet ref: 991.5. The trauma of the event and subsequent torture carried out to determine his level of knowledge of the signal and accompanied activities had damaged his psyche to the point where he had become mute. Further details of the damage his brain sustained and the likely effects can be found in the medical report by Drs. Kevan, Marsh, and Liao, within evidence packet ref: 991.6.

From Vanguard defendants Howe and Patterson, we learned that Luca Doe took personal responsibility for Mr. Mazzari and what he saw as, "his own damn fault for letting that bastard discover the signal." This responsibility led to his using Mr. Mazzari as a living, breathing experiment for his own brand of psyche manipulation, the basis of which, according to Patterson, was, "to develop a framework of obedience with which to develop and codify the new instructions for the unlinked abbots." Patterson added, "no one within Vanguard, especially Project Inception, saw the validity of transposing human conditioning to an AI-driven mind." And that, "Luca was losing his own grip on reality and defied Vanguard on numerous occasions." Howe has testified the accuracy of this account and suggested that this schism was the reason why Luca Doe apparently went rogue within the organization, transferring his base of operations to Earth.

There is still conjecture as to the internal politics of

Project Inception, and whether this is an accurate account of Luca Doe's motivations. My own evidence is insufficient to recommend an alternative in lieu of the aforementioned defendants' reports. Any further investigative activity will be sent as is appropriate.

HARLAN STRETCHED his arms above his shoulders and stood up. There was more to add to the report: boilerplate legal stuff, but he'd joined all the necessary dots and referenced all the appropriate pieces of evidence. It was now down to Kallstrom's legal team to piece it all together into the final coherent account for the courts.

At least now, those in Vanguard would be brought to justice, and Bella could finally put her poor brother to rest and attempt to move on now that she had her answers. He wasn't sure that knowing her brother was an experiment-gone-wrong was any kind of solace, but it was the only one available, and he figured that was better than not knowing. At least she would have her say in court and would see those left alive in Vanguard pay for their crimes.

It was not nothing. He'd come to learn that over the years. Some of the most hideous crimes could affect the relatives of a victim in ways beyond comprehension, and yet he'd seen it so often that the conclusion of a case, and the meting out of justice, helped the victims and those around them find a slither of light in the all-consuming chaos of universal indifference. That tiny crack of goodness, of righteousness, helped light their path to acceptance so that they could live again, knowing that in this world of suffering and struggle, there was something out there diligently working as a bulwark against the darkness.

And it was that realization that drove Harlan to do what he did.

The music stopped.

He went to the door, opened it, and stepped into the living room. Irena turned to face him. "Hey. Report finished?"

"All the important stuff is done. You want some coffee? We've got a few hours to kill before we have to submit the report, and I could use a break."

"Sure.... But there's something I need to tell you."

"Oh?"

"It's Leanne. She came by earlier while you were working. She didn't want to stay, but left you a note over there on the kitchen counter. I didn't read it."

She blushed as she said this. He waved it away. "It's fine. I trust you. Did she say anything else? She was due to meet with her legal team today. I still can't believe she agreed to testify."

"I have a feeling those plans have changed."

Harlan walked across the room and picked up the polymer envelope. A hand-written letter was inside, along with a data card. The note simply read:

Harlan, I'm sorry.

I cannot face what is to come. I've always been a coward, and I can't escape my nature. Don't wait for me any longer. You deserve to move on.

Please don't try to find me; you will only find pain.

I will always love you.

Leanne.

HIS SKIN PRICKLED WITH HEAT, and his fingers trembled. He thumbed the data card over his terminal and looked at what Leanne had given to him: a decree nisi for a divorce. He collapsed forward onto the counter as a wave of emotion rose up in his chest.

Irena placed a hand on his shoulder. "Are you okay?"

He took a deep breath, stood up, and faced her. "I think so. Leanne has given me the one thing I've wanted for the last decade. Finality. I can now let her go." With that, he leaned in and kissed Irena. She returned his kiss with eagerness.

After a few moments, they broke away. Harlan looked into her eyes and saw a new world of happiness and completion staring back at him. She smiled and laughed out loud, then wrapped her arms around his neck. His terminal chirped with a series of notifications, but he ignored them. The world of justice could wait, just as he had waited so long to be whole once more.

Finally, he could live a life worth living again.

Finally, he had a measure of his life again.

AFTERWORD

Dear reader, thank you for reading my book. I hope you enjoyed it. If you did, I would be most grateful if you could leave a review. These help us small authors a great deal. Fewer than 1 in 100 readers tend to leave reviews, but they're easier than you might think. Just a sentence of your thoughts will be fine and a star-rating. These help Amazon market books and enables me to continue writing you stories. Thanks!

ALSO BY A.C. HADFIELD

The Carson Mach Adventures

The Atlantis Ship

The Terminal War

The lost Voyager

Blackstar Command

Prominence

Magnitude

ABOUT THE AUTHOR

A.C. Hadfield is a pen name of Colin F. Barnes. Under Hadfield, Colin writes space opera novels across a spectrum of pulpy adventure (*Carson Mach series*) to classic hero's journey tales (*Blackstar Command*), and explorations into post-Earth colony life *(Vanguard Rising)*.

A.C Hadfield's newsletter: http://eepurl.com/dISpxL

Visit Website: http://www.colinfbarnes.com/achadfield/